When the Bough Breaks

Elizabeth Mapstone

When the bough breaks
©2021 Elizabeth Mapstone

The right of the author to be identified as the author of this work
has been asserted in accordance with the
Copyright, Designs and Patents Act 1988.

ISBN 978-1-910779-82-8 (Paperback)

Cover Illustration by David Wilcox.

Typeset by
Oxford eBooks Ltd.
www.oxford-ebooks.com

To David Wilcox - a very special friend

1

Madge

The desert was cold and grey. The sun had gone, leaving only shadows beneath the sandhills which rose on either side. The golden sands had become grey and the sky was grey so that in the grey distance she could not tell where the desert ended and the heavens began.

She was alone in the desert. She could see herself, was outside herself looking on as a spectator, and she could see that it was true: she was entirely alone. No one was beside her as she stood on the undulating sands, a forlorn grey figure in the grey expanse of shadows.

Sadness was all she felt. Strange that, she thought. She did not even know why she was there, why she should be all alone in a desert of shadows, of molehills turning into mountains. She could see them growing, knew that this great slope on her left had been but a tiny hillock in the sand some minutes before, and now it was heaving and bulging as it grew in size, clouds of sand leapt into the air and foamed like waves on the sea before tumbling back onto the heaving mass which now towered above her head. Strange indeed that all she felt was an overpowering sadness, and no fear.

Fear. Oh, why had she introduced that thought? For Fear was there, of course he was. Just waiting for her to think of him before making his attack. Fear was lying in ambush as he always did; she could feel his very presence even before he appeared, the flesh on her back crawled as though his clammy fingers caressed her and the hair on her neck rose of its own accord. In spite of herself, of her better judgement, she turned her head. She must know in what form he had clothed himself this time, even though she knew that if she just stood still and directed her thoughts elsewhere, he might change his mind and go away. Fear was stronger than her better judgement. She knew that.

And Fear was at her back, a monstrous bird with great scaly neck stretched forth, and bulging eyes and sharp curved beak. His wings were huge, domed, flapping behind her, she could feel the waves of torn air on her neck, his talons were sharp, waiting to dig deep into her flesh.

She must escape. She must run like the wind to the edge of the world where he could not reach her. She must leap like the sun over the mountains into the limitless heavens. But she could not run. Her feet would not rise from the ground. Why, oh why would they not obey her? Slowly, oh so slowly she moved her heavy limbs, and she could feel Fear behind her, mocking, playing with her cruelly as a cat torments a mouse, and the ground hurt her feet, sharp flints cut her soles, spilling her blood.

Then the ground ended, and she was falling… falling…

NRRRRRRRRRRRRRRRRRRRRRRRRRRRR………..

Her body jerked and her head hit the pillow, and she lay there trembling, though already she had forgotten why.

Gerald snorted and turned away. She could see him out of the corner of her eye, a great hulk of blue pyjama half hidden by the sheet his hand was holding firmly over his shoulder. Her heart was pounding wildly as though she had been running, or frightened, or fallen. He lay barricaded behind the bedclothes and the alarm was ringing. Ringing. Ringing…

Oh, that alarm clock... If he must have an electric one that never runs down, why can't he wake up in the morning and turn it off? I don't want to have to lean over him, my body against his, how I hate that one unchanging note, God, will it never stop? Gerald, please, I'm not saying it aloud, but please, please wake up, that long scream jars the rhythm of my heart, it's wearing away the sheath of my nerves. One day I'll go mad and start screaming too. With the clock, or instead of the clock...

Still blind with sleep, Gerald lifted one arm, and in exasperating slow motion groped for the keening clock, and pushed the switch. Peace. Then he collapsed back onto his pillow, his eyes closed.

How annoying men could be. It was always the same, every morning she was jangled out of a good night's sleep by the alarm he took for ever to turn off, and then he would lie there for ages, peacefully dozing as though nothing had happened. Her heart was pounding away inside her rib-cage until it seemed to her the whole bed shook, but he never noticed. And he had a train to catch.

"Gerald," she said. "Time to get up."

In a violent eruption of movement, Gerald threw back the covers and heaved himself out of bed. Swaying slightly as though still drunk with sleep, he stumbled into their adjoining bathroom and banged the door.

Madge pulled up the bedclothes that Gerald had thoughtlessly torn from her, snuggled back into the warmth of the bed and closed her eyes. Slowly her jangled nerves unwound and her heart eased its violent beat. Each day it seemed to take imperceptibly longer. How she wished Gerald were not so abrupt in his movements. Somehow everything he did these days seemed to affect her physically.

At last calm prevailed, and she was able to open her eyes to greet the new morning. Sunshine was gleaming through the green figured curtains, falling in pools of gold on the window sill, and contentment warmed her limbs as she stretched them under the bedclothes. It was always a pleasure to lie in bed in the morning, once Gerald was up and she could stretch her arms and legs without hindrance. She liked the green glow cast by the brocade, and when the sun shone brightly outside, the way the light glinted on the crystal dishes on her dressing table, and changed the brown tortoiseshell of her hairbrush to the richness of a topaz. Her birthstone. She always noticed that. As the ancients consulted entrails, so she studied the sunlight in her bedroom. The lustrous gleam of topaz was a good omen.

Time she got up and started breakfast. It need never be said she let her husband go off in the morning without a good breakfast inside him. Bacon and eggs, toast and marmalade, that was what a man needed. And she could do with a cup of tea herself.

Gerald emerged from the bathroom, his long lined face freshly shaved, his dark thinning hair gleaming with water and slicked down close to his skull. Without glancing at his wife, he strode to their large walk-in closet and began to dress. His back was towards her, the door partially closed.

Madge reached for her beige woollen dressing-gown and turned away from him as she drew it on, just in case, not particularly thinking of what she was doing, for so she had dressed herself in her husband's presence for years beyond recall, out of habit, out of conviction. Immodesty was deplorable.

Her turn in the bathroom, and she did not glance in the mirror. She knew too well how she looked and it gave her no pleasure. He'd left the lavatory seat up again, and the cap off the toothpaste. It was so inconsiderate. Why did he do such things? She would never know, it was incomprehensible. Men were incomprehensible.

She hurried downstairs. Put on the kettle, start the bacon, set the table, dispel with purposeful activity that strange empty feeling that threatened invasion. But when she heard Gerald start the car to take it outside, as he always did, she found herself standing with a plate in her hand, staring out of the kitchen window. He'd be in pretty soon and she'd hardly started. What had got into her?

Gerald's being so predictable was a great help. She knew exactly what he would do in the morning, just as she knew what he would do in any situation: after she had come downstairs and made the tea, she would hear him start the car and take it outside, every morning without fail; he would then be another three or four minutes checking the post, and sometimes he would bring her a circular from the W.I. or a notice of a meeting of the Church Ladies' Circle, or even very occasionally a letter from Father or Cousin Ruth; so that when he walked into the kitchen, she could put his breakfast straight in front of him as soon as he sat down. It was a matter of pride with her to time it right.

She could read him like a book. He hated to wait, ever, for his breakfast, his dinner, if she were delayed and they were going out, as though his time were infinitely precious, each minute a drop of liquid gold. But it was a matter of pride with her that her husband should have no ground for complaint, however trivial. If he measured out his moments like an apothecary, each second a precious grain, then her timing would become as delicate and precise as an atomic clock. She knew his game and he would not win. And there he was, dark and sleek, standing dramatically in the doorway, as though to announce his presence. Men could be so irritating. As usual, she said nothing, just watched his pomposity slowly subside like a leaking balloon. Abruptly he strode into the room, lifted out one of the shiny wooden chairs and sat down at the table. She put his plate in front of him. She had done it again.

He never really looked at her, and this bothered her in an obscure way. After all, it was natural that after so many years he'd be inclined to take her for granted. She found herself watching him as he ate his breakfast, she sitting opposite with a cup of tea. The bony structure of his face seemed risen to the surface and all his skin sagged towards his chin. His brows converged in glowering blackness, every line on his cheeks deepened and pointed downwards, and dominating all was his nose, bony and sharp. Even his body, once so tall and broad of shoulder, had become somehow deformed, stooped, round-shouldered under some imaginary burden, potbellied even, and his hair was plastered down black on his bony skull. He looked like a caricature of a bird, a dark brooding menacing crow.

She shivered. His silence, however usual, had become oppressive.

Some music would help. She turned on the radio, and the voice of a young male singer rose out of the box and filled the room with harsh sounds. She did not really care for the songs of today with their strange insistent rhythms and crude words, infinitely preferred the lovely melodies and moving sentiments of the songs of her youth. But she wanted to bring the world into her kitchen. Thousands, maybe millions of women all over the country were listening to that song just as she was, and she could imagine a mystical bond, in the air so to speak, linking them all. Then she did not feel alone.

"Do you have to turn on that noise?"

"I'm sorry." She turned it off. It was a ritual. Every time she turned on the radio he complained. She stood up, went over to the window. The slightest criticism always precipitated a battle between anger and tears within her breast. As usual, she subdued them both. But her stomach felt tied in knots as she listened to him noisily crunching toast. Why should he always object if she wanted to listen to the radio, in her own home?

He drained his cup, stood up.

"Will you be in to dinner?"

"You know I'm always late on Friday."

"Yes. Of course."

She followed him into the hall, watched him pick up his briefcase, throw his raincoat over his arm. What was it on Fridays? Board meeting? Conservative Club? Masons? Local council? She couldn't remember, it had been so long. Not that it mattered. Just so long as he looked after himself.

"You will make sure you have a decent meal, won't you? All these late nights working can't be good for you, you know."

"Don't worry about me, I'm fine." He opened the front door. "Bye now. Have a good day."

She watched him walk briskly down the path, take command of his shining Rover 2000. Then she closed the door. He was gone for the day. Secretly she was glad he had to leave the house every morning: a parting sanctioned by custom, by necessity. Every man left home in the morning to go to work, that was the pattern of modern life, and every evening he returned.

Time the children were down. She went to the bottom of the stairs.

"June! Robert! Hurry up."

As if on cue, her 18-year-old daughter came dancing down the stairs, bubbling with high spirits. Madge found this unbelievably precious – her daughter sparkling with laughter. How had she managed this miracle?

"He's still not up, Mum," June said as she swung round the newel post, and blew her mother a kiss. Then she disappeared into the kitchen.

2

June

June was tall and slim, eighteen last June (why her parents had to be so *obvious* she couldn't imagine), and so far as she could see, she had been given all their worst features without any of their good ones. Her hair was like her mother's, fine and dull mousy brown and thin, not dark and curly like Dad's. Her face was long like Dad's, and she had her mother's eyes, small and sort of nondescript, not blue or brown or even grey. But this morning, in spite of these unfair handicaps, she felt she had achieved marked success with her appearance.

Her new dress fitted perfectly; it was purple, with a tight tucked bodice trimmed with lace, and long full sleeves caught at the wrist with lace, and a full maxi skirt falling from just below her bust (which had developed beautifully now she was on the Pill). She had on black shiny boots, gorgeous button boots laced to her knees, and, greatest pride of all, lying on her bed beside her suitcase waiting for her to leave, a mid-length cloak in purple wool. Lined. No wonder she felt good this Friday morning. Not only had she achieved beauty against fearful odds, she was also going away for the weekend, straight from work, and wouldn't be back until Sunday night.

"June dear, what *have* you got on?"

June popped a slice of bread in the toaster. "It's a maxi dress, mother."

"Oh. Well, let me see it then."

June pirouetted a couple of times to show off her new dress, then submitted to a long examination by her clearly anxious mother.

"Very pretty," Madge said at last. "Very quiet and demure. Yes, I like it. I suppose Hetty is having a party then?"

June eyed her mother knowingly. "Come on, Mum. Don't start."

"What are you talking about? I just said I think this is a lovely dress. A bit old-fashioned perhaps. And hardly suitable for work."

June sighed. "I do wish you wouldn't always go on about my clothes. All the girls wear maxis these days. It *is* nineteen seventy, you know.'"

"My dear, I can't help being old-fashioned, and I'm sure Hetty's mother is too. What is she going to think if you arrive in that get-up?"

"Nothing, of course."

Her mother poured them both a cup of tea, but she was frowning.

"I do wish you'd think a bit, dear. She'll be bound to imagine you haven't been brought up properly. You wouldn't wear a dressing gown to go shopping, would you? In the same way, you shouldn't wear a party dress to work, or to visit a friend for the weekend." She hesitated. "Of course. I don't want to interfere or anything."

June laughed good-humouredly. "Oh, no. I can see that!"

"I'll tell you what," her mother said in a gently reasonable voice. "You go and change into that nice blue dress with the white collar and cuffs, and I'll wrap that lovely dress in tissue paper for you so that it will be fresh for your party. How about that? Don't you think that'd be a good idea?"

June raised her eyes to the ceiling, but said nothing. Placidly she continued with her breakfast.

Madge suddenly strode over to the kitchen door, which she threw open and shouted loudly: "ROBERT! RO-BURT!!"

"Yeah," came a gloomy voice from upstairs.

"For goodness' sake, HURRY UP! You should be leaving now."

Then she slumped into her chair, clearly overcome with bewilderment at how difficult it had become to persuade her own children to behave as properly brought-up children should. Poor Mother, she simply had no idea that things had changed from when she was a kid. Presumably she'd catch up eventually...

June stood up, and plonked a kindly kiss on her mother's forehead. "Bye, Mother. See you Sunday."

Madge caught her daughter's hand. "Bye-bye, dear. Take care. Are you sure you have everything you need?"

"Course I have. Don't be an old fusspot."

June skipped up the stairs and banged on her brother's door. "Come on, Bobby. You'll be late again."

Then the great moment. She put on the purple wool cloak and examined herself in the long mirror. Yes, she looked marvellous. Even with her face. Dad would say: "You look a million dollars." She knew he would. What a pity he couldn't see her. Never mind, the world would.

She ran down the stairs, out of the front door, called "Byee, everybody!" before she slammed it shut. Away for the weekend, her heart sang as she danced down the path and out into the road. Two whole days of freedom, of doing just what she wanted to do and no one would know. Two days of bliss.

She laughed aloud with joy, before composing her features for the boring trek to the bus and to work. Life was great.

3

Madge

Madge went into the lounge and drew back the curtains. Horror-struck, she watched her daughter's progress down the path: a cloak as well. No wonder the girl had skipped out so quickly.

Both love and pain mingled in her breast, for June looked so lovely in that extraordinary get-up, like the heroine of a romantic serial on TV. But Madge peered anxiously from behind the nylon lace curtains, praying no one was about. There was a hope, given the time, everyone might be busy in their kitchens. Lucy next door was probably cooking breakfast, that was one good thing, and she could see no sign of any of the others from where she stood in the bay window. June might not have been seen, and when she came back on Sunday night it would be dark, all being well, so they might be able to smuggle her inside again with no one being any the wiser. There was a chance they might get away with it.

But what a way to behave! What made her so flamboyant? Why was it the girl never stopped to consider her mother's feelings? Everyone wanted freedom, of course, she could understand that, it was only natural. But was it too much to ask her own daughter to curb her more extreme impulses, to take account of the exigences of this respectable and conservative neighbourhood? After all, Madge was going to live here for the rest of her life.

To relieve her feelings, Madge shook out the olive-green cushions on the settee even though the maid was due to arrive shortly. Then she marched into the kitchen feeling very cross.

Where was Robert? What had got into the boy? Could it be that his father was too critical of him just lately, as though he had forgotten what it was to be sixteen, as though he were jealous of the easy life his children had? How she hated to feel critical of her husband. Her stomach was in red hot tangles. She wanted to throw something, or burst into tears.

Robert drifted into the kitchen as though he had all the time in the world, in green blazer and grey school trousers. He looked as though he had freshly shaved.

"Morning," he said gloomily.

"Good morning. Do you plan to go to school today?"

"O'course." Gloomy still.

"Oh. I did just wonder."

"Have to, don't I?" The gloom if anything deepened.

She put his plate in front of him. "Come on, Robert. It can't be as bad as all that."

"You'd be surprised." A sudden grin lit up his face, then was gone. "They're all a bunch of morons."

"That's not a nice way to talk." He sighed and raised his eyes to the ceiling. Really her children had acquired some most unpleasing habits. "Robert dear, if you would only do some work and pass your exams, then you could go to university where everyone is as clever as you."

"Waste of time. I've told you. University's all part of the system. Nietsche says..."

"Oh, no," she interrupted, "not Supermen. I don't want to hear another word about them." Supermen don't fail their O levels, she could hear Gerald sneering, and Robert shouting, Supermen don't *take* the bloody things, and Gerald shouting back, No son of mine is going to be a good-for-nothing drop-out.

"You see? No one ever listens." Dispiritedly, he poked at his egg, took a couple of mouthfuls, stood up.

"You really should listen to your father, you know. He has your best interests at heart."

"I'm doing what he wants, aren't I? I don't want to resit any exams. Total waste of time as far as I'm concerned."

"Yes, dear, I know. But your father knows best." She looked at the clock. Eight thirty and she wasn't even dressed. And her head had begun to ache. Sometimes it seemed to her that her family didn't consider her feelings at all. "Robert, please hurry up. You must go."

"All right, all *right!*" A note of hysteria tinged his voice. "I'm going, aren't I?"

Impatiently she watched him open the back door, letting in draughts of cold September morning air, and with great reluctance take his bicycle from the covered porch. Then she hurried upstairs. She certainly couldn't let the maid find her like this.

When she had washed, she sat at her dressing-table, and for the first time that day looked at her reflection. Without hope and with little charity. She knew too well she looked more than her forty-four years, that deep lines were etched on her forehead, round her mouth and chin.

It seemed unfair. Other people appeared to win more battles against time than she. After forty, some said, you couldn't blame Nature for your face, you had made it yourself. But what should she have done differently? Surely her mouth had been beautiful once. Sometimes she could see her lost girl-hood in June's pretty smile. But now her lips seemed narrower, set in a thin line that drooped always downward. And her eyes too seemed smaller, and the colour of rainwater in a puddle. And her brows were sketchy, not eyebrows at all when you thought of how film stars looked, just two straggly lines of mousy brown hair.

Ah well, she'd never been a beauty, and looks weren't that important. No one looked their best first thing in the morning. Nothing she could do about it anyway, just try to grow old gracefully, and avoid looking like mutton dressed as lamb.

She smoothed in some of that new cream with Royal Jelly, then dusted nose, cheeks, forehead and chin with powder made of silk. Then she put on her new pantie corselette that really did give her a good shape, stockings, a good petticoat with lace inserts, a cream blouse with hand-embroidered panels, a green Scotch tweed skirt and toning Scotch wool cardigan. She brushed her permed grey curls with her Mason Pearson hairbrush, clipped the Majorca pearls around her neck, and she was ready. That was better. Now she felt more like herself.

No niggling irritations would undermine her composure now. She walked downstairs, ready to face the day.

She liked her house, despite its limitations. It was only ten years old and one of only a dozen like it in a new luxury estate outside Godalming in Surrey. All their neighbours were successful men like her husband – stockbrokers, company directors, a doctor, a solicitor – and all their wives were nice, well-spoken people who did their bit when it came to the Women's Institute or raising money for charity. They had asked her to be Secretary of the Ladies Circle at the Church this year, and everyone had quite understood when she told them how sad she was she couldn't take on such an important job, because of all the demands on Gerald's time now he was on the Council.

The basic framework of the house had lent itself to individual variations, and Gerald had insisted on a large study downstairs, taking up far too much space so that they had not been able to install a cloakroom where everyone else did. She had always found this hard to forgive. It was not at all adequate to send a guest upstairs to wash his hands: it always felt degrading somehow, a diminution of her status to have to send guests into such a private part of the house. Perhaps she was super-sensitive. Gerald had never understood.

But the lounge pleased her, for it had a grey stone fireplace, windows facing both front and back, and off it a large square dining area overlooking the patio, so that the room was like an L and the two rooms could be separated by sliding doors. The fireplace was, of course, not used as fires are messy and they had central heating; but she liked it as a focal point in the room and had had installed a very ingenious arrangement of hidden coloured lights and moving parts so that it looked just like a glowing fire.

The colour scheme was subdued: she hated ostentation. She wanted her house to be a tasteful background, a foil for her personality. Everything had been new when they bought this house (she had insisted on that), and the beige fitted carpets, the olive green suite, the twenty-four inch television set in its oak cabinet, the oak dining suite were the very best she could find. On the wall was just one picture, a brightly-coloured painting of a small girl with enormous dark eyes, which she had bought one day on impulse because she thought it looked like June.

Goodness gracious, how time was flying! Friday was always a busy day. She had to explain to Rose, the maid, exactly what cleaning and polishing she must do to leave the house immaculate for the weekend, and make sure she knew exactly where to put each item when the weekly order arrived from Marshall's the grocers; there was her hair appointment at eleven; and she simply must pop into the butcher's and change the order for the weekend. There would be just time for a little something for lunch, and then her bridge afternoon. Lucy's turn today. Perhaps she would have a bite to eat in that new restaurant everyone said was so nice. That would be something to tell the girls about.

She must hurry. She really looked forward to the afternoon games with Lucy and Barbara and Vanessa. She played a pretty good hand, though she said it herself, and in between times they would discuss their children and the problems of the younger generation; then they would discuss their husbands and the little everyday irritations. Lucy would say Jeremy was perfect, and they would all raise their eyebrows and laugh, and wonder secretly to themselves. Babs would no doubt recount another example of Ted's violent temper, and they would sympathise and say they couldn't see how she put up with it, and secretly they would think she probably brought it all on herself with her nagging. Vanessa would say she just wished she were a man, that's all, which was stupid, and they would tell her so. And then Madge would say Gerald worked much too hard and they would all commiserate, and they'd say how glad they were he was on the Council, it was time someone took a serious interest. And she would say, yes, of course she was proud of him and did her best to give him every support. They might end with a real heart-to-heart about how hard it is to keep going without appreciation because men always take everything you do for them for granted.

4

Patricia

Patricia Patterson walked out of the Board Room smiling. A very satisfactory way to end the week, she thought: the big contract with the detergent company signed and sealed, and only five o'clock on Friday afternoon, all weekend ahead and in two hours she would be with Gerald.

"That was advertising at its best," said Maurice Morris, who followed right behind. Patricia savoured a further thrill of triumph, for this small pale man, so easily overlooked and under-estimated, was Advertising Director of the detergent company and well-known for his brief and caustic comments. The other men followed them into the corridor, and she stopped, looked at Pete Castle, her chairman. He walked round behind her, stooping as usual from his ungainly height, put one long lean arm around her shoulders.

"Wonderful, Patricia darling."

"Thank you. I'm delighted our meeting went so well."

"That campaign your people gave us will shoot us to the top of the league, Pete," boomed Will Kenton, the detergent company's Marketing Director. "And Patricia, we'll be seeing a lot of you next year, I know. You must come and have a drink with Maurice and me, to celebrate."

"Thanks, Will, but I have an engagement. Another time perhaps." She smiled at him and realized from the way he gazed deep into her eyes he had his own ideas about their future relationship. He was an attractive man too, with dark brown eyes that held her and sent a shiver down her spine. But the momentary thrill was replaced by resentment: why was it that every man who fancied himself a Casanova took her independence of ties as an invitation and a challenge? She had supposed that rank and hard competence would in the end defend her, but all that changed was that those who dared approach her were tougher, financially more successful, their advances more assured and not necessarily more subtle. Sometimes she wished she could acknowledge Gerald, just to stop these womanisers in their tracks.

Deliberately she filled her eyes with cool rejection, though she knew that bruised pride might make him more critical at future meetings, then turned away.

"Goodbye, Maurice," she said, shaking his hand. "Goodbye, Will. We'll be in touch with your people next week. Please excuse me now, I must leave you."

"Have a good weekend, Patricia," Pete said, and she knew he wished to help her on her way. "See you Monday."

News of the contract had reached her office before her, and there was much joking and playing the fool as the tensions of the past weeks were broken. But she was anxious to get home, and escaped as soon as she decently could, left them all to their celebrations. She wanted some time to herself before Gerald arrived.

The disadvantage of leaving the office early, she thought as she crossed the London square and joined the crowds converging on the Underground station, was that it was not early for almost everyone else.

Holding herself tightly contained within invisible armour, she plunged down the steps and was immediately absorbed by the steady stream of bodies that flowed like lava down the accelerators, through the tunnels and caverns beneath the city. The stream flowed on relentlessly, bubbling through the opened doors of a train, and she tried not to notice the five people who were all in close physical contact with her, two backs, several arms, a few legs, a broad masculine chest. Usually she read a book, but tonight that was impossible, she could not have held it so that she could see the print if she could have dug it out of her capacious leather bag which she was holding somewhere in the region of her knees. At each station, people pushed and pummelled their way off the train only to be replaced by even more, until she wondered if she might actually not be able to breathe and whether it was indeed her own bag she was hanging on to so grimly, it was so long since she had seen it. When the crush increased so as to be literally unbearable and she was about to cry out if only she could get some breath, she noticed a blond young man try to hold the press away from her and their eyes met in mutual commiseration. But that was all. The British habit of remaining remote in the most dismal travelling conditions seemed to her the only possible way of getting through this sort of horror in a civilised manner.

The kitchen was chilly when she made herself a cup of coffee, so she took it into her bedroom with its glowing gas fire. What did Gerald think of this flat? she wondered as she relaxed on her bed. It must be so different from his home, yet he had said several times, with pride, "I have a very nice house." She imagined it as something in an out-of-date issue of Ideal Home Magazine. So what could he think of her flat, the converted ground floor of a rather decrepit house in Hampstead, where the décor was not so much planned as evolved around her most important possessions?

She loved her bedroom: dominating the room was a bed she had fallen in love with, its ornate back representing a peacock's tail in full splendour, while long French windows opened onto a small tree-filled garden, and the sun came in every morning, filtering through the leaves of a large flowering cherry.

Her large living room had grown around her books, her collection of pottery and ceramics, her records, her stereo equipment, and a very large blue and green and purple Spanish rug. The colour scheme stemmed from the rug: white walls, black chairs, hanging paper lampshades, two white, one blue, and carefully chosen curtains, cushion covers, ashtrays to pick up the colours of the rug which she had bought one day, long before this flat, because she thought it was beautiful.

Time to get washed and dressed. But after she had bathed, she sat at her dressing-table and examined her face coolly, objectively in the triple mirror: signs that she was approaching forty were unmistakeable. Though she had devoted much time and a large proportion of her income to the preservation of her youthful beauty, already her eyelids drooped, faint lines could be traced on her forehead, and certain blemishes on nose and chin seemed ineradicable, so that she took care never to be seen without make-up any more. Her dark hair too did not keep her secret as well as she wished: beautifully cut and cared-for by a Bond Street *coiffeur*, it had begun to take on a lacquered and artificial look. She was getting old.

Her green eyes had gone pale and cold as she examined the progress of years on her once beautiful face. The strain of the last few months had given her new lines, a drooping mouth and a certain slackness of skin. That, as much as any pain she had felt, decided her.

She must push Gerald.

"Would you marry me if I were free?" he had asked. The sun had been shining that day in April, nearly five months ago. Yellow forsythia had glowed in the London square where they had gone that lunch-time, and daffodils, so they had sat in the sunshine, and he had explained that he had to go on an unexpected business trip so he couldn't take her out to dinner that evening as planned, and he had something important to say to her. Suddenly she had known what it was to be, and he had said, "Would you marry me if ..." and she had said, "Oh, darling, yes, of course". And had gone back to the office radiant, almost bursting to tell the news, but no one to tell it to. Fortunately.

All he had meant was that. He was not free, he was married with two teenage children. He had just wanted to know, to hear from her, to caress this knowledge in secret: that a beautiful woman would have him if she could.

Nothing had changed. He had continued to come back to her flat two or three times a week, to have dinner and talk and listen to music, and to make love. He had bought her flowers, and perfume, and a gold bracelet. They had even managed a weekend in Paris. He had been brighter and gayer than she had ever known him, but not another word about marriage had been said.

She had waited. To be successful in business as a woman, you had to be patient and bide your time. So she knew how to keep her own counsel, even though she wondered sometimes how she had succeeded in avoiding the subject so constantly on her mind: had he meant he was asking for a divorce?

But now it seemed to her unreasonable. Here she was thirty-five, going on thirty-six, having spent the last three important years of her life devoted to a man who was not free. Half her life gone, surely now she could ask for permanence. Had he not talked of marriage? It was not even her idea, it was his.

Amazing how even the most sophisticated could find themselves entangled in cliché situations. She, Patricia Rhea Patterson, Bachelor of Arts (London), member of the Board of Directors of one of Britain's leading advertising agencies, cool, competent business-woman with a future, was now just another member of the Eternal Triangle.

The situation was not exactly new – she had been the Other

Woman more than once over the past twelve years. But until recently, she had found the cliché aspect amusing and slightly absurd, and had brushed aside any notion that she was no more in command of her life than all the other women she lumped together as Suburban Housewives, for whom she wrote advertising campaigns and dismissed in her mind with mild contempt.

The meaning of her existence could never have been invested in love for a man. She had seen too clearly when her father was killed that a wife could lose too much. Nor had it been possible for any youth to fill the image she had carried with her for so many years of an older man, tall, lean, strong as a hero, striding forth to slay the dragon of oppression. She was as good as any man she met, and had been determined to prove it. Only Gerald turned her world upside down. Their meeting had coincided with her Directorship, and the synchronicity of events seemed to her to hold a meaning: at the culmination of her career, she met the man whose love made her feel complete.

Yet... was it not strange that it should be he when there was such a yawning chasm between his tastes and hers? In some ways, though she loved him more than she thought it possible to love any man, he was a stranger to her, in some ways terrifyingly conventional. Living alone, she had indulged her own tastes to the full, but with Gerald she would have to compromise, his tastes were not hers. Was she prepared to give up all this? No. The truthful answer was that she was not. However crazy it might seem to set such store by pots and pictures and a peacock bed, they were to her part of the very fabric of life. But surely with Gerald that would not be necessary. With him she could be herself. With him she would be safe, and her beautiful things would be safe too.

Shouldn't I be worrying about his wife? she asked herself. If I press him, he will surely come to me. What of her? But she found it impossible to imagine that that foolish woman could really care if Gerald left her, she had made it so clear so long ago that she no longer loved him. The marriage was one in appearance only.

She had never believed it was possible for her, or for any woman like her, to break up a marriage. She had known many married men, and felt completely sure that when a man took a mistress, it was a sign of a rift but not the cause of it. A marriage was an intricate web woven by two people and only they had the key to its pattern. No outsider could enter and learn its secrets until one, or both, pulled the web apart. And then it was a marriage no more.

Now she wanted to learn this secret, weave her own mysterious web, become one of the mystic sisterhood of the truly married. Now she wanted to end this life as the Other Woman and become the Wife.

She had found her role painful in its loneliness, but this was not her reason. It was as though their relationship had become a power outside themselves, something beyond their control, an almost tangible presence that haunted her at every moment of the day. She knew deeply and with absolute conviction that their love affair had reached that point where it must be transformed into something permanent and solid, like marriage, or be ended for ever.

5

Gerald

Gerald lay in the bath, contemplating his navel.

He was a tall man, broad of shoulder but lean, with a hush-puppy face and greying curly hair, somewhat thin on top. His stomach was still youthfully flat despite his forty-six years, and his navel made a hollow that held water if he raised his body until he was floating on the surface. Last night, Patricia had poured wine into his navel, and lapped it up.

What a magnificent woman, he thought. His penis thickened and rose as his mind filled with memories of passion shared.

It was late Saturday afternoon, and he had just finished mowing the lawn. He supposed that later that evening, as usual, they would go round to the King's Arms and drink with all the neighbours, and the thought filled him with overpowering boredom. Better far to stay here in the bath and contemplate the navel from which Tricia had drunk wine. He knew that so long as he remained in the bathroom, he was quite safe. He would be left alone. Madge would not come near, not if she were to burst, he thought cruelly, not if he stayed here for five hours. Stupid female, to be so afraid of a man's naked body. A husband's phallus. What's it for then if not to go inside his wife? Memories crowded his head of times without number when Madge had shuddered and turned from him, black, ugly memories which pained his eyes as he saw himself cravenly pleading with her to masturbate him if she would not allow him inside her body. And she holding it as though it were a piece of meat. I don't know why she didn't wear gloves, he thought viciously, I'll buy her a pair of long ones, right up to the elbow. Not that I want her to touch me now, thank you. I'm finished with that sickness. Oh, Tricia, Tricia, thank God for you.

He wondered again, as he had wondered this last year every day he had found unpreoccupied with work, when he could or how he could rearrange his life so that he was with Tricia. Inevitably this posed the question of divorce, and however much he tried to shy away and find gentler, less destructive solutions, yet divorce ended by appearing the only honest way.

For Gerald was essentially an honest man. But a cautious one. He had pulled himself up the hard way, knew too well that his background was a poor preparation for his present position as Technical Director of a large cosmetics manufacturer, and that as the son of a railway guard at Willesden Junction, he had only managed to get to university thanks to the fortuitous intervention of the war. So many members of his generation had reason to thank the war for the opportunity to be educated, to escape the poverty of their working class backgrounds that he found within himself a profound guilt in his dealings with the unions which he feared might lead him to be harsher than necessary at times, and a deep pity for those who had not escaped. Among his colleagues though he noticed no pity, very often only contempt, and he wondered in his idle moments which of these hard brutal negotiators had had a father or uncle out of work during the thirties. Now he was a successful man, with his beautiful house, his company car and his £8,000 a year. He had made it. And he wanted to keep it that way.

Last night, Trish had said: "Do you remember April?" and he had crushed her in his arms, for of course he remembered. How could he forget? Then she asked, "Did you mean that you were going to get a divorce?" and he had not known what to say. Naturally he had had that in mind. He asked her if she would consider marrying him if he were free, to find out if he should pursue the thought of divorce any further. Obviously, if she had not been interested, there would have been no point in pushing the issue around in his head. But he had only said *if* he were free. He had not meant to imply anything more. He had not *decided* anything, one way or another. Divorce was a big step.

Besides, how could he be sure he deserved a better life? Even when he told himself his marriage was an empty shell, had been a worthless convention for years, he was not sure it was up to him to act. Had he the right? Had he not made this hollow mockery of a marriage just because it was the only sort of marriage he was capable of making? For their failure could not be the fault of Madge alone, however much he might resent her coldness, her frigidity. That he felt unwanted in his own home, even by his own children, was this not perhaps his fault?

But he could remember with bitterness going outside to sit in the car to read because he could find no peace at home – Robert with his damned guitar and June's pop records and the television and that infernal radio with its inane chitchat and that appalling noise they called music. Madge had that damn radio going morning, noon and night. Whenever he came home it was blaring away, and even in the morning the first thing she did was turn it on. Good God, you'd think a man could have a little peace and quiet in his own home.

Really he felt very often his only function in that house was to make money for them all to spend. When he came home, no matter what the hour, no one bothered to greet him, they just carried on with whatever they were doing. Perhaps they were happier without him, just as he was happier away from them. So that to go away and make a new life with Tricia would be a satisfactory solution for all of them. The children, if they missed him, might realize that he had feelings too.

But marriage, after all, is a social convention. He had never wanted to flout convention, merely to lead a reasonably contented life without hurting anyone, and to know the pride of doing his duty. As far as he knew, he had done his duty well, had served his King and country in the Royal Air Force, had fought to preserve freedom and the British way of life from the forces of evil, had lived an upright moral life, worked hard and loyally for an important British company, fed, clothed and cared for his wife and family, now as a Councillor contributed to the welfare of the community.

And yet, somehow this did not seem to be enough.

Perhaps the world had changed, and values were different. For now it seemed to him it was important to be true to himself. His life was more than half over. Was it not time now to opt for life and love while he could still make this choice? Did he not deserve some happiness? Well, if not deserve, he thought hastily, did he not have the moral right as a human being to try to find it?

The most serious problem, he felt, was that Madge's pride would be hurt. She was a very proud woman.

Then again, did he really want to marry Tricia when he got right down to it? Was it sensible for a man of his age to start another marriage when he had just made a mess of the first? Would theirs be any better? And what did he really know of her anyway? Why was she not already married? There was nothing so very special about him, a balding middle-aged man with a frigid wife and two teenage children, that he should make her feel differently from any other man. There must have been lots of other men, he thought suddenly, probably dozens with whom she had contemplated marriage. Who had rejected whom then? She knew so much about love-making too. Sex with her was an art, an exquisite pleasure eternally renewed through her infinite variety.

He found himself racked with jealousy, tortured by his own thoughts. She would be angry with him he knew, for she had never denied the lovers of the past, of the time she had not known him.

"Oh, yes," she said ironically when he reproached her. "I'm second-hand, third-hand, tenth hand. Why, I've been through so many hands, I must have the patina of an antique."

Other men had kissed her lips and breasts, tasted her smooth bitter honey, seen her stomach heave and heard her cries of passionate frenzy. Other men had been caressed and kissed by her, and endured the ecstasy of her wonderful mouth, sucking, licking, probing.

"But it was never like this," she said. "Love gives sex a totally new dimension. For the first time in my life I really know what is meant by 'making love'." But how could he be sure?

He had never had reason to suppose he was a great lover. Indeed, his life with his wife implied quite the opposite. Perhaps her frigidity was his fault. As far as he could remember, things had been fine at first. He hadn't known then what he knew now, and she had been a virgin and scared, but he had been gentle, and surely he remembered she enjoyed sex then? It was June, really. She had hated having June, and the pain had racked her so long, she swore she would never have another baby. And then that night he took her by force. They had been to a party, and she had flirted with their host, and he had been very tight and amorous, partly jealous of her flirtation and partly proud that she had aroused another man, for she had been so pretty and gay that night. And they had gone to bed, happy, laughing, and he had made love to her with passion, even though her laughter died and she shrank from him, tried to push him off. Robert had been conceived that night.

You could say that night was the end of their marriage if you wanted to put a date to it. One night in December 1953. And it was his fault. No getting away from that.

Except that was hardly reasonable. Any normal man expects to be able to make love to his own wife, not every day perhaps, but often and certainly when they have just been to a party and have been bright and flirting, and reminding each other, I am a man, I am a woman.

Madge didn't really like being a woman, did she? Having babies is the most female thing of all, and she hated that. Even though she was a housewife and cooked and made beds and so on, she was not really feminine. Not like Tricia. There was a strange thing: Tricia, a successful business woman in a man's world, was a far more feminine woman than Madge. It was not just looks, it was a whole approach to life. Tricia liked being herself.

This thought seemed to lead him in the right direction, show a way out of this maze of contradictions. For with Tricia he was happy because he could be himself. If the answer to these problems was that one must be true to one's self, then with her it was at least possible.

"If I were truly honest," he said aloud, "I couldn't live this lie." The bathwater suddenly felt cold, and it was time to soap himself all over, shower it all off and rub himself dry.

If only Robert had not failed his 'O' levels, he thought as he rinsed out the bath. Now he'll need another year at school. When is he going to pull himself together? You can't just wander out into the world at his age without qualifications, just because you want to discover the unknown. It really isn't good enough.

Gerald

Having successfully diverted his mind, Gerald concentrated on the short-comings of his sixteen year old son, for whom he felt a warm but baffled sympathy. It took only half an eye to see the world was in a terrible state. Where was any hope for the future if young people with ideals just frittered away their time in idleness and self-indulgence? He felt old and tired sometimes. Could he not look to his son for help? Poetry, guitars, wandering in the sunshine – self-indulgent drivel. He'd like to ban them all.

6

Gerald

Going to the Club before lunch was a pleasant enough habit, Gerald thought to himself as he crunched over the gravel, even if the same faces, the same opinions, the same jokes week after week threatened him with the boredom he went there to escape.

"Good morning, Mr Hunter."

"Morning, Wilson. Fine day."

The uniformed doorman respectfully held open the door as Gerald stepped into the spacious dimly-lit hallway. "Yes, sir. Mr Gardner left a message, he wants to see you special, sir. He'll be in the bar."

"Thank you, Wilson."

Immediately his spirits lifted, restored at the prospect of something more stimulating to discuss than sports or gardening or cars. That was the advantage of a club like this: important business or political matters could be dealt with quietly and in comfort. He smiled to himself. Today he could receive a message like that from his bank manager and feel pleased. His own father never had a bank account at all, had kept what little surplus he could scrape from his meagre wages in Post Office savings stamps. No doubt it was something to do with the findings of the Council Amenity Committee. Gerald chuckled appreciatively as he opened the door: they'd only drafted the report on Thursday.

The room was crowded. He caught sight of Freddie on the far side of the room, watching the door, and waved. Freddie's glass was full. Might as well get a drink on the way.

"Hey, Gerry. I was hoping you'd be in."

There was Derek Malley grinning at him, and suddenly Freddie Gardner was a pompous bore. Why should he expect to be able to discuss confidential reports of Council committees? Better by far to drink with Derek. There was something about this chap, very blond, very handsome, early forties, legal eagle for a powerful industrial conglomerate …

"Good to see you, Derek."

"Glad you're here, old chap. I wanted to tell you my news before the scandal breaks." He laughed embarrassedly. "Here, sit down. I'll get you a gin."

Derek made his way to the bar, and Gerald sat in one of the armchairs at Derek's table. Scandal? What scandal? The very word was intimidating and conjured up horrific pictures of embezzlement, which was out of the question in this case, or sexual orgies – which also was out of the question. Even when he regained control of his brain, and exchanged excessive fantasies for more realistic ones like, well, like divorce for instance, the picture still didn't fit. Derek and Tina were the only really happily married couple he knew. And then he wondered briefly what Derek thought of his marriage, it probably looked all right on the surface.

No, no, he was letting his imagination run riot. It was probably something simple like a driving offence, and that could be unpleasant. Still, if he had a word with Ted over there, puffing away at his pipe like an old factory chimney, he'd make sure it was kept out of the local paper. Why else was a dull chap like that a member of the club if not as editor of the local rag?

Freddie Gardner folded his newspaper and his glasses, put them carefully on the table, and stared fixedly at Gerald who waved. "Did you get my message, old boy?"

"Yes – I'm on my way to join you, but was waylaid by me

learned friend."

The bank manager rose from his chair with a resigned air, and carried his glass over to Gerald's table.

"Getting hold of you can be a devil of a job, old boy," he told Gerald, sinking heavily into a chair beside him. "The nuisance is that I'm due at the station in half an hour to pick up the wife's mother, and there'd be the deuce of a row if I were late. But we must have a chat about that report you fellows have just got up on the future amenity needs of the area."

"Come now, Freddie. don't tell me you are taking an interest in Art and stuff," said Derek, returning with two full glasses. "Not at your age."

"I'm always interested in Art and stuff," said Freddie, his round red cheeks puffing with indignation. "When it has commercial potential, of course."

"What are you two talking about, for heaven's sake?"

"Your Council Amenity Report, of course. Wake up, old boy."

Gerald burst out laughing. "Oh, that. Who have you been talking to, Freddie? It's got nothing to do with Art. It is about preserving our natural heritage from the encroachments of industry, and more especially protecting us from motorways."

"I did not mention the word Art," said the bank manager with hauteur. "That was our frivolous soliciting friend."

"I do beg your pardon," said Derek lightly.

"Now Gerry," said Freddy, ostentatiously ignoring Derek. "I do have some idea what is in that report of yours, and that is why I want to talk to you. Green Belts are all very fine in their place, but it won't do, you know, to drive out industry completely. We'll all go bankrupt."

"Come off it. You know better than I do that land values have gone up more than ten per cent in this area just in the past year."

"Precisely. And why do you suppose that is? Because better roads and faster cars mean we can get to London in less than an hour. And now you and a few other fellows want to put paid to our growing prosperity and reroute the proposed motorway right away from here. It's a bit much, old boy, really."

"No one is saying there should be no motorway, Freddie. We want one to take the heavy goods vehicles off our tiny roads. But the issue is where."

"That's just it. The Minister has put forward a perfectly good plan, and it's all set to go. Who needs you to start rocking the boat, telling the powers that be that a few minor figures in a tiny community in the backwoods of Surrey don't want them to put their multi-million pound road here, it must go there? You won't get anywhere, of course. All you'll succeed in doing is to make a lot of fuss and waste a lot of time. And investment in the area will just melt away."

"Have you seen the proposed route for this wretched motorway?" Gerald could feel his temper rising, and he knew that was a mistake. "Let me describe to you what this 'perfectly good plan' would do to Godbridge. So the powers that be, in their wisdom, have decided to slice right through the middle of our upper village, and to eliminate the public right of way through the woods, as well as the farmhouse itself, and then they propose to tear down a wide swathe at this end of town, eliminating hundreds of houses, and running – get this – two hundred yards from the new Secondary School building. Can you imagine those poor children, trying to work with heavy lorries crashing past the window?"

"Ridiculous," said Freddie dismissively. "Obviously a clerical error. In any case, those people don't mind living near noisy main roads."

Derek spluttered into his gin, while Gerald exploded:

"Freddie, how dare you be so callous?"

Freddie shook his jowls and smartly-suited spare tyres with simulated mirth. "A veritable knight in shining armour, ha, ha! Looking for dragons to slay, ha, ha!" He then adjusted his countenance for serious business. "Come now, Gerry, you're a man of the world, can't make an omelette without breaking eggs."

"It's sheer vandalism to destroy people's homes when there are perfectly good alternative routes." Gerald felt so angry he knew he was liable to lose his temper and say things he'd regret. "It can't have escaped everyone's notice that if the motorway were allowed to move closer to the golf course, almost all the loss of houses in Godbridge could immediately be avoided."

"A somewhat fanciful idea, old chap, ha,ha!" Freddie stood up. "We must talk more about this before it goes to Council. You must not be stubborn, you know."

"I don't mind talking.," Gerald said drily. "Why don't you give me a ring tomorrow?"

"I'll do that. Bye. Must dash."

Gerald watched the dark-suited bank manager waddle across the deep red pile and ooze round the door out of sight, and his head felt painful and heavy.

Derek exhaled a wave of laughter. "Cheer up, Gerry. He's such a pompous self-centred ass, you don't want to take people like that seriously."

Bitterness held Gerald round the throat. "Too many people are like that. He doesn't care about anything that does not immediately concern him. He knows he's all right in that house up on the hill, and he never goes anywhere except here or the Golf Club. And he knows his clubs won't be endangered. So why should he care whether Godbridge is ruined or the countryside scarred for ever?"

"You sound a bit sour."

"Just a bit disillusioned, that's all. Never mind. Tell me about your scandal?"

Derek looked down at his glass, hesitating. "It's going to sound like one more case of egotism and crass stupidity."

"I'm sorry," said Gerald. Then he laughed. "You *are* an ass."

"Well," Derek said, and took a deep breath. "I've quit my job. We are moving, beds, brooms and bathmats, to the West Country."

He paused, and Gerald was silent.

"I knew you'd be shocked," Derek said with disappointment in his voice. "Really, you know, this is the best thing that could happen to me."

"I'll believe you if you say so." Gerald gave a small laugh. He lit a cigarette. "Come on, tell me more. What happened?"

Derek leaned forward enthusiastically. "You remember in the summer we found a cottage we wanted to buy?"

Gerald nodded. He could hardly have forgotten, Derek and Tina had never ceased their eulogies of a country cottage way off down a farm track, completely secluded in a fairy-tale glen with waterfall and sparkling stream. A country cottage for holidays. Not to live in.

"Naturally, I tried to arrange a mortgage through our department, and immediately my boss was on to me: what was the idea? Was this the first step to leaving the company? It was none of their business, and in any case, I didn't plan to leave yet. So then he pulled various wires, and we were refused a mortgage on the grounds we were not living there. Tina said she and the boy would go and live there. So the goddamn company stepped in once more – can't allow this, it will break up your marriage. I was pretty cheesed off by this time, and finally managed to raise the necessary somewhere outside the clutches of Big Brother. So we signed the contract. And then last Monday, Big Brother told me I was to be promoted – Company Secretary of a new engineering company we have just acquired. In Glasgow. Refusal would be seen, I was told, as proof my loyalties no longer lay with the company."

"So you quit?"

"Right."

"That was a pretty courageous thing to do."

"Listen, Gerry. I'd had all I could take of their trying to run my life for me. They had my body. Apparently they wanted my soul too."

"What does Tina say to all this?"

"She's right in there with me, pitchin' as our American friends would say."

"That's great. And of course, now you can start your own practice, can't you?"

"Yees," Derek said somewhat dubiously. "Though all my work has been in company law, and I don't imagine there will be a crying need for much of that in Cornwall."

"Why not stay here, then? Lots of the men here would be glad to give you their support to start you off." Gerald began to feel enthusiastic, but Derek shook his head.

"No, Gerry. I'm just a drop-out. I want to get away and make my own life, out of the business rat race. It does something to your soul, the everlasting politicking and manoeuvring. I want to do something different. I don't know, open a shop or a restaurant or run a guest house or something."

"I didn't know you felt so strongly about all this." Gerald felt an immense sadness, for he realized Derek was about to walk out of his life.

"Yes. Sometimes I think it is terrible the way people never talk of the things that really concern them." Derek leaned forward earnestly. "Look, I'd like to tell you something very important that happened to me. I don't know whether you'll find it very interesting, but I'd like to tell you."

"Go ahead."

"I've been doing a lot of reading lately, trying to find things out, and somewhere I read how William James spent a night alone on Mount Marcy. He couldn't describe the significance of the experience, he said, but he knew that its influence permeated the whole of *Varieties of Religious Experience.*"

Gerald's sadness was overburdened now by a sense of futility. He had heard vaguely of a writer named James, but he didn't think it was William; he supposed Derek had mentioned a book title, but he had never heard of the book. He felt rather the way he had in Belgium near the end of the war, when he found himself lost and everyone speaking a foreign language. Derek was still talking.

"The same thing happened to me, Gerry. I went down to the cottage after we had signed the Contract, just to look things over, there was nobody living there then. And that night I decided to spend it in the glen, alone. I don't know if I can describe it, being awake all night and absolutely alone, no people for miles around, nothing but rustling branches and trickling water and moonlight dancing over the ferns and leaving magical patches of light and darkness. I can't tell you how important it was. William James had written about it, and there it was, something tremendous happening to me too."

That at least was something Gerald could understand. Talking of religious experience seemed to him irrelevant, but he knew the mysterious pull of nature, the earth and sky, the wind, the sun, the sight and smell and sound of woods and grassy downs, the immense impersonal grandeur of the sea.

"So that's why you are going to drop out," he said slowly. "I see."

"I'm glad you do."

"When are you leaving then?"

"In a month."

"So soon." They were silent. Then impulsively Gerald held out his hand. "I know I'll see you before you go ... but I want to wish you lots of luck, Derek. I guess I'll miss seeing you around."

Derek clasped his hand. "Thanks, Gerry. You'll be coming to stay with us before you know it, don't forget that."

Gerald had driven home, eaten the lunch Madge prepared, gone into the garden to mow the lawn, and all the time there had hung around his heart a heavy sense of depression, of having been betrayed.

Odd, he thought now, catching himself with this thought, never realized I'd got so fond of the chap. Pity he's going. Damn fool idea too, burying himself in the country.

September leaves drifted past the window, and he got off the bed, stood looking at the bright golden clumps of chrysanthemums, the leaves skittering in the breeze over the freshly mown lawn. Dear God, how he'd like to leave too. Was it possible? Worlds could be changed, lives were not necessarily set in concrete. If Derek could say, I want something different, so perhaps could he ...

There arose before him a vision of a stone cottage, set in a garden luxuriant with flowers, surrounded by undulating farmland, a wood, a stream, a thatched roof, roses round the door, sweet-scented herbs, a log fire blazing in the hearth, copper kettle, oil lamp with round opal glass shade, comfortable chintz chairs, and Tricia – her hair down, glowing with country air, smiling. A big brass bed like his grandmother had, with white lace cover, curtains blowing in the breeze, sunshine, flowers, love ...

7

Madge

Madge was resting. Saturdays were always hard work, what with everyone home and meals to cook and beds to make and messes to clear up, and no one ever around to give a helping hand. By four o'clock on a Saturday afternoon, she was worn out, and was glad that Gerald usually took it into his head to have a bath, so that she could have a bit of a rest. Not that he gave her any warning, and it could be quite awkward sometimes since he always blocked up the bathroom for hours. But he never did think of other people. She should be used to it. He couldn't help it, men just were naturally inconsiderate.

She sat in her beautifully furnished lounge, with a tray of tea and biscuits in front of her, a magazine on her lap, and beside her the radio playing her favourite light music. The brightly-coloured painting above the fireplace brought a smile to her lips. It was a lovely picture – amazing what little treasures one could find even in an establishment like Boots if only one were endowed with discrimination and taste. The little girl with untidy black hair and enormous dark eyes was charming, and to the discriminating eye, quite remarkably like June. She felt great pleasure in having thus symbolically hung the portrait of her daughter over the fireplace.

June was the best thing in her life. Other mothers were worried sick by rudeness, sullenness and terrible suspicion, other daughters had shameful secrets, but she knew her June did not hide things from her. Their relationship was so precious. Without her daughter, what would she have left? Her husband was so seldom at home.

He really does work hard, she thought, and wondered again if it might be bad for his health to have so many commitments. After all, it was her responsibility and she always read magazine articles about middle-aged men and their health and how their wives could keep them fit. Men were so awkward, though, and never would do as they were told, even if it was for their own good. One magazine article had even talked of the "male menopause" and how men in their mid forties often feel the need to have an affair before it was too late. That was really shocking, and worried her at first. She could remember last Spring, around Easter time, she had a vague apprehension he was carrying on with someone. Yet even at the time it had seemed very unlikely, and now she felt certain it could not be so, sex just wasn't that important to him any more.

Madge didn't like sex. Vaguely she remembered there had been a time many years ago when it had been pleasant enough, though how it had been and how her body had felt, she had really no idea. Now that they were getting older, they could fortunately dispense with it altogether. For over a year now, Gerald had made no demands on her. Not even to do it for him, which she hated, but she did because it was better than having to go any further. He could not know how her body cringed from his. He could not have asked such things of her if he did.

It was a comfort sometimes to be getting older, for the demands and pressures seemed to diminish with the years. She had never been a beauty, she knew that, and had had to struggle to keep her end up. All those curlers in her hair, and lotions and lipsticks – she was glad she needn't worry now. It was June' s turn.

She thought of herself at June's age. At eighteen. But that was 1944 and she was already engaged to marry Gerald. Growing up during the war had had its advantages, for she had never lacked boyfriends after they opened that airfield near her home in Berkshire, and it must have made her mature more quickly somehow. She couldn't imagine June getting married, for she was still little more than a schoolgirl.

Had it not been for the war, she would never have needed to work; but since she was expected to help the war effort, her father had found her a job as a clerk in the Ministry of Food. Then she joined the W.V.S. and three evenings a week served tea on Waterloo Station. Sometimes she could not get home at night, so would spend the night with Clara, a large forthright woman who took Madge under her wing, for she had three daughters of her own. Or she might take refuge in the Underground and feel the comradeship of Londoners in peril fill her veins, so that she would raise her head high and want to sing aloud.

And Gerald seemed to confirm her love of life, for he was cheerful and made everyone laugh, so that they were always surrounded by hosts of people.

She remembered the first time she saw him. He was tall and slim and handsome, his uniform was freshly pressed. Army uniforms weren't as nice as Air Force ones anyway, and sometimes they used to look as though they'd slept in them for weeks.

A vision of a trainload of weary soldiers filled her head, young boys with grey faces and enormous packs on their shoulders and long rolls dragging, staggering over to her counter while she slopped out hundreds of clumsy cups of hot sweet tea and saw that some of them were wounded, filthy bandages round arms and hands and heads, and some leaned on sticks, and all were stained with mud and blood. And behind came Gerald, marching smartly in his blue uniform with gold wings, cap jauntily perched on his dark curly head – how dared he walk so gaily through this mass of weary soldiers who had been over there, sleeping in mud and spattered with blood, fighting for our liberty? Why was he not wounded? How did he escape scot free when every true red-blooded Englishman was laying down his life?

Strange what crazy thoughts one can have. She pulled herself up short, for he had done his bit. He had dropped bombs on sleeping German cities and fired on German fighters in the air, seen planes explode and comrade or enemy plummet in flames. And that terrible time he was reported "Missing, believed killed", and his belongings sent on to her …

Robert appeared suddenly, crashing open the door and ambling in with shoes covered in grass cuttings and leaves. His jeans were filthy and his tee shirt looked as though it had come from one of her jumble sales.

Blood rushed to her head, and she had to close her eyes and swallow before she could speak. "Do you think," she said slowly and carefully, "you could take off those disgusting shoes and clean up the mess you have just made?" She compressed her lips tightly, and felt the blood pound at her temples as her son stared at her uncomprehendingly.

"Did you hear what I said?" Her voice was rising, she knew. It never failed. She would promise herself time and time again not to lose her temper with him, and then he would do something as thoughtless as this. The times she'd told him to clean his shoes before coming into the lounge. That lovely beige carpet had cost the earth, and she wasn't having it ruined just because he didn't have the courtesy to think what he was doing.

"How *can* you be so stupid!" Her voice was rising to a scream. "Take those horrible shoes off immediately. Look what you're *doing!* Oh, for God's sake, get out of here! You make me sick."

Robert left the room with his head down and his shoes in his hand, and Madge immediately began to regret her ill-temper. She collected the dustpan and brush, and then a bucket of soapy water so that she could rub away the marks, glad of something practical to do to relieve the pressure of emotions that filled her head. It must be a passing phase, for he didn't appear to enjoy these sessions any more than she did. And yet, was it so awful of her to ask him to consider her feelings? So many years of her life had been spent in sacrifice to others, could she not ask her son at least to think of her?

8

Robert

It was Robert's experience that he could do nothing right for his mother. He had come in from the garden quite cheerful for a change, wanting to show her a poem he had just written out in the garden. 'I should know better,' he muttered to himself, but somehow he continued to nurture the illusion that his mother, who said she loved him, might one day understand.

Once again, she was too angry to listen.

Robert, as usual, had found it impossible to answer his mother. The retorts that immediately came to mind would only have made matters worse, so he had stood there, shifting his feet, and dropping grass cuttings and dead leaves all round. Unfortunately, that seemed to make green stains on the wretched carpet, so he did take off his shoes, and then found he was trapped, quite unable to defend himself.

Best thing was to leave the room as rapidly as possible. He did not try to make sense of incidents like this, merely to live through them.

Head down, shoes in his hand, mind in a whirl, he found himself in the kitchen, wandering aimlessly round and round. Eventually, he left the shoes on the table and went up to his room, not because he intended to be provocative, but because he gave up trying to decide what to do while standing in the middle of the room, and just dropped them on the nearest clear space before escaping to his own sanctuary.

9

Gerald

"What the blazes are these shoes doing on the kitchen table?"

Gerald's outraged voice shattered the peace of the afternoon, and jangled Madge's nerves as it reached her through closed doors, through walls, as she was listening to a moving rendering of 'Galway Bay'. She hurried into the kitchen, her nerves taut.

"Please don't shout like that."

"What do you mean, 'don't shout'? I'll shout if I feel like it. Look at that!"

Angrily, he gestured towards the yellow formica-topped table. In the middle sat Robert's tatty corduroy shoes, once beige but now stained with bicycle grease and ingrained with dirt, and mounds of fresh grass cuttings and dead leaves stuck to the torn soles and scattered all around as they had dropped off.

Madge picked up the shoes, dropped them outside the back door, then proceeded to clear up the mess.

"Least said, soonest mended," she said. "I really don't see why you need make such a fuss."

"For Christ sake! Anyone would think it perfectly normal to park filthy shoes on the kitchen table. ROBERT!!"

"Oh dear, please don't start on at him again."

"Are you trying to tell me I shouldn't speak to my own son?"

"Of course not, dear. But you should try to calm yourself first."

"Calm yourself! Calm yourself! That's all you ever say.

Can't we ever speak one word of truth in this house? How can I calm myself when I'm drowning in a sticky morass of lies and sentimental crap!"

"Gerald dear, you'll give yourself a heart attack. You mustn't let the children get you down like that." Madge tipped grass and leaves into the rubbish bin, and then set about washing the table. "I really don't think you understand young people these days. Never mind."

"I see," said Gerald tightly. "I don't understand anything about young people these days, so I must not speak to my own son. Very well." Keeping himself very carefully under control, he walked through the dining room into the lounge, closed the sliding doors and turned off the radio. He then poured himself a gin and tonic, without ice because that was in the kitchen, walked over to the window and stood looking over the back garden.

At least the grass wasn't growing so quickly now. With a bit of luck, it might stop soon. But look at the weeds. You'd think with two grown children he'd have a bit of help sometimes…

It occurred to him that June and Robert hardly ever lifted a finger, not in the garden nor in the house as far as he could see. He was overwhelmed with a terrible sense of failure, for surely it was their job as parents to make sure their children contributed to the family unit, and it reflected his failure as a father that he could ask nothing of Robert or of June. They were spoiled brats.

And where was June anyway? He hadn't seen her at all today, so he supposed she was staying with a friend or something. But wasn't it a bit odd that a father should not know where his daughter was? And that no one should bother to tell him, or even maybe ask him if it was all right? Did he really have to be cut off from his own children?

Well, even if June was lost to him and no one listened when

he said she should study, not waste her time in that awful record shop, he'd make damn certain Robert got a decent start in life.

Not that it would do a damn bit of good, he could see that now. The minute he took off the pressure, Robert would be away, dropping out, bumming his way round all the sleazy parts of the world. What was the use? Why go on flogging yourself to death when there was no value in it, no one gave a damn whether you lived or died?

Madge came in. "There we are. All neat and tidy again." Then she saw his glass. "Oh no. You're not drinking already. It's only five o'clock. What can you be thinking of?"

Gerald turned round, carefully put his glass on the table in front of her, then walked to the door.

"I'm going out," he said, and went.

He drove to Hampstead, to see Patricia. He had never done this before, Saturdays did not belong to them. He could not even be sure she would be at home for he did not know how she spent her weekends. He had not wished to talk of his family life, of his drab mundane existence in his suburban villa, and so had been unable, except in the most general way, to ask her how she spent her time without him. But today he felt that everything had conspired to drive him into her arms. She could not but be there, waiting for him.

The weather itself seemed to tell him he was right, as though the universe had looked down upon this puny mortal in trouble, and had chosen this day to show him the path to happiness. As he set out, the sun emerged from behind grey clouds and its light sparkled on the shiny bonnet of his Rover 2000, gleamed on the metalled surface of the road, urging him to speed all the way to London. But as he drove, he began to reconsider, and black clouds rose from the horizon and darkened the sky, and a great storm of rain beat upon his car. He continued on his way despite misgivings and concluded that he must see Tricia now, if only to preserve his sanity; and miraculously, as he turned into her road and his heart beat with fear that she might not be there, the sun came out once more, low over the rooftops, brilliant, clear, washed clean of darkness by the rain.

He rang the bell, dreading beyond words the need to return without having seen her, and after only a brief agony of suspense, she opened the door. Astonishment flashed across her face, and then she threw the door wide and her face bloomed in welcome.

"Darling! How wonderful! Come in, come in."

He leapt across the threshold, pushed the door closed behind him with his foot, and took her in his arms.

"Trish, Trish," was all he could say. He felt as though he might burst into tears at any moment. The soft yielding lusciousness of her lips, the warmth of her body, her own special odour mixed with perfume obliterated all sense of the forbidden, of the extraordinary. She held him and he thought that all he wanted was this gentle, almost maternal love which enfolded him in the warmth and comfort of her arms. The sort of love, a tiny voice wept inside him, he had never experienced before in his life. No longer did he feel he had searched the length and breadth of the earth in vain. His dreams had become incarnate. This marvellous miraculous female was the Ideal Woman, and she was here, in this house, and he was in her arms. This was where he belonged for ever.

A little later, she telephoned, for she was invited out to dinner, and Jill and Leo insisted that he come too. He was glad, and surprised that he should be happy to share her with anyone else on this special evening. But to go out to dinner together on a Saturday night would set a seal on their relationship. They were a couple. They too were socially acceptable.

He was concerned a little about his appearance, for he had walked out of the house in grey flannels, a blue turtle neck pullover and a tweed jacket. He didn't even have a shirt and tie. But Patricia assured him he didn't need a tie, that he looked splendid as he was and the blue pullover matched the blue of his eyes. Well, if she was happy about it … There was no nothing to be done in any case.

When they arrived at the Roth's spacious late-Victorian terrace house, he was thankful he had not been able to dress as he would have chosen. A tie would certainly have been out of place, and even his degree of casualness was formal compared to the other two men in the room.

Leo, their host, looked extraordinary and so unlike their last meeting that for one moment Gerald imagined there was a joke. But no. This was his staying-in-in-the-evening get-up, apparently, plum-coloured skin-tight trousers (there was no doubt he was male), plum shirt open right down to his waist and displaying all the black curly hair on his manly, if somewhat overweight chest. Among the hairs glistened a stainless-steel star medallion on a chain, on one stubby finger lay a large steel ring, and round his wrist what could only be called a bracelet. Unusual in design, but certainly a bracelet. Patricia commented on it, but with delight rather than surprise: it was a wide smooth steel band designed to encircle two-thirds of the wrist, inset at intervals with large claws holding large unpolished semi-precious stones.

"Leo, this is absolutely marvellous. Where did you find it?"

"I made it myself," said Leo, not with any undue modesty either, Gerald thought. At Tricia's cries of astonishment, he carried her off to his basement workshop, leaving Gerald alone with Harry and Ellen James. Sounds of children could be heard far away upstairs, so presumably Jill was still putting her youngsters to bed.

A sense of unreality engulfed Gerald. Although he had met the Roths several times, he realized he had known nothing of them because he had not been inside their home, and he didn't feel he understood very much yet either. This lounge was so curious and outside his experience, all black and white and chrome and glass, with a strange snake-like lamp in one corner, and large mounted black and white photographs covering every wall. But he was exhilarated, as though he were on the brink of a discovery. All the people he usually saw on a Saturday night, ordinary intelligent business-men, lawyers and so on, he understood them, but almost without exception they filled him with boredom. They were so predictable. This was new, different.

Harry James was pouring beer at the other end of the room, not carelessly but with concentration. Gerald liked to see that, beer could be the queen of drinks when handled correctly. The chap was a writer apparently, of plays for television and such. He didn't look as though he was starving anyway, for he was large in every way, tall, wide, verging on fat, and apparently didn't care much about his appearance either; his trousers were baggy, his shoes down-at-heel, he wore no jacket and only a very ordinary pale blue nylon shirt open at the neck, sleeves rolled up above the elbow. His greying hair was combed straight back, his face was pale as though he sat too much out of the sun, with huge jowls, a large nose and tiny pale eyes set deep in his pasty flesh. But when he turned to Gerald to hand him a foaming pewter tankard of beer, a smile lit up his face and showed a long row of very large, very even, very white teeth. His voice was low, melodious, hypnotic.

"I guess you don't go much on jewellery for men, Gerry," he said. "Neither do I."

"It's a new thought to me," Gerald admitted.

"The women, though, they love it," Harry said confidentially, taking possession of the only really comfortable armchair. "It must be the new mating signal. Time was you could get by with a sports car, or more recently long hair, or in my case, the scent of genius. But now we're going to have to doll ourselves out like fairies, or we're dead ducks. A sad thought."

A low laugh came from the region of the bookcase. "Your mating days are supposed to be over, Henry dear. You don't need to worry."

The thought flashed across Gerald's brain – Henry James? - but then he could think of nothing but this new woman. Ellen James could not be the wife of that slob. He had not seen her properly before, for she had been kneeling beside the bookcase and introductions were not made in this set. Now as she walked towards them, he saw that she was beautiful. Slender and graceful, she was dressed in a long clinging dress of some green stuff, her pale golden hair was swept up Grecian style, her nose and brow were firm and her mouth delicate. He could not imagine how she came to be here, married to that crude oaf: she should be dressed in silks and diamonds, guarded and cherished by rich men in dark suits and shiny limousines, she belonged in great halls lit with crystal chandeliers, with fountains and marble statuary and the sound of music...

Her voice asking him to tell her about himself brought him back to earth, and he saw that she was pale and interesting, but not beautiful like Tricia. The very banality of their conversation gave him time to reflect, to wonder what had come over him just moments before. His mind did not seem to be under control. He had better be careful.

Jill came in with Patricia, followed by Leo and a very dark chap. Gerald stood up to greet the ladies, and Jill reached up to kiss him on both cheeks.

"Gerry darling, I'm so glad you came. This is the way it should always be." Tricia looked at them both and smiled. Jill's round pink cheeks and light brown eyes filled Gerald with tenderness, and he put his arm round her shoulders and hugged her impulsively, before letting her go.

"Salut, Vincent, mon vieux," said Harry from the depths of the black armchair, evidently disdaining the niceties of civilised society where a gentleman stood up when ladies entered. *"Ca va?"*

The dark man shrugged his shoulders gallicly. *"Comme ca."* His black eyes seemed reluctant to look anywhere but Tricia.

"Sit down, everyone, make yourselves comfortable," said Leo genially. "Vin, come and meet Gerry. Vincent Lemieux, Gerald Hunter."

The two man shook hands warily, and Gerald struggled to remain afloat in the flood of unexpected experiences. The man was a Negro, black as the things of night.

"I'm so sorry I neglected you all so long," Jill was saying, "but we had a crisis upstairs. Julie dropped her night-night in the bath ..." She continued to talk incomprehensibly about babies and baths and tantrums and tears, and Leo handed round drinks and everyone found somewhere to sit, making splashes of colour in this black and white room.

Keep calm, you fool, Gerald told himself. French-speaking blacks are obviously common-place in this circle. But what really stirred him up was the realization that this Vincent chap had no wife with him. Tricia had been expected alone. Therefore the implication was ... just for this dinner party, of course ... but Tricia and that Negro ...

Tricia sat on the floor beside his legs, gently laid her arm along his thigh and lifted her face to him with a warm, loving smile. The dark hair framing the perfect oval of her face, the pearliness of her skin, the depths of the green pools in her eyes, all these told him of her love. He put his hand on hers and squeezed it. There was nothing to worry about. This hideous pairing-off was not her fault. He just wished the chap would stop staring at her like that and direct his nasty brown eyes somewhere else.

They were still talking of children when he tuned back in.

"All children seem to have something," Leo was saying. "Mark used to have a rather nasty piece of blanket with a satin ribbon, and it was a major crisis if Jill wanted to wash it. And Jenny had a teddy bear."

"Still does," said Jill.

"Your two were just the same, weren't they, Ellen."

"Oh yes, indeed. And when Jimmy had his tonsils out and then developed complications, heaven knows what ghastly consequences that would have had if he hadn't been able to have his piece of blanket with him. I've always felt grateful to that night nurse who let him hide it under his pillow. She was a truly good human being."

"In my opinion, that sort of indulgence is bad for children," said Harry, leaning back comfortably with a tankard of beer in one hand and a cigarette in the other. "Ellen and I had quite a fight about it, until I decided to opt for the easy life."

"So I should think," cried his wife. "Imagine! He had this crazy theory that a baby should be prevented from sucking its thumb and given no toys in bed, and just look at him with his beer and his cigarettes."

"Ah, yes, but I need cigarettes now because I was allowed to suck my thumb in childhood. It's entirely my mother's fault."

"Nonsense. You need cigarettes because you are addicted. And you probably became addicted in the first place because you were deprived as a child."

"I do hate the way you psychologists always blame the

parents," protested Jill. "I mean, we all do our very best. No one knows how to be a good parent till they've been through it, and then it's too late."

"I don't think we always blame the parents," said Ellen a little huffily. Then she laughed. "Well yes, I suppose we do. But then we see the casualties. I find it very hard sometimes not to get upset and angry and remember that seriously incompetent parents were themselves brought up badly, and so it goes on, back and back."

"Oh, Ellen," objected Vincent from across the room. "That is surely too simplistic a theory. People are not simply a product of their environment. Surely you will accord them a measure of free will."

"Of course," Ellen began, but Leo interrupted:

"The thing obviously is to present valid choices. If all a child find in his life is violence, anger, hatred, if he never has any experience of love..."

Gerald's mind shut off.

He could accommodate no more of this argument for the whole conversation was beyond his experience. Where he came from, women discussed children and babies, separately and quietly among themselves, while men talked cars or football or politics. Here the men were discussing childcare as a matter of course, as though they were involved. Extraordinary. And yet he had felt for years that there was something odd in an arrangement where he was expected to make pronouncements *ex cathedra* so to speak, while the everyday problems of his children's lives were held to be outside his province. It had never occurred to him that what a child took to bed might affect the sort of adult he became – was that what they were saying? To his shame, he could not even remember to what, if anything, his own two children had been so attached it might be the leaping off point for a similar conversation in other circumstances, at other times.

Of course, what these people were talking of was feelings. In his life, he dealt with facts. It would not do to exaggerate. Just imagine the effect if he got up at the next Council meeting and said, "Gentlemen, the hooligans and drug takers who threaten to wreck our town need our sympathy, not our anger. They attack society because their parents did not love them."

He looked around at the colourful group collected in the black and white and chrome room, the privileged and beautiful people: Jill, leaning forward, drawing through her hands the garland of purple nuts hung round her neck, short brown hair disarrayed, eyes alight; Ellen, pale and golden, delicate, her graceful contained way of sitting betraying her as older than he had thought, emanating a vital intellectual force; Patricia, darkly, richly beautiful, leaning against his knee, listening; Leo, planted squarely on the black stool, using hands and arms to emphasize his words, dark, virile in spite of his Christmas tree decorations; even Harry, slouched in the deep armchair, had a definite presence and indefinable charm. And Vincent, the black man, the foreigner, an alien force with which he must reckon.

What was he, Gerald, doing here? Did he really belong? Did he even want to? The question felt important: these bright, colourful people set against a black and white background, moving, talking, gesticulating as though for his benefit, he could choose at that moment whether to become part of this vision or to refuse it on the grounds of its unreality, its detachment from those things that he knew and understood, and so it would fade away. For ever.

Jill leapt up and disappeared into the kitchen. Gerald was relieved to note that even here it was the woman who cooked dinner. And Leo opened the wine.

Presentation was half the pleasure of food, Gerald thought as Jill ladled out the French onion soup from a shiny dark brown tureen into pottery bowls. Even the dishes here were different, not white china decorated with flowers or a tasteful border of gilt, but brown pottery and stoneware, rich against a mustard yellow tablecloth and yellow linen napkins. The flavour of the soup was subtle and delicious, admirably supported by crisp croutons and just the right amount of melted gruyere cheese. This looked like being a memorable meal.

The black fellow was on Tricia's other side, and since the table was circular, Gerald could watch him easily. He'd never met a Negro socially before. Strange how the palms of his hands were so pink, with the lines standing out darkly against the pale skin, and a sudden change from pink to black on the edges of his hands. They say black men are not black but brown, but this one was so very black he looked almost navy blue in places. The inside of his mouth and the whites of his eyes were so prominent against his blackness, their pale vulnerability was almost obscene.

As Jill removed the soup dishes and he told her had found the first course superb, he could hear a conversation between Tricia and that chap. Much as it pained him to eavesdrop, he had to find out what their relationship was.

"Qu'est-ce que tu fabriques avec ce beau type-la, ce gentleman avec le sourire sec et l'air froisse?" Vincent demanded in a low voice, leaning towards her in a repulsively intimate manner.

"Vin, tais-toi," said Patricia, and she glanced round the table. Gerald was relieved to note that Leo, Ellen and Harry were absorbed in a discussion of a Mastroianni movie, and he pretended to listen to them. *"C'est mon futur mari."*

"Quoi? Impossible. Incroyable!" Vincent appeared shaken, and Gerald felt a sudden sense of exultation. She was right.

Dear, beautiful Patricia thought of him as her future husband, and that was what he would be. He allowed himself a brief vision of a future consecrated to her. When he returned to reality, the chap was still going on at her.

"You are wasting your life in that advertising shop, manipulating people. And for what. You are not doing it for the power. I think not even for the money. You are manipulating people just for pleasure. *Ah ma chere amie,* do not throw away your life like that. People like you are too rare. Marry me. Come with me to Africa, do something worth while in my unhappy country."

"Dear Vin, you know I hate being put on a pedestal. I can only fall from there one day, and when that happens, you will hate me."

"Tu me desesperes."

"I don't believe you. *Tu te desesperes toi-meme.* You should have returned to Africa a year ago, and *voila,* you are still here."

So he wanted to marry her too, did he? Poor chap. You could hardly blame the poor fellow, though it was a pretty outrageous idea even to think of. But he couldn't help being born the wrong colour, and presented with such a beautiful white woman who obviously was kind and friendly, no wonder his head was turned. One could feel quite sorry for the chap.

Jill's *boeuf bourgignon* raised Gerald's spirits even further. Such excellent cooking was rarely found in a private home. The pieces of dark red meat were perfectly tender, the mushrooms and tiny button onions firm, the dark gravy rich and deliciously flavoured. These people took the importance of wine and food for granted, while he had had to go to the Festive Board or find a French chef in an expensive restaurant. What a fool he had been all these years.

Wine, food and laughter. It was amazing how these

simple things made him come alive. He felt taller, straighter somehow, his head was clear, his stomach no longer in knots. The glow from the ruby liquid in his glass swirled down his backbone and he was master of his fate to be sure. All things were possible. He had only to choose.

10

Madge

Saturday evening dinner was a disaster. Madge was very upset. Mealtimes often were uncomfortable these days, and she really did not know why. She always did her best to create a proper family atmosphere. Now June had taken to going away for the occasional weekend, Madge had begun to feel quite lost sometimes without a friendly face in the kitchen or a joke or two over the washing up. Of course, Robert had a lovely sense of humour: he could be quite hilarious, making up funny rhymes which he set to music on his guitar, and sometimes his friend Matt would turn up, and they'd entertain her while she whipped up a fresh cake for them and then they'd eat it straight from the oven. She didn't mind the mess they made one tiny bit. But it hadn't been like that this weekend. Far from it.

Partly it was her own fault, for shouting at Robert like that. She really did not understand what got into her sometimes, she never lost her temper with anyone else. Just Robert. And then she said things she didn't really mean, and could hardly even remember afterwards. Not that he seemed to bother much about it. But it bothered her.

However, he had stupidly put his filthy shoes on the kitchen table, and as she pointed out, it was his fault his father was not there. He should know by now what an impatient hasty man his father was, and should avoid at all costs doing stupid things like that to set him off. When Gerald lost his temper, it set a blight on the house for a week.

Robert had begun to argue then. The two of them were

alone at the dining table: June's chair was empty because she was at Hetty's, and Gerald had not yet returned, and she obviously couldn't keep the chicken waiting more than half an hour or it would have been spoilt. It could have been such a lovely evening, just the two of them, once they had cleared this business of Gerald and the shoes out of the way. But he had to argue, even while she was serving him his favourite portion of chicken and lots of roast potatoes and tiny green peas. She could have wept.

"It's stupid to make such a fuss about a bit of dirt. It doesn't hurt anyone."

"Civilised people do mind dirt, dear. It harbours germs."

"But going on about it, it's so petty. So what if I put my shoes on the kitchen table. I know it's not usual, but it's not a crime, for Christ sake."

"No one said it was, dear. Please don't swear."

"Well, he's behaving as though it's a crime, walking out of the house as though we're not fit to be in his presence. Must be a raging maniac."

"Robert! Please! Don't talk about your father like that."

"Well, he is. A bloody tyrant, with a mind as blinkered as an old carthorse. Look at you. You're scared out of your wits because he lost his temper, and all he's does is slam out of the house like a spoiled brat. He's the one who's behaved badly, not me."

"Robert," Madge said faintly, "I will not have you criticise your father."

The blood rose to her temples, throbbing wildly. She put her hand to her breast, felt anger choking her so that she could not speak. Robert looked at her in consternation.

"Gosh, Mum. I'm sorry."

She scarcely heard him. Hammers beat against the shell of her skull, and flashes of sharp light confused her vision.

Anger, deep red violent anger that would tear her apart, what was she to do with this violent emotion which was not, could not be, whatever Robert said, could not ever ever be fear?

"This is intolerable," she said at last. "First you behave stupidly, then you try to brazen it out instead of apologising, then you attack your father. And the cap it all, you blaspheme."

"I did apologise."

"If you can't pull yourself together, you'd better go to your room. I really can't bear any more."

Robert leaped up, banging his chair against the wall. She saw the dent where it tore the wallpaper and spattered plaster even as she knew he was throwing himself across the room.

"I swear the whole bloody world's gone mad!" He slammed the door behind him.

She was left to contemplate her beautiful meal, perfectly cooked and barely touched, the indescribably painful evidence that her family was disintegrating and she didn't know why.

In a brief flash of resentment, she contemplated putting the whole lot in the dustbin. But she wasn't like that. It was all good food, and she had been well brought up, she knew it would be a sin to waste it. Had her nanny not told her many times, 'Think of the starving millions' when she had been tempted to leave scraps on the side of her plate? No sensitive person could waste good food when little children, little black children in dirty uncivilised countries, but children nevertheless, would go to bed that very night with nothing in their tummies. So she wrapped it all in silver foil and put it in the refrigerator, and then she washed all the dishes, even the greasy roasting pans, and put everything away, so that in the end there was no sign the meal had ever existed.

Fortunately, she remembered to telephone Lucy and Jeremy, or they would have been round at nine as usual on the way to *The King's Arms*. She said she had a headache, which was true enough, nothing about Gerald's not being there. Then she sat down with a pot of tea to wait for him.

She really did not understand what had happened. Were men always so unpredictable? Or was it a question, as her mother had said, of class and heredity? It was true that there were great differences in their backgrounds, and that Mother had said, 'You are marrying beneath you. It can only lead to unhappiness.' But that was more than a quarter of a century ago, surely not worth considering now.

But what if her children were tainted with undesirable traits? Could that be the explanation for Robert's rudeness? June's flouting of convention? Perhaps she would never get them to behave correctly, they would resist her influence and drift away, and she would never be warmed in her old age by the glow of their success.

Obviously on her side there was no problem. The Leicesters, her father's family, were all respectable men of business, and her father had been a civil servant in the Ministry of Food. Many a time as a child, she had sat on a stool at her mother's knee and listened to her father expound the glories of working for the government, he standing with his back to the fire, his hands lifting his coat tails to warm his back. And her mother's family had all been something to do with the law. Once she had visited Uncle Malcolm Wagstaff's office in Banbury, a large dark musty room with fading yellow paint, walls of shelves loaded with worn dull-green folders tied with bright pink tape, a glass-fronted bookcase with heavy leather-bound volumes, and an ancient safe, its bulging green door fitted with wheels. His desk was large and dusty too, covered with papers and folders and pencils and pens and glass dishes for pins and clips and two big chipped inkpots. Two upright chairs for visitors stood in front of the desk, and the one she sat in had a red scratchy seat and a curious hollow towards one side. Mother said Grandfather Wagstaff had had that office and that it hadn't changed ever, and the Wagstaff on the sign downstairs was grandfather's name too.

But if Class, Birth, Heredity were really important, surely her father would have said something when she wanted to marry Gerald. She hadn't listened to her mother's forebodings: no one cared about class in those days, everyone was equal. She felt so proud to walk out with Gerald, she knew all the girls envied her hanging on the arm of a handsome airman with curly hair and blue eyes and lovely blue uniform with wings. If the differences in their background had really mattered, her father would have said. Instead, he had approved of Gerald even though his father was only something lowly on the railway. 'People like him are the backbone of the nation,' he would say. Her heart still glowed when she remembered these words.

But that didn't mean there might not be something not quite nice hidden in his background. She had never met his mother, who had been killed in an air-raid, but secretly Madge thought it was probably a blessing she hadn't been around, for from what she had heard, the woman sounded a right battleaxe. Gerald's father had never really counted at all: when she met him, he was already a frail old thing, wounded in the war while guarding a petrol dump, and his wounds had left him unable to care for himself, so until his death five years ago, he was essentially a drain on their assets. Not that she would ever have said such a thing in Gerald's hearing: he loved his father, as any son should, and insisted on taking the children to visit their grandfather from time to time. She learned very early on to avoid even the faintest hint of criticism, for she hated his explosions.

Not that any of this meant she criticised her own husband. Naturally she did nothing of the kind. She did get annoyed with him sometimes. Her mother had warned her: 'Men are selfish and inconsiderate,' and occasionally she found it hard to remember he couldn't help it, and then she did feel cross. But these were small minor irritations. She loved her husband as every wife should, and after twenty-five years of marriage, you had something that almost stood by itself. All those years of living together through the good and the bad, they made a relationship as solid and sure as the Bank of England.

She didn't even know why she was thinking about her marriage at all. It was not the sort of thing she needed to think about, so it was very odd that in the past few days she had started to wonder what her life was all about. It would have been a comfort if she could have talked to someone when, just occasionally, for a brief instant, she questioned whether it was all worth while.

But who? Vanessa and Barbara and Lucy would talk about husbands and children and marriage in general, and they'd all agree it was hard to be a woman. But that was not quite what she wanted. After all, you couldn't really open up your heart to your neighbours, they'd be bound to think something dreadful. Like when Vanessa said she wished she was a man. Everyone could see what she meant, it was obvious that men have the best of it. But it was a stupid thing to say, you couldn't wish you were something you were not, she might as well wish she were the Queen of England. In any case, it could be they didn't feel trapped and bewildered sometimes, as she did. Perhaps she was odd. All the magazine stories she read and all the nice family programmes on television showed that women could find fulfilment in being good wives and mothers. She had her position to maintain. She couldn't let them suspect that on rare occasions, very briefly, she felt a little inadequate.

The Church didn't really help either. She knew it was sinful of her to question God's purpose, and it was her duty to accept the burden of womanhood with patience and cheerfulness. And she did try. But patient acceptance did not prevent her from asking why women had to suffer. The monthly pains that only got worse as years went by, the excruciating agony of labour and childbirth – men had nothing comparable in their lives. The years and years spent waiting, watching, while your husband made his life in the world, and all you could do was try not to give him any cause for complaint.

Original sin was Rev. Frost's explanation, and secretly she was angry. How typical of a man. She had to spend her years on earth in misery just because Eve, some wanton hussy, gave her husband an apple. It was all so terribly unfair. She didn't like the way the Church blamed women for all the sins in the world, Eve in the Garden of Eden had nothing to do with her, she would never walk around naked or listen to snakes talking. And anyway, if Adam knew better, why did he not say No?

'God is Love," said Rev. Frost, and GOD IS LOVE was painted in tall letters on the notice board outside the church. But she did not believe it. God was masculine, He was the Father and the Son, therefore he could not love.

The only person she could have talked to about these things was her mother, and she was dead. Her loss still brought pain though it was more than five years now, and she could still remember how empty she had felt and how no one had understood. Gerald had said all the right things, and patted her on the shoulder, and gone right on with his life. Father had told her to pull herself together. It was strange that she had felt so lost, for after they retired to Cornwall, she had only seen them twice a year, in summer and at Christmas. Yet she had felt as though a light had gone out inside her and there had been no way of finding what to do.

And then one wonderful night, her mother had come to her. She was lying in bed, feeling very alone, and suddenly she had known that her mother was with her in the room. Until that moment, she had never understood that there could be a life after death. The joy of it came with a glorious certainty: one day she would be reunited with her mother in Heaven. There would be no business parties then, no trips abroad for her mother, no nanny to hold her forcibly back, no nursery to be locked in, no maids to torment her. Just herself and her mother. She realized that after all she was lucky to have no brothers and no sisters, though she had longed for a playmate for years, for now she would have no brother and no sister with whom she must share her mother for all eternity.

She decided to go to bed. Ten o'clock, and Gerald was not home yet, but she really didn't feel like waiting up for him. He was probably drinking somewhere – she was glad to have been spared that at least. He was beginning to drink far too much. But she couldn't worry about that now, she had put up with enough for one night.

Robert she presented with a sandwich and a glass of milk because she really couldn't let her own child go to sleep hungry. He grinned at her worriedly: "I didn't mean to upset you."

At least he had the decency to apologise. His father wouldn't, that would be too much to ask.

It did seem unfair that women should have to devote themselves to such cold, selfish brutes as men invariably are, but the memory of her mother had strengthened her. Only women know what love is, and a mother's love can transcend the grave. It was a real comfort to know that.

11

Patricia

As Gerald drove them to her flat, Patricia rapidly reviewed the state of her bedroom and made a mental note of things she must do as soon as they arrived: turn up the fire, put on the bedside lamp, hide the clothes on the chair, get brandy and glasses. She felt as though she were planning a campaign and her entire future depended on its success. She was convinced that if Gerald did not make his choice tonight, he was lost to her for ever.

He was smiling and happy, he did not look as though he was on the verge of a momentous decision. She could not let this opportunity go by default. Her own integrity was in question. Did she or did she not mean it when she said she loved him enough to sacrifice her freedom of action to him? And if she meant it, could she then be so cowardly as to let him slide away from her, out of the orbit of this new life he yearned for and had not yet realized he could reach out and grasp, just because he did not act, did not say enough?

She did not subscribe to the inhibitions of a former age where men and men alone made all the important decisions. This was her life too. And although she could not for one moment envisage trying to force Gerald into doing something against his will, she certainly believed she should do all in her power to persuade him to do as she wished. She saw them both as free and equal agents, at liberty to use argument and persuasion upon each other, but always understanding and protecting the other's freedom of choice.

"You manipulate people," Vin had accused her. "That is the

very essence of advertising, to persuade people to buy things they would otherwise not even think of. Basically what you do is immoral."

But to her the key was choice. No one was forced to buy something they did not want just because she had arranged for an advertisement to be published saying they should.

"It's a game," she told Vin. "Everyone can see the moves, there's nothing hidden. The advertiser pays to have the virtues of his product broadcast to the public, but if it turns out not to be what the public wants, too bad. No one buys and the advertiser loses his money."

Vin was wrong. She did not manipulate people: she had too much respect for another's integrity to try to impose her ideas, however strongly felt, on others. But that did not preclude persuasion. What was the human voice for if not to communicate with others? What the invention of language, of words, if not to convey ideas and feelings, to make us feel less alone?

But she did believe implicitly in the other's power to edit or reject. So she did not see the outcome of her important campaign as certain. Except that she loved Gerald and Gerald loved her, and such love as this had never visited either of them before. By the very nature and essence of this love, there could surely be only one true result.

That was how she believed one should live: for truth and love. If Gerald only saw this too, then together they could impose a meaning upon existence, discover that secret sought by philosophers and poets for centuries, the secret that true lovers claim to know.

Gerald did not give her a chance to carry out her plans once they reached her flat. He turned up the gas fire himself, and then took her in his arms, both standing in the middle of the bedroom floor, still fully dressed as they had come in from outside.

They did not speak. She began to say, "Darling..." but he covered her mouth with his own, and as they kissed, tongues of flame rose and licked their limbs and liquid fire smouldered in their loins. Slowly they removed each other's clothes and shuddered with exquisite pleasure as they felt the vibrance of their naked skin upon skin. Every inch of their bodies was alive, responding to caress, to kiss, every sense awoke, touch and taste and sight and sound and smell. With hand and eye and lip and tongue they examined God's creation and found what he had made and saw that it was good.

The miracle of creation they discovered and recreated themselves, in a welter of flesh and bone and sinew and the primeval waters of the sea. Over and over again, they discovered that there were heights undreamed of, fit only for gods and the chosen few, heights that they had perhaps reached before and then forgotten, but now claimed as theirs. Until at last, in a final volcanic eruption, the whole earth shuddered and was moved. Then all was still except the beating of their hearts and a slowly flowing river of sweat between their breasts. They smiled at each other in pride at the power, the glory and the ecstasy of it. Rapture transfigured their faces and joy was in their hearts.

They lay together for a long while, his arms clasped close around her, her head on his breast nestled among the curling hairs which tickled her nose.

"I do believe you enjoyed that," he said at last, gently teasing.

"Oh, I don't know," she replied in the same gentle mocking tones. "The earth only moved out of its orbit tonight, and scattered the stars in the heavens."

"You are right," he said, and his voice was serious. "Worlds have gone off course tonight."

She pushed herself up onto her elbows, and looked into his face, scarcely able to breathe.

"You mean you have made your choice?"

For a moment he looked at her with incomprehension.

"But of course," he said. "I had decided some time ago. I must have you, so I must leave my wife."

12

Gerald

Gerald left the flat before six in the morning. He could not stay to savour with her the laziness of a Sunday morning, lie in bed with her and caress her limbs, drink coffee and eat breakfast as though worlds had not gone off course in the middle of the night. Yet he had to sleep beside her to affirm their love. To make love and leave her as he had done so often before would have made mockery of his new decision. So he left in the cold grey of a September dawn, and Patricia said nothing to hold him back.

After half an hour, he had left behind the sleeping conurbations of Kingston, Surbiton, Esher, and drove slowly through the darkness of the common, negotiated sprawling Cobham, then on into Surrey's gentle countryside. The dawn was lightening as he stopped the car, and waited to watch the pale sun rise, glowing faintly through the mists of the Thames Valley. Alone in his car, isolated from the world, he sat for an hour, maybe two among the grey blanketed hills, and watched the sun chase the swirling mists and the green fields emerge fresh and sparkling and the trees glow green, yellow, gold in the rising sun.

It seemed to him in the cold light of this new morning he had made the most obvious and sensible decision, and was staggered to think how long it had taken him to make up his mind. Slow and steady like that damn tortoise, he thought wryly, but at least it won the race.

Facing Madge was going to be difficult, of course. The real problem was that he was a coward. They had been living this farce for so many years, it was like a bad habit you can't give up. Madge had probably only hung on so long to avoid a scandal which might wreck his career. But what the heck, he could do without politics, and he'd take his chances at the office. He'd explain how he had come to this decision so late in the day, and the old girl would understand.

He told her his decision carefully and gently, sitting in their impeccable lounge, one on each side of the fireplace with its ingenious arrangement of logs. He touched on their years together, their estrangement and keeping up appearances for so long, how concerned he was not to hurt her, what an excellent mother she had been, and how grateful he was for her support in the past. He would not abandon her, of course, would make sure she was adequately provided for, and he was sure she would agree how much better it would be now for both of them to make a new life while there was still time. He would leave now, as soon as he had packed a few essentials, and would arrange about the larger things and what to do about the house later, when she had had a chance to see a solicitor. It was only right to let her do that, though of course she must know that he would be more than generous. He didn't want to disrupt her life too much. But he knew she would agree, a break now would be best for both of them; the children were nearly grown up, they would all be happier living their lives honestly instead of keeping up appearances for fear of what others might say.

She sat in her armchair and appeared to listen to him talking, but said nothing.

It disturbed him that she refused to speak. He supposed she was angry with him, and it was true that her life would be disrupted to some extent. But he would be generous to her, she must know that. It was not like her not to say a word.

Was it possible that the idea of divorce had come as a shock to her? It was true they had never talked of it. But then they never talked of anything that mattered, had not actually talked to each other for years. He had no idea what she actually thought about anything, though he rather inclined to the conclusion that she didn't think at all. He had known her for a quarter of a century, and she had never once produced an original comment.

She was probably trying to punish him. He had spent a long time, nearly two hours it must have been, trying to elicit a response from her. Well, he had done his best. Too late now.

Eventually, he went and packed those things that seemed essential, though how he was to choose seemed almost beyond him. Shirts, socks, underwear, a couple of suits, ties ... What was the weather going to be like? Cold maybe, and wet. God. Well, if he left anything really essential, he could always buy another, and he'd get his secretary to help sort things out. The sooner he got out of here the better.

June was still away apparently, and Robert was still in bed. How to explain to a sixteen-year-old boy? He sat on the edge of his bed, and tried to make it clear that he was not leaving his son, he was leaving his wife, and his son was still his son. He would see him again very soon.

"When did you decide this?" Robert's voice was hollow and dark.

"Last night. Why? Does it matter?"

"I see." The boy turned away, closed his eyes, his face to the wall.

"What do you see?"

"Nothing."

"This is very painful for me," Gerald said, but his son did not move. Gerald felt driven beyond the boundaries of decency, and rushed from the room.

Now he was desperately anxious to escape. Robert clearly was terribly hurt, and he just had no idea what he should have done or said.

He had planned to drive straight back to London, to Tricia's flat. But he felt he would rather be alone for a while, so he stopped for lunch at a pleasant inn on the Hog's Back. There the enormity of what he had done struck him forcibly, so that he spent the rest of the day and part of the evening wandering across the downs, wrestling with his conscience and weeping openly, tears running down his cheeks and sobs tearing his breast, as he thought of the years of hope and goodwill and hard work now crushed into nothingness with his open admission of failure.

13

June

June hoped for a lift from the station on Sunday night, and telephoned. But her mother said, "Your father's not here," which wasn't so unusual, so she had to take a bus and then walk. It's so stupid not to drive, she thought for the seven hundred and fifty sixth time. Mother could have her own car like everyone else, and then I wouldn't have to walk all the time when Dad's not there. She resolved to ask for driving lessons for her Christmas present, and then perhaps she could get a car of her own. It wouldn't be that difficult, Don had picked up a jalopy for £20 and it went like a dream. Or maybe a scooter, that would be better than nothing. Dad would be bound to make a fuss about an old banger, but even on a scooter she could ride to work every day.

But more important things were on her mind.

Her conscience was heavy laden for she had spent the weekend, not with Hetty as her mother thought, but with George in his scruffy flat in St John's Wood. Not that she felt guilty about sleeping with George, for she was in love with him and what was more natural? But she had lied to her mother and she was afraid of being found out. And then there was that old harridan on the floor below, who had abused her on the stairs that morning for disturbing the sleep of decent people because they had played records and danced and sung last night – and the old bat had called her 'a dirty whore'. She had rushed up the stairs and thrown herself on the bed, half angry and half scared because perhaps the old bag was right. Was she a dirty whore?

George had laughed and put his arms round her, and Bill and Philip who were sharing the other room came out and laughed too. They all swore they would vouch for her blameless character, and they put on another *The Who* record very loudly, and she fried them all eggs and burnt them all toast.

It was a miracle to her that he should say he loved her. George was red-haired and handsome and a student at the Slade, and surely had the pick of all those talented girls studying with him. But then she was lucky because they had known each other for so long, for four years now, and theirs was a true romance that would last for ever. She absolutely did not believe the absurd tales she had been told by certain jealous females, who seemed to think she would accept that her beloved George took advantage of every available woman he met. He was so lovely, so gentlemanly, it was absurd to imagine even for one instant that he could behave so badly. She knew him better than that.

On her return journey, she had been wondering how she could manage to leave home. At the moment, she did not know what she wanted to do, or where she would go, or who she wanted to be. But a small bud of independence had begun to grow inside her. She realized she had a life and it must be lived. With George perhaps? Or perhaps even not.

When she got in that evening, there was a terrible air of gloom everywhere. Bobby didn't even say, 'My god, what have you got on?' as she expected, he just got up, brushed past her in the doorway and mooched upstairs.

"A fine way to greet your sister," she said to his back. But he just kept going.

"What's eating him?" she asked her mother, flaunting her beautiful cloak a little as she took it off. But her mother didn't react. She just sat in her chair, staring at the phony fire.

"Mum, is something the matter?"

"Why should there be?"

"I don't know. You seem odd somehow. Are you ill?"

"Yes, that's it. I'm ill. I've been stabbed to the heart."

Her mother's toneless voice making this melodramatic statement was so shocking, June almost laughed. I wonder she's not more careful about bleeding all over her precious carpet, she thought. But then she was ashamed of her stupid sense of humour. The poor woman was obviously upset about something. She knelt down beside her mother, put her hand on her knee like a dog to comfort her.

"Who did it?" she asked fiercely in spite of her good intentions. "Who's the villain?"

"Your father..." began Madge.

Not Dad, oh no... She had a wild vision of her father in his pinstripe suit gesticulating madly on the rug in front of them, a briefcase clutched in one hand – and the carving knife in the other.

"He says he wants a divorce. He says there's another woman. And he's left me. Left us … But it can't be true ... It simply can't be true ..."

"But why?" cried June. "Why?"

Her mother said nothing more. Her eyes were closed on her pain.

June sank to the carpet at her mother's feet.

So this was what it felt like when the bottom of your world fell out. Dad, Dad, why did you leave me, why couldn't you wait for me, take me with you? Why didn't you even say that you were going?

A bitter hatred arose in her heart for the unknown woman who had stolen her father, for now she knew he could not love her. She, his "little June bug" whom he used to carry across the sands in Cornwall, now she was nothing. Only the other day he had said, "You do look pretty, little June," and he had kissed her on the forehead, but it had all been a lie. He had been pretending all the time. If he loved her, he couldn't just go away like that and not say a word. Could he?

"Why, mother?" she said again. "Why did he go?"

"No, no," said Madge opening her eyes. "It's all a mistake, you'll see. He couldn't be so stupid. He'll be back."

She put her arms round her daughter, and they sat together in desolation before the flickering artificial fire, waiting for the car to drive up or the phone to ring.

Grey emptiness invaded June's room that night, a greyness no lamp could dispel; it swamped her pictures, her china ornaments, stole the colour from the flowered curtains and the blue counter-pane. So grey and empty was the world, the harsh outlines of her furniture hurt her in their crudity, jarring against her hands, her arms, her legs as she moved about. She became aware of the muscles in her limbs and the bones within her flesh, and no longer felt quite sure she knew how to walk across the room, how to unbutton her boots or unzip her dress or even how to brush her own hair. When she lay down, she was uncomfortably aware of the texture of the sheets, the shape of the pillow, the undulations of the mattress. Her bones were cold, and her muscles ached, and her skin was raw. The greyness would be hidden if she turned out the light.

But she was afraid of the dark.

Then into her mind came that most difficult of all Girl Guide Laws: 'A Guide smiles and sings under all difficulties.' She had been a Girl Guide for so short a time, it was amazing she should think of this. But she could think of no better help. So she got out of bed, wrote down the law on a blank piece of paper which she propped on her dressing table.

She would not cry.

14

Madge

Three days of silence passed.

The telephone did not ring, and cars went by and did not stop. Dazed, Madge wandered from room to room, stood looking at the beige telephone on its shiny table in the hallway, cold and silent, went to the window and looked down the road at other cars stopped outside other houses. The pressure in her breast grew and grew until she could hardly breathe.

Upstairs in their bathroom she could see no bottles, no shaving things; in their bedroom, his side of the bed was untouched, and in the closet, few clothes of his, no suits, no shirts, no shoes, a scattering of ties. Panic filled her as she realized he had taken everything that mattered: his bedside clock, the leather stud box June had given him, Robert's painting of a clown, his volume of Rupert Brooke.

But not the beautiful ashtray she had given him. She picked it up. Why had he left this? Did he really hate her so much? What had she done to deserve this?

And there was June, wanting her to talk, to explain. How could she explain when she did not understand?

"I don't understand," she moaned aloud, holding on to the bannisters as she swayed, dropping the ashtray she had given her husband some years ago because she had thought he would like it. It bounced on the stair, then slid down the carpet to the floor below where it broke in two. Why?

"Why did he do this?" she cried. "Oh, God, tell me if you can. Why has he left me after all these years? Why am I all alone?"

June rushed to her mother, who collapsed on the stairs, weeping and pulling at her hair, swaying to and fro, sobbing that she did not understand, did not understand.

There must be a way to get to him, to bring him back, she thought. Perhaps if she just telephoned him at the office, she could tell him he must come back and explain why he was behaving in this cruel way. But he might tell his secretary to say he was out; she could not bear to be so humiliated. June should do it, he would speak to her. So June did telephone her father's office, and was told he was away for a few days, expected back next week. The secretary's tone implied surprise that she did not know.

A letter was the answer. She could write to him. Not to the office, though, that wouldn't do at all. Had he given the Post Office a change of address? Had he planned that far ahead? There was one way to find out: she could write to him and address it here, to their home, and if it didn't arrive she would know he had got it all arranged. So she wrote him a letter, a short note pointing out the impossible situation she was in. The letter was posted, but not delivered to Godbridge.

If I were ill, he'd have to come then, she thought. Even if I don't know where he is, the Police would find him. They would broadcast an appeal: "Would Mr Gerald Hunter, vacationing somewhere in England (he must be in England), rush to the local hospital where his wife is dangerously ill." He couldn't ignore that.

But supposing he didn't hear the appeal, didn't listen to the radio as any normal person did?

Someone would be bound to tell him. And then he'd be upset, as he should be, for he'd realize what a terrible thing he had done to her.

And she really began to feel ill, for the incomprehensible

loss had left her with a growing pain in her breast, and the terrifying feeling sometimes that she could not breathe.

The doorbell rang one evening, and June opened the door to find her Uncle Hubert on the doorstep.

"Good evening, my dear," he boomed, patting her on the head, then pushing his way into the hall. "Run along, there's a good girl, I have to talk to your mother. Ah, Madge my dear," he added as Madge appeared in the doorway to the lounge. "This is a sorry business, don't you know? A sorry business."

"My dear Hubert, I can't imagine what you are talking about. But do come in. June dear, please fetch your uncle a drink. I'm sure you'd like one as usual."

Madge led the way into the lounge, quietly concealing her indignation. The way this brother of Gerald's tried to take over her house was always unacceptable to her. Pompous fat man with his bristly moustache and military bearing, always trying to bulldoze his way everywhere. She couldn't help thinking his pot belly made him look ridiculous, with his trousers hanging below like a windless flag at half mast.

"And how is dear Ena?" she asked. "And your lovely Shirley? It's such a long time since we had the pleasure of your company."

"Very distressed, as I am sure you can imagine. As are we all. You are bearing up magnificently, my dear, I can see that. Always knew you would." Hubert took possession of one olive green armchair. "You have my deepest sympathy."

"You are very kind, Hubert. But I assure you, there is nothing amiss that need concern you."

"Of course, my dear, of course," he said soothingly. "But I want you to know that it is my wish to stand by you in your hour of need." He paused dramatically. "This is a most distressing situation, for both of us. When my brother asked me to act as go-between, so to speak, at this very difficult time, I ask you to imagine my feelings."

"Gerald asked you to act as go-between?" said Madge in disbelief, ignoring Hubert's feelings. "What for?"

"Ah, my dear Madge, what for indeed? Thank you, thank you," he added, turning to June who plonked a glass of whisky and a soda syphon onto the table beside him. "And now, this is a private adult conversation if you don't mind. I'm so sorry I can't pay you my usual avuncular attention this visit."

"Uncle Hubert, I heard you the first time." June's cheeks were flaming with anger. "I don't think I need point out that I am an adult too, for I have no intention of remaining in this room a moment longer. Good night."

"June!" gasped Madge, but her daughter was gone. "Hubert, I'm so sorry..."

"No, no! A grand girl," cried Hubert, and laughed heartily. "A grand girl. A fine spirit. Such a shame when parents can't sacrifice their more selfish feelings for the sake of children like that. I do understand my brother's needs, of course," he added musingly. "But no English gentleman feels it necessary to wreck the very fabric of society, just because he feels like kicking over the traces once in a while. One must maintain the home front if only for the sake of the children."

"You may understand your brother," said Madge icily. "I do not. And you clearly do not understand me. I must ask you not to subject me to a moral lecture."

"No, no, of course not," he said hastily. "Quite out of place. Ahem. Let us get right down to the major question in your mind. Ahem. Yes. I have naturally impressed upon my brother the necessity for a handsome financial settlement, and he has now agreed – upon my insistence, I may add," he gave her a knowing smile, "to put the house in your name. I realize of course that you will probably find it too big and will wish to purchase a smaller house for yourself eventually. But I am sure you will agree with me to talk of selling this house while you still have a boy at school is somewhat premature."

He put up his hand as though to forestall her objections.

"Yes, yes, I know it is not my business to tell you what to do. I just hope you will not take it amiss if I say that I pray you will not be too hasty. Naturally everything must be done to make proper provision for your financial well-being, and Gerald agrees with me that the family must stand together in this hour of crisis."

Madge remained frozen in her chair as he paused. She could not believe that Gerald could so totally misrepresent her feelings.

"My dear Madge," continued Hubert as she remained silent. "It is my fondest hope that you will look upon me as your brother in your hour of need. Naturally, I am unable to act for you legally, but I hope and pray you will trust me and perhaps put off consulting a solicitor until you have both had a chance to think things over. A divorce in the family would not reflect well on any of us." He paused, but Madge made no move.

"Gerald says you are angry with him. Just between you and I and the gatepost, I am angry with him too. But at least I have one piece of good news for you, a ray of light in the darkness of this stormy time."

Madge looked up hopefully.

Gratified, Hubert continued: "I have with me a cheque. A very large cheque in fact. I believe this very handsome sum will help you over some of the difficulties of these first days. Naturally the bills for the house are still Gerald's responsibility, and if you would like to pass them on to me, I will make it my job to see that he deals with them. But this handsome cheque will, I believe, make a great difference in your feelings towards your erring husband."

With due ceremony, Hubert removed from his breast pocket a long white envelope and produced Gerald's cheque. Madge could see his signature as Hubert made an arc in the air and grandly handed it to her. But she could not bring herself to take it. She could not move.

A great weight pressed upon her head and throbbing filled her ears and throat. Her eyes would not focus and Hubert seemed to swing before her, sometimes looming large like a menacing giant, sometimes far away and tiny like a child's toy.

Betrayed. How could he do this to her? How could her own husband abandon her so cruelly? It was impossible. She had done nothing to him. It was impossible that he could really mean to abandon her totally, leave her entirely alone. Yet there was his ugly fat brother leering at her – what was he doing here if Gerald had not sent him?

She had done nothing to deserve such treatment. What terrible thing was inside her own husband that he could torture the woman he had sworn to love? Oh God, dear Lord, could it be that she had been married all those years to a monster?

"No, no," she moaned aloud. "No. No. No! I won't have it, I won't. It's too much. Oh, the lies, the lies, the lies ..."

"My dear Madge, calm yourself. Just take a look at the cheque. I am sure it is better than you imagine."

"Oh, no. I can't bear it any more. I can't bear it!"

Madge stood up, swaying, then stumbled around the room, banging her shins on the coffee table, swooping against the sofa, sliding against the window, but not noticing, not knowing where she was: imprisoned in a dark world of blank misery.

Hubert ponderously rose to his feet and went to her assistance. She shuddered violently as he touched her arm, and swung round and hissed into his face, so that he cringed away from her: "Get away from me, you. Leave me alone!"

Involuntarily, he held out his hand to her, and in it still lay the cheque. This she snatched from him and tore it into little pieces which she attempted to throw into his astounded face.

Darkness exploded in her brain. "How dare you suggest I can be bought with a paltry cheque? How dare you? And in my own house. That's what I think of your precious money. Go tell that to your cowardly brother. Go on, go away, go tell your pathetic brother what I think of him and his beastly family..."

Her voice broke and she rushed stumbling from the room, up the stairs and into her bedroom, where she slammed the door with such force that the jamb splintered and the whole house shook.

"How dare he! How dare he!" Her body raged with a passion she had never known. Heavily she fell against the dressing table and glared at her distorted face in the mirror. "Look at yourself. You're an ugly old hag. He doesn't want you now, and you'd better realize it. You're fit only for the rubbish heap."

She slumped with her forehead on the glass over her baby photographs, and ran her fingers through her hair, felt like pulling it out, tearing it out by the roots, as though to tear away this last vestige of her feminine attractions would bring relief. A horrible stench assailed her nostrils. For a moment, she was nonplussed; then she knew. The smell was the smell of fear. No, not fear. Of anger. In her hair, oozing from her pores, anger had reached her very core and turned her rotten. There was nothing left for her now but to die. She was old, cast off, stinking of putrefaction. She had had her life, and now it was finished. She should kill herself. She was good for nothing else. In a last paroxysm of energy, she swept the glass dishes off the dressing table to smash them on the floor, then collapsed in utter despair.

15

Reactions

June was hovering on the landing wondering whether to go to her mother, and she leapt forward at the sound of crashing glass, found her mother curled in a ball on the floor. But as June went to her, Madge edged away in a crouched position, cutting her ankle on the broken glass but not noticing, trying to get into a corner.

She couldn't believe her mother would ignore her offers of help. But it was clear that something had frightened the woman, who took no notice of her daughter, simply muttered, "Leave me alone, leave me alone."

Very worried by this unexpected behaviour, June rushed downstairs and reluctantly asked her uncle for help.

Hubert, whose dignity demanded he leave, but whose good will and decency insisted he stay, hovered in indecision in the hall.

"The poor woman's gone mad," he muttered. He intended no clinical meaning in the words, but he could not leave his sister-in-law in an apparently unbalanced state of mind until June had reassured him she would be all right. So it was he who called the doctor when June came down the stairs, her eyes staring. And it was he who insisted that June could not cope any longer, once Madge had been taken to hospital collapsed with nervous exhaustion, and that she must go home with him,.

He told Gerald the news as soon as the medics had taken charge. He did not exactly enjoy his role, but he did feel a certain satisfaction in the poetic justice of the situation, and he did not refrain from pointing out to Gerald the moral implications of what had happened, nor from explicitly stating what Gerald ought to do now.

He had telephoned because that was quicker, though he would rather have liked to see Patricia's face. She'd be stricken with remorse, he felt sure, and he hoped so, for any suffering she might undergo was only due punishment for having tried to break up a marriage. Gerald had no choice now. He would have to go back to his wife, and their little idyll would end.

Patricia was, in fact, angry. She saw immediately that Madge's collapse was a hysterical attempt to regain her husband's attention, and she deeply resented the emotional tangle this was to create in her relations with Gerald. Or with anyone else. Could she not have been content with what she had, the sympathy of the entire society? Was she not already the Englishman's favourite pet, the underdog? Did not the abandoned wife represent all that was Good and Wholesome about Our Way of Life – home, children, stability? A middle-aged man with grown children was undignified running away from home, and his greying wife, lonely in her machine-filled suburban house, would have everyone's sympathy. 'Staying together for the sake of the children' had become accepted as the norm for English married life, and it was expected that if you could manage to stay together that long, habit and inertia would keep you together for the rest of your days.

Her sympathies lay with June, who apparently had coped marvellously with a situation beyond her years. If Madge had had some courage and dignity, had shown some consideration for the feelings of her children, I might be able to empathize with her, she thought. Her heart went out to June, on the threshold of womanhood, trying to make sense of the emotional muddle her parents had created. She wished she could meet the girl, offer her understanding, but this hardly seemed the appropriate time.

She said very little that evening as Gerald pondered, for she was afraid to say too much. She might be angry with the woman, think her a bitch, but she must avoid saying any such thing to Gerald. Women tearing each other's hair and scratching each other's faces were a horror and an abomination, and she could not bear to demean herself by indulging in such vulgarity. And it was his problem to solve. She would help if asked, but she wanted to know how he would react.

16

Gerald

Gerald did not know what to do. He felt deeply that Madge was punishing him, that this was the sort of emotional blackmail he should fight with every fibre of his being. But what if she were seriously ill, and it was his fault? He really couldn't abandon his wife if she had something seriously wrong, if she needed him to care for her. 'In sickness and in health' said the marriage service. He couldn't choose this moment to walk out on her.

He telephoned the hospital, and was told she was under sedation and sleeping quietly. He arranged to see the doctor in the morning.

He and Patricia made love that night, as they had done every night since he came to stay in her flat. But it was not as usual, they felt estranged in some way, discovered that sex was not as good when their minds were not in tune. A dark cloud settled around them. But love will overcome they said.

At the hospital, Gerald found Madge still under heavy sedation. An atmosphere of hostility seemed to him to pervade his dealings with everyone, the nurses, the ward sister, even the other patients. The gloom invaded his spirit, and he began to believe she was lying there, in that bed, grey and lined, because he had cruelly mistreated her.

The doctor alone appeared not to blame him. Dr Barber was a short, bustling man, with a small moustache and bright eyes, always cheerful, always in a hurry.

"Your wife has high blood pressure, but this should respond to treatment. Seems to have been poisoning herself with her own hormones, you might say, but nothing to worry about now. She'll soon be back to normal."

Gerald arranged for private accommodation, for which BUPA would pay, that was the least he could do. Get her away from the prying eyes of the witch in the next bed.

"Oh, so you're the husband," she said in a piercing voice. "Poor woman. Brought in here all of a shake she was, and where were you then? Men are all the same. Take, take, never there when you need them. In terrible pain she was. It's her heart, I know, you can't fool me."

He had stood there hypnotised until the nurse has shushed the woman. But they had told him little until the doctor arrived, only that she had required sedation to quieten her. He looked at her lying in the hard bed, sheets tucked tightly around her. She looked old and ugly, and his heart ached as he remembered her years ago, bright and gay, never really pretty but vivacious and full of laughter. She must have the best of care, a private room, nurses, anything she needed.

When he left the hospital, he decided to go for a drive to clear his head. No point in going back to the office, he'd never be able to concentrate. And it was getting late anyway. He didn't even want to talk to Tricia, not at the moment. She wouldn't say anything he hadn't already thought of, and either she would be all sympathetic about this crisis, which he couldn't stand, or contemptuous of his vacillations, which he couldn't stand either. Or else she'd just sit there like a bump on a log and say it was his problem so she couldn't interfere. Women were never any good at helping a chap with a sticky problem, there wasn't any point in giving her a chance to try.

Of course, he was quite clear in his own mind what the approach to the problem was. His marriage was a failure. He had left his wife. She had become ill. Question: as a responsible man, what should he do now?

He drove out along the Hog's Back, and then because the sun was shining and it was a lovely afternoon, he parked the car in a layby. Walking alone in the countryside always restored his sense of perspective.

The scent of bracken filled his nostrils as he plunged down a track leading into the valley, and already, here and there, piles of crisp golden leaves crackled underfoot. Flies zoomed importantly along the path and into the bushes, and grasshoppers sang cheerily in the warmth of the sun. The smells and sounds were reminiscent of a summer's day, yet they had less clarity, less vibrance, and the yellowing leaves on the trees nearby, the patches of brown and red and gold splashed across the hills, the way the greenness of the leaves and grass had dissolved from a certain, vivid colour to the subtlety of a Sisson painting, all showed that autumn now reigned. A jay flew past, calling loudly, and he stopped to watch the noisy policeman of the woods with its dusky pink breast and blue and white streaked wings. Words no longer revolved in his head. He thought no thoughts at all as he descended deep into the Devil's Punchbowl, and the inexorable impersonality of nature held him in thrall.

A clearing, a patch of thick green grass beneath a silver birch, and he lay down, his face shadowed by the waving branches, his body warmed by the afternoon sun. Idly he watched a small brown bird clean its beak on a branch, high above him in the tree. Two plump wood pigeons flapped clumsily into the clearing and waddled erratically across the grass, the delicate pink, blue, mauve, dove grey plumage incongruous in the view of the lack of intelligence in those dull beady eyes. Stupid birds, he thought, you'd be better off in a pigeon pie.

However, this was getting him nowhere. He had come here to think. The enveloping clouds in his brain must be dispersed. He was perfectly capable of thinking logically, for heaven's sake. And since no answer had come to him spontaneously, logic must be applied to his problem.

Right. First, Madge was in hospital. She was ill, that was a fact, doctors and nurses were looking after her, right. Second, he was her husband. Indisputable fact. Right. Third ... but what was the logical connection?

So start again. Patricia. He was in love with Patricia. He wanted to marry her. So he had to leave home, obviously, had to divorce Madge, obviously, no problem. But Madge became ill. So he couldn't marry Tricia.

No, no, no. That was all wrong. There was no logical connection between Tricia and Madge's illness.

He looked up into the tree, and watched the blue sky and the patterns made by the yellowing leaves which fluttered gently above him in invisible currents of air. Gerald, he said to himself severely. You are farting about like a complete goddamn fool. The problem is obvious. Madge is ill and you think it is your fault. That's what the problem is. Now solve it.

He closed his eyes and looked on darkness.

All right then. Madge was ill, and he thought it was his fault. Was it? Was it possible she had been so upset by his leaving that she had become hysterical and collapsed? The answer was obviously Yes, it was possible. Obviously.

But was it likely? That was what Bertie said had happened, granted, but then he was really an old woman, loved making mountains out of molehills. He'd have *wanted* it to be like that. That was it, the bloody sod. He *wanted* it to be like that. He was jealous, and wanted to break up their 'little love nest' as he so puke-makingly put it.

Gerald sat up, filled with anger at his brother's self-righteous presumption. How blind he had been, not wanting to see. Bertie's eyes had nearly popped out of his head when he met Tricia, obviously the chap couldn't bear the thought of their happiness when he was stuck with a wife like Ena, fat, frumpy old bag. Of course, Bertie's answer was to keep a tarty dyed-blonde bit in a tiny flat somewhere. From the stories he told, she was a wild one too, Gerald had never even heard of doing some of the things Bert said they got up to. A bit odd, kinky really, if what he claimed was true, which it probably wasn't – more like a prurient middle-aged man's fantasies. In any case, that sort of thing wasn't good enough for a sensitive man of integrity. There was more to life than just sex.

Not that he was underrating sex. Far from it. But for that one didn't have to leave home. He had left home for Love. Nourish sex with love and you had something extraordinary, unbelievable, shattering.

Love too meant a whole new way of life. Exciting people, places, food, wine, music, theatre, art. All the important things in life were in reach at last. He couldn't be expected to turn back now. Not yet.

He had strayed right off the point again. He lay back. Was it *likely* that Madge had collapsed because of him? That was the question he was supposed to be considering.

That question posed all kinds of other awkward ones he couldn't answer either. Perhaps the only thing would be to ask Madge herself. Was she really upset? Had he really hurt her that much? That would mean she really cared, if she were genuinely upset and not just her pride hurt. But if your pride is hurt, you don't become ill. Angry, yes, but not ill. So that if she were ill – and she was – that would seem to imply that she was really upset. And if she were genuinely upset, that must mean she must care about him, so perhaps their marriage was not a total failure after all.

He could understand her misery if she really did care. Had he not spent an entire day walking in this very area, weeping openly at the pain. It was not the sorrow of parting, it was the agony of destroying something that had taken so many years to create. A quarter of a century they had lived together, and brought up two children, their marriage was like an old gnarled tree, its roots hidden underground, entangled in the very foundation of life. He had taken an axe to the tree and tried to cut it down, not realizing that the stump would remain, and beneath the stump, the entangled roots immovable around his heart.

He had not believed it possible that she still cared for him in any way. But her illness made him think she did. In that case, his duty lay with her. He could not think only of himself, he owed it to his past, to his own sense of responsibility to care for the wife he had chosen so long ago if that was what she wished. "For richer, for poorer, in sickness and in health..." Marriage vows were not mere words, they were a commitment for life. He could not do any more hurt to her, his own wife.

A tidal wave of misery engulfed him then, and he lay on the green grass beneath the silver birch praying that this might pass. For he knew that he must leave Tricia. All his hopes for a new life were shattered, all chance of true happiness lost. He must turn his back on the one person who meant most to him in the whole world. He must renounce everything he held most dear. The unaccountable cruelty of a Fate which snatched him back at the very threshold of Paradise filled his breast with pain, and he turned on his face and wept. After a while, he was no longer sure why he was weeping, the whole world was filled with such black pain, no light was left.

He lay with his face on the earth, his body racked with sobs, while the sun sank behind the hills and the valley was filled with darkness. The black shadows were cold as they touched his legs and back, and he shivered as he sat up.

I'm not much of a man, he said to himself bitterly. But it's all a question of how much hurt you can stand to do to another person. I'm just a coward.

He shook himself and stood up. Courage, old chap. Lying there, crying like an old woman, that's enough of that. No one ever said life had to be fun, that's what Mother used to say. I guess she's right. It's no rose garden, that's certain.

He began to walk briskly up the hill and his limbs ached with stiffness and cold. It had taken courage to leave Madge in the first place, and would probably take even more to return. If she'd have him. But she would. They were too much married.

As he reached the road at the top and walked towards his car, golden rays of the setting sun gleamed unexpectedly on the horizon, making stars of its light through the branches of a distant tree. The sky was glowing crimson and rose and gold. Once again he took the shining of the sun as a symbol, his personal sign that he had made the right decision. He must renounce Patricia and return to his wife.

There was not much point in returning to London. The best thing was to telephone Tricia from home and spend the night there.

June and Robert were both in when he arrived, but beyond looking up and saying, "Hello, Dad," neither seemed to have much to say to him. In fact, they both appeared to be waiting for him to say something. But he had no energy to cope with them that night, there would be plenty of time. He would have been willing to talk, but if all the energy had to come from him, they would have to wait.

He went into his study and telephoned Tricia.

"Darling, where are you?"

"In Godbridge."

"Oh." She was silent for a moment. "How was she?"

"She looked ill. And rather old." His voice sounded lifeless. "I see."

Perhaps she does, he thought, and hoped so, for he knew

he was a coward and did not want to tell her. "I'll phone you tomorrow," he said.

"You're staying there then."

"That's right."

A silence. He wanted to cry out, It's all right, I don't mean it. But he couldn't. Then he said urgently, "Trish, I do love you."

"I love you too." She sounded as though she might be crying.

"I'll phone tomorrow. Good night," he said hastily, and put down the phone. What a ghastly situation. A nightmare. If he took care of one, he hurt the other. Whatever he did, he just couldn't win.

He poured himself two stiff gins with tonic, one after the other, and smoked five cigarettes. Then he listened to the news, and went to bed.

17

Patricia

Patricia was indeed crying as she put down the phone, though she was angry with herself for so far losing control. Tears were a useless sort of self-indulgence, all they did was make her feel a sodden mess, with red nose and swollen face, and usually a headache at the end of it. Why cry, you fool? she asked herself angrily. It's perfectly understandable. His conscience is hurting him, and so he wants to be on hand, just in case. In case of what, she wasn't quite clear. But she could quite understand his wanting to be around while his ex-wife was in hospital. He'd be back soon enough, once he had discovered there was nothing seriously wrong.

All her sensible self-counselling did not make her feel any better. Several cups of coffee later, she found herself wandering round her flat, picking up books and putting them down, putting on a record then changing her mind, going to fetch something to eat, then feeling nauseated at the very idea. Into the bedroom, and she looked out of the window. Nothing but her reflection, just darkness out there with herself looking at herself, the outline of her face ghostly in the glass. No wonder he left her if she looked like that. A witch in the night.

Cigarettes and black coffee. "I was born to sing the blues." A perverse streak made her put on Shirley Bassey, and she found the tears gathering in her throat again. "Tonight my heart she is crying, Tonight my heart she is sad." A pain grew around her heart. "Love is de bird dat spread de wings and fly away."

Just one cliché after another, she thought despairingly, and now her heart was aching, a truly physical pain. She had forgotten how love could make you suffer.

Did she really believe Gerald might leave her after all? After only two weeks of happiness? Surely it could not be possible.

But perhaps he had not been ready to come to her. It had been her fault, she had pushed him, perhaps if she had said nothing, he would not have come. But for heaven's sake, they couldn't have gone on for ever like that, in a half world, where their intimacy was as though they were married, and yet he still lived the lie with Her. That just wasn't good enough. He couldn't spend the whole of his life vacillating between the two of them. He had had to choose. Naturally she expected him to reject dreary Convention and outmoded Duty, and to embrace Life and Love.

But suppose he didn't. Suppose that by putting pressure on him, she had pushed him into making a decision too quickly. If he went back to Her, he would be making a terrible mistake. Surely he must realize that the sort of love they had found was rare and precious. She knew. She had tried many kinds of love. The miracles that they experienced together only happened once in a lifetime.

Therefore, he must come to her. The logic of her thinking was inescapable, but it didn't make her feel any better. A terrible pain enclosed her heart, and steel bands had somehow wrapped themselves around her rib cage, so that she could not fill her lungs with air and felt she might suffocate.

She ran a bath to try to relax, and eventually the warmth of the scented water helped comfort her aching body. The pain in her chest subsided, and a new wave of tears rose in her chest and filled her eyes. She knew in the warmth and privacy of her bath that Gerald might never return. He had said he would come to her, but his commitment was not complete.

What she should do was telephone him as soon as she got

out of the bath. She owed it to him. She would tell him he must choose what was best for himself. No. She must go further. She would tell him that she would fade right out of the picture. Half measures would not do. She couldn't allow him to come to her if he really felt his duty demanded he remain with his wife. He must not do anything just because someone else wanted it. He must know in his own mind, absolutely certainly, what he wanted to do. And she would abide by his decision. If he chose to remain with Her, then she would say nothing to hold him back. No reproaches. He needn't worry about her. She could take care of herself.

As she dried herself and dressed in her long blue dressing gown, she was determined to telephone Gerald. She would fade right out of the picture. No half measures now. Let him tell That Woman that, and she'd be better soon enough.

Slowly she walked into the living room and picked up the black telephone.

Supposing he believed her? If he believed she really meant that it was all over between them, he might never come to see her again. That would be disaster. She'd be left with less than she started with, not more. No, she couldn't do it. Far too risky. She put the receiver back in its cradle.

He might think she really meant it that she could manage without him, when that wasn't what she intended at all. She realized then that she had secretly hoped that her magnanimous gesture would show him what a noble, generous, loving person she was. Then he would never be able to leave her.

Miserably, she sat in one of her black swivel chairs, staring into the middle distance until everything was blurred and out of focus. What a rotten bitch she was.

Playing games, trying to manipulate Gerald when the very essence of Love was to be honest. People said, 'All's fair in love and war', but that only proved how corrupt was the human race. Love was not war, could not be compared with war, the ultimate form of inhumanity, and she had been about to use the very methods she most deplored just to get her own way. Love had no value if abused like that.

She would have to go to bed. Even if he was no longer there, and a dark empty space yawned beside her. She added an extra blanket and her limbs still ached, because he was not there. A cigarette, hot milk flavoured with nutmeg and cinnamon, Eliot's *Four Quartets* because poetry was good to read when you were miserable. Pray to the gods they would send her to sleep.

But the words of the poet reached a quivering centre in her. Renunciation. She could not tell what Eliot had in mind, for all she could think of was love. To renounce love. Oh, no. The agony would be too great. There were too many years ahead to bear contemplating a life of greyness, without the warmth, the vibrance, the joys of love. That could not be what Gerald was planning.

The book was no comfort at all. He knew too much.

She pushed back the covers and got out of bed. How to sleep? Back to the living room, where she poured herself a very large brandy. Desperate measures were needed.

Misery embraced her as she returned to her lonely bed, and wondered what he was doing. Sleeping alone too, but in his marriage bed. What should she do?

Probably he had decided nothing yet. If only she could talk to him. The telephone was no good – too dangerous, it was too easy to misinterpret, misunderstand when you could not see the other's face. The wires distorted voices until you were just as likely to end up fighting as vowing eternal love. But if she could see him, talk to him, remind him of all they had meant to each other…

The brandy warmed her and swirled round her head, bringing

promise of sleep and the hope of a new day. They could not have got so far only to lose the first battle. Of course it was going to be a struggle. But surely he realized how precious was the love they had found. It was a miracle, and miracles only happen once in a lifetime. There was not so much love in the world they could afford to throw away the love they had found.

She turned out the light, and lay alone in the darkness praying to the gods that give love. She would have faith. He would return.

18

Madge

If I am in the desert, she thought, I should feel warm. The sun should beat down upon my head, filling my body with fire and the air with brilliant light. There was no light, only a uniform greyness, and the vault of the heavens above was black. It is not just, she thought, that I should be alone still in the grey nothingness. She walked by herself in the immense grey desert and she knew the sun had burnt out.

Cold crept after her and caressed her body with icy fingers. She could not remain here alone, without warmth, she must escape, and so she ran and ran, not knowing where to go, but needing to fight this terror. Still Cold pursued her. Even as she stumbled blindly on, she knew she would not win. A mantle of snow lay across her shoulders and all around her ice was forming, until at last she could not move. She was imprisoned in an immense eternal block of ice.

In anguish she cried aloud, 'But the Ice Maiden was beautiful!'

He came forward then, her Enemy, and she saw him for the first time – tall and gaunt, wrapped from head to foot in a long flowing black cloak. She could not see his mouth, only the sharp hooked nose and the piercing eyes like rapiers. Sounds of a wailing wind filled her ears and the folds of his cloak flapped like the wings of a gigantic bird, mocking her immobility. Through the wind came the sounds of evil laughter to assail her ears, and now she could no longer cry out in protest.

'Yes, she was beautiful and beloved,' he sneered. 'You do

not have even that.'

He left her then, alone, his evil laughter still ringing in her ears through the void.

Fear had her prisoner at last. So many years she had fought him off, but had not thought of this emptiness. She was lost. For ever.

She knew she was in bed. But it was not her bed, for it was hard and narrow, the sheets held her tightly, and if she moved her legs, the rough cloth rasped her skin. Her body felt light and strange.

Experimentally, she pulled her hand up from beneath the covers, up to her face, and slowly opened her eyes. The hand looked like her hand, paler perhaps but familiar. But it felt like an alien hand. With an effort of will, she moved the fingers one by one, and shafts of vermilion heat shot up her arm. She shut her eyes and dropped her hand on her breast.

Where was she? Why? A pain lay over her right eye. She knew if she moved, that pain would attack her ear, her neck, her teeth, surround her forehead. Yet move she must for she could not remember where she was or why. It was of the utmost importance that she find out. She must see the window. Were there bars across it? What was the unknown force holding her here? Was she in prison? Had she committed some terrible crime so she must be incarcerated for ever?

It took a great effort to open her eyes a second time. Rapidly she scanned the room while her heart pounded. Pale green walls, white ceiling, curtains – ah, curtains in a prison cell? - and a window. Without bars. Open. Someone crashing dustbins outside, far below.

She raised herself on her elbow. The room was stark enough for a prison cell, just this narrow bed, a chair, a washbasin. But the curtains blowing in a slight breeze were reassuring.

The man with the dustbins was whistling gaily and tunefully, and it came to her that she must be in hospital.

Yes, that was it. On the wall was a bracket holding a glass of red liquid and a thermometer; beside her, a jug of water and a glass on a tall square cabinet; across the foot of the bed, the usual hospital table on wheels; and pinned to the sheet, a bulb-like contraption on an electric cord which must be a bell.

But why? Why was she in hospital? Hospitals meant pain. And death. Birth and death. What was she doing here in hospital, she wasn't about to have another baby, thank God. Had she had an accident? Mentally she scanned every part of her body, and it was all there, she had not been smashed up in a car crash. Was she there for an operation?

A comet of fear seared her through, swooping from her throat to her belly. Operation meant knife, blood, scar, pain, pain, pain. No. No. She had sworn she would never have another operation after last time, she'd rather die than have someone cut up her body with knives, leaving her with more pain than she had before. And now she realized that pain held her everywhere, her head, her neck, her back, her stomach, her legs, her arms, her hands, even the tips of her fingers hurt her, and the ring on her left hand felt like a lead weight. Not gifted with a sense of humour, she thought such widespread pain could only mean serious illness, and she rocked from side to side in desperate fear, crying aloud for help.

When Gerald came to visit her again, she was quiet and calm. Dr Barber had explained that her blood pressure was high and she must keep quiet, and that had seemed an adequate reason for a private hospital room and the attention of doctors and nurses. Dr Barber was so kind, tears rose to her eyes when she looked at his red cheeks and bristly moustache, she wanted to kiss him. Naturally, she would be a good patient and keep quiet and calm to please him. That she could not remember being brought here was still remotely disturbing. But the important thing was she was in good hands.

"Here is your husband, Mrs Hunter," said a nurse briskly, showing in a tall, thin, stooping man in a dark business suit, and closing the door behind him. Madge looked at the frowning, awkward figure standing near the foot of the bed. What was this man to her? The window was behind him and his face was in shadow. He reminded her of a stooping black crow.

"Hello, Madge," he said. "How are you feeling?"

Ill, of course. Why else was she in hospital? Or was she supposed to say, 'Very well, thank you'? She said nothing.

"Here, I brought you some flowers. Thought they might cheer you up a bit."

Thank you, how very kind. Chrysanthemums. She didn't like chrysanthemums, they had a funny smell.

She did not move, so Gerald laid the huge bouquet on the table across the foot of the bed, then pulled up the visitor's chair.

"Tell me how you're feeling now." She did not look at him, just continued to stare at the bronze flowers she had always disliked. "Dr Barber tells me you're doing fine. You'll soon be out of here. Then we'll be able to start a new life." He took one of her hands in his own. "Oh, God, I do hate to see you here like this."

She looked at the dark, bony man sitting beside her bed, holding one of her hands, and it came to her suddenly, a flash of light across her brain, this man they called her husband was her enemy. He had betrayed her.

She snatched her hand away,

"Don't push me away, Madge. I know I have behaved terribly badly, and hurt your feelings, and made you ill – but please, listen to me. I want you to take me back."

She knew now what she had been fearing for so many years: it had happened. He had imprisoned her in the ice of isolation, unwanted and unloved.

"Look, I'm sorry. I really, truly am. I didn't want to hurt you, truly I didn't. You must believe me."

They said a prisoner grew to love his bonds. She'd see. Better to know where you are than to live in fear.

"Madge, why won't you answer me? I'm trying to make amends, I really am. Look, I really didn't think you cared very much any more. It wasn't as though we had much in common, not for years. Don't you agree? And our sex life, well, if you'll forgive me, it wasn't exactly the greatest, was it? We both knew that. So you see, I thought we'd both be better off if I left."

Perhaps her dreams would be better now. She'd be glad not to have to run from Fear, for he could no longer torment her. Imprisoned is imprisoned after all.'

"Why won't you *say* something? I'm trying to *explain* to you, I see things differently now."

She had watched a cat play with a field mouse and did not want that role. She imagined the mouse might die of fright.

"Christ, Madge! What are you trying to do? Punish me? OK, I agree, I deserve punishment. But will you, for chrissake, say something! I am trying to tell you, I see I have been wrong, and I want to come back. Will you have me?"

She couldn't risk going through all that again, haunted by fears she could now put a name to, but no less dreadful than in their earlier, formless days. She would know it had happened once, and so it could happen again. No. No. Fear was stronger than her better judgement. She was afraid of Fear.

Gerald stood up and paced the room. "Don't you realize…?" he began, and then stopped.

"Don't I realize?" she said, suddenly breaking her silence. "What? That you're guilty? That you know you've made me ill, and you don't like the way it feels? Even though, if you had stopped to think long ago, you could have foreseen I'd be shocked and the shock would make me ill."

"At least you're talking," Gerald turned to her in relief. "Of course I feel guilty, Madge. But how could I have known you'd be so shocked? I had no idea."

"No. You never did have any idea how I felt."

"I guess it works both ways," he said, goaded into self defence.

"That's right. It's always my fault. I suppose it's my fault I'm now in hospital."

She didn't really know why she was saying spiteful things to him, but something inside her wanted to hurt him. She would have liked to stab him through the heart and watch him writhe in agony.

"For God's sake, let's see if we can talk without throwing accusations at each other. Look, I don't think you can have heard what I am trying to say to you. I am trying to say, I am sorry, and please, can we try again."

"Why?"

"Because you're my wife, and I think you need me."

"I was your wife before. So what's changed?"

They were both silent.

"You're not to be trusted, are you? Men never are. I should have known. All the lies, all the lies you must have told. Pretending to be a respectable member of the community. Why you even thought you might become Mayor, didn't you? And all the time you were behaving like an animal with That Woman. I'd never trust you now, never as long as I live. My mother warned me, men are selfish, deceitful and selfish, so I tried not to care. For years and years, for so many years I could weep just thinking about it, I have sat quietly at home, waiting. Watching and waiting. Looking out for you, thinking of nothing but you, of being a good wife to you. And what did I get in return? I'll tell you – nothing. No love, no caring. Just nothing."

Madge continued in this vein for several minutes. All the resentments accumulated over the long years of her married life suddenly and unexpectedly found expression in this austere and virginal bed. All the things she had never said, had never intended to say, leaped to her lips, jostling and falling over each other in their haste to reach the light. Long years of repression had changed their shapes, the tiny irritations and misunderstandings of their life together were warped and twisted, and their expression became a parade of ugly images from the dark and fetid depths of her primeval mind.

19

Gerald

At first, Gerald had attempted to reply and his anger grew. Had he not come that very morning prepared to sacrifice all he held most dear for her sake? But as Madge's tirade continued, he realized that any sacrifice he could make would never in her eyes overcome his failure to live up to his marriage vows. Nothing he could ever do would compensate her for his having an affair with another woman.

He went over to the window and stood looking out, his back to her. His love for Madge had been long a-dying, he saw now, a long and lingering death unnoticed in its progression by either of them until it was too late. Yes, he had wept that day on the downs, for the death of his hopes and dreams and the death of his love. Now it was buried. Mourning was over. Chief among the grave-diggers was Madge herself.

Clearly their life together, for all their youthful hopes, had been a disaster. Misery and bitterness marked them both. A new life apart was their only hope.

His anger faded, and he felt calm, clear-headed. He regretted very much his cowardice in accepting Hubert as his messenger; from now on he would arrange everything himself. And he must take care of the children. All that he must do would be done.

When he left the hospital, he telephoned Patricia.

"I'm coming home."

Lying in bed peacefully, blissfully, pillows piled high against the peacock's tail, looking at the window bright with sunshine, the first thing he apprehended consciously was the glow of colour outside: the glorious golden leaves of the maple, the green of the elms now yellowing with the fall, the diversity of the flowering shrubs by the garden wall all seemed to gather round her window. Sunday morning, and always the sun was shining.

Perhaps we never make love when it rains, he thought idly as he ran his hand over her thigh and down her leg.

"Darling, your face is so different," she said, touching his cheek.

"You too. You look about twenty-two."

These days, it was always the same. They made love and the tensions of their lives outside dissolved. His face, long and thin and deeply creased with worry and the conviction of being unloved, now took on a smooth glowing roundness. She imagined she must know how he had looked as a youth. But it was not his boyhood face she saw, it was the face of a mature and happy man.

"It's all so unbelievable, it's like a miracle," she said, and her face seemed to glow with the same joy that filled his heart.

He crushed her to him, and thought, Thank god, thank god, this is what it means to be alive. More than half his life gone, and never before had he known what true happiness could be. It had seemed impossible that a beautiful, talented, successful woman like Patricia could possibly love a very ordinary, rather dull man like himself, and he had fought against the notion for months. And yet it was true. It could not be otherwise, for she had shown him unmistakeably since he had made his choice that he, Gerald Hunter, was the great love of her life. He would never understand it, and now it seemed sensible not to try. He would accept this great gift with humility and be glad.

And yet, perhaps in some way he had not yet understood, he did deserve this happiness. Was it really possible that joy could come to a middle-aged man unpaid? He had had little enough joy in his life, god knew, so it seemed right and just that he should be granted a measure before his life ended. He had give his half century entirely to the service of others: he had fought for his country through five long years of fear and horror, he had been an upright member of society, serving the community through charities, through politics and on the council, had followed the strictest possible moral code, had never taken any of the many opportunities to line his own pockets, there had been nothing in his life of which he had been ashamed, nothing of which he feared scrutiny. Until Patricia. And she was the very best part of his life, a tiny fraction of it, but the best. All the rest had been dreariness and boredom, but a preparation for the greatest joy a man can have: true love in his maturity.

"Perhaps we have both been preparing for this all our lives," he said.

"Oh, yes! I know I have." Her voice was vibrant with happiness, but she was serious. "It's as though somehow I spent all those years searching for the right man. You know, darling, I realize you don't like the thought of my having had other lovers, but really I would never have discovered what kind of man I can truly love without their help. They led me to you."

"There must be many men you could love, not only me."

"Until I met you, I really thought I had become too fussy, too selective," she said seriously. "I never doubted there must be someone somewhere, but that I would meet him, that he would be free to recognize me, that became more and more unlikely. I feel somehow our love is a gift from the gods."

"To be treated with reverence."

"Yes."

They were lying in each other's arms, and he felt like a

young god himself, powerful, virile, sure of his own strength.

"I wonder how many people have found such love," he said complacently.

"Everyone wonders that," she said laughing.

"No, no," he insisted. Such miracles could not be for common mortals, he was sure. "Probably you have to go through the kind of experiences we have had to find it."

October, November … the year was dying, but for Gerald and Patricia it was as though the world had been renewed and a new era begun. Such happiness they found hard to believe possible, and yet each day brought more joy in learning to know each other. Every small act took on a new significance, their interest in the world, in their jobs, in their friends was not diminished, but rather heightened. It was as though they had discovered a secret elixir, a fountain of life which bubbled inside each of them.

"You give me so much love, I feel it spilling out all round me," Patricia said, and Gerald felt this too. Their joy was so deep, so concentrated, renewed without fail each evening and existing still each morning, he truly believed that they were the chosen, the blessed.

Gerald found that his heightened perception showed him worries, pain and fear even when nothing was said. Occasionally colleagues began to talk to him about their private affairs, though he felt in no way equipped to deal with other people's emotional situations. Yet he was grateful for what he felt was an accolade, and if he could prevent other people's worries from becoming his own, he felt their intimate confessions created a multi-coloured backcloth to his life. He could not avoid thinking this was the ultimate arrogance, yet how else was he to cope with this new rich abundance of life?

The scandal of his elopement was not as devastating as he at first feared. A small item had appeared in the local paper, but it had been carefully worded in view of libel laws and because the Chairman of the Council was a friend of the editor, merely stating that Councillor Hunter had resigned because of private matters and it was understood that he planned to leave the district. Not that it took long for the poison pen purveyors to winkle out much of the truth, and he had been almost glad that Madge stayed so long in hospital so that he had been able to prevent her from suffering this particular outrage. Whatever the intention of the anonymous writers, he had been chastened. In the quiet backwaters of civilized England, it was not often one was confronted by the black horrors that can twist men's minds.

As far as his office was concerned, he found that his position was a guarantee of discretion and not an invitation to scandal. That there were sniggers and crude jokes at his expense he did not doubt. The chairman and his immediate colleagues had to be told, briefly, of his new domestic arrangements and he did not imagine the matter could end there. But the unexpected result was that he learned of a great deal of unhappiness among his colleagues, and that he was far from being alone in regretting a marriage hastily undertaken in youth so many years earlier. Only Peter, whom he had considered a friend, told him coldly one day, he and Meg had discussed the matter, and they could no longer receive him in the same house as their sons.

His own children, however, gave him serious cause for concern. He wished most heartily he had been a better father, for he realized he did not understand them at all. Yes, he could understand they would be upset. But what really was going on inside them? June he found incomprehensible. He had telephoned her, asked her to meet him, and she had fallen into his arms hysterically crying, 'Dad! Dad!' But now she would have nothing to do with him, put the phone down when he tried to speak to her, ignored his letters. What had he done wrong? Why had she turned against him? Had he said the wrong things that day? He couldn't remember clearly, but it seemed to him he had been calm and reasonable, tried to explain to her why he had left, and she had gone quiet, deathly quiet as though the life had gone out of her. In the end, he had not known what to do so he had put her on a train back home. Dear god, what good was all the love in the world if you could not have the love of your own daughter?

Or was it that Madge had been poisoning her mind against him? That was more than likely since he had always had a good relationship with June, now he came to think of it. The stupid wicked woman, could she not allow him even this, the love of his own daughter? The inevitable would happen, his lovely June would change from a happy outgoing girl into a woman with a warped and twisted mind. And what could he do? Nothing.

Robert, on the other hand, was at least around. Sometimes he was around far too much. Some odd quirk had driven him to leave home and follow his father to London. Tricia was very good to him, and had made up a bed in the spare room, and now he seemed to come and go as he pleased. She had made it clear she did not consider it a permanent arrangement, but if ever he was in desperate need of a bed there was one there, and he had accepted her offer as though it was the most natural thing in the world. Sometimes Gerald suspected his son slept out, in Regents Park perhaps or by the river, but he would never say. It was worrying not to know what he was doing, and the nights were frosty now, surely to god he could pull himself together sufficiently to get a room at least. Gerald had in fact found him one, and paid a month's rent in advance, but Robert had never been there when he called. He would give him until Christmas, that would be three months of going haywire, then insist he pull himself together. So he wanted to leave school, had left school, very well: then let him clean himself up, get some decent clothes and throw away those old rags, get a job and live like a decent human being. Just because your father decides to make a new life for himself is no reason for going to pot.

Gerald was sitting in his office, staring at a print of Picasso's Don Quixote on the wall opposite, a pile of papers marked URGENT unheeded beneath his elbows. Cold fear gripped him as he thought of the possible implications of that expression he had heard his mother use so often and so had incorporated into his own store of cliches. Yes, it was more than likely Robert was on pot. At the very least.

Dear God, please, let it not be worse than that, he prayed. Oh God, please let there be a God, don't let my son get hooked. Let me find him, let me get through to him. Oh God in Heaven, please don't let me do this to him.

It was clearly of the utmost importance to find Robert and warn him of the dangers. He roamed London, sifting through the vagueness of his memories to find a clue, asking advice of sneering taxi-drivers – Piccadilly Circus, the Embankment, underground stations one after another – finding many long-haired and dirty youths slobbering in corners and jabbing needles into bruised and scrawny arms, but thank God, never Robert among them. Until at length he returned home to Patricia's flat, exhausted. Robert was there, scruffy, sprawled on the floor.

"Do you take drugs?" he asked fearfully.

Robert laughed contemptuously. "Of course."

"You're not on the hard stuff, are you?"

"Don't be a fool, Dad. Do you think I'm stupid or something? You haven't got a monopoly on life, you know. I'm gonna live too."

20

June

June went to visit her mother every day, and Madge was six weeks in hospital. The doctor could see that the girl would collapse in her turn if required to nurse her mother, and he muttered to himself that the daughter should be his patient: youth was on her side and he could have guided her through her bewilderment into perfect health. But she asked for nothing. She was not ill in body and was reasonably sensible and intelligent, though the practised medical eye could see that she was wandering in confusion. Something had died inside her, and she was as yet only half conscious of herself as a separate human being, so she could not identify her hurt, her loss, her pain. The light had gone out of the sun, and she knew no way to turn it back on.

So Dr Barber kept Madge in hospital and treated her for high blood pressure. She was a private patient, and was herself in no hurry to leave. The constant attention was a balm to her wounded spirit.

Madge's bruised mind, unaccustomed to introspection and beclouded with drugs, picked over the words Gerald had said and the words she had said, rejecting and selecting like a French housewife picking over plums, until she was left with an interpretation of recent events worthy of the Mediaeval Church: there was Good and there was Evil, there was Right and there was Wrong; she, worthy handmaid to her husband, had at all times behaved with piety, innocence and grace, had struggled against fearful odds to maintain the dignity of a virtuous woman; her husband, weak and sinful as men always are, had hearkened to the Devil, and was lost; he had had a second chance, her collapse, which was occasioned entirely by his wrong-doing, had at the same time given him an opportunity to atone, but he had refused it. He had abandoned her for a harlot, and all the world should know.

During her weeks in hospital, she perfected this theory, trying out possible variations on the nurses, on Lucy and Barbara who visited from time to time, on June. It was agreed that men are beasts, are selfish, want to be indulged like children, that her husband was unusually self-centred and mean, that the depths to which some men could sink were unbelievable, that no man worthy of the name could leave his wife to languish in hospital for weeks on end, no grande passion (one of the nurses was of literary bent) could possibly justify abandoning two children and a wife who was so terribly ill.

At first, June refused to play her mother's game. But as time passed, the arguments became persuasive. She was lonely, she was heartsick, and she found a wonderful warmth, the joy of regaining human contact when she tentatively one day agreed with a lesser point. And so it grew, the pleasure, the exhilaration of unhappy women huddling together, warming themselves at the funeral pyre of another's reputation.

Maybe Mum was right, maybe men really were selfish beasts. Dad certainly didn't seem to care much about the mess he'd left behind him. Even when he came home that night, after Mum was taken to hospital, he didn't bother to say anything, to explain. It was all very well him keeping on telephoning now, but when she did go up to London to see him, all he could do was go on and on about what a marvellous creature this Patricia person was, as though she cared. And it obviously never even occurred to him that she had had to take time off work to see him.

George was always so busy too. It was understandable, of

course he wanted to do well, but it wasn't much comfort. She'd have liked someone to talk to. And now even Bobby had gone.

He'd gone around moping and miserable, and getting into worse and worse trouble at school, until he had a flaming row with that horrible form-master, and he came home all in little pieces which she stuck together with tea and sympathy. He kept saying he was no good and only made Mum worse and he was a discredit to the family and he'd better get the hell out. What do you say when your brother gets as low as that? She told him not to be such an ass and carted him off to visit at the hospital. But he'd been so morose. He almost seemed to think Mum's grumblings about men and their selfishness and disregard for others' feelings had been directed at him. Sympathy was so wearing: she'd felt exhausted.

When they left the hospital, and he walked blackly along, dragging his heels and answering only in monosyllables, in the end her patience snapped.

"Oh, go away then if you want to! You're no help to anyone when you go on like that."

So he did. And she was left alone to cope with Mum, while God alone knew what he was doing. She'd phoned Dad, and apparently he had turned up at his office and Dad was looking after him. So presumably he was all right. What a mess.

She shouldn't have lost her temper with him. She really should have known better. But he shouldn't have flung off like that either. Why did people behave so badly to each other?

Ruth, her mother's cousin, came for the weekend, and June wished she could have stayed. Ruth was fifty, medium height but thin and gaunt and angular, so she looked taller, with untidy grey hair cut very short. She wore no make-up, principally because she had never had the patience to learn how, and her skin was rough and red. She had never married. Some said it was no wonder with her acid tongue and a face like an Aztec shrine, but she had been attractive in her youth and had been asked more than once. She had loved three men in her life and been loved in return, but now she lived with her widowed, arthritic mother and wrote papers for scientific journals on maze-learning in rats. Few signs were left of the brilliant young girl who had set out to probe the exhilarating mysteries of science despite the disadvantages of her sex. Only her eyes, beneath straggly brows in need of shaping, glowed warm and brown with kindness and intelligence.

It had been a strange weekend, with Ruth sitting there talking about the liberation of women and being independent and making a life of one's own, sitting in this house where there was only one sex (no second sex) and that was a dirty word, where Women's Liberation was an invention of the devil; or going to the hospital, sitting beside Mother's bed and listening to the two of them talk about an unknown past and watching Ruth try to ginger Mother up with exhortations and laughter. She had been more cheerful too, for a while. What a pity Ruth had to go. It was rather like having a fuse in the main box and you don't even know where it is. Ruth had put the lights back on, but now they were out again, perhaps for good.

"Oh God, oh God, How weary, stale, flat and unprofitable seem to me all the uses of the world," she quoted, to her own surprise, and laughed a brief laugh at the thought perhaps her schooling had not been a total waste of time. She had learned a few words in which to clothe her dreary thoughts, before she gave up any attempt to think at all. It was all, even thinking, even talking to herself, such a waste of time.

In the haberdashery department of a big store, pushed and

pummelled by a crowd of dowdy women in dull dark coats, with ancient handbags on their arms and bulging shopping bags banging legs, June decided to steal something.

Her face was hot and flushed and her back still clammy, for she had been remembering with shame that English lesson at school, in her last year, when she had hysterics. Why she should be thinking of that now, or why she should still get upset about it, she really didn't know – that was part of another life, another era. The 'most embarrassing experience of her life' as dim-witted interviewers tended to say on dim-witted radio programmes, no matter how often she reworked the material in her memory, she had to face the fact she had been a fool. The class had been studying *Canterbury Tales* for A level, and they had got to that bit in the Clerk's Tale where the marquis tests Griselda by taking away her child, she could remember the words still:

> *"And like a lamb, she lay there, meek and still,*
> *And let the cruel fellow do his will."*

That was when she started screaming.

Really, it had been rather funny, she could still see Miss Wood's face, the way her jaw dropped and her mouth fell open, just before she stood up and started to slap June's face. That was the bit that made her suffer most. In memory. At the time, she had hardly felt the blows, she was so involved in the horror of this woman having her baby taken from her and just lying there "like a lamb, meek and still". But now, in memory, she hated the woman for hitting her, slapping her in the face, this dried up old spinster dragging her back to what she called Reality, which was to accept everything written in a book as a Revelation From On High. So she had not taken Eng.Lit for A-level, and everyone had thought it was because she was afraid to return to class, because she was ashamed of her outburst. Which it was, partly, but mainly because she was ashamed for Miss Wood, and the way she had slapped her face because she had had a genuine personal reaction to a Classic and it was unacceptable.

What all that had to do with her current decision she had no idea. Probably there was no connection. The desire was still there, not to have something she could not pay for, no, she wanted to steal something, anything, just to see if she could defy law and order and get away with it. Of course, she was rationalising, she knew that, but she felt if she could take some object, any object, the most worthless thing on the counter say, if she could make herself take it in defiance of all she believed, all she had been taught, all society stood for, then her fears for her individuality would be lessened.

But if she were caught? Then she would take her punishment, for she would know that rebellion was not for her. Perhaps her punishment would not be so bad if all she had stolen was a baby's teething ring. That was the cheapest thing there. What they were doing in haberdashery she couldn't imagine, but there was a long rack of them, white plastic rings for 10 pence each.

Success. It was so easy to slip the ring off the rack and into her pocket, she was amazed. Half of her was expecting a heavy hand on her shoulder as she moved through the shop and out into the street, but the other half knew that she had succeeded. No one had seen. How easy it was.

Now what to do? At home she examined her ill-gotten gains: one baby's teething ring worth 10 pence. She had no use for such an object, knew no one who had a baby or was likely to have one for years. She felt a certain contempt for herself for having chosen so useless and foolish an article. Was that the value she set upon independence and freedom?

Ten measly pennies?

But that was the point. She had not wished to steal for gain, she had no desire for a life of crime. With a certain amount of pride she knew now that she could steal if she wished, and she would not.

Her desire had been to impose her own will on events. Such a minor, puny, insignificant event. But far-reaching in its implication, for she knew now she was not necessarily doomed to subjugation. She could choose to affirm her independence.

And what if she were to reverse the process, so to speak, and return her ill-gotten gains? She would walk into the shop, take the ring out of her pocket, openly, and put it back on the rack. Everyone would see, and there would be nothing they could do. Laughter bubbled up inside her. That would be the best revenge of all.

"To take arms against a sea of troubles," she quoted jubilantly. But her way would be to affirm life, not end it.

21

Madge

Madge left the sheltered cocoon of her private hospital room for the harsh reality of her empty house.

June hovered still in the background, but she was at work all day, and had her own friends. Robert, she discovered with a sharp pain, had left home: he had come to see her a few times in the hospital, and was now apparently with his father. The maid had not let her down, thank goodness, but that was all. There was no one to look after her now, and quite genuinely she felt ill.

Lucy Jones, her next door neighbour, did her best to ease things. She was a bright, cheerful woman who had an immaculate house, a glorious garden, a studious teenage daughter, and a successful, cheerful husband. What secret sorrows this shiny facade concealed she never said, though some said her biggest fault was her tongue. Her second fault was her curiosity, a vast all-embracing inquisitiveness which allowed her no peace until she should learn all the details of the interesting debacle next door. But she was warm-hearted too, and practical. She organized the laundry, chivvied the maid, got in groceries. She galvanized Madge into sorting out bills for Gerald, bullied June into cooking a decent meal. And she listened.

But people were a disappointment to Madge. She found herself thinking, they should have made Gerald come back by now, six weeks in hospital should have been enough. She had to laugh a bit, crazy thoughts one could have.

Though it was time he came back. But she could wait. She

would be patient like Griselda in that lovely tale her mother used to read to her. She would win in the end.

Lucy valued the solidarity of wives against the erring husband.

"You must make him pay," she said authoritatively. "Sue him for everything he's got. Every penny you can. You mustn't let them get away with it. There's going to be a new law, you know, and then he'll be able to divorce you just like that. Casanova's Charter, that's what Lady Summerskill called it."

"But I don't want a divorce!" cried Madge in horror. How would she ever be able to hold up her head again?

"If you don't divorce him, he'll be able to divorce you. That's what my paper says. Go on, you do it. You're the innocent party. You can make him pay."

Make him pay. Make him pay. Lucy was talking of money, but Madge's mind tossed the words around, trying out meanings until she found the one she wanted: pay for his crime, punishment, atonement. Yes, he should atone for all the suffering he had caused her. Oh, if only she could make him suffer.

She was innocent. Like Griselda. If a Judge told the world that, they could not argue then. June would see she should not criticise her mother, she would realize the extent of her father's wickedness, would know you can never trust a man. A Judge in a white curly wig and scarlet robes would bang his gavel and proclaim from his carved throne, "Gerald Hunter, you have wronged your wife. You must pay for your sins. Go languish in prison for ever." And Gerald her husband, her enemy, would be dragged away in chains. Then the Judge would turn to her, and declare in ringing tones: "Margaret Leicester Hunter, I hereby tell the world you are innocent." People couldn't argue then, they couldn't point the finger or whisper behind her back. They would know on the highest authority she was innocent.

But she did nothing.

It was November. Some days it seemed the sun never shone at all, the house was as though wrapped in a cloud, a soggy blanket that dripped, dripped through the long lonely days. The lawn was choked with leaves and scraps of old newspaper and chocolate wrappings, and the swirling grey mists seemed to be encircling her, choking her in their dark, cold, damp shrouds.

The day the central heating broke down she burst into tears. It was all just too much. Lucy, who seemed to have an instinct for those in need, found her weeping at the bottom of the stairs, took her home and gave her a cup of tea, phoned her husband who promised to fix it that evening.

It was almost unbelievable luck to have a man in the house again. There were so many little jobs that needed doing: the kitchen door handle had come loose, one of the electric light fittings looked a bit dangerous, so many little things that only a man could manage. She fussed around Jeremy and brought him innumerable cups of tea, while June nagged in whispers, "For heaven's sake, Mum, the poor man will feel he'll never get away." But Madge knew that Jeremy was glad to help his neighbour and his friend.

"I must go now," he said at length, put his arm round her shoulder and kissed her cheek.

Madge recoiled in horror. "What do you think you're doing?" she gasped. "Dear Heaven, all you men are the same!"

Jeremy scuttled out of the back door, his face fiery red, and June shouted at her mother: "What on earth's got into you? The poor man was only trying to be friendly, to make you more cheerful."

Madge turned her back on her daughter who understood nothing. She was shaking with anger and with fear. So that was what men thought of abandoned wives, was it? Abandoned in more ways than one, easy meat for any man. If that were so, she could not face anyone ever again.

Thoughts of her mother could no longer warm her now. She did not want her mother to know her secret, that Gerald had left her for another woman. So she could not call to her spirit through the black abyss of space that divided the living from the dead, she dared not ask her mother's ghost for comfort.

What if she blamed Madge for Gerald's leaving? This was, of course, highly improbable, but supposing. Or she might be angry with her daughter for not having hung on to her man in spite of everything, for women had to sacrifice their all, their bodies, their hearts, their pride, their very souls to the man they married. So Madge had failed. Except that she really could not see how, she *had* sacrificed her all. Gerald in his blind wickedness had thrown her sacrificial ashes to the winds. It was Gerald who had failed her.

But she did not dare to call to her mother's spirit, and her mother did not come to her.

At Christmas, she decided to visit her father. For many years since her mother's death, he had spent the season with her, but this year his rheumatism was bad and he did not want to travel. He had retired eleven years earlier to a house he had built in North Cornwall, and her mother was buried in St Endellion. Now he lived in comfort, with a secretive dark-haired local woman to care for him. Madge had occasionally wondered at their relationship, for it was unusual in the extreme for a Cornish woman to live in as a housekeeper for a 'foreigner', and if sometimes they would help out a few days a week, this came to a halt during the tourist season, for earnings were richer elsewhere. But Mrs Coates had remained, doggedly loyal in the face of Madge's attempt to patronise her, grim-faced, taciturn.

When Madge arrived at Bodmin Road station, her courage all but forsook her. Robert had chosen to stay in London, with Gerald she supposed, and she had not been given an opportunity to argue. But June was with her, and it was she who determined that no car was waiting to meet them in spite of several letters outlining arrangements. Mrs Coates wouldn't give them a thought, she knew that: "They'm ony furriners, inn'ut." But it was unlike her father. Could he be ill? He always enjoyed organising people and cars and travel schedules. She had noticed he enjoyed that part of the funeral, especially when he came up against the thick stone wall of Cornish procrastination. Though naturally he had mourned his wife.

First off the train grabbed the taxi, and buses didn't meet trains in this part of the world. Madge sat on a hard, draughty bench in front of the new ticket office while June wasted several sixpences trying to locate a taxi, until a hire car arrived at the station with a fare nearly an hour later. When they arrived at Trebetherick in the gloom of a December night, she could not but feel she was an intruder, unwanted, in the way.

Her father looked much older now, as though he could feel the weight of his 76 years. He was thin and frail and bent, and shuffled around in carpet slippers and long shapeless cardigans and scarves round his neck. She was shocked to see his grey head seemed shrunken, emphasizing the bristling eyebrows above tiny wrinkled eyes, and his once firm mouth now seemed slack and sloppy. His brief comments thrown into the conversational void that evening were confined entirely to his own state of health. Mrs Coates bustled around him, looking at Madge and June with a gleam in her eye, scolding and petting her charge like a mother a spoiled child.

They were expected though, so they had a hot meal and

freshly aired sheets to lie between. Exhausted from the journey and the joyless reception and the misery of the past months, Madge escaped to bed as soon as she dared. It would be all right in the morning.

The next day was Christmas Eve, and she tried to help as best she could in the mammoth preparations. But Mrs Coates appeared torn between wanting this other woman out of her kitchen and resentment at being the only one working her fingers to the bone, so Madge could do nothing right. She felt too crushed to be arrogant, had no wish to put this member of the serving classes in her place. Indeed, she vaguely wondered what this woman's place was, for she ran the house as though she were its mistress by right. But eventually she could no longer tolerate the woman's veiled criticisms and silent rebukes, and decided to let her get on with the the work on her own.

She would go for a walk. June said she would come too, and together they took the road up and round and then steeply down a sharp, winding hill because June wanted to watch the waves on the surfing beach at Polzeath. It was a dull day, a nothing day, neither sunny nor raining, not hot nor cold nor windy nor calm, just a day for walking and thinking of other things.

So Madge thought of her father as she trudged along the road. She wanted to talk to him, she desperately needed a sympathetic ear, but it was almost as though he was avoiding her. Every time she sat down beside him, he would find some pretext to shuffle off, to call for logs or for more hot toddy, and was only comfortable when Mrs Coates was there and he could ramble on about the sad state of his health. But he was her father. She felt sure he would accord her some shred of comfort if only he knew how desperately unhappy she was.

Then they came round the corner and there was Polzeath

Bay, the grey waves foaming and crashing white in a series of
curves, and June ran down the steep hill like a child and onto
the wide expanse of sand. Madge followed slowly, her weight
pressing on the soles of her feet as she tried to maintain her
balance down the sharp incline. She was definitely fatter than
usual, her skirt felt tight and her feet more uncomfortable, she
had the nasty sensation she might be waddling down the hill
in her heavy brown shoes.

She watched her daughter dancing and skipping across the
sand, stopping now and then as though to greet the ocean,
spreading her arms in a wide embrace. Let her enjoy herself
while she can, such antics were for children. Madge would
rest herself on the nearby rocks, and watch the turbulence of
the sea.

With considerable difficulty, she hoisted herself onto the
cold grey rock, and tried to find some repose there on the
edge of the sea, to ignore the cold and hardness against her
body, to lose the tensions she carried with her everywhere.
Idly she watched the gulls wheeling and swooping and crying
harshly. Always the gulls impinged on her mind when she
came down here, and their mewing like cats seemed to fill her
dreams at night. Birds, always birds. She did not like birds,
hated them for their arrogant freedom, the way they could
lie on the wind and float to the corners of the earth. They
were cruel too. She would watch the birds in the garden at
home: blackbirds were the worst, would never let each other
alone, always one chasing another away, or several attacking
one unfortunate lone thing until she would go to the window
and frighten them off, and watch their victim make his escape
with feathers dropping to the ground. How could people turn
to nature for consolation? Nature was cruel, implacable.

Several gulls had settled now on a rock not far from her,
out in the sea. A grey speckled one attracted her attention: it

looked angry, its head jutting forward belligerently, its sharp curved beak opening regularly to emit a wailing cry. As she expected, it soon took after a companion, a beautiful white gull with grey wings and golden beak. But to her astonishment, the white gull did not retaliate, merely moved out of its way, obviously thinking, 'For Christ sake, leave me alone'. Madge was irresistibly reminded of a man, of a husband wishing only for a peaceful life, trying to escape the importunate demands of his unhappy wife.

That was what these two gulls suddenly seemed to be, must in fact be: husband and wife. The speckled gull, the wife, seemed sad to her now. Perhaps even seagulls had unhappy marriages, husband gulls made their wives miserable. The speckled gull was weeping, crying out her woes.

The white gull flew up and circled the rock once before slowly alighting and returning to his perch. The wife – it must be the wife – went to him, head down, shoulders hunched, her wailing never ceasing. Like a sad wife trying to make up, she nuzzled her husband, cried to him for sympathy, for understanding, for love. He turned away with ill-concealed irritation.

At length, the white gull's exasperation grew so strong, he flew away. And did not return. Madge watched the abandoned speckled gull, the wife, and felt a part of its agony. Were all living creatures at one in sorrow and desolation then? For they certainly were not united in any other way.

The gull continued to lament. Its wail was softer now, yet it pierced her heart. Its misery was obvious. Many other gulls stood by and none came to offer any help. When she rose to leave, maybe twenty minutes later, the gull was still crying weakly. The white gulls stood round in silence.

Christmas was a time of sorrow for Madge. Memories of

childhood Christmases haunted her, those years when the season had been one of coloured lights and sparkling tinsel and music and laughter. She remembered the huge tree they used to have in the sitting room, reaching right up to the ceiling. Her mother always decorated the tree herself, the servants being left to deal with streamers and holly, and Madge could feel again the pleasure, the excitement, the pride of being allowed to help. In her hand she could feel again the fragile glass balls, with gleaming colours that changed and swirled as she moved them in the light, and the icicles of clear twisted glass that held rainbows and were so fragile that every year one broke, and the flying angels made of twisted gold thread, and the brightly coloured Christmas animals, all lost now and never to be replaced. When she was older, she had been the one to put the fairy doll at the top of the tree, leaning over from the top of the wooden step ladder with her mother holding her ankles. And one year, she must have been about eleven, she had completely redressed the doll, had made a white satin dress trimmed with sparkling tinsel and wings and a crown and a magic wand, and had prepared a special bed for her in a shoebox, lined with a piece of blue velvet, so that she would be comfortable when she was taken down from the tree and had to sleep all through the long year.

And the candles. No one had candles any more, but they used to light wax candles on their tree. Putting the candles on the tree was a very important job, and it was not until she was at least twelve that she had been allowed to do that, for the holders had to be firm and the candles held away from the upper branches so they would not catch fire. Nothing was as beautiful today, candlelight was softer than the electric lights people had now, more alive, and the glass balls gleamed in the flickering light and the tinsel sparkled, and you felt for a brief moment transported to fairyland.

"You can't have Christmas without a tree," June had said after their walk, and she had gone into the village and returned with a small straggly tree and some boxes of coloured balls. But the problems this created seemed insurmountable, for she wanted to put the tree on a table in the lounge and to borrow a flower bowl to stand it in as there was no proper pot.

"Mother had a proper stand," said Madge, and her father and Mrs Coates stared at her coldly.

"Don't fuss so, Maddy," her father said irritably, so June said she'd make do with a kitchen mixing bowl and crepe paper, but the tree had to stand on that table.

Madge couldn't say a thing in this house, it seemed. All she meant was surely Mother's stand was in the loft. But he had never liked her to ask him anything, was always saying, "I like people to stand on their own two feet." Which was reasonable enough as a comment, but now she came to think of it, bore little relation to reality. What about that stupid incident over her watch strap? She must have been fourteen, and her watch strap broke. It was only a cloth one and very frayed, and he had said: "The only reason I'll give you a new one is that I can see you have tried to mend it." A new watch strap because she had put a few stitches in, but when she wanted to go abroad with the school, he had objected, and when she had talked of going to college or taking up nursing, he had said, "It's a waste of money, you'll never pass, you'll only get married." The Bentley, the maids, the furs for her mother, and the jewels, you'd have thought he could have spared his only daughter something.

She had really wanted to become a vet. For years she had dreamed of caring for animals, any animals, dogs, cats, rabbits, horses, especially horses. She had filled her bedroom with pictures of horses, and all her relatives gave her china animals, and there had been that glorious year when she was given a riding outfit for Christmas, hat, crop, jodphurs, boots, and had been allowed to take lessons. It was true she was not very good at it, she had always been ungainly. But was that a reason to stop the lessons quite so soon? She remembered her riding things left forlornly in the cupboard, and going secretly to put them on when her mother was out, and dreaming of galloping over the hills.

Of course, the war had made things difficult, the maids all gone, and of course she had to work. Even so, it would have been nice if she had been consulted, there must have been a million things she could have done to help the war effort rather than land up in that boring clerk job in the Ministry of Food. Still, it was her own fault really, she never said anything. Even when she had longed for a dog of her own, all she had done was burst into tears when he said "No!" and nurse her misery in secret. He might have relented if only he had realized how much she needed one.

The only thing she had insisted on in all her life was to marry Gerald. That had been easy too, because he hadn't really seemed to mind. He had been glad for her, hadn't he, in her happiness, glad that she had won the heart of such a brave and handsome young airman, and had insisted amazingly little on the differences in their backgrounds. He had wanted her to be happy. Surely now he would help her find the way again.

It was not until after dinner on Christmas Day that she was able to speak to him alone. June was in the kitchen with Mrs Coates, washing up, and Madge felt she must, absolutely must talk to her father right then or dissolve in tears.

"Father. You didn't ask me what happened."

"Eh?" he said, lighting his pipe with great puffs.

"I mean, you never asked me about Gerald, where he is and … so on. And Robert. Don't you want to know?"

"I figured you'd tell me if you wanted to."

"He's left me. Gerald … he's living with another woman."

The horror of this statement was upon her. Her father would know now that she was a failure as a woman. But he would comfort her, if only he would take her in his arms again, how her body longed to touch another's. Fat and misshapen it might be, but if someone, if her own father could only take her in his arms, it might assuage all the hurt, she might then find the strength to carry this terrible burden.

He sat there in his chair, puffing at his pipe which threatened to go out, a little grey old man. Three months it was now, and she had not told him before because she had been afraid.

"Did you hear me, Father? He wants a divorce." Madge's voice rose hysterically. "Father. Say something, for heaven's sake! Don't you understand? Father!"

His pipe went out and he sat in his chair, looking at the black charred bowl with watery blue eyes.

"I'm disappointed in you, Maddy," he said. "I was looking forward to spending this Christmas in my own home for a change. It may be the last I shall ever spend on this earth. And now you have ruined it for me."

Dazed, she stood up, walked out to the hall, put on her green coat, a scarf, opened the front door and her father said not another word. She had to walk, to get away from there. Her eyes blind with unshed tears, she strode down the hill the other way, towards Daymer Bay, a bulky middle-aged grey-haired woman in heavy brown shoes, brown tweed skirt, three-quarter length jacket, and a silk scarf figured with dogs round her head.

The tide was high, and children were playing on the shortened beach, so she turned seaward from the mouth of the river and walked along the cliff path towards the ocean. The wind caught her as she emerged onto the springy turf beyond the scattered houses, and cotton-wool clouds scudded across the sky. It was a turbulent day. Waves crashed rhythmically against the rocks below, and occasionally spray was carried against her face by the wind. She was not alone. Whole families seemed to have chosen Christmas afternoon for a stroll along the cliffs, so she strode on faster round the promontory, past the old rusty wreck held fast by the rocks, hoping to find a sheltered spot where she could be alone before she came to the cliff hotels overlooking Polzeath.

The sun shone intermittently as the clouds were blown across the sky, but the wind was cold. It felt like a knife on her face, and pierced her eye, so that she knew she would have a sick headache that night. Finally, exhausted by battling against the wind and the unaccustomed exercise in walking so far, she sank down on the long grass at the edge of the path. A hollow in the ground protected her from the wind here, and she rested, watching the white gulls wheeling on the wind, listening to the sound of the waves beating on the rock far below.

The wind and waves seemed to invade her soul as she lay there, the sun warming her tired, unwanted body. Why could she not be free like a seagull riding on the wind? It grew on her that the sea could give her peace, for it was mighty and deep. The waters at the edge might swirl and sway, and throw great gusts of spray into the air, but only the surface was rippled by the wind. In the deep blue depths of the sea there was peace.

If she were to stand up now, and walk over to the edge, she could walk out of the pain of the world. She could walk into the soft gentleness of the clouds, into the calm of nothingness, and drop gently into the peace of the sea below.

She wanted to do this, to walk out into space and leave the anguish of the world behind. It was not fear that held her back, for she did not think at all of her body smashed on the rocks below. But the voice of reason still whispered in the back of her mind, and though she felt as though she could bear no more pain, yet she remained lying in her sheltered hollow until the strength of this desire should ebb. She lay there a long time, until her limbs ached with the cold and she staggered as she walked back, for she had discovered deep within her a desolate longing to end her life.

22

Madge

The hut was made of mud baked golden in the sun, and the floor on which she lay was dark dry earth packed solid beneath her limbs. She was content, glad to lie on the smooth dry earth in the gently caressing darkness of this small round hut. The day shone dimly through the small low doorway, and she knew she must get up. She must exert herself, must squeeze her heavy body through the small opening, for she was expected. Someone was waiting for her out there in the light.

Then she was outside.

She walked round the side of the hut, and there it was. The desert again. Stretching before her as far as the horizon, nothing but an expanse of sand. And then the hut was gone, and even at her back there was just sand, she was in the middle of a heaving, swelling ocean of sand.

She knew she had been here before, she had a sense of acquaintance, of familiarity, of intimacy even with these swelling golden mountains, and the deep dark valleys between. So she belonged here perhaps. She did not know, but it felt like her desert, as though a voice whispered in her mind secretly, "This belongs to you."

She walked over the sand towards a golden mountain on her right, and the ground was warm to her feet. The sun shone down from a clear blue sky, warming her body, and it was good to be in the heat of the sun after so long in the cold. Yes, she remembered now, once she had been enclosed in an icy prison, but now she could walk free in this immense expanse and the sun would warm her.

Beside her walked another woman. She knew this was her Friend. Together they climbed to the top of the golden mountain in the warmth of the slipping sand, while the sun rose inexorably in the sky and the heat increased. She could see that it was not a mountain, merely a very minor hill, for vast ranges of mountains lay ahead, each one higher than the last, an infinite stretch of golden peaks gleaming into the illimitable distance.

Below were the valleys in black, black shadow.

The Friend raised her arm, and the blue folds of her long flowing cloak fell back, and beneath the blue cloak she wore a gown of purest white and round the hem a heavy border of gleaming precious stones.

"That is where you must go," said the Friend, and pointed down into the deep black shadows of the valley below.

No, no! She could not return to the blackness. She knew too well what awaited her there, she had been chased by demons before. Fear would reappear in a thousand disguises, and she would never escape again.

"I will show you the way," said the Friend. "Take my hand."

"There must be another way," she said.

The sun rose in the sky, she could perceive its passage, its rise was like a comet searing through the heavens. Now it was overhead. It was twelve o'clock.

"Farewell," said the Friend. She descended into the darkness of the valley, and her clothes had turned to rags.

The sun was a raging furnace of flame, and the heat swirled around her head and burned her body, and she threw off her clothes, and still the flames licked at her skin, yet she was not consumed. She felt to the ground and tried to bury herself in the sand, and prayed that the fire of the sun would burn out.

And then the sky darkened, and the sun in a vermilion arc swooped down the sides of heaven and sank into the abyss at the edge of the world.

She lay in the sand, and she was naked, and it came to her there was something she could do. There was another way. The grains of sand that lay beneath her, and around her, which partly buried her tired body, they were not black or white as she had imagined. She looked carefully at the sand in her right hand, and she could see that every grain was different from every other. Just as snowflakes were said to be different so that of the millions and millions that fall in a year, no two were ever the same, so now she knew that grains of sand were different, and glowed in blues and greens and pinks and purples and yellows and browns and many shades of black and white. They could help her. If she examined every grain of sand in the desert, and divided them up and counted every grain, she could hold the demons of the valley at bay. So she lay on her front and began to count. She must hurry. How much time did she have? Hurry, hurry. She counted more, and then she looked around, and saw that the sands stretched for ever to the edge of time, and it was impossible. She could never count her grains of sand before the hourglass ran out.

Darkness began to enclose her then, and all around rose wailing cries of demons come to haunt her. Then she knew. She would not go down to that valley, so the valley had come to her. Where was there to flee? Who could help her now? She called in despair to her Friend, but she did not come...

Shaking with fear, Madge fought her way out from under the bedclothes, fumbled for the switch of her bedside lamp, for light to dispel the darkness. All around was as usual. The green brocade curtains were drawn against the night, the door to her bathroom and closet were closed, her bedroom was calm, unruffled as it should be. But she did not venture out of bed.

The door opened, and June looked in sleepily, her long hair tousled. She was wearing nothing but a flimsy pale pink nightgown.

"You all right, Mum?"

"What do you mean?"

"I thought I heard you call out. You sure you're alright?"

This was her own flesh and blood, there was no reason she should pretend to her own daughter.

"I was dreaming," she confessed. "Something horrid. I'm sorry I woke you."

"Would you like a cup of tea? It might help you get to sleep again."

"What a lovely idea. If it's not too much trouble."

So June went downstairs, while Madge tried to remember why she had been so frightened. But she could recall nothing except a terrible sense of doom, and a conviction that one day the demons would catch her. A cup of tea, and June for company, that would pass some time. Such black shapeless fears haunted her dreams, it might be better not to sleep at all.

She felt restored by the light in the room, the familiarity of walls, furniture, curtains, clothes folded neatly on the chair, hairbrush and hand mirror in her dressing table. She smiled at her daughter when she returned with the tray of tea, and was glad of her.

"Shall I phone Grandfather in the morning?" June asked as she poured out.

The blood in Madge's head was swirled high, as a tornado lifts the waters of the sea and spins it dizzily in the air, a whirling vortex in her brain.

"He told me he was worried about you," said June as her mother remained silent. "You remember, on Christmas Day?

When you went to bed early with a bad head after that long walk? He said he thought you were not well, and I was to let him know if there was anything he could do."

Madge lay back on her familiar pillow in her familiar bed, and watched the familiar walls sway to and fro. Flashes of red streaked from one side of the room to the other, while darkness lurked in the corners. The ways she saw things, and the way others saw things no longer were the same. Her mind no longer functioned as it should. One more reason for Fear to grab her by the throat. She was totally isolated. She must be going mad.

During the days and nights that followed, she felt trapped by a demonic restlessness. She slept little, fearing the helplessness of dreams, and waking early even after fatigue had driven her to bed. No longer could she bear to sleep in her marriage bed, not even for a few hours, so she moved to the small square guest room that held fewer, different memories. Her father had slept in this room, and now she knew she disliked her father. He was selfish, cruel, and he did not love her.

The desolation of this thought drove her to wander through her house, from room to room, upstairs and then down again, searching for some consolation but finding none. For if she disliked her father and he did not love her, it was possible then that he disliked her too. Then all things were possible, the door had been opened wide to all the ills of the world.

If her father did not like her, who did? Gerald? But Gerald was selfish and cruel too, and did not love her. Perhaps he actively disliked her? But why? And she, did she really like him if she were brutally honest, and what was left but to be brutally honest?

No. She did not like Gerald. She disliked him intensely. She hated the way he was so sloppy and messy in the privacy of their bathroom and bedroom, she hated the noise he made when eating, caring as much for her sensitivity as he did for the floor under his feet. She hated the way his eyes glazed over when she tried to talk to him, about anything. She hated his vile, brutal temper, the way he was constantly picking on Robert, the way no one could say anything without his walking out of the house in a bad mood. Yes, she disliked him all right. She was better off without him.

So perhaps, if he felt the same, he might never return to her. Then she would never be able to punish him for his wicked cruelty, as he deserved. What then would be the point of living now?

Could he really dislike her though? Why should he? What had she ever done to deserve this cruel treatment? Why, oh why would he not return and explain, for if something was wrong she just did not understand what it could be. That was cruel too, leaving her a prey to black thoughts and not saying what had really been wrong, what really had driven him away. That must be what is meant by mental cruelty.

She wandered around and around this house of which she had been so proud, and hated it. It was ugly and not the sort of house she wanted at all, the cream walls were dull, the beige carpets dreary and never clean enough, the maids never seemed to stay these days, and the furniture was all wrong, she hated it, she wanted to smash it up and burn it all and make an end. So she wandered to and fro, and June kept saying, "Mum, shouldn't you see a doctor?" As though doctors were any help. Dr Barber was a man, wasn't he? He was like all the rest.

A letter arrived from Ruth, not saying much but cheerful, suggesting a trip to Nottingham. Let her be cheerful then, it was her privilege, she didn't have the burden Madge had to bear.

"It's sometimes so difficult to get out of that deep pit of depression," Ruth wrote, "without the help of a friend. Someone to talk to, someone's shoulder to cry on. I do understand. I remember it takes a long time to blur the pain of desertion. So why not come and spend some time with me, Maggie? It can't be worse than stewing alone in that house of memories, and it might help."

She probably meant well. After all, Ruth was her cousin, and family should stick together. But Madge could hardly travel all the way to Nottingham in her state of health, and she certainly wasn't planning to sit in the house all day with old Aunt Glad muttering away to herself in the corner.

In any case, Ruth must have a short memory. Many years ago, she had refused to talk to Ruth about things that really mattered, and she couldn't see that she would start now. Did she not recall those terrible words she had said so long ago? They were burnt with fire on Madge's brain, so horribly shocking they had been.

"Maggie, you're emotionally constipated," Ruth had said one day when they were both very young women, and Madge still felt shaky at the memory of those cruel words. Even if Ruth were three years older, that didn't give her the right to be so terribly rude. What did it mean anyway? Nothing. It was just Ruth's way of putting ugly words together, just to be hurtful.

Men did that sort of thing. Perhaps Ruth was like a man, not womanly enough to get married, her thoughts contaminated by the acids in her laboratory. She was always having affairs too, the way she told it. So she was immoral. Madge couldn't quite see why she still had anything to do with her, except that she was her cousin, and had been her only friend as a child. And she did know how to laugh.

Laughter, there wasn't much of that nowadays. A waste of time anyway. Life was too sad, too grim, it showed a superficial sort of mind that could laugh in the face of universal misery.

Madge was not emotionally constipated anyway. She could remember many times she had lost her temper and shouted at the children. That was showing feelings, wasn't it? But such memories brought shame, for she knew it was wrong to lose your temper like a fishwife, and shout at children who didn't know better, even if they didn't always listen as carefully as they should. She remembered now those long years of shame when she just never did seem able to restrain her tongue, however often she promised herself she would. Life was so full of disappointment, you never thought of that when you made your good resolutions.

The pain in her head would not leave her. It lay over her eyes, and pinched her forehead, pressed into her skull and clung around her neck. Although she dared not sleep, she needed to rest her aching head on the pillow. But when she lay down, the day-light beat in sharp rays through the fabric of the curtains. She covered her aching eyes with a cloth wring out in cold water, and it dripped damply into her ears and onto the pillow. Her back ached, and her arms and legs, everywhere ached, while all she desired was to lie in bed and shut out the world.

But memories haunted her then.

She remembered her babies, how strange it had been to look at the long scrawny body of her newborn baby girl, and realize she was now a woman. Like her own mother. No longer a young girl, but a woman, she had joined the mystic sisterhood of the mothers. She had not been sure she wanted to join this sisterhood in truth. Freedom, irresponsibility, music and laughter given up in exchange for a husband, a house, and a position in society. The compensation for what she had lost did not seem worth while. But she had no choice, it was society's will. And the initiation ceremony, the birth of the child, was too cruel to contemplate. No wonder her mother had never told her what to expect.

And then her boy baby. A tiny, fully-formed man child, entirely dependent on her ministrations. A sense of power had filled her at first, at the thought of this helpless male needing her for survival, but the exultation soon faded. He was a stranger to her. She would look at him lying in his cot at night, and know that she would never understand him, that even through her own son she could never know what it was like to be a man. They were so different, so obviously different: the trousers, the shirts, the short hair, the heavy boots, the bicycles, footballs, trains, aeroplanes; the noise, the mess, kicking things, guns, anger, bombs, 'I'll blow you up!". Obstinacy, delinquence, Borstal, fear, anger, resentment. It could never be otherwise. He was a stranger born of her body, living in her house, but a stranger, as her husband was a stranger.

But there had been consolation. She could feel again the tender softness of a baby's head nestled against her neck, the fragile sweetness of a tiny pulsing creature who needed her, no one but her, dependent upon her for food, for drink, for rest, for sunlight, for life itself. Tenderness filled her heart before the helplessness of a child, and she had known love. The gentle touch of a child's hands on her knees, the hug of its arms around her waist had brought her happiness. It was good to remember that.

When not lying down, she would eat. She could not stop eating, she felt urgently hungry all day, and eating cake and chocolate and bread loaded with butter and dripping with honey gave her a momentary pleasure she could find nowhere else. Inevitably she became very fat. Her clothes began to burst at the seams until there were fewer and fewer things she could decently put on. But what did it matter?

One dreary day in February, she sat in her bedroom with nothing on, and looked at herself in the mirror. No wonder her skirts would no longer do up, and her blouses gaped at the front. Her belly was distended as though she were pregnant, and great rolls of fat bulged where her waist once had been. Her massive thighs were streaked with dark blue and purple veins, as were her huge breasts which flopped down to her belly. She lifted them and they were heavy on her hands. But these were her breasts. They belonged to her, Margaret Cecily Leicester Hunter, and her husband had kissed them once and loved them. She stroked her own breast in memory, and a terrible longing overcame her, her breasts wanted hands to smooth and mould, and lips to suck, and her whole body felt aflame. All gone, all wasted, she moaned and she rocked her aching body back and forth.

The doorbell rang. She threw her dressing gown round her naked body. It was the milkman. Only a lifetime of reticence and habit prevented her from dragging the man inside and throwing herself upon him, for he was a man. Not an attractive one, not young nor even very clean, but a man. And when she had paid the bill and closed the door, she was overcome with horror and shame at the thoughts she had had, and the violence of her feelings. The most appalling, devastating thought of all was that he would have been repelled. Her body was ugly and fat and old, and no man would want to take it. She knew then, with absolute conviction, that she was rotten, a failure as a human being, a sordid mess. She had no right to exist.

Gerald came to discuss disposal of their property. She was incapable of discussing anything with him, all she could say was that she hated the house, so he said he would buy her a new one, a smaller one perhaps, she had only to tell him what she wished. When he took some books and most of the records, and asked if she agreed to that, she could only stare at him dumbly and watch him pack a part of their home in cardboard boxes. She wanted to kill him. She imagined picking up a kitchen knife, a long sharp one, and plunging it into his back. But she just sat in the upholstered chair and stared.

"We had better arrange the rest through solicitors if you can't even talk to me," he said. "I'm sorry you hate me so much. I don't hate you, you know. I feel very kindly towards you. Please believe me."

"Yes, I can see that," she said bitterly. "Why don't you go away and leave me alone?"

"Very well. I'm going. But do look after yourself. You don't look at all well."

"I'm not at all well. I'm ill, sick in the head and sick at heart. I shall probably die, and then you might care."

"Don't talk like that, for god's sake," said Gerald irritably.

She turned her back on him and waited for him to leave. The bitterest thing she knew was that if she were to die, he would not care at all. Merciful heaven, he would find it a relief.

June said she wanted to leave home. She wanted to share a flat with friends, or go to France, or to Canada. She was concerned about her mother and did not want to hurt her, but since she would not go to a doctor, what more could she do? Madge listened to her daughter talking of the dark black force which possessed her mother and which would drag her under and drown her too if it could, and recognized this as true. But she had nothing to say. June wanted to escape, to live, it didn't matter. She could neither help nor hinder her daughter's plans, for to take action she would need charity or faith or hope.

Madge saw now that she had failed. At everything. She had failed as a wife, since Gerald had left her and would never return; as a mother, for Robert had gone and June would soon follow; as a daughter, for her father did not love her and now her mother no longer brought her comfort. Deep, deep sadness filled her heart as she saw that she had failed at everything she had ever attempted: at school, where her efforts were never enough; at horse-riding; even the puppy she had longed for all her childhood and finally acquired when she was married – as soon as the war was over and Gerald was back, they had gone to buy a puppy, and she had failed to keep him safe, and he was run over. One moment he was bouncing along the path beside her, and the next he was under the wheels of a car, and he was dead. She knelt in the road beside him, and the driver kept saying, "I'm sorry, I'm sorry, it wasn't my fault, he just ran out, I'm terribly sorry," and she just knelt in the road beside her poor battered puppy, until a woman from one of the houses nearby ran out with a blanket and wrapped her puppy in it, and put the bundle in her arms. And she had walked home with the puppy, and the life had gone from him. She never knew what happened to the driver or the woman, all she knew was that she had failed and her puppy was dead. So she never had another. It was better that way. And now she had failed at life, her own life. It was better she should end that too. She had no value as a human being.

Why not let go? There was nothing left to hold her back. The darkness was in her brain. If she thought of Gerald, of her marriage, of a possible future, she saw nothing but black clouds and she did not have the strength to dispel them. Nor the courage. She did not want to look inside her head. She just wanted to end this misery for ever. If only her mother did not reject her on the other side. That was the only thing of value she had left.

She began to see death everywhere.

It was late February and the trees were dark and bare, the garden bleak after the long winter sleep. But when the crocuses pushed their heads above the soil, she saw only their eventual inevitable death and decay. She looked at the robin, and saw only a flat, insubstantial two-dimensional shape moving about the drear yellow flatness of the lawn. Life was colourless, without substance, all around her was doomed to rot away. And she herself with her gross aching body was a walking mound of rotting flesh. The heavy bleeding she experienced now only served to justify her fears, and she would sit in the bathroom, having poured out her life's blood, horrified at her malfunctioning, waiting expectantly but in terror for the end.

Sounds of hooves clopped sharply in the cobbled street, and the pale traveller reined in his horse in the moonlight, and waited. He did not pull the rusty bell nor bang with his whip upon the door, he sat in his silvery cloak in the moonlight, while his grey horse snorted and threw tendrils of warm breath into the night air. She stood beside the window looking down upon the traveller, wrapped in his silvery grey cloak, sitting so stony still. The hand that held the bridle was long and thin, like bones in the silvery light.

Why did he not call her? Why did he sit so arrogantly, knowing that she must go to him? She would change her mind then, she would remain behind. But he looked up at her as she stood by the window, and his eyes were sharp and cold, black fires smouldered in his skull that were never warm. So the die was cast. Her thread was spun and the third weird sister had lifted the shears. So be it. She was glad.

Was she not young and slim and beautiful? The pale rider below had been bewitched by her charms, had ridden through forest and thicket, over mountain and marsh and plain, not stopping for rest until he should reach her humble dwelling and carry her away. For this was her wedding night, she was young and golden and dressed all in white, and she lifted her long skirts and ran down the stairs, out of the door into the cool moonlight to meet her lover.

He lifted her upon his horse, and she was in his arms, and he flicked his whip and the grey horse reared, and they were away, galloping as fast as the winds of time to the edge of the world.

This was not her lover. She saw now she was in the arms of a dry skeleton with no flesh, a skeleton wrapped in a silvery cloak which billowed out behind him in the flight of the wind. Nor was she young and beautiful, and if this was her wedding night, it was a cruel jest for she was a grey, lined, fat, flabby old woman who had wasted her life. She had been overjoyed at the thought she would ride this horse at last, but now she could see, was outside herself and could see herself, a fat and flabby failed female in the arms of a bony skeleton hastening to the edge of time.

But it was as though there were another self, for she could see this same fat, flabby, ugly woman lying on the floor of a tiled bathroom, sprawled in the smelly, bloody, sticky mess her body made as its machinery failed and spun in sickening disorder to an end. She was surprised to see herself lying on the tiled floor, and could hear herself crying aloud: "Help, help! Have pity someone, oh help!" She was crying aloud and she could feel the horror of the crying woman, and yet she was no longer with this woman, for her demon lover held her in thrall.

Then she was alone. Horse and rider had disappeared, and she was alone on the edge of the abyss. What ties were left to sever? Who wept for her now? Who must she comfort before she threw herself into the blackness? She saw Gerald laughing with a beautiful woman in a strangely coloured room; she saw June naked and making love with a handsome youth; she could not see Robert, could not find him, his heart was closed to her. So be it. It was finished.

She let go and sank into the depths of eternal night. Her life had ended and she had found no value in it.

23

June

Death was an outrage. It made a mockery of everything. What was the point of talking of good and evil, of right and wrong, what was the point of anything when in the end you had to die? Everyone on earth was a prisoner, condemned to death.

"I won't have it, you hear?" June shouted in anger. "I won't have it!"

She was standing in the bathroom, in the middle of the white and green tiled floor, looking at the washbasin with its bar of Imperial Leather soap, and the glass shelf above with the flowered plastic cup and her mother's toothbrush and half-used tube of toothpaste reflected in the mirror, and the towel rail with the fluffy green and white Jacquard towel dipping to the floor, and the wide window-sill of green tiles and the flowered make-up mirror, and the two big windows of frosted glass framed with blue and green and pink flowered curtains. But it wasn't really such a good idea, standing in the bathroom where her mother died, sprawled on those shiny tiles beside the green boxed in bath.

She walked back into her parents' bedroom, and did not look at the big double bed or the dressing table where lay her mother's brush and comb and mirror, walked instead over to the wide window and looked out at the dull grey February day. Two blackbirds were searching for worms among the dead leaves on the lawn. Fresh air might blow away the cobwebs in her brain. She would go into the garden.

Down the stairs, through the kitchen, open the back door. Bob's bike had fallen over and was going rusty in the rain dripping from the edge of the porch. She picked it up and propped it against the garage wall. It must have been lying there for weeks and she had never noticed. The cold and damp outside penetrated her flesh and crept around her bones, so she went inside again and shut the door, walked over to the window. A blackbird tugged a worm out of the ground and gobbled it up.

Good thing about Mrs Johns anyway. She would go back next door in a minute. Good that Mrs Johns had let her stay the night because she didn't even feel like going into her own bedroom at the moment, let alone sleeping there, alone in the house. She shivered. Perhaps she should go and get a cardigan. In fact, she had better go and change into something different, she was still wearing the long purple dress she had put on yesterday to see George. It felt silly and pretentious now instead of glamorous and feminine. Slowly she turned from the window, trailed her hand along the edge of the table, walked round the chair that stood in her way, out of the door into the hall, up the stairs, turn right, into her own room. shut the door. Why did she have those stupid pictures on the wall? Pop singers with long hair and conceited smiles, she should take them down, she was beyond all that stuff now. She sat on the edge of her bed, rested her chin on her hand.

If only Dad would come back. It was lonely here, spooky somehow. He had gone off with the funeral people. With the body. He must be back soon. The body … God! Fancy thinking of your mother like that. What must it be like to be a body? It couldn't be like anything, of course, stupid, that was the point, being a body was being nothing. Not being.

What did it look like then, her body? No one had let her see her mother, as though there must be something horrific about seeing her own mother dead. Mrs Johns had even stopped her coming into the house last night. She had been waiting for her, must have been hours and hours, amazing if you thought about it. Anyway, there she had been waiting when June arrived home late last night, and instead of letting her go into her own house, she had taken her next door. Strange how you could just let yourself be led away like that, and think nothing really except, "What's got into her?" Nothing like "My God, there's been an accident." Everything was so different from normal, you'd think you'd have sensed it, and yet all you said to yourself was, "Whatever is the matter with her?" Sort of as though it wasn't really important.

She had been made to sit in an armchair in front of the fire. She could remember that very clearly, the warmth of a real fire with yellow, orange, vermilion flames dancing round the dark grey and brown logs, and the white fluffy rug and the turquoise chair she sat in, and how Mr Johns had looked at her so sadly, and that know-it-all Linda hovered near the door in a short pink nightdress, staring with wide dark eyes. Mrs Johns had knelt beside her and put her arms round her and said, "I've got some terrible news for you, my dear. Your mother has died."

June almost said, "Thank you very much. Now can I go home?" before the words penetrated.

It just wasn't possible, no one could die just like that. Anyway, it made June feel very cross and sort of put in the wrong for this strange woman to tell her her mother was dead, when she knew perfectly well her mother was waiting for her to come home right next door, and would probably launch into a tirade the minute she stepped inside the house if she didn't get a move on. She was late already.

So she got up to go, and that stupid Linda who should have been in bed hours ago burst into tears, and June said, "Thank you, I'd better go now," and the fire swung in front of her eyes, and the white rug came up and hit her in the face.

Everyone made a lot of noise, talking and clucking, such a lot of fuss, she just let go for a while. Which was stupid really as it just made everyone fuss even more, and the doctor came, and they put her to bed in their spare room, and the doctor said he knew Dad's new telephone number, and all the time they kept stopping her from going home, and she knew her mother would be angry. Now it was too late. She couldn't let her know she was sorry, she did care, she would have helped if only she had known how. But it was too late, she was gone for ever.

"Oh, hell!" she said aloud, and stood up, unzipped the dress and stepped out of it. It looked a mess. Somehow she felt as though she had lost some time somewhere, maybe it wasn't yesterday that it all happened. Her head felt like a gooey mess of mashed banana. Yecch! A cup of coffee might help. She washed her face in the messy bathroom she and Bobby shared, and brushed her hair, then put on a dark purple sweater and a pair of jeans, and some soft blue corduroy shoes. That felt more comfortable.

She went downstairs and into the kitchen, put on the kettle, took out a cup and tipped in a spoonful of instant coffee and some sugar, then went and looked out of the window again. Mr Johns said his wife had a blood-hound's nose for trouble, which wasn't a very nice way for a husband to talk, but was probably a good thing really, otherwise goodness only knew what June would have found when she came home alone that night. Her mind veered away from a brief imagined version of her mother lying dead in the bathroom, and concentrated instead on Lucy Johns persistently ringing the door bell and wandering around the house, peering in the windows, convinced that something was wrong, as though she had ESP or something, then a vivid picture of her trim figure climbing in through this very window. She probably had climbed in as beautifully as she climbed into a car, delicately lifting one stocking-clad leg in after the other without even getting a ladder. Lucy Johns was like that. So she called the doctor and left a message at Dad's office (which he apparently didn't get) and got someone in to clean up the mess in the bathroom, whatever that meant. June didn't really want to know, yet it bothered her, this vague 'mess' she was not allowed to see. As though death were more disgusting and horrific even than she imagined. As though it was degrading, even though it came to us all. Why wouldn't people talk of it? If only Dad would hurry up and come back.

She turned on the radio loudly and her mind was swamped with the rhythmic beat and clashing unmelodic sounds of a current hit. But after two minutes she had had enough. Usually she found pop music a good way to escape, the noise and rhythm would invade her mind, her body, pulling her muscles this way and that in rhythmic time to the beat of the drums, she would be outside herself and like it. But today she did not want to be dragged outside herself, nor invaded inside herself. It was all she could do to contain herself in anything like one piece so that she would not just give up again and faint or dissolve in tears or something equally feeble and banal.

This death business was for the birds. Yes, let them have it. Let all the birds in the world drop dead, she wouldn't care. She just didn't want her mother to be dead. It hurt. She wanted her back here, in this kitchen. She wanted her to walk in right now, grey and fat and frumpy, with a frown on her face perhaps, but her mother. June would go to her and take her arm, nothing too demonstrative or she'd be frightened, and squeeze her arm a bit and say, "Come on, Mum, come and sit down. I'll make you a cup of tea." And her mother's frown would fade a bit and she'd look a little surprised, and she'd sit down at the table and say, "Shall we have some of those nice chocolate biscuits?" So June would take down the tin, and put some biscuits on a plate, and they would both sit at the table and drink tea and eat chocolate biscuits, and just be glad to be together for a change. She put her head in her hands and hot tears oozed between her lashes for it was too late for that, and mostly they hadn't been glad to be together just recently. All June had done was criticise, criticise, not realizing her mother was ill. Dangerously ill. For she was dead.

A car pulled up outside the house, and shortly after she heard a key turned in the lock of the front door. Dad was back. But then her heart sank into the region of her knees as she heard voices and realized he had brought Uncle Bert with him. What for, for god's sake? She did not move, frozen with her cup in her hand, her elbow on the table, as she heard them walk through the hall into Dad's study and shut the door. Whatever was that man here for? She would go back next door, to the Johns and wait for Dad to come to her there.

Like a fool, she had left her bag upstairs. She couldn't just leave it there, for if Dad forgot and went off without seeing her, she'd never get back in again. Damn. As quietly as she could, she slid off her chair and crept to the door. No one was to be seen. Slowly she tiptoed across the hall and up the stairs. How ludicrous to tiptoe like a sneak thief in your own house, she thought, and nearly giggled aloud as she avoided the sixth stair because it creaked.

"The only place I can think of is the bedroom," said her father's voice, and there they were in the hall and she was caught. "Hello, June. What are you doing here?"

"Going up to my room, if it's all the same to you," she snapped. What are you doing here, indeed. It's my goddamn house too.

"Now, now, June my dear," boomed Uncle Bert. "We both know you are upset. Terrible state of affairs, don't you know?

Terrible."

"Quaite," said June, and she ran the rest of the way and slammed her door behind her. Damn men. Damn them. They were following her upstairs too, damn them. "Go away," she shouted. "Just go away."

".... what's got into the girl," said her father's voice.

"Don't you worry about her, Gerry my boy. You have enough on your plate. Ena and I ..." Their voices faded, and she knew she was doomed if she didn't do something fast. She couldn't stand being cooped up with Ena and Bert again, it would be better to stay here. She began to pack her overnight case, sponge bag, nightdress, clean underwear, clean jumper. After all, if Dad didn't want her, she could stay next door till the funeral and then she wouldn't mind being on her own. She'd get a flat or something then.

Voices again, and her father was saying, ".... can't have made one then."

"As I say, she'd never let me handle it for her, you know, old boy. Always a little hostile to me, for some reason, God rest her soul. But there, I never let it make any difference to me. Women are funny, whimsical creatures, don't you know?"

There was a knock at her door.

"Yes?" She would have to open the door in the end or, as adults, they would assume they had the right to barge in without her permission.

"Can I come in?" asked her father.

"I suppose so." He opened the door, and there was Uncle Bert hovering ponderously in the background, peering round his tall thin brother, trying to see into her room. If only Dad would come right in, she could shut the door in his face.

"Are you all right, June?" The silly man was hovering half in, half out – how was she to close the door?

"Of course," she said indifferently. "Why not?" She felt

cross with herself for answering this way because she wanted his concern. But really, such stupid questions.

"Did your mother ever say anything about having written a will?" Gerald asked.

So that was it. Not even buried yet, and they were worrying about what she might have left behind. Hyenas howling over a body still warm. "No," she said shortly.

"No problem, dear boy, no problem. Let me look after it."

"I see you've packed already," her father said. "So you don't want to stay here? I don't blame you. I don't feel like sleeping here tonight either."

"I'm going next door," said June hastily, knowing exactly what was coming.

"Come, come, my dear," intoned Uncle Bert as she knew he would. "You can't stay with a perfect stranger when you have family to take care of you. No, no," he put up his hand as she was about to protest, "I won't have another word. You must come with me. Don't you worry any more about your daughter, Gerry. She will be in good hands. We know what is best for her at a terrible time like this."

"No, Dad, please," said June, praying he'd understand. But the frown remained on his forehead, and he said, "I suppose it might be best. Can't keep on taking advantage of our neighbours, can we? I know they are marvellous people, but there is a limit..."

"You bet there's a limit!" June cried angrily, then gritted her teeth and would not say another word. Marvellous. Just marvellous. Trust her father to help her out of a tricky situation. Rely on him any time. Well, she just abdicated. She wouldn't do anything, she wouldn't eat, drink, talk, nothing, just be the puppet on a string they seemed to think she was.

So Uncle Bert carted her off in his blue Wolsely and subjected her to a sickening lecture all the way to Harrow on how normal it was to grieve but sinful to grieve too much for it was the Lord's will and death came to us all in the end. When they arrived at his horrid little house with the phony leaded diamond windows and flounced net curtains, June had not said a single word. Nor would she say anything to moon-faced Aunt Ena. She knew the woman was not at all pleased to see her, so why not give her the satisfaction of having something real to moan about for a change? Spread sweetness and light, that was June's motto, make everyone happy. She knew how her aunt would go on:

"That niece of Bert's hasn't even the decency to say Please and Thank you, she's so self-centred she expects everyone to wait on her like Lady Muck, and she doesn't even shed a tear at her own mother's passing."

Hypocritical prig. Let her carp on. At least the house had a guest room, she could shut herself away in there and let them get on with running her life.

There were two unforeseen drawbacks to the Veil of Silence. One was that she couldn't use the telephone and so couldn't call George and tell him what had happened. The other was Shirley.

Shirley was her cousin. She was eleven years old, fat (all that family was gross), with a lovely creamy skin and pretty fair curly hair, but such a sulky expression and such piggy eyes, you couldn't feel anything but prickles up and down your spine when the brat came and lounged in the doorway and wouldn't go away. She came in after school that day, and she leaned against the door jamb in her in her dark green school uniform, licking at a sticky red lollipop, staring.

June was furious. She leaped up and marched over to the door, gesticulating angrily to the girl to disappear and firmly shut the door again. But no sooner was she back in her chair, gazing moodily at nothing, than the door slowly inched open again, and there was the Sticky Monster once more, staring. In the end, she had to break her Vow of Silence, and tell the S.M. in no uncertain terms not to dare come near her again.

That evening she heard Aunt Ena's voice raised in anger, and knew she was the object of contention. Of course, one should not listen to others' conversations, but she did not feel that normal considerations of decency weighed on her here, and it would be interesting to hear what was being said. Might add to her store of human knowledge. So braving the danger that the S.M. might catch her eavesdropping, June opened her door quietly and crept down the stairs to listen.

"Anyone would think I had nothing better to do than wait hand and foot on someone else's lazy good-for-nothing brat. Never lifts a finger around the house ..." Aunt Fruitsalts was as predictable as a pop record you had heard twenty-seven times. "Last time you brought that niece of yours, when her mother took off for a nice long rest in the hospital, unlike some of us who never have a moment's peace, why she wouldn't so much as dry a dish unless I nagged her into it. And look at her this time, moping around, won't even walk out of that room, acting as though it belongs to her. The way she talked to our Shirl, let me tell you, Bert, I won't have it. You hear? Where does she think she is? In a rest home or something? Now I suppose she is waiting for me to take her meal up on a tray, Miss High and Mighty..."

"Come now, Ena. Remember the girl's mother has just passed away. We must do our duty by her in her hour of need."

"I know the girl's mother has passed away. That's just like you, Bert, always stating the obvious. And I don't want you saying I'm hard-hearted either, nothing could be farther from the truth, as you should be the first to know. Of course I realize she should be upset and all that. But in fact, between you and I and the gatepost, I wonder if the girl has any real feelings at all. Unnatural, that's what I call it, never a tear on her face. I mean, if she was crying and carrying on all the time, I'd understand, that would be normal for a girl whose mother's just passed on. But this one thinks of nothing but herself, just sits there rudely ignoring anything I say, expecting everyone to run around after her at every turn. I wouldn't put up with it in my own daughter, and I certainly won't put up with it in someone else's."

"Charity begins at home," said Uncle Bert piously.

"That is exactly what I say, Hubert Hunter. "Charity should begin at home. So why don't you remember that before you bring home another lazy good-for-nothing stray? I have enough family of my own without having to bother with yours."

June sat on the stair, on the grey patterned carpet, and stared at the walls which had been papered to look as though they were panelled in wood. What was the time? She looked at her watch and hoped it had not stopped, then shook it and wound it just in case. It said five minutes to eight. What sort of time was that? A nothing time, smack in the middle of the evening, not a time to start doing anything, yet time one was doing something. Some people were sitting down to dinner, some waiting expectantly in the theatre for the curtain to rise, some on their way to meet friends, or a lover. She was sitting in torn blue jeans on the stairs in a dreary semi in Harrow while her aunt and uncle haggled over her body. Not her soul though. They wouldn't recognize one if they saw it. They were still going on with their sanctimonious bickering, but she stopped listening. Should she go out? What for? Where would she go?

Suddenly she felt terribly, terribly tired. She would go to bed. She would have a good sleep, and heaven help the S.M. if she came near, and in the morning she would find some way to get out of here. Wednesday night now, the funeral was on Friday. It would soon be over.

24

June

The next morning June climbed the walls of sleep up to the new day, and heard Uncle Bert's voice drone about shaking a leg and putting her best foot forward and everything being for the best in the best of all possible worlds. She kept her eyes closed and waited for him to get tired. It took a long time. Most people liked the sound of their own voices, but he would have won prizes in a marathon. He had to go to work (thank god), but he knew she would appreciate the importance of showing gratitude to dear Aunt Ena, whose sole concern was for her welfare, not to mention himself and his own not insignificant contribution, family was family, they must help each other in times of crisis, blood being thicker than water …
And bile being thicker than blood, she suddenly leapt out of bed and dashed to the bathroom, where she was sick.

"Are you all right, my dear?" twittered loving Uncle Pangloss outside the bathroom door, and she did not deign to reply. She should have eaten something last night, it was as though her guts were being torn inside out. But she would not eat anything in this house. She would go out, she could leave this morning, go back home maybe. Anyway she could go to a cafe and buy a decent cup of coffee, and maybe a sandwich. The retching which had taken her body out of control began to subside, and she knew she was going to feel better any minute now.

"For heaven's sake, what's the matter with you?" The dulcet tones of Florence Nightingale's solicitous enquiry reverberated from tile to tile, so June got up from the bathroom floor where she had been kneeling beside the loo, and washed her face with cold water and dried it on some tissues. Naturally there was no towel for her and her flesh crawled at the thought of using one of theirs. Then she went to the door and waited until the Lady removed her Lamp, which took no time at all for the gentle nurse did not bother to wait for a reply, but had already turned and started downstairs. "You'd better hurry if you're going to have some breakfast," she said over her shoulder. "I haven't got all day to wait on girls who can't look after themselves. Shirl! SHIRLEE! Haven't you gone to school yet?"

"Yes, Mum," came the Sticky Monster's voice faintly from the kitchen.

What a family. No conception of the meaning of the English language. She had never made a more sensible decision than when she decided never to speak to them ever again.

June dressed slowly, for she felt dizzy, and in any case did not want to re-encounter Uncle Pangloss. Her hair needed washing and she could do with a bath. Never mind. She repacked her overnight bag – she would not be staying here again.

Was she being unreasonable and badly behaved though? She thought about it as she sat on the edge of the bed, and had to admit she probably was. Aunt Nightingale and Uncle Cant were being as kind as they knew how and she certainly wasn't making it any easier for them by being so rude. Yes, she was definitely very rude. But what the hell? It served them right. All that phoney claptrap about family and blood ties, the real thing was someone had died, for god's sake. They didn't give a damn about her mother. So they could go to hell. Which they would. Self-righteous, sanctimonious, hypocritical prigs.

Uncle Cant and the S.M. must have gone now, leaving only kindly Aunty Hyena, who was probably stuffing herself with chocolate creams over a hot stove. She crept down the stairs with her bags. This was her Year of the Creep. Thank you, guardian angels, for tidy button-down minds, all the doors closed. Carefully across the hall, past the old-fashioned hall stand, open the front door with its red and green coloured glass, out into the cold fresh air.

To slam or not to slam, that was the question. Yes, to slam. She wouldn't give a damn. Poetry. With a marvellous sense of freedom, she took hold of the loop of the letter box, swung the door in and then towards her with a deliciously house-shaking CRASH. That felt great. Crash bang to them all, slap in the face, slap, smack, pow! Don't come telling me what to do any more, you hear, when you don't give a shit about me one way or another. You hear? Up yours!

She made an obscene gesture, then skipped down the path and through the gate, and she heard the front door open behind her and Lady Bountiful shout, "Hey! Where do you think you're going?"

June turned and said with venom: "Drop dead!" But unluckily the woman didn't, and waddled down the path in her nasty flowered nylon dressing gown, providing the neighbours with a lovely titbit of gossip. She made a grab for June's arm and hissed: "You can't do that. You can't rush off like that, not at this terrible time. You've got to stay right here until the funeral."

June threw her aunt's hand off, and a light exploded in her head like a kind of madness, and laughter seized her as she saw faces appearing behind nylon curtains all along the road.

"Just try to make me, you great lump of lard, you nasty, mean, two-faced, mingey, stingy, grudging, sanctimonious hypocrite."

The madness was in her head, and she turned from her aunt and waved regally to each window in turn while her aunt tried to grab her bag, so she kicked her on the shins, then walked away. At the corner, she turned to make a final flourish to her apoplectic relation who now was scuttling indoors, then she ran all the way to the bus stop. Well, she had burnt her boats now, and no mistake.

Harrow was one hell of a way from Godbridge, which was a good thing most days, but right this minute a damn nuisance. The only way to get there was to go right into London and then out again. So first she would take a bus to the station and have a cup of coffee if there was a place open, then take a train into town.

Strange. She didn't really feel hungry at all, just a bit light-headed and dizzy, and a slight burning sensation in her throat. Not what you would call hungry. It was strange to be among all these people on their way to work, knowing they all had to be somewhere at a certain time and it mattered, and not to be one of them. Strange not to be in a hurry, not to know how the rest of the day would be spent. Strange. Yes, everything felt strange. She really felt rather peculiar.

Off the bus, she went into a seedy-looking cafe where two workmen in blue overalls were thumbing pictorials and drinking tea in a corner and a dark thin man was wiping down the counter. The coffee she had promised herself was obviously going to be undrinkable English stuff, not the fragrant brew you got in Espresso bars, so she asked for a cup of tea, strong brown and hot. She took a packet of crisps as well, as she thought she'd better eat something. She hadn't had a thing since breakfast at the Johns's the previous morning, and then she'd only been able to eat a slice of toast. She was off eating for a while.

She paid and sat down at a grey topped table with dirty ashtray, red plastic ketchup holder and thick glass salt and pepper shakers. Money was going to be the next problem. When she had to fork out for this much needed cup of tea, she realized she hadn't got enough to get back to Godbridge under her own steam. She'd have to ask Dad to give her a lift. Damn and blast. Money might be the root of all evil, but it certainly was the key to freedom. With it you could do what you damn well pleased. Without it, you were a prisoner.

Her head in her hands, she contemplated the stupid situation she had got herself into. Perhaps it wasn't such a good idea to phone Dad after all. Supposing Uncle Cant had been on to him, or worse still, Lady Bountiful herself. Which was more than likely, she could hardly keep such a juicy tale to herself, could she? And even if by some lucky chance Dad had not been told the scandal of the morning, there was still the danger he might insist she go back to Hubert's Happy Home for Waifs and Strays, and if he insisted she was going to have a lovely time explaining why she couldn't possibly. Best to let sleeping dogs lie.

She decided to phone George. Maybe he wasn't in class this morning. If anyone would care about her, he would, and he didn't even know yet that her mother was dead. A terrible longing overcame her to lie again in his arms, against his broad firm chest, kiss his soft warm mouth and run her fingers through his red curly hair, feel his animal warmth fill her once more with a sense of being alive. Her shoulders felt empty without his arm around them. She opened her bag and found a coin. Somehow she felt almost afraid at the prospect of phoning him like this, first thing in the morning, without warning. But she was not worried really, he wouldn't mind. It was excitement at doing something unexpected that set her heart beating a little faster and set butterflies dancing in her tummy. She wanted to hear his voice, and to tell him her mother was dead. She would not say she must have died while they were in bed together, the last time, only two days ago – to say that would somehow put a shadow between them and lay a blight on their love for ever.

The number rang for a long time, and she could see the pay phone in that dingy hall ringing, ringing, and each person in that three storey house hoping someone else would answer. Lazy buggers. It was past nine now, most of the lodgers in those horrid rooms must be at work now, or in classes. He probably wasn't there, why would he be? But she felt he would be there this morning just because she needed him, if he loved her.

She was just about to put the phone down because obviously no one was going to answer when the receiver was lifted the other end and a male voice barked: "Yes?"

She had to swallow a lump in her throat before she could answer. "Can I speak to George … George Rand, on the second floor?"

"Who is that?"

"Phil? Is that you, Phil?"

"That's right."

"It's me, June."

"Hey, June baby. Holy cow, d'you realize you just got me outta bed?"

"Lazy good-for-nothing, you should be in classes at this hour, shouldn't you?"

"Yeah, sure. Hey baby, you at a fire or something? You sound kinda breathless."

The lump came back and was bigger this time and took longer to swallow. "Is he there?" she asked at last.

He didn't answer immediately, then finally said: "Man, I'm sorry, you're just outta luck today. He actually made it to class this morning."

"Oh." She tried to joke: "Must be a nude model, I guess."

"Something like that. Hey, June baby, you got problems or something?"

"Oh, nothing much."

"You gotta message I can give him?"

"Will he be there this afternoon, do you think?

Phil hesitated again. "Well, I just don't know what his plans are, baby. Shall I ask him to ring you or something?"

"No. That won't do at all. Oh God..."

"You in trouble?"

"Phil, I just want to see him. He will be back this afternoon – or at least this evening, won't he?"

"He will. Man, I'll drag him back by his long red hair, you'll see him today."

"You won't have to do that Just tell him I'll be there, what, about three?"

"Make it four, baby. See you."

"Thanks, Phil. Bye."

She bought another cup of strong hot tea.

"You all right?" asked the dark man as he took her coins and rang up the till.

"Yes, thanks." She smiled a little to make him feel OK, before returning to her grey table. Nine twenty-five. Hours to go. Seemed stupid really, but you couldn't expect other people's lives not to go on. She put her head in her hands again, and realized she had a headache. Damnation.

A baker's van drew up outside and a white-coated driver struggled through the door with a wooden tray piled with pies and pastries and doughnuts. God, that smelled good. She opened her purse and tipped the contents onto the table: three large silver coins, two small, forty P, four coins for the telephone, plus three ones, six halves, that made 54 P. Better not. She still had to get to St John's Wood, and then right through till past lunch time. She put the coins back in her purse and closed her bag. The tea was good.

The baker returned with an armful of sliced loaves wrapped in striped waxed paper, the till rang, the two men exchanged noisy greetings, the door slammed, and there was silence. She held her fingers against her throbbing temple and contemplated the descending level of the brown steaming liquid in the thick white cup.

"Here," said a voice, and she found the dark counter-man beside her, holding out a plate with a doughnut.

"No, it's all right, thanks."

"Go on, you can do with it," he said, put the plate down and walked away. "No skin off my nose, never sell this lot in one day. Better you should eat it than let it go stale."

She contemplated the crisp round sugar-coated ball and its aroma rose and assailed her nostrils, and saliva began to gather in her tongue, and course down her throat.

"Gosh." She looked at him behind the counter now, leaning on his elbows, reading a newspaper. They were alone. She hadn't noticed the other men leave. "You sure?"

"Course I'm sure. Go on, eat it." He laughed a little, then returned to his newspaper.

She gazed unbelievingly at the crisp fresh doughnut and decided she didn't care about warnings against taking things from strange men, if he had any funny ideas she would deal with them later. "Thanks," she said, and then devoted her entire attention to the delicious flavours of the fried dough, crisp and sugary outside, still faintly warm inside and sweet with strawberry jam. She licked her fingers and ran her tongue round her lips, chasing the last vestiges of her banquet, and realized she had been hungry after all. She leaned back in her chair and sighed audibly. The Good Samaritan looked up.

"Gosh, that was good," she said. "Thanks."

"Think nothing of it."

She couldn't sit here all day unfortunately. In fact, it was almost as though her acceptance of this stranger's unexpected gift had place a stronger barrier between them, shining in its newness and impossible to ignore. He had done this Good Deed, and since unlike the Good Samaritan he was in his own land, it was up to her to leave. He must want her gone.

The obvious thing was to go on to St John's Wood by Underground and leave her bag there, so she said goodbye to her new friend. Then on the train, she thought perhaps the station might not have a Left Luggage Office, so she stayed on until Baker Street. She still had hours and hours ahead, and very little money. What to do? She could go to Madame Tussaud's perhaps, or the Planetarium, except that would take all her money and she'd still have hours left. So in the end, she decided to go to the Zoo.

At least it wasn't raining as it usually had been whenever Dad brought her here as a child. Funny that, the Zoo to her was principally dripping cars and pools at the turnstiles and quick dashes between the Aquarium and the Reptile House where you could spend long dry hours discovering the weird creatures that swam under the seas or slithered through untamed jungle.

Birds were singing in the trees as she reached Regent's Park and began the long trek up Broad Walk. Spring was coming at last – she could see buds bursting into leaf here and there, and even daisies in the grass. It was as though she was suspended between lives, for a few hours no ties held her, no duties called, she had been given the gift of non-time where hours have no meaning, only what she might feel as she lived through them. But the pleasure of that thought faded as she reached the turnstiles, and she knew that she was seeking her childhood.

Within the zoo, her childhood seemed as far away as ever.

She found she was walking through a tunnel she didn't remember, into the famous aviary she had never seen. Cages for birds should never be allowed she firmly believed, though grudgingly she had to admit this one was magnificent. The sides of the cage swept in long geometric lines into the sky, and then the path became a bridge and she looked down upon rocks and a stream, and her eyes were level with nests in the trees. The exotic fowl took no notice of her presence and she watched them wheel and swoop above and then below her, beneath the bridge, to the waters. It was a beautiful cage. But she didn't like it. If she stayed any longer, she might burst into tears. So she hurried to the other door and let herself out and wandered along the green banks of the canal where daisies and celandines were blooming.

It was as though she were suddenly lost, for she didn't know where to go. But it was peaceful here, so she sat on the grass for a while and just let the tears roll down her cheeks for they insisted on being shed, and she watched the waters flow past and the insects busy in the grass and listened to the birds calling, and refused to think, just let the water in her eyes drain away. Eventually it stopped.

Time had passed anyway. As she made her way back, she saw numerous mothers with babies or little children too young to be at school, in reins or pushchairs or on their mothers' backs, and lots of little boys in short shorts and little girls in woollen dresses running to and fro and shouting, while their mothers chatted in twos and threes. All these women, some barely older than her, some bright and some clearly stupid, yet they all knew how to be a mother. How very odd.

Back at the entrance, she went the opposite way this time, and began to recognize the place. In the monkey cages, various species of the non-naked ape swung from bar to bar inside the roof, or chattered to the staring children hoping for peanuts, or sat in corners eating a banana, or groomed one another, picking off the fleas with long fingers and popping them into their mouths.

Then came the cat house, which she hated but entered anyway, and her stomach burned with fear of these animals that live on blood and flesh. As she looked at the burning eyes of the tiger sitting staring in his corner, and the deep raging eyes of the lioness prowling up and down, up and down behind the bars, she could see they knew her fear and were contemptuous, and would spring on her if the bars were not there and plunge their claws into her flesh. She hurried through to the outside, and the lion shook his mane and roared as she left, and her knees trembled as she moved quickly down the path and took deep breaths of fresh air to dispel the stench of big cat.

She was full of nameless fears, and as she walked she wanted to look over her shoulder. None of the big houses of birds or fish or reptiles appealed now. The only animals in the Zoo she would feel happy with were the elephants. Strange how she loved them for she did not imagine she was in any way like them, nor did she want to be. She was perhaps more like a cat that smouldered with anger when held back by bars, and what distressed her was the knowledge that freedom could be taken away and such anger could exist. The elephant would climb mountains in the snows and storms of winter though its home was hot and humid, with cooling waters and green leaves to eat, it would cross mountain passes with honour and dignity. Without making war on Man.

Make love, not war. Hah! That's what she did and Mother died. That's what Dad did, and he left home and turned his back on his daughter, and Mother died. Poor Daddy. Her heart suddenly filled with pain for her father who must be suffering now with the knowledge of what he had done. She remembered him now: she had walked along here holding his hand, and his eyes were twinkling as he told her stories of the animals in the jungle, of Kaa the snake and the Jungle Boy, of the Cat that walked by itself, of how the elephant got its trunk and why the crocodile smiles. She felt a terrible desire to sit down and just cry. This was getting ridiculous.

She needed to phone her father. The idea of seeing George and being independent and all that jazz was all very fine, but she had to get back to Godbridge, and she needed Dad to give her a lift. The funeral was tomorrow morning, and she didn't know when or where, and she had to get home to change her clothes.

What could she wear anyway? Should she buy something special, a black dress or something? But what with? She didn't care what people thought, but just this once she wanted to do things right and not get people upset with her for no reason at all.

By the time she reached the station, she felt so hot and sticky she simply had to spend a penny to change her purple jumper for the thinner yellow one, and then she really needed to buy a bar of chocolate because she was starving. Then she went to telephone. After the coin dropped, she had one 5P left and one 2P. That wouldn't get her anywhere.

Fortunately big offices always had people to take messages, but she felt sure he'd be there now, it was after two. Then his secretary answered and said he wasn't there, she'd just missed him, for heaven's sake, he'd left to go to Godbridge by goddamn car, so she was stuck, and to her absolute horror and shame, she burst into tears, practically deafening the poor old thing the other end. Disgusting. Dear old Mrs Mac came through like an angel though, and when June explained she only had 7 P in her purse, told her to jump into a taxi and the doorman would pay when she arrived, and she'd lend her money to get home, but first she should come right upstairs to Mrs Mac's office where there would be a nice cup of tea waiting.

She was afraid the driver might be cross if she said she hadn't any money, so she explained before she got in that someone would pay the other end and she wanted to go all the way to the City. But he was ever so nice about it and told her to hop in, and then she felt a bit like a fraud with people looking at her sitting like a queen in her own chauffeur-driven car, not caring in the least how much traffic there was or how long it took, and the numbers on the meter kept on clicking up and it didn't matter to her any more.

Mrs Mac had been Dad's secretary for as long as she could remember, and every time Dad was promoted to a bigger office, Mrs Mac moved into a bigger office too. Often during school holidays, she had popped into Dad's office and chatted to Mrs Mac, who never seemed to mind however busy she was. And now Mrs Mac came to meet her at the lift, and took her hand in both hers and squeezed it gently, and then took her through her huge Exec Sec office with its machines and filing cabinets and vases of flowers, into Dad's room with its ankle-deep carpet and enormous teak desk, to the corner with armchairs and coffee table. This marvellous woman had provided not only tea but sandwiches and biscuits, so June settled comfortably into one of the leather armchairs and gobbled the food, while the dear woman warbled on about how sad she was, and what Dad had done about the funeral and who was coming (Ruth, thank heaven, and various obscure relations) and what time and what to expect, and not to worry if she wanted to hold someone's hand because most people did, and had she thought what to wear, it was always such a difficult thing to decide, but thank heaven no one had to wear black these days, anything dark would do. And June really began to feel better with this kind-hearted woman going on, somehow just hearing about all the practical bits made it feel real and not a horrific fantasy.

So she confided that she really hadn't got a thing to wear, only trousers or minis or one maxi, and they all seemed a bit extreme. Mrs Mac quite understood and said she'd just have to lend her some money. And they both went down in the lift and round a few corners, and there unexpectedly was a very nice boutique where she found a super dark brown midi skirt with a short jacket that Mrs Mac said would do perfectly, and it wasn't dreadfully expensive so she felt terribly tempted to buy a lovely golden brown floppy hat which looked absolutely stunning. But she wasn't supposed to be enjoying the occasion, so she turned her back on it and thought about shoes and a bag, and decided she could make do. Then Mrs Mac bought her the darlingest brown silk scarf with white spots to tuck in the neck, and would not take 'No' for an answer. So when they said goodbye, June just had to kiss her, and it was a bit of an emotional scene really, terribly un-English in this terribly English company with its titled lords in the Board Room.

Then she found herself in a sleek navy blue Daimler, surrounded by bouquets and wreaths of flowers, being driven out of the City by a uniformed chauffeur. Mrs Mac's brainwave: she had spent a few minutes on the telephone organising people, and lo, June was to be driven home and then the flowers delivered direct to the funeral parlour. She sat in the corner of the luxurious Daimler clutching the enormous bag with her new suit, and looked at her battered blue overnight case, her torn jeans and scuffed shoes, smelling the flowers which would lie on her mother's coffin, and she felt a little sick. But it seemed an appropriate home-coming after Hubert's Game of Happy Families.

25

Gerald

The first Gerald knew of Madge's death was a phone call late Tuesday night from Lucy Johns: apparently Dr Barber gave her the number. What happened to Lucy's message at the office he never knew, but a temporary on the switchboard no doubt figured it wasn't her problem if she couldn't locate his secretary, he'd get the news when he arrived home. He drove out to Godbridge immediately.

June was asleep by the time he arrived, thanks to Doc B's magic pills, so after a couple of stiff brandies from Jeremy's bar, he went next door, had another brandy from his own store, and went to sleep in Robert's room.

Next day his head was blessedly fuzzy. He made his way through the formalities as though dealing with a business problem. He supposed he must have a turmoil of feelings, but he sure as hell wasn't going to look. The only feeling he could recognize was anger, which hardly seemed comprehensible or appropriate.

The funeral was arranged for Friday morning. His jaw set, he pushed his way through bureaucratic fumbling and procrastination coldly and ruthlessly. Hubert drove down to help search for a will, for he held Gerald's but not one for Madge, and took June back with him to Harrow.

Gerald felt badly for his daughter, wanted to comfort her, but did not know how. Women understood these things so much better. He would have liked her to stay with Lucy, but as Bert pointed out, it was too much of an imposition on good neighbours, however kind and generous they might be, especially when there was family to turn to. Ena was a woman after all. He couldn't do anything for June himself. She was quiet and funny, as she had been ever since he had left home, and he could see no way to reach her. She did not want him.

Relatives had to be told, Madge's aunt Gladys and cousin Ruth in Nottingham, her cousins in Banbury, her father in Cornwall. He sent them all telegrams, and Ruth rang up to say she'd be there.

Robert still did not know. As soon as he could, he drove back to London to find his son. How to find a boy in London who, when not in his father's company, chose to keep his whereabouts secret? But he was not a young boy – he kept forgetting. He was a young man. Or part boy and part man, and a father cannot always tell which part is which.

It was after six when Gerald got in. Patricia was not there, and he was no nearer a solution as to how to find Robert. He poured himself a strong drink. His mind had stopped functioning.

Patricia came in at six thirty, and Robert was with her. What a woman. Without saying a word, she knew what was needed and went out and did something about it. A great burden slid from his shoulders.

Robert stood in the hallway, arrogantly, his weight on one leg, one hip jutting with the wide belt standing out around his hip bone, a peep of flesh showing as his dark sweater carelessly rode up his lean chest, one hand holding his brown jacket behind his back. This young man, as tall and lean as Gerald, his rather pimply face framed by long brown wavy hair below his shoulders, this was his son. But Gerald did not dare put his arms round this arrogant stranger, even though he recognized a part of himself standing there in the hallway, daring anyone to come near.

"Pat said you want to see me," Robert said, and it sounded

as though he meant, It had better be something good.

"I'll make some coffee," said Patricia. "You two go on in there, and I'll bring it when it's ready."

Gerald nodded. "Good idea. Come on, Bobby. I have something important to tell you." He turned back to the lounge, trembling a little. Why was it he saw his son as a stranger, and at the same time felt him as a tender, vulnerable baby? He had just reverted to his baby name, and they had not used it for six years.

Robert followed, and stood a careful six feet away, hands in pockets, slouched arrogantly like a cowboy in a Grade B movie. For a moment Gerald felt outside the scene, as though he were observing it from the window so to speak, two tall men confronting each other, one in sober dark business suit, blue shirt and Rotary Club tie, the other young, irresponsible, hairy, in tatty blue jeans and brown jacket, standing in a room where neither belonged, a design-conscious room with black modern chairs, hanging paper globes, pottery, books, records, and a colour scheme subtly emphasizing the woven wool rug that lay between them on the floor. He wondered how he came to be there, and hoped he would acquit himself properly.

"Bobby," he said at last, "I have some terrible news. Mummy has died. She died last night, very suddenly."

"Oh." That was all he said. He stood looking down at the floor, and all the arrogance oozed out of him, from his head, his neck, his shoulders, his hips, down his legs and out through his toes. Gerald saw it happen and put out a hand to steady his son, who suddenly found he needed to sit down, put his arm round the boy and held him close. Very briefly, the barriers were down and he had no need of thought to understand the needs of this boy, his son, who had lost his mother.

"Jesus," Robert whispered at last. "It can't be true."

"I know, son. I know. But it is."

"But why? How? What happened?"

"It was her heart. Apparently she had a heart attack yesterday and died in the bathroom. Lucy Johns found her, and telephoned me last night. I've been down there all day, sorting things out."

"But ... why did she die?"

"It was her heart the doctor says."

"Yeah. It would be. Her heart ... Jeesus." He sat in the chair, his head drooping over his knees, and did not say another word.

Gerald went to the kitchen to fetch Patricia. He was drained and in need of her help.

Robert did not touch the coffee she poured for him, just sat staring at nothing. Gerald made another attempt to find something to say that might help.

"Do you want to see her?" he asked. "The body? It ... she is at the funeral parlour, of course. I could take you tomorrow?"

"JeeSUS!" Robert looked up, his eyes staring. "Are you kidding?" He stood up. "Pat, d'you mind? I think I'll have a kip."

"Of course," she said. "The bed's made up. Go ahead, you know where it is."

He went, in a hurry, leaving the living room door wide open, but slamming the spare room door shut behind him.

"My God, I made a mess of that," Gerald said dismally. "But what can you *say*?"

"Darling, don't worry about it. It's a terrible shock for both of you, and there's no way round it. You both have to live through it and it can only be bad."

Strange sounds came drifting down the hall, and they realized Robert was crying. Patricia got as far as the closed door before she understood her instinct to comfort someone in distress was inappropriate here. Her role in this drama was too equivocal, she could bring him no comfort. Slowly she returned to her chair.

"I can't go to him," she said. "I must not know."

They sat in silence for a few minutes. She looked at Gerald while he looked at the dark side of his soul.

"I daren't" he said at last, gazing at the floor. "I would only make things worse."

She was sad for him then. She knew he too was in pain, the bad comfortless pain where you see your own failures rise up from their slimy murky depths into a quagmire, the Slough of Despond and no Help in sight. Because of his guilt and his own need for comfort, he was failing his children who surely ought to have first claim on his attention and compassion. But that terrible word 'ought' again – she resolved to eschew that word for ever. He would choose whatever he could tonight, and she would help him cope with what was left.

"What gives you solace, darling? Music? Reading? Do you want to talk?"

"Dear God, I don't know. Drink, food, making love, I guess. But I have no energy. Everything is all wrong, all topsy-turvy."

"All can be provided," she said smiling, gently joking. "I'll bring you a gin and tonic, then I'll make a meal. You sit here quietly. Would you like some music?" She stood behind his chair, stroked his hair, nuzzled his head a little.

He raised his hand to hers, squeezed it gratefully. "You love me, I guess."

"Of course, I do, silly. You know that."

She put on Tchaikowsky's *Pathetique* and brought him a drink, then she left him alone. For some minutes, he sat and let the music wash over him and through his head, cleansing his mind of the black thoughts that had been haunting him all day, unclear and unspoken, but there. But as he sat quietly and that infinitely sad melody in the first movement began, different darker images arose in his mind. He had never been able to sit and listen to music without some other occupation – and now the music was tearing at his vitals, grabbing him by the balls. He turned it off.

Perhaps he would read something. To turn on the television, which was his first impulse, would be cowardly escapism, besides television was a bore, newspapers were a bore, news magazines were a bore, everything was a bore. But he did not like smoking and drinking and generally wasting his time, he felt inexplicably embarrassed and uncomfortable.

He turned to the bookshelves. Kipling perhaps. He'd like to read some of his poems again that he'd learned by heart as a boy. There was a man who understood.

> *'If you can keep your head when all about you are*
> *losing theirs ... tum tum ...*
> *If you can meet Triumph and Disaster and treat those*
> *two imposters just the same...'*

There! And that smugglers' song, how did it go?

> *'Laces for a lady, letters for a spy,*
> *Watch the wall, my darling, while the Gentlemen go*
> *by.'*

Marvellous.

But Patricia didn't have any Kipling as far as he could see. Then he discovered that by great good fortune his own volume of Rupert Brooke had been tidied away on the shelf. A strange, warm sentimental feeling overcame him as he took it down, a small volume with a shiny white cover, like the prayer book every girl used to receive for first communion. He often carried this book with him when away on business, though he did not often open it. Just to have it was a comfort. He knew many lines by heart – he might not be widely read, but what he had read, he had read well.

> *'God! I will pack and take a train,*
> *And get me to England once again!*
> *For England's the one land I know*
> *Where men with Splendid Hearts may go.'*

Yes, yes, his own sentiments exactly. Then he turned to *The Fish*, and his spirit was soothed by the flowing water words, his very heartbeat slowed down and share the pulse of the poem where 'music is the exquisite knocking of the blood'.

But his peace was short-lived. Turning the pages, relaxed and unwary, he found his favourite poet had been preoccupied with death. He had remembered sex and love, but now he found only death – death of love and death of girls and death of young men. And finally his heart was twisted and scorched with remorse as he read a poem entitled *The Dead*, and thought of Madge, and he knew that her life had been woven of more cares and sorrows than joy and mirth.

> *'These had ... gone proudly friended;*
> *Felt the quick stir of wonder; sat alone;*
> *Touched flowers and furs and cheeks.'*

Was this Madge? When had she felt the stir of wonder, gone proudly friended? He could not know, of course, yet he felt there had been little joy or wonder or even friendship in her later years. And why? Was this his fault? No. She was a dull, unfriendly, rather stupid woman without the ability to find joy and pleasure in the world. But what a waste. What a waste! And what was the use of reading a book like this if all he found was pain and remorse? Better not to think at all.

He walked around the room, picking up pottery bowls and books and terracotta animals, but not seeing any of them with his brain. He prowled up and down the room with an ache around his heart and a pain in his head no material thing on earth could assuage. He thought of his children: his daughter, his first born, alone with her dying mother, and now alone with Bert and that self-centred Ena – he should comfort his daughter, should he not? But how? He did not know. And his son, half man, half boy, lying in this flat alone in that impersonal room, made for overnight guests but otherwise not used, lying in the narrow bed, weeping for the mother he had not seen for months. What had he, Gerald, done? He felt in some terrible inexplicable way to blame for all the unhappiness around him, as though he would drown in all this misery, for he did not know what he had done that was so wrong, nor what he could do now to make it right.

26

Patricia

Patricia went out to buy a bottle of wine. She was glad of an excuse to leave them alone for a while, for she felt the emotions in that flat were tearing her apart. She needed a brief respite, to be alone before she returned to be the tower of strength she knew they both expected her to be. She would do her best. She never refused a cry for help when it was within her power to do something, had never wittingly done so since she learned what it is to be alone, and had understood how no person is an island.

How was it, though, that she excepted Madge Hunter from this knowledge? If every person's death diminishes me, how was it she felt detached from this death, as though she had not died a little when Madge died? The bell tolls not for me… Ah, but this was not so. She realized as she walked down the benighted street, between the pools of light thrown by the lamps, it was rather that she felt she had died too much. Madge's death had diminished her more than it should. A light had dimmed in her soul. The belief she had cherished to protect herself against the cruel sharpness of material reality, that the human spirit might be indomitable, this keystone of her faith had been undermined.

The woman could not have died of a broken heart. Unless she, Patricia, had so far misread the situation and understood so little of what makes a marriage that she might now be held criminally responsible. But Gerald had not believed she loved him, and surely he must have known. Without love, can there be a broken heart? Was it lack of courage then? How was it possible to die of that? It is not possible to wish to be dead, and then to be so. The human body is strong, people live and live and live in the most appalling circumstances. There obviously had to be some physical disability. So why was she torturing herself with these foolish questions?

Was it really possible to die of hysteria? Was that her fear? That she had helped drive this weak woman to a state of hysteria, in ignorance but what sort of plea was that? She remembered that Vin had told her of psychosomatically-induced fatal illnesses, that fifty percent of complaints taken to a doctor were psychological in origin, and that included tuberculosis and cancer and heart disease. It was not possible. How was it then that people survived the horrors of concentration camps? Of forced labour prisons? And yet a tribal African, many miles from his village, when condemned by a witch-doctor's curse, may sicken and die. Just like that, as though the life had gone out of him. The life had gone out of her...

She pushed open the door of the shop that stayed open until 11 pm, and the bell jangled. Forget it. Get on with living. She bought three frozen trout, some petits pois and a packet of sliced almonds; a french loaf and unsalted butter; a bottle of Chablis and some wafer mints.

Then she walked back through deserted streets, and rain was falling. Would Robert want to eat? It was a good thing she had found him, though not difficult: she thought perhaps he did not want to disappear entirely from his family, for he had let the information as to where he was staying (in a student house, with an Italian named Maria) drop casually, as though by accident, and she had known she should make a note of the address, and that he did not want his father to know. Strange how he trusted her. She was glad.

Having deposited her parcels in the kitchen, she went to

listen at the guest room door. No sound. She knocked.

"Yeah?"

"It's me, Patricia. Can I come in?"

She heard the bedsprings creaking, heavy footsteps and the door opened.

"I just wondered if you'd like some supper."

He put his hand to his mouth. "Oh. What is it?"

"Trout and almonds. And Chablis. Sound nice?"

He shook his head, turned back to the bed where he sat down, his head between his knees. "Gosh, Pat, I'm sorry. Just not up my street."

She went over to him then, put her arm round his shoulders, felt his animal warmth through the dark knitted jersey. "I'm sorry, Robert. It's really beastly. The strongest men weep when their mothers die, you know. Why don't you? It might help a bit." He looked up and smiled wanly. "Look, I'm sure you could do with a little something to eat and then, why not go to bed? I could make you a poached egg?"

"OK... I'll be there in a minute."

"Good. I'll start cooking."

She returned to the kitchen. He could eat quietly on his own, and then go to bed. And she would be able to give her full attention to Gerald. Her man.

Robert came in, very pale with the pink acne spots standing out redly on his nose and cheeks. He sat at the table, fiddled with the salt and pepper shakers until she put the plate in front of him, then listlessly ate but finished it all. He refused anything more.

"I'll bring you a hot drink in bed."

"OK."

She prepared a tall mug of hot milk with brown sugar and whisky. No doubt a sixteen-year-old should not be given whisky. But she was offering him this potent nightcap medicinally, and she felt sure its effects on his over-heated brain would be nothing but beneficial.

He took the hot milk obediently, lying in bed and eyeing the liquid with raised brows as she turned on the bedside lamp and turned out the overhead light. But he drank it anyway, and turned to her appreciatively as she stood by the door.

"It's nice to be mothered when you haven't got a mother," he said, and his lips drooped and he looked down at his milk once more.

"Sleep well. See you in the morning." She blew him a kiss which he caught. Then she shut the door.

Now for Gerald. She would feed him and give him wine and take him to bed and make love because of love. Then he would sleep.

She hoped she would too. For some strange reason, she felt caught in darkness, in black weaving shadows. She thought inexplicably of the ancient goddess Ishtar who caused the waters to flood the world, and then wept to see the havoc she had made. She was caught in the dark night of the moon.

27

Gerald

He was in a dark vaulted cellar, walking between rows of wooden casks, along a cold stone floor, rough, unfinished, the middle worn smooth by the feet of ages. Spiders had woven webs draped from cask to cask, and in his nostrils was the smell of must.

He was searching for a fine wine put down many years ago. He held a candlestick in his hand and the light flickered on the dusty shadows. It was important that he find the wine now, or it would never be his. He turned to the right, between rows of casks, and there in a dark corner, in a deep stone recess, was a rack of wine bottles. It was a good thing he had searched diligently, he knew that, for otherwise he would never have found it. With the greatest care, he withdrew a bottle from the rack, unhesitatingly choosing the right one. Yes, the label told him so. The label was wide and ornate, with a gold embossed crest and a picture of a hunter drawing a bow. The date was hidden in dust.

Cradling the bottle in his arms like a baby, he stroked it with one hand and streaked the dust and webs. Slowly, exultantly, he moved through the vaulted cellar, for he knew the Gentlemen had smuggled this in for him one dark and moonless night, secretly from a foreign land.

Then he was in the kitchen in Godbridge. He knew it was his kitchen, though the walls had been painted, divided horizontally all round, the bottom half entirely black, the top a tangled frieze of trees and briars in greens and greys. With great skill, he manipulated his corkscrew and drew the cork.

But as he lifted the bottle to pour wine into a silver goblet, he found the bottle had grown impossibly large, and he could not hold it and it tipped of its own accord, spilling the contents.

"What a waste," he thought, and held the silver goblet under the mouth of the bottle as it lay across the table, pouring the purple liquid to the floor. As he lifted the goblet to his lips, the liquid rose all around him as a lake, and he saw in the depths Madge was lying, drowned. He tasted the red wine, and it had turned to vinegar.

He bent forward to pull Madge to the surface, and saw that the wall of the house had gone. June came floating towards him, lying on the waters of the wine that was vinegar, her hair trailing all around her as she sang:

> *"Say, is there Beauty yet to find?*
> *And Certainty? And Quiet kind?"*

All around was the blood red sea that smelt of vinegar. Madge had disappeared, and June was floating away. Robert swam by in a black wet-suit and frogman's mask and flippers, snorkelling in this blood red sea. What did he hope to find in those murky depths?

He saw Patricia then, her back to him, sitting on a rock, gazing at the moon. But the waters were rising and would drown her too. He must swim through the waves which rose in his face. He tried to call to her, but no sound came, and he could not make his limbs move as the waters rose higher

Gerald awoke then, and lay panting in the grey before the morning light, and saw that the red wine sea had receded. Tricia was there beside him, sleeping peacefully. What an extraordinary dream. He shivered with remembered horror even though he knew that dreams are just that, dreams, and meaningless. In any case, he never dreamed. Odd that he should dream this night. But no, not so strange really, after all, a death in the family was a bit disturbing to say the least. Poor Madge. Extraordinary that he should dream of her drowned whether the sea was wine or vinegar.

Still, that was nothing but morbid introspection. Never got a man anywhere. He'd be better off getting up and making some coffee. Odd, he always thought of coffee in this house whereas he had always drunk tea in his own. Just after six – a bit early. He'd go and have a quiet bath and then make coffee. Tricia would like that.

Quietly he got out of bed, gently moving the bedclothes so as not to disturb her, though she felt him leave and snuggled into the warm hollow he had left. He kissed the corner of her eye, then drew his dressing gown round him and closed the door softly behind him.

A light was shining under the kitchen door. Robert sat hunched at the kitchen table, and the face he lifted was drawn and haggard.

"Hello, son. Couldn't you sleep?"

"No. Yes. I had enough."

Better see his son was all right first. "I'm going to make some coffee. Would you like some?"

"OK."

Gerald filled the kettle and plugged it in, found the coffee beans in the cupboard and poured a measure into the grinder. The whizzing whirring crunching of the grinder sliced painfully through the silence of the early hour, and both relaxed visibly once it stopped.

"It's not fair!" Robert burst out suddenly, and slammed his fist on the table. "It's not bloody goddamn fair!"

Gerald tried to communicate his sympathy with a look, but the boy was imprisoned in a private world, his eyes fixed broodingly on his long brown hands clenched into fists on the table before him. Then as though he felt his father's eyes upon him, he turned in sudden anguish:

"I didn't mean to hurt her. You know that, Dad, don't you? I didn't mean anything."

"Of course you didn't," Gerald said soothingly. "No one ever imagined you did. A boy has to leave home some time, we all know that. You have nothing to reproach yourself."

"Innocence should be a defence in law," Robert said, shaking his head from side to side. "It should be. I meant nothing. Nothing. How was I to know it would lead to this?"

"Here, drink this," said Gerald handing him a mug of steaming coffee. "There isn't any call for you to blame yourself for anything as far as I can see, so do stop torturing yourself for nothing. If anyone should be torturing himself with remorse, surely that person is me. And it doesn't seem to me the situation is that simple anyway, so I am not going to. Come on, son, drink this coffee. It will make you feel better. You know, I don't suppose a woman dies in the world without some man or boy wishing they had treated her better while she lived. That's life, I guess."

"Yeah, sure." Robert sat very still, his jaw clenched.

Gerald laid one hand on his shoulder and squeezed it gently, then he left the boy alone. He had no idea what the boy could be worrying himself about, but supposed it was normal to find that death left you with vague feelings of guilt and remorse, and adolescents anyway were susceptible to excesses of emotion. He didn't feel so hot himself. He supposed the world would blame him for Madge's death, and couldn't help feeling he would do the same in different circumstances. But blame and guilt and remorse didn't achieve anything, and he had things to do this morning. If only the ache in his throat would fade a little. He found it hard to swallow. And he definitely had a touch of indigestion after that meal last night, better lay off fish, never did a man any good.

He was a little detached now, he discovered, which was as it should be, best way to keep emotions under control. Even when Tricia put her arms round his neck and kissed him still warm and cosy from sleep, he was not moved. He shaved and dressed slowly and efficiently, not thinking of anything and not wanting any intrusion either. Tricia in her usual tactful way let him be.

Before he left, he called through the bathroom door to Robert who had, for some reason, locked himself in.

"I'll phone later this morning, so make sure you're in. OK? We'll meet early afternoon and I'll take you back to Godbridge. Right? Robert!"

"Uh, uh," was all the answer he got.

"Look after yourself, darling," Tricia said and kissed him. "See you tomorrow night."

What a time of year to have a disaster, he thought as he drove to the office. He was going to have the devil of a job to get the business plan completed even without this catastrophe, especially in view of Britain's projected entry into the Common Market. And now there was that financial crisis in the parent company hanging over their heads... This was no time for personal affairs to intrude into his business life. He'd need all his wits about him in the next few months.

Mrs Mac, his jewel of a secretary, had already begun her final check on arrangements for the funeral when he arrived, had drawn up lists of relatives and how they were arriving, where, at what time, who needed to be picked up by car, who would stay for the funeral tea. Flowers had also arrived in his office, for some reason. The scents rose and swirled around him and he found it impossible to swallow again, so he was glad when Mrs Mac assured him she could cope perfectly well with all the last minute arrangements, and he could leave for an important meeting on certified colours. Flowers made him shudder. He should have added to the *Daily Telegraph* announcement, 'No flowers by request'.

His absorption in work was interrupted however by a very apologetic Mrs Mac who said she could no longer hold off the importunities of his sister-in-law, so could he please speak to her. Ena sounded hysterical. It was impossible to make sense of her story, for it seemed that June had leaped upon her aunt in an access of madness, and then run away in shame. And apparently his daughter had inflicted so much physical damage upon her aunt, she could barely get to the telephone. He was naturally appalled. But Ena had bathed her wounds in so vast a quantity of self-pity, any further sympathy would have been superfluous. So he was able to direct his thoughts to June, and realized that due account must be taken of Ena's penchant for exaggeration, and his daughter must be in need of his help. He must find her. Poor girl, she needed her father at a bad time like this.

He got Mrs Mac to try the Godbridge number every half hour, just in case. Lucy wasn't in either. He decided he must get down there as soon as he could, June would be bound to turn up there eventually.

He rang Robert as promised. He would pick him up in half an hour to take him to Godbridge, so that he could sort out suitable clothes for the funeral tomorrow.

"I can't come. It's not right."

"You certainly will," Gerald told him angrily. "You have to. You have to pay your last respects to your mother. I don't want to hear any more nonsense."

"You can stuff that phoney crap up your fucking ass!" shouted Robert, and slammed down the phone.

What had got into his children?

Why was his own family so undignified? Other people were able to behave in a civilised manner, but his family, as soon as there was a crisis, seemed to behave as though they belonged in the jungle. What had he been doing wrong all these years? He would have a bad headache if he didn't watch out, one way or another. He'd get Mrs Mac to give him an aspirin and then he'd be on his way. At least she was civilised. But no relation.

Death seemed to bring out the best in other people, as though confrontation with mortality suddenly sobered and softened everyone he encountered. Except his own family. David phoned, all former reproaches forgotten, and Derek from Cornwall, and Babs popped in with a casserole for his evening meal. He was deeply touched. He longed to tell these people, his friends, how grateful he was for their human kindness, but was unable to find the words.

So that when the dark blue Daimler drew up at the gate with its bower of flowers and June inside, shaken with emotion and brimming with tears, he knew how to take her in his arms and kiss her hair and help her into the house; knew how to hold her as the tears overflowed and she sobbed and sobbed and her body shook with the convulsions of grief; and he did not let her go until her grief was spent, and she had the strength again to stand alone. Then she washed her face and he made some tea, and they sat together at the kitchen table and talked a little of what must be done, and they were at peace.

28

June

June travelled to Nottingham with Ruth immediately after the funeral. She didn't particularly want to go, but then she didn't particularly want to stay either. She didn't know what she wanted really, having only a swimming sensation of fatigue and nausea and general misery. So when Uncle Bert made ominous noises about "knowing what was best for his own brother's daughter" (and that in spite of the ostentatious bandage on his wife's leg), she had turned beseechingly to her mother's cousin and had accepted the immediate invitation with alacrity.

"You don't want to make up your mind about anything, Junio, not just now," Ruth said. "Best to get away for a while."

So she found herself in a corner seat on a train speeding up to Nottingham, looking out at the vague green blur of fields and trees, or the grey and red blurs of buildings, aware only of a numb gratitude to this one kind-hearted relative who had rescued her from the limbo of London. Much to her surprise, when they arrived at the house they found Aunt Glad sitting by the window, dabbing her eyes with a damp handkerchief, and she was moved to kiss her great aunt with more warmth than she had expected to feel. Someone cared after all that her mother had died. It was a great relief. And she was able to smile and shed a few unashamed tears herself before settling into the small neat room they offered her.

People said that once a person was buried – or cremated – you knew it was final, and so life could begin again. It was true, of course, you knew it was over. It was better than that terrible waiting, as though by some miracle it might turn out to be a mistake, and she would find her mother sitting in her olive green armchair wanting to know where she had been. No. Now she knew irrevocably. Her mother was dead. She could say it out loud: "My mother is dead." She knew it was true. Nothing remained but a few handfuls of ashes.

But this did not ease the pain she felt when she thought of her mother and father and her past life in Godbridge. She couldn't let it alone. Like an aching tooth, her mental tongue felt compelled to explore the ugly cavities in her past. She had loved her mother, she knew that, and oh God, surely her mother had known that too? But she hadn't always been very kind to her, had even laughed at her old-fashioned ideas and her continual worry as to what the neighbours would say. Poor Mum. She hadn't been able to enjoy much with her constant looking back over her shoulder to see who was watching. And then when Dad left, she hadn't really been as sympathetic as she might have been. The truth was, she had rather admired her father for finally taking such a romantic step. If only he had included her, that was what hurt – to be excluded like that. But now she realized her mother had been hurt too, badly hurt. No one in the family had realized how badly she must have felt. It had made her literally ill. How terribly blind and self-centred they had been.

And Dad. What could he be feeling? Did he realize how much to blame he was? At other times, in another place, could he not be arraigned for a crime? Was this not … murder?

June's heart moved sideways in her breast, then dropped suddenly like a stone. What a terrible appalling ghastly thought to pop into her head. She couldn't have that. Ridiculous. Only a hysterical teenager could possibly have such stupid thoughts. She had better stop, fast.

That Other Woman though … she was clearly to blame. It

was all her fault. There couldn't be any doubt about that.

June didn't sleep well that first night. For some reason, she kept expecting to see her mother and continually felt compelled to sit up and peer around in the light thrown through the curtains by the street lamp. Vague fears haunted her, memories of wild animals lurking in dark corners and evil men hiding under the bed returned from her childhood, and she became very impatient with her own stupid fears, but was quite unable to chase them away. She was glad to hear Ruth stirring early next morning and know it was all right to go downstairs.

"Oh dear, did you have a bad night?" asked Ruth, noting June's pallor and the dark rings round her eyes. "I *am* sorry."

"Thanks, it wasn't so hot. I sort of felt haunted, though goodness knows why."

"How horrid for you. I must give you a sleeping pill tonight, so don't let me forget."

"I was such a selfish bitch, you know, Ruth. I didn't know she was really upset – I just thought she was worried about what other people would say." Ruth nodded, and June's thoughts jostled each other in their haste for expression. "She was, of course, worried I mean. But deep down, I think she wanted to be loved, and oh … I don't know … I seem to have failed her there too. She feels so lonely to me now. I never thought of her that way before. She seemed to have lots of friends and so on, and she was an adult. And my mother. But now it feels as though no one really cared for her at all, and she was all alone. Oh God, that's terrible … terrible."

June covered her face with her hands and tried to prevent more hot tears from bursting out. Really, there was a limit.

Ruth put her arms round her shoulders. "There now, cry if you want to, June dear. Tears are good. They wash away the pain in the end."

"It's not my pain I'm crying for, it's hers. And that's so futile. It's too late for her. Oh dear God, why couldn't I *see?*"

"You did stay with your mother," Ruth said gently. "You can't do everything. Only your best." She walked over to the window, and stood looking out at a slow drizzle lit by the kitchen lights. "When you lose someone you love, I think you always remember things you regret. You can't help it. No one ever had a perfect relationship." When she turned back, her eyes were bright. "You do get over it in the end."

Later that day, when she had helped Ruth do the weekend shopping and they were back in the kitchen preparing the evening meal, June burst out:

"My mother was an awfully nice person, you know."

Ruth smiled. "I do know."

"It's so difficult to say how. She didn't do anything spectacular. In fact, I think her life must have been terribly boring. But she was always nice. I mean, she'd worry a lot about whether we were being brought up properly, but ... oh, I don't know ... she was nice to be with."

"What a lovely thing to have said about you."

"I don't understand why Dad left, you know. I know Mum was getting older and she didn't really make the best of herself, but then so was he. Getting older, I mean. We always used to have such a lot of fun when we were kids, I don't know why it all had to change. I remember going on a picnic to Haydon Ball ..." June's face shone with the memory of that happy sunny day. "We played tracking, Bobby and Dad and I, while Mum stayed on the blanket under the trees, guarding our 'home'. It was marvellous – the bracken was so high, you could move for miles without being seen, all across the sides of the hill and down into the valley. I wish I could go back."

She stood at the sink, a half-peeled potato in her hand,

gazing at the past. The heat of the sun, the smell of bracken and dust in her nostrils, the buzz of insects, earth between her fingers and scratches on her legs, it was as though they had all returned and recaptured her senses. That was the last time they had been together as a family, properly. Four years ago.

"Mum and Dad didn't really talk to one another even then. I wonder why."

"Relationships never stay the same," said Ruth. "They either grow like plants in the sun, or they wither and die."

June was caught in the treadmill of recollection, and until she could share her burden of memories, she would never escape, forever returning to the place from which she had begun. The potatoes forgotten, she talked of holidays in Cornwall before her grandmother died, when the sun always shone and they went swimming and pony-trekking and built sandcastles and explored caves and ate fish and chips and icecream and candy floss, and her mother smiled and was happy.

"I never thought of this before," she said suddenly, "but I think a light went out in my mother when Grandmother died. She was never the same. Ruth! You don't think that will happen to me, do you? Imagine living a life with no life inside."

"No, Junio, I don't think it'll happen to you. You have so much to live for."

"Do you mean Mum didn't have anything to live for?"

"Not enough, perhaps. Though she did have children."

"How sad to be married to a man and not be happy with him."

"Yes. So many people are. I think it's when people expect things to happen to them instead of realizing that life means work, and you go out and make things happen."

"My mother certainly didn't do that. She was afraid, I think. Poor Mum."

"You don't have to repeat your parents' mistakes, you know. Perhaps you can learn from them, and make yourself a new life."

Ruth stopped, as though fearing she had gone too far, and June caught this echo of her own earlier thoughts: "make a life of your own, of your own". If only she could. If only she could see how.

"It will have to be my own," she said, and in her own ears she sounded bitter. "No one else cares."

"Loneliness is part of the human condition," Ruth said gently. "Only love can bridge the gap."

Love. What a small word to hold the salvation of all the world. Perhaps I don't know how to love. Oh God!

"Ruth, should I have done more for my mother? Should I have made sacrifices instead of wanting all the time to get away?"

"Good heavens, of course not!"

"But you do. I mean ... Aunt Glad." June was suddenly terribly embarrassed. The blunt straightforwardness Ruth said she preferred could go too far.

"No. I made no sacrifices. My life is basically the way I wanted it. I would be ashamed if it were otherwise. My mother and I are together because we both prefer it that way."

"But ... marriage?" whispered June, feeling she may as well be hanged for a sheep.

Ruth smiled, her brown eyes full of warmth and kindness, but behind them June had the impression of a faint stirring of an ancient pain that had taken long to blur.

"The one I wanted wasn't free. The luck of the draw. He had to choose too. He said, I can't leave her, it would kill her, you must understand, and so I had to accept his decision."

Sudden clarity of vision seared June's brain, while horror clouded Ruth's face as she realized what she had said.

"I hate that woman," June said, and venom was in her tongue. "I hate her."

She wrote to George that night, telling him of her mother's death and why she had not turned up on Wednesday, and she gave him Ruth's address.

It was strange to realize that Ruth was a relation and that they shared some of the same blood, for June did not think she had known any other woman in her family so strong, so firm, so free of fear, and so lacking in all feminine charm and guile. No one could call Ruth passive or weak.

Nor, for that matter, could anyone say that of Aunt Glad either. She was physically weak and ill, it was true, crippled with arthritis and often in pain, yet she fought like a beleaguered fortress town besieged by overwhelming forces. She knew she must lose in the end, but she was not going without a struggle.

Is it worth it? June asked herself. She would take her great aunt a cup of tea and watch with painful apprehension as the old lady struggled to raise the cup to her lips without spilling any of the contents down her front. And then, when her aunt asked her if she would read to her for a while, she realized with a stab of horror that the old woman was almost blind.

"How old are you, Aunt Glad?" she asked one day, knowing by now that such bluntness did not offend.

"I was born in 1892, my dear. Queen Victoria was on the throne."

"Gosh, that's a long time ago. You must have seen an awful lot in your lifetime."

"Yes, I've had a full life. When I was a girl, we still had gas mantles to light our rooms, and horse-drawn carriages and chaperones for unmarried young ladies. I have seen the arrival of electricity and motor cars, of radio and television, the telephone, aeroplanes, the atom bomb, and even men landing on the moon. It is perfectly incredible.

June watched her aunt's hands as she made this long speech, enunciating each word with care, preserving the breath it was such a struggle to draw into her lungs. Those long white hands folded in her lap reminded June of her own mother's long pale fingers. In spite of the arthritis, Aunt Glad's fingers were only slightly bent and swollen at the knuckles, and the nails were still firm and smooth. June had thought all old people's hands became gnarled like an ancient apple tree and speckled with dark blotches. She looked down at her own. Yes, she had inherited that too. It was a good inheritance, though often she had thought she would have preferred a better line in eyes, larger ones, with well-shaped brows.

It was the mouth and jaw that were so different. Aunt Glad's face was all wrinkled like a withered fruit, but still the strong firm chin she shared with her daughter was there, defying the world if it should try to take dominion over her. What of my own chin? June wondered. If I were to set my face against the world, determined to make my own way, would I end up with a granite jaw and a face like an Aztec shrine? Or did it mean that I must fail in any attempt because my chin is small and my cheeks thin? Do these things really have any meaning? She looked at the faint lines traced on the palm of her shapely hand. So few lines – too early to tell her future.

"What about you personally, Aunt? What happened to you?"

Aunt Glad crinkled up her already wrinkled face in an amused smile. "I'm not interesting, my dear. Just one woman among many."

"You can't say that!" June protested. "Ruth is always telling me, 'Look at my mother, one of the first women ever to earn her living in law, years before women were officially permitted to enter.' How on earth did you manage that?"

"Oh, there's usually a way if you will. I had to learn to typewrite first, of course, in order to enter an office. Then I used to read up on all the new company laws, and my father helped because he'd got all the books in his chambers. You must have seen his chambers? Wagstaff and Wagstaff. Lovely musty, dusty place in Banbury. My brother Malcolm had it later, till he died. Anyway, I read so much that in the end I knew more about company law than most, so I became quite useful. It was pleasant to be able to earn a living doing something so interesting."

"I wish I was interested in something like that," said June despondently. "Ruth keeps saying 'Find out what you're interested in'. But how? She says we girls are dead from the neck up, walking zombies who think it's unfeminine to be interested in anything but clothes and pop music. And she may be right. But what do you do if you don't have any particular talent?"

"You must be able to do something, my dear. Everyone can. Don't you think it would be undignified to spend your entire life as a parasite? Most women do. I believe they should be ashamed."

"Gosh, are you a women's libber too?"

"I have not heard that expression. What does it mean?"

"You know, Women's Lib. The liberation of women, equal rights, equal pay for equal work and so on. Women's Libbers burn their bras so that men will not look at them as sexual objects."

"Plus ca change," said Aunt Glad with a low chuckle. "In my day, it was the vote and chaining yourself to railings. Naturally I am in favour of the liberation of women. But in my view, women are their own worst enemies, secret slaves to a frantic need to be loved. They spend their lives waiting for

satisfactions which never come. Learn to be alone, my dear. That is the best I could wish for you. And the secret is – learn to love yourself."

June felt as though all her most cherished ideas had been tipped into a coffee grinder and whirled around and broken into such tiny pieces they could never be the same again. Love yourself? That was supposed to be the biggest crime of all. Think of others, not yourself, that was the rule she had always been taught. How could you love yourself anyway?

Yet these two who said, "Live your own life. Think of yourself. Even love yourself," these two women were much nicer people to be with than most. Certainly a million times nicer than a certain other pair of relatives she could think of who were always carping on about Christian charity and "Doing one's duty to others" and "helping people in their hour of need". Sanctimonious prigs.

Maybe that was it. If you honestly faced the fact that everyone has to think of himself – or herself – because you have to live with yourself, inside your own body, all your whole life, perhaps a compensatory quality arose from somewhere. How else explain that when Ruth and Aunt Glad claimed they thought of themselves, they were in reality thoughtful of others and generous and kind? While Uncle Cant and Aunt Hyena mouthed all the right words and were as self-centred as you could get? Heaven help me, she prayed, please don't let me be like them.

Dad telephoned. But he might have saved himself the bother. He had phoned a couple of times before, but it was no good. The telephone was a monstrous machine of non-communication.

She wrote to George, a long letter, and told him how badly she missed him. The days went by, each one the same as the next. She wrote to George again, reproaching him for his long silence. There were few occupations more painful than watching for the postman and the struggle to regain equanimity after he had passed, leaving nothing.

It took three weeks, that was all. One week to recover from the shock of the funeral, one week to assess the situation, and one week to pluck the courage to leave.

One evening, Ruth said quietly, "In a time of sorrow you can choose how you will be. You can choose weakness or strength." And she had chosen then to go to George. She longed for his arms about her, his body on hers. Did she not belong with him now that she was forsaken by both mother and father, should she not cleave to him as her man? Had he not sworn to love her, as she loved him, for ever?

Besides the situation in this house was undignified. No self-respecting person could tolerate it. So she wrote a note to Ruth while she was at work, because she was too cowardly to face her, packed her suitcase, took some money out of the Post Office and caught the train to London. George didn't know she was coming. She wished he had written. The ache in her breast was very painful when she thought of his neglect and what it might mean. Secretly she was afraid to telephone him, though of course it was far too expensive to call from Nottingham, besides the longer she put off speaking to him, the longer she could count on what had been, the longer she could cherish his love. But that was nonsense. She was walking out of one more house to go to him. She would hardly do that if she were not sure of him, would she? She must be able to count on his love, for she was burning all her boats behind her.

Ruth's face, hurt and bewildered, haunted her mind. She knew perfectly well she should have had the courtesy, not to say downright human decency to say goodbye properly.

After all Ruth had done for her too. She was perfectly well aware of all that, there was no need for her mind to trap her in another treadmill, no need at all for her body to tremble with hot sticky shame. But Ruth would understand. At least she wouldn't interfere or tell Dad or anything. She would respect her decision. OK, she'd apologise abjectly one day and make up for it somehow. But in the meantime, she had to make her own choice, even if that did involve hurting other people. She did have to live with herself.

At St Pancras, she had to wait a long time for an empty phone booth. At least he must be in this time, she thought as she listened to the ringing in that dingy hall, and knew that everyone in that horrid house would be waiting for someone else to answer. At last a husky woman's voice said, "Hello."

"Can I speak to George Rand?"

"Is he that gorgeous hunk with red curly hair?" asked the female voice breathlessly.

"Sounds like him. On the second floor."

"I'll see if he's in."

June waited a long time, hearing voices and laughter far away, but no one came to the phone. She had to insert a second coin, her last, and she was feeling pretty annoyed when the voice returned, bubbling over with inappropriate gaiety. "He said, who is it? He was in the bath, you see."

"Tell him it's his rich Aunt June, who is coming over right now to find out why he hasn't been feeding the goldfish." You'd think if she were going to be sour, she'd be sour to some purpose. But her mind had addled.

"It's your rich Aunt June," shouted the voice. "Says she's coming over."

To her immense relief, she heard George calling, "Hey, wait. Don't let her go."

And then he was speaking to her. Oh, delectable deliverance.

"June. Is that you? Where are you, me old darling?"

"Oh, George," was all she managed.

"Hey, come on, old thing. Chin up and all that. Are you back? Can't wait to see you, you poor darling, after all you've been through."

"I want to see you too. I'm at St Pancras."

"Great. I'll meet you in our coffee place, OK? Half an hour do you?"

"Yes, I'll manage that. Wait for me, won't you, if I'm late?"

"Silly girl. See you soon."

So it was all right. She had known it would be. She walked down long tunnels, took an underground train, up again into London streets on the way to 'their' coffee place, and all the time she felt she was not walking, she was gliding, floating, for her body was so light, ethereal, now it no longer carried the burden of anxiety and suspense.

29

Gerald

Gerald shut up the house which he intended never to visit again, left the keys with Guildford's two main estate agents, and instructed them to sell, fast. First with the contract, he said, and left it to them to work it out. He could expect a good profit in the current seller's market. Then he drove straight to the office and immersed himself in work.

He found it was necessary to work until eleven most evenings, to work Saturday and Sunday, that Britain's probable entry into the Common Market combined with poor profit situation had doubled the amount of planning necessary this year. He had to travel to Frankfurt, Milan, Brussels, subsidiaries in Italy, Holland and Germany required his personal attention. It was not a question of trying to escape his personal life, he was one of a new breed of senior executive for whom the computer had created immeasurably more work rather than less. Demonstrably, the hours he worked he did not work alone.

A major source of frustration and delay was travel as thousands of European businessmen tried to fly from capital to capital first thing in the morning, which was why he found himself paying off a taxi at Victoria Station one Sunday night before taking his berth on an overnight sleeper to Brussels. He fumbled and dropped money on the kerb, so he knew he was tired and perhaps overwrought. The best thing would be to buy a book to take his mind off everything for a while and get straight into bed so that he'd be able to concentrate tomorrow.

A good rousing masculine story was what he wanted, none

of that dreary pornography. James Bond was too escapist, but Hemingway was supposed to have written real he-man stuff. He chose *For Whom the Bell Tolls*. A flaxen-haired woman beside him at the well-stocked stall suddenly said: "Why don't you try this? It's very good. I know you'll enjoy it." Without really knowing why, Gerald also bought the book she pointed out, thinking with half his mind that Tricia might like it since it was history, for the book was a detailed analysis of the Charge of the Light Brigade entitled *The Reason Why*. Only standing in his pyjamas in his first-class sleeper and looking at his purchases did it dawn on him that the book titles had significance. Who was the woman then?

Neither of the books did much for him after all. Thank heaven he always carried a supply of sleeping pills for emergencies. This seemed an appropriate moment to benefit from such foresight, he'd never sleep otherwise. The British Rail bunk was surprisingly comfortable, with fresh linen, a plump pillow and a fluffy blanket. The drug, the motion of the train and the pleasure of having discovered a civilised way of travelling put him to sleep very quickly.

A buxom flaxen-haired wench came and stood beside his bed. Would she join him? He imagined burying his face between those enormous soft breasts and tasting the luscious skin with his tongue, and he leaped up to claim her. But she said, "No," and then she led him to a hill top overlooking a lake where the wind blew cold and the trees bent their bare branches to the ground. Down below, men were hacking with pick-axes at the thick ice which covered the lake, and as he watched, the hole widened and an ugly misshapen man with matted grey hair and grey skin and grey shabby clothes was dragged from under the ice. He wanted to see this man more closely, but could not see the way down. And then the man was gone.

Gerald

The woman took his hand, and the weather changed. The temperature rose and the heat of the sun melted the ice on the lake.

At the water's edge was a rowing boat, and he was to pay for their ride, but all he could find in his pocket was an old bent penny and a foreign coin. The boatman was angry. The sun had now risen high in the sky and it was very hot, and he thought they could swim in the water instead. But the woman whispered in the ear of the boatman, who smiled and nodded and walked away. They climbed into the boat, and the woman took the oars, rowed them to the middle of the lake. He trailed his hand in the water, and it seemed to grow hotter and hotter, until he feared it would boil, and he saw that it was the colour of blood.

"Not again!" he shouted, and stood up in the bows, waving his arms around.

"You will drown," said the woman, "unless you do as you are told. Sit down."

"Hussy! Traitress!" he shouted, and then he fell into the blood red lake and the waters closed over his head because he was going to drown if he did not wake up ...

Struggling to wake through the mists of drug, he felt still as though he were drowning, for he was drenched in sweat and suffocating from lack of air. The train was in the hold of a cross-Channel steamer, and the heating appeared to be operating at full blast. Gasping he tried to open the window. It was stuck fast. Fumbling in the half darkness, he rang for the attendant. But he couldn't wait, he could scarcely breathe, every one must be dying on this train. It was as well he had woken in spite of his pill. He opened the door to the corridor. No one was about. There was no sound at all but the ship's engines thundering. He could not open the corridor windows either. It was a nightmare. Perhaps he would wake up soon.

He stumbled down the corridor to the attendant's cubby hole and saw that it was empty. He was not dreaming. Of course, the attendant was up in the ship's bar, and everyone else was asleep because they all knew about the heating and had made preparations accordingly. He had got to get that window open by himself. The heating was already off in his compartment, so no relief to be had there.

Half of his mind told him he looked ridiculous fumbling away in the middle of the night in his blue pyjamas, his brain fuddled with drugs and lack of air. If he could have found anything to smash the glass, he would have gladly wrecked all the windows in sight, and to heck with the consequences. At last he discovered how to move the handle and the window moved slowly down. You'd think they could give instructions, he muttered blearily, it couldn't be that he was that stupid.

The air from the bowels of the ship was comparatively refreshing, and he leaned out for a while and looked at the long carriages anchored to their iron cage, and wondered why it was he saw no movement, no sign of life anywhere. But thanks to the pill, he was very sleepy, so he crawled back into bed.

The next thing he knew was that he was frozen. And the blind he had drawn to exclude the light from the ship's hold was billowing out into the night and making an unholy racket. The train was now rushing across countryside, through a raw wintry night, and it was high time to close the window again. This too was easier thought than done.

First he had a battle with the blind and feared at any moment to see it whipped away over the darkened fields. Then he couldn't get the handle to move in reverse. He was so weary, so sleepy, so fed up with all the ridiculous farce, he just wanted to forget about it all and go back to sleep. But really it was too cold – and the noise was driving him crazy.

At last he found the knack and got the window within two inches of the top, where it stuck. The blind still flapped and rattled, but he couldn't be bothered any more. It would do. He needed more sleep. He would sleep until early morning coffee arrived.

Banging and rattling his door awoke him and he looked at his watch. Quarter to nine. Was that the coffee? It was very late. He couldn't remember what time the train was due to arrive. Someone was shouting outside and the train was not moving. He struggled out of bed, and lifted the blind. At least it was not Brussels. He had not realized the train stopped anywhere, they must be nearly there. He had better hurry up.

More rattling at the door reminded him to open it. Outside he found piles of linen heaped along the corridor and an irate Belgian with a mop pouring abuse into his ear in a foreign language. The words were wasted, but he got the general idea: he was preventing decent people from getting on with their work. Where were they? Schaerbeek. Where was Brussels Midi? Passed long ago, no doubt. The chap was still going on, leaning blackly on his mop handle, though communication was in vain. He had to get dressed. The chap started to move in, so Gerald shouted: "Allez-vous en! Fermez la porte!" which served beautifully, and he thanked the Lord for his lessons in Basic French.

How was it possible he could have overslept? What of Customs and showing his passport? What of his coffee? Hastily he threw on his clothes, locked up his case, he'd have to find somewhere to shave on his way into the city. Just as well this wasn't a trans-continental train or he'd have ended up in Poland or somewhere. His mind was obviously not entirely under control. He'd better be careful.

Where was Schaerbeek anyway? He finally found a station

employee who deigned to understand his rudimentary French, and was told a commuter train was just arriving destined for Bruxelles Midi. The perfect solution. He would return to the station where he should have arrived in the first place, and go on to the hotel from there. He could shave in the men's lavatory before going up to the conference room. With a bit of luck, he might hardly be late at all.

He tried to focus his mind on the coming meetings for big changes were in the air, and now he was being asked to go over to the States for a couple of weeks. It wouldn't surprise him if a takeover were in the offing. No more drugs, that was certain.

His head felt as though it was floating in space, his brain detached from his body, swinging through an empty void on a pendulum. With an effort of will, he tried to catch hold of the real world, concentrate on concrete reality, on work. He opened the papers he would have to discuss at the meeting this morning, but he found that each word had become a separate entity, rather like round pebbles which had been scraped clean and dipped in clear water. They lay detached from each other on the page, without meaning, round stone pebbles shining in the light.

Perhaps he had been more deeply disturbed by Madge's death than he had realized. Probably. But he had no time for that. He'd think about it later, when his business problems were cleared up.

30

Gerald

Four days later, it was Good Friday. He had been to meetings in Germany, Holland and now Brussels again. Patricia flew to Zaventem to join him. He felt worn out, tired beyond words, and longed for the comfort of her arms and the solace of her body. As she walked towards him through the baggage hall to where he stood behind the Customs barrier, he thought she had never looked more beautiful. Her hair was lighter than he remembered, and she was wearing a well-tailored honey-coloured trouser suit with tan accessories which reflected the colour of her hair, a gleam of gold on her lapel and round her wrist, she looked to him then like a golden girl coming out of his dreams.

He was proud of the envious stares of other men as she came up to him, smiling, looking searchingly into his eyes to see how he had fared. He touched her bottom briefly, possessively, before taking her case and hurrying her outside to the car he had hired. Once there, they kissed deeply, and he felt angry at the restriction of her clothes, that her jacket was fastened, that she was wearing a bra, that she objected when he tried to feel between her legs. Gently she tried to extricate herself and talk of the flight and what they might do in Brussels, and he resented her cool acceptance of their long parting, her rejection of his caresses. He wasn't going to rape her in a public place, for Christ's sake, he just longed blindly to bury himself in the warmth of her body to reassure himself that she was there.

She did still love him though. He could tell from the

tenderness in her blue-green eyes. That was the important thing.

His head was filled with her perfume as he drove into the city. He would take her straight to the hotel and they would make love before going out to dinner. He needed her. All the muscles in his body felt knotted, every nerve fibre buried in his flesh was stretched to its limit. Thank God that this time he was blessed with a sensual woman, one at last who understood his needs and how to minister to them.

Sensual images flowed through him, searing his flesh with flame as in his imagination she lovingly explored and caressed every part of his body while, in reality, she sat beside him in the hired car erect and remote still in her business uniform. Driving in a strange city on the wrong side of the road demanded the largest part of his attention, but he was still able to glance at her lovely creamy skin, and think of the beauty hidden beneath those clothes. He could undress her in his mind, and find the mole beneath her breast, the scar on her abdomen, and know that the secret forest guarding his well of contentment was dark and rough. Possessively he put his hand on her curving thigh, and she put her hand on his and squeezed it. Yes, she loved him still. Thank God.

The promise of their joyful union in bed was like the promise of a drink to a thirsty man, a warm scented bath to a hot and dusty woman. For the first time in his life he could count on fulfilment of his deepest needs without fear of disappointment. His mother had ignored his existence, his wife had turned from him in disgust: but Patricia, his one and only Love, would always give him whatever he asked. Only thus could he be certain of his value as a human being, as a man.

Upstairs in the hotel, he practically threw the bellboy out of their room, and roughly took her in his arms. She clung to him as their lips met, and he could barely contain himself, he wanted to rip her clothes off her beautiful body and throw her onto the floor and rape her, so overwhelming was his desire. As she came up for air, he threw off her jacket and started on the buttons of her blouse which, with only the greatest self-control, he did not rip off, then glued himself to her mouth and started on her trousers. She wriggled and struggled, and he thought he'd tear these clothes off her if she didn't help, the flames in his flesh were licking his brain, why was she as though in armour? Why did she not undress him too?

She pulled herself away from him, and said, "No, darling, not like that."

Freezing water dripped from his aching body. "Why not?"

"I'm sorry, darling. It doesn't feel right." She began to restore her clothing.

A surge of terrible anger quenched the flame of desire. "Why did you lead me on then?"

She frowned. He could have hit her then. He was deceived. Betrayed. She stood up and walked over to the dressing table, and she wasn't even beautiful, she was too short and too fat, women of that shape shouldn't wear trousers. Why had she built him up only to knock him down? He sat on the bed – the bed they were to share – and gloom settled like a vulture on his shoulder, flapping its dank wings with a sound like despair.

"You obviously don't understand what it's like to be a man."

"Let's not fight, darling. Making love is too precious. It must be right for both of us."

"There's always a reason these days."

She frowned again, sitting on the stool across the room, miles from him. "Why do you say that?"

"The last few weeks, the last couple of months maybe, you

haven't wanted me to touch you at all."

For a few moments she just sat there, staring at him, then got up and walked over to him where he sat on the bed.

"That isn't true. You know it isn't." She knelt in front of him, put one arm round him and kissed the top of his bent head. "Please don't let's fight about it. Maybe we need time to relax and get used to being together again. Everything will be fine."

But she felt remote, like a being from another planet.

"You used not to need to get used to being with me."

"Shall we go and have a drink?"

"What do you want to do?"

"Darling, I just made a suggestion."

"Oh. Right. Let's go then."

As they descended in the lift, she didn't even look at him. He was having problems enough as it was, he didn't need her to create new ones. Had he not given up everything for her sake – home, children, good name, political future? The least she could do was give him her love without reservation. It was not unreasonable of him to expect her to console him, stroke his fevered brow when he was overwrought, return his passion when he was consumed with desire. He had hoped he could rely on her not to let him down. Was he doomed to remain always utterly alone?

They stopped for a drink in the Cafe de la Grand'place, a rambling picturesque place of wooden tables, wooden staircases wandering upwards towards rickety wooden floors at unexpected levels, with life-size puppets in mediaeval Flemish costume hanging by their necks from the ceilings, and festoons of inflated papillotte bags hanging like grapes above an everlasting gas fire.

"Insane – a damned firetrap," muttered Gerald sourly, and he insisted on taking a table near the door.

They were served fairly quickly, to his surprise, and he began to feel a little less stressed as he sipped his drink. Tricia leaned back and smiled. Dammit, he told the discontented voice inside his head, I'm going to enjoy myself, so shut up.

"I guess you're right," he said. "Travel does take it out of you."

"I expect we both have business masks to shed - all that armour and pretence." She laughed. "You look quite human now."

Hope flamed as she touched his arm. "Not human. Animal. Just you wait."

Arm in arm, they walked out into the famous square. The splendour of the ancient guild buildings raised his spirits, their gilt facies a flamboyant reminder of the tenacity of the little man, the simple man, the man of the earth who stands and holds his ground while tyrants wage war around him. Untouched for centuries, these handsome houses had stood about the cobbled square, blind witnesses to crimes of tyranny and oppression, while ever upward soared man's spirit, symbolized by the upward flight of the spire on the Hotel de Ville, seeking union with the Great Architect himself. He did not trust himself though to express these thoughts aloud.

They made their way out of the square and down a winding narrow cobbled street, where every other door offered gastronomic delights until they came to the restaurant recommended to Gerald - a long room lined with blue tiles and long wooden tables crowded with Belgians. There was just room for them, one on either side of a long table, and they agreed this was the place for them to savour their first meal out together for many weeks.

Gerald approved the unexpected delights of dining in such basic accommodation: no wasted efforts on separate tables and white table cloths; simply a small choice of excellent wines, and a very restricted menu which clearly appealed to a discerning crowd. The food was delicious. To him the pleasures of the flesh brought enormous comfort, and he could not understand how another person would not be consoled by a good meal and a bottle of wine.

He was puzzled to see Patricia's struggle: she barely drank what was a first rate wine, though she assured him it was perfectly lovely; and when the food arrived, seemed more inclined to push it around than to delight in the flavours it offered. It was difficult for him to know what to say or do. She evidently didn't want to share her difficulties, indeed she seemed to retire into a shell whenever he tried to get close. He didn't dare to push her too hard. Something had upset her, that was obvious, but he felt worried that she could not tell him. He had no idea why, nor any idea of what he could do to defend his love.

His deepest fear was that she was turning from him, and it hurt. But deep, deep within him lay the conviction that this was only to be expected. He loved her for she was honourable, and no honourable woman could continue to love a man as despicable as he.

They made love that night. She was still his.

The next day they drove to the Ardennes and into Luxembourg. The sun shone in a brilliant blue sky, and on the hills the trees were putting forth new green. This was the best thing they could have done, they agreed, leave the dirt and deafening haste of the city, the tensions of their work, and drive together towards sweeping hills and forests. The miles fell away. She sat beside him, relaxed and smiling, in bright yellow slacks and sweater, huge round sunglasses like saucers shielding her eyes. He put his hand on her rounded thigh, and she turned her head and smiled, put her hand on his and squeezed it. He moved his hand possessively between her legs as they sped across the countryside. She gently moved it back.

"You don't usually mind," he said.

She laughed. "Not when you're driving."

Playfully she slapped the hand that persisted almost of its own volition in exploring this precious territory.

"You don't usually do that," he said.

"Silly thing. Now now."

He could sense that his need to make her feel as he did would precipitate a fight, but he was pressured by inner forces. Why didn't she understand his needs? What was wrong with a private feel inside a private motor car? If she loved him, she should want it too.

"Darling, don't."

He sank into a cold black pool. So that was it. She had turned against him already. He should have known.

"I'm sorry," he said. "I must remember not to touch you any more in future."

"Darling, what *is* the matter with you? I didn't say anything like that."

He negotiated the confusing intersections at Bastogne, noting the World War II tank which stood at the cross roads as a startling reminder of what happened right here, but not feeling it was the moment for one of his orations on the superiority of the British bulldog character to which he always felt inspired by anything that reminded him of Churchill and Dunkirk.

"You've changed," he said. "You used to like me to touch you. Not any more."

He could see her frowning as she looked straight ahead without speaking while they sped through the heat and dust and monotony of the Belgian countryside. What was the point? Why carry on like this? Why not drive into the ditch, there, where the road curved sharp round a bend, why not carry straight on? It would look like an accident. End it all.

Self-preservation was too strong an instinct, and he turned the car with the road. Where there was life there was hope... Hah!

"This makes me very unhappy," Patricia said at last. "I don't know why we have fallen into such misunderstanding, but it's making me feel physically quite ill. Do let's stop."

"Of course, I like it," he said . "Naturally, it's all my fault."

She leaned back, clutching convulsively at her belly.

Why did women always make such a song and dance about feeling ill when there was trouble? He didn't feel so marvellous himself, but did she care?

There was the frontier. As he slowed down, she took off her sunglasses and turned to him, and there were tears in her eyes. Pain stabbed his chest as he realized what a prize prick he had been. What had got into him? He pulled over.

"Trish darling, I'm sorry. Can you forgive me?"

Tears ran down her cheeks as they clung to each other with mute promise. He would not behave like a brainless bastard again, he swore to himself, surely Gerald Hunter was capable of behaving like a decent Englishman. They kissed with gentle lovingness and caressed each other's cheeks. As they crossed into the green and pleasant Duchy of Luxembourg, he knew he must take care not to hurt her again.

With some good navigation and considerable good fortune, they found the village of Kautembach and the small hotel recommended by a gourmet for their lunch-time stop. A dozen houses, a large square church, a wide winding stream gurgling over stones, and an abandoned railway station and goods yard – that was the village nestling in a valley between wooded hills.

They sat on the veranda of the small hotel, drinking cool Moselle wine from wide green glasses, watching children play in the stream and the sunlight dance on the water. The meal was an hour and a half coming, and superb: boeuf en croute, the *specialite de la maison.* Madame, it transpired, cooked like an angel, Monsieur cherished his wine, his son was learning the business which clearly was thriving, daughter-in-law laughed and chatted with regulars and fetched and carried, and cuffed and caressed her two small children and dog as whim predicted. At the back of beyond, and they were lucky to find a table for Saturday lunch-time. They took the last double room, there seemed no point in moving on.

If only to work up an appetite for another meal, they set out on one of the signposted walks through the forested hills. The sun shone still, and the sky was pale with the haze of heat. New life burgeoned all around them, buds burst open, birds flew busily to and fro with twigs and grass for nests, insects buzzed and danced. Relaxed and happy together at last, they walked hand in hand and talked of moving into the country. Would they not be happier after all to leave the world behind? They could buy an old cottage, in Sussex perhaps or Kent, with farmland all round and lambs in the springtime.

Yet that evening at dinner, when he began to talk of political things to avoid any of the painful topics nearer his heart, she appeared deliberately perverse. Whereas before she had always listened to his views with interest and respect, it was as though she had now decided to take up the extreme opposing position on any opinion he cared to voice. It didn't matter what, she disagreed vehemently and at length – on Ireland, on Biafra, on Ted Heath and the Common Market, on rich and poor, sickness and health. Even when he broached the subject of her cleaning woman, as delicately as he knew how, she jumped down his throat. He had imagined, foolishly, they might be able to agree on this at least since some of her friends were Negroes.

"I am surprised that you employ a coloured girl as a cleaning woman," he said in a conversational tone.

She gaped in what was clearly intended to convey total incomprehension. "You what?"

"I am surprised because I should have thought it against your principles of equality to employ a black woman as a servant."

"You mean I should employ a man? Delighted, if one would apply."

"Come on, don't deliberately misunderstand. All I meant was, you often complain that coloured people can't get decent jobs, and here you are, perpetuating the situation by employing one of them in a menial position."

"You mean I should discriminate against her just because she is black?"

"Of course I don't mean that. Don't put words into my mouth."

But there wasn't much point in continuing. The conversation degenerated still further so that by the time they were served coffee and brandy, she had accused him of chauvinism and intolerable narrow-mindedness, and he had pointed out her blind arrogance and potted thinking. He could not help thinking she was unjust, unreasonable and downright impossible.

Nor did they sleep well that night for the bed was lumpy and uneven, the mattress shaped rather like a hammock, and the pillows hard.

Easter Sunday, and the bells rang joyfully through the village, echoing in the surrounding hills. Patricia slid out of the lumpy bed where they had in the end, but uncomfortably, lain in each other's arms, and leaned out of the small square wooden-framed window. Below, the village square was thronging with people – old men in black suits and black hats, some leaning on sticks, old women in long black skirts and shawls over their heads, young men and women in more modern but still sombre clothes, children of all ages washed, combed, polished. Everyone was hobbling or walking or skipping or dancing through the streets to the church, though it was not quite eight o'clock. They must be the only people in the village left behind.

"I wish I could believe like they do," she said from the window, still watching. "Sometimes life just doesn't seem to make sense. Don't you wish you could go to church like them?"

"Whatever for?" Gerald lay back in bed wishing she would come back to him, wishing she would not startle him with comments like that out of the blue, unrelated to anything that had gone before. So a lot of ignorant peasants were pouring into that ugly stone church. So?

"I'd be a Catholic if I converted," she said. The last of the stragglers went up the steps, and the doors of the church were closed. She waited while the sun rose at last above the hills opposite and poured light into the valley.

Gerald was appalled. The gulf between them seemed to take on the dimensions of the Grand Canyon. If ever there was a religion he despised it was Roman Catholicism – worshipping the Pope as infallible when he was only a man was more than any intelligent person could take. And the very idea of going to church on Sunday seemed to him hypocritical. For important events perhaps, like marriages and births and death, since that was how our society worked. But religion patently had very little to do with life itself.

"I thought you didn't believe in God anyway," he said

accusingly, for really one never knew where one was with her these days.

"I don't," she said sadly.

He clapped his hand to his forehead and raised his eyes to the ceiling. Was ever a man more badly used?

"I just wish I did," she explained, and climbed back into bed. She was cold, and there would be no point in going downstairs to breakfast for some time.

Gerald regained some of his former tenderness for her as she snuggled up close and their bodies entwined. He couldn't help feeling though that it was absurd to expect to find a meaning in life beyond themselves.

31

Patricia

Grievous admission, she actually felt glad to see him wave and disappear through Passport Control. He'd be in the States for a week, six days for her to breathe again and renew her strength to cope with his dreary moods, his incessant demands. It was the second Sunday after Easter, two weeks since their stay in Luxembourg, almost exactly a year since he had asked her to marry him. What had happened to them that their wondrous love had withered into bickering and mistrust? Were they then just like everyone else? Had their miracles become miraculous no more?

Maybe I'm not good marriage material, Patricia thought miserably as she returned to her car. She knew she had retreated in the face of his dogged concentration on business, his flight from tenderness, knew she had wrapped around herself once more the protective shield of the single business woman. Years of habit made it necessary to guard her heart from threatened harm. What sort of idiotic divinity had decreed that only the innocent youthful teenage heart can give and not count the cost?

But oh, he was so trying, so exhausting, so prone to resentment, so quick to misunderstand. Heaven knew she had tried to be sympathetic and understanding, for it was obvious he was suffering because of Madge's death. A death is always distressing, but a death when you already feel overburdened with guilt ... Yes, she grieved for him and felt pity in her heart for his unavoidable misery. But why, oh why should he turn against her? Could it be ... surely not ... was it possible he wanted to burden her with the blame?

Patricia drove back to London with steel knives through her heart. Was she to blame? Was she a Scarlet Woman who had used her evil wiles to steal a man from his loving wife? Was that really the utter nonsense she was sure it was? She had never met the woman, how could she be responsible for her weakness? When called to account on Judgement Day – if such a thing were to happen, which it wouldn't – what other answer could there be but, "Am I my sister's keeper?"

"Convenient for you, anyway," Jill had said, "her dying like that."

It might look that way from the outside. But from her own point of view, it made everything a thousand times more difficult. Living, Madge could be forgotten. Husbands leave their wives all the time, and it was up to women to make something of their lives apart from marriage. But now, dead, Madge held power. Her ghost entered everywhere. Perhaps it was her ultimate revenge, and she would haunt Patricia for ever.

She returned to her flat as a sick animal hastens to its hole, to huddle alone in dark warmth and isolation until health is restored. She wandered through her rooms, savouring her solitude, touching her pots with light fingers, looking possessively at her paintings, the pewter work done by her mother, the little clay horse, the Italian ceramics. She chose Mozart's *Clarinet Quintet in A* for Gerald did not care for chamber music, set it to play loudly, glorying in the subtle interplay of superb instruments and the golden voice of the clarinet. Yes, her beautiful things were safe and filled her with pleasure still.

She was glad to be alone, would not phone Jill or Ellen, would see no friends to fill her empty hours. Peace and solitude were what she craved, until she could make sense of the torments that had shattered their love.

If only Robert did not come. How could she have been so stupid as to encourage him? She had not seen him often since that day he had slammed so rudely out of the house, just before the funeral. But apparently he had the idea that she had understood even if his father had not, and he had turned up several times, always while Gerald was away. It was as though he wanted something from her he was afraid to ask – sympathy perhaps, or understanding, or reassurance, she did not know. He never said much, just lounged on the floor, drinking coffee and smoking, staring into space, or sometime he paced up and down the room restlessly. But she did not want him there this week. He was waiting for something from her, and she did not have it to give.

But as the days passed, and her deliberate solitude was tinged with a hint of loneliness, it was borne in upon her that she was failing her love as soon as demands were made upon it. For the first time in many years she was asked to consider others before herself, and every instinct was selfish. There was no virtue in love that could be generous only through happiness. That was too easy. To give when love was joy only increased the measure of joy a thousand-fold, for then indeed it was true that to give was better than to receive. But when your lover is too sick at heart to accept your gift with joy, is that the moment to withdraw, and say, So you don't want me after all? Had her self-centred way of life left her so incapable of true love that she must fail as soon as the way became difficult?

No. No, she could not accept that. That Gerald needed her now, more than ever, there could be no doubt. She had failed him in the beginning, but it was not a necessary failure. Now that she understood where she had made her mistake, she could regain her faith in him, in herself, in the love they shared.

She would not waste her time grovelling in guilt. What use was it, eternal soul-searching, the everlasting sense of *mea culpa*, of apology for phantom faults that hovered like shadows across the springs of life? If she had failed, she must try again. Life was to be lived. She must do something.

She was not deficient in courage, she knew that. That it takes courage to commit oneself totally she had only just discovered. But she had that courage. She chose then, with only her conscience as witness, to stake everything on their love, for it was good.

Robert was standing on the doorstep when she returned that Friday evening. His brows were knit with a look of thunder, and for a moment she stood still in fear of him. He was as tall as his father, and broad-shouldered and strong, and the force of his smouldering anger smote her in the face.

But she would not fail now. Robert was Gerald's son, and part of him, and so she would love him too. The tide of her fear subsided, and she walked towards him with a welcoming smile.

"Where the hell have you been?" he snarled at her. "I've been waiting here nearly an hour."

"My dear Robert," she said tartly, "if you don't bother to let me know when you are coming, you can hardly object if I am not there to greet you." No longer worried for she could see that he was just an unhappy boy in need of help, she opened the door. He retained sufficient self-control to stand back like a gentleman, and allow her to enter her own home first, though not to take from her arms the bag of groceries.

"I'll go and make us a pot of coffee," she said over her shoulder. "Go in and make yourself at home."

As she ground beans and boiled water, she could hear him

pacing up and down in the next room, picking things up and putting them down distractedly, and her heart contracted as she thought of his breaking one of her precious dishes.

Irritably, he walked through to the kitchen door. "What the hell are you doing?" In his hand was a shallow blue ceramic bowl with an unusual interior texture, and he saw her face turn pale.

"Please, Robert," she said quietly, "go and sit down. I'm tired too, and we both need a cup of coffee before we talk. I'm just coming."

He knew then how to hurt her if necessary, and felt calmer with such a simple weapon in his hand. He went and sat in one of the black leather armchairs which he swung and rocked on its axis.

She carried the coffee into the living room and set the tray on the low table.

"What have you been doing?" she asked him as she poured out.

"I didn't come here for small talk," he said rudely.

"Oh, Robert. How can you be so unkind? That's not small talk, I really want to know. Have you a job? Where are you staying? Don't you know we care about you?"

"Yeah, sure."

"Well, tell me then. Are you still at that garage?"

"Listen, I didn't come here to talk about me. I came to tell you about June. There's something you should know. Or Dad should know, so I'm telling you."

Great heavens, she thought, please, not another disaster. "Tell me then, what's happened?"

"She's pregnant."

Robert did not believe in wrapping things up, but he was dismayed at Patricia's reaction. She was a sensible woman, for Christ sake, and she'd never even clapped eyes on June, so what was there for her to get steamed up about? Jeepers, she surely wasn't going to let him down and have hysterics or something, because someone had got to do something, and he sure as hell wasn't going to risk confronting his father.

Patricia sat for a long time as if stunned. Her emotions were in a turmoil and she had great difficulty in sorting them out. Her first thought was selfish, Lord no, not another crisis, and then of Gerald and how shattered he would be, and then tumbling over each other, guilt, for she could not believe otherwise than somehow, inexplicably, this was their fault, and fear for June, and compassion.

"Poor June," she said at last.

"Is that all you can say?" Robert exploded. "Poor June," he mimicked, "poor June my ass. What are you gonna *do*?"

"Oh, for heaven's sake, stop acting like a spoiled child. I don't know what I'm going to do. Tell your father for a start, I suppose."

"Money is what's needed."

"Money?" she said astonished, for her mind was still grappling with the emotional situation.

"Yeah, money. You know, filthy lucre, the root of all evil, dough, bread, the stuff my father has so much of he can do what he fucking well likes."

"Robert, you are really being so offensive, I just can't take much more."

"Tough titty."

She closed her eyes and her mouth was set in a hard line.

"Just tell me where June is living. And then go. I'll speak to your father when he returns."

"Oh, you rich expensive tarts," he sneered. "Nothing touches you, does it? You never had to suffer, not like the rest of us. Just put out your hand and take, you don't notice you are trampling our faces in the mud." He stopped, feeling his impotence. She was so still, so secure in her own beauty, her intelligence, her competence. She would never understand.

His parting gesture was to smash something, just a gesture, a symbol to her of what had happened to others. But he respected her collection too much to destroy something very beautiful, that blue bowl for instance, so he chose the most worthless object he could immediately see, a plaster replica of a reclining horse, crude and primitive.

With great deliberation, he picked up the horse and dropped it on the floor where it broke into many pieces. And when she did not move, he threw down the blue bowl too. Then he turned on his heel and left.

He could not have known – surely – that of all her things he had chosen the most precious. That small black and white horse had been made by her young sister when she was ten, the year she died. It serves me right, she thought, I shouldn't put my memories into breakable things. She is gone, now no more than before Robert came.

She knelt on the floor and began to pick up the pieces, but there were so many – the unbaked clay had crumbled, the only thing to do was to sweep them up. Still she hesitated when it came to putting the pieces in the dustbin. It was so irrevocable. But the damage was done. Why hesitate? It was only pieces of painted clay after all. The sooner she started caring about the living rather than inanimate pots and things the better.

Take what you want, God said. Wasn't that the quotation? *Take what you want, God said, and pay.* Payment was never what you expected somehow. But she had made her choice. And her secret self said, You shall not be bankrupt.

32

Gerald

Gerald hated Montreal from the start. The moment he got off the plane he realized that Milan and Montreal might be on the same latitude, but Europe's balmy spring sunshine had been left far behind. Winter still held Canada in its icy grip. To Montrealers there were many signs that winter's six-month-long siege was lifting, for the brown piles of snow along every road-side had begun to disappear, the winds no longer knifed you through, and heavy furs were now too warm. But Gerald was repelled by everything he saw – the yellow laden sky, the dirty brown slush, the women in their dark coats and heavy boots, lights on at 4 o'clock in the afternoon and it was April. These days the weather, which he normally didn't even notice, had begun to affect his mood.

He had taken the airport bus and fortunately it took him directly to the doors of the hotel, so that there was absolutely no need to go outside again. He would have a drink and a meal and go to bed. But Sunday afternoon, out of season, Reception offered him afternoon tea, and he was pained by a glimpse of morning-coated waiters and the colonials' nostalgia of silver-plated teapots and potted palms. The bars were not open, none of them, and no one was in the kitchen. It was now past 10 for him, and he was getting hopping mad: surely these bumbling fools had had trans-Atlantic visitors before, where else in the world would you meet such crass lack of consideration? He had sent word that he would use Sunday night to become acclimatized and adjust his internal clock, but was glad when Art Mendel telephoned to greet him and invite him to dinner. By the time he had telephoned Patricia and had a wash, he found a bar open after all, and was feeling considerably mellowed when he tipped one of the doormen to get him a taxi.

He knew nothing of the geography in this part of the world, but the drive seemed to him a long one. The driver was French-Canadian too, so he would have been doubly watchful if only it could have done him any good. Still, they arrived eventually, and by London standards the fare was not excessive, and the chap had even stopped beside a gap in the snow, so that he could get out and step onto the pavement without struggling over a filthy mound of sand and slush. Snow was falling, sparkling in the lamplight, the world was hushed, resting peacefully beneath the gentle soft white blanket. Gerald could see that snow held charm when it was fresh and falling gently and not very cold.

The Mendels were very hospitable, plied him with bourbon and water, and showed him all over their modern split-level house of which they were inordinately proud and, in to him typically American fashion, naively certain he would be as interested as they. But he felt swamped by acres of maple panelling with worked copper fittings, vast picture windows, the enormous refrigerator, the freezer, the washing machine and drier, the wall oven and fitted cupboards, the basement playroom with its twenty-two inch colour TV and ping-pong table, the jungle of potted plants. Sarah Mendel had obviously gone to a great deal of trouble to prepare the meal, cold consomme (which he hated), some sort of chicken casserole, and an enormous strawberry shortcake (made inevitably, he supposed, with frozen strawberries) and ice-cream. He had to admit to himself as the evening wore on, he was in a lousy mood.

Perhaps it was their Jewishness, he thought as he rode back

to the hotel in another taxi. Patricia would object, say he was chauvinistic, but they *were* different. Why try to pretend? Even in front of him, a stranger, they had not been able to hide their marital difficulties either, and Sarah for all her appearance of warm motherliness was a typical nagging Jewish momma. Their little boy was only four now, but heaven help him in another ten years. In the meantime though, she was taking it out on her husband, you could see that, pushing him like an upholstered steamroller. He felt sorry for Art, for whom he had a lot of respect professionally. He, Gerald, was no racist and he wasn't prejudiced either. It was a lot of nonsense to say a man was prejudiced when he could see differences with his own eyes.

Tricia just didn't know what she was talking about. In fact, she was becoming very tiresome with her moralising about having an open mind and brotherly love and all that guff. You only had to look at the world with half an eye to see the British were more civilised that any other race, so why talk of chauvinism when presented with an indisputable fact?

Look at America, so-called bastion of the free world. You couldn't walk the streets at night without danger of a knife in your back. Even in the New York Hilton, the switchboard telephoned you to make sure you locked and chained your door from the inside. And their legal system was a joke, judges bought and sold, gangsters running city councils, the gun-happy police no better than the criminals they are supposed to be protecting society against, ready to torture teenage girls campaigning for civil rights.

Yes, she had said, these things are true, but they are also distortions. Cultures vary the world over, that's obvious, and what societies will accept varies too, even from year to year in the same place. You are kind and gentle, she said, but do you know how much of that is thanks only to your good fortune in being able to live successfully like that? Given the right circumstances, how do you know you would not lie and steal and cheat? How do you know you could not kill?

Well, he had killed. For his country, during the war, he had killed hundreds, probably thousands at a distance, by bombing German cities from the air. Could that be what she meant? That was ludicrous, for war meant you had to do things that no civilised man could do under any other circumstances. You had to because it was your duty to defend your country. Pacifism was indefensible. Only a coward would refuse to fight for his country, even to give his life if need be.

By the time he reached the hotel, he was feeling very angry, and had to have another drink even though he had drunk too much and was very tired. It was as well they were not going to see each other for a week, for Patricia's criticism of his long-held convictions had always annoyed him, and today the memory of her voice, so confident, and of her face, so friendly and smiling, filled him with such anger he wanted to strike her across her face and make that smile disappear, hit her so that her head jerked and she lost her self-assurance.

But when he was in bed, and put out his hand to where she usually lay beside him, it came to him with a cold sense of horror that she could be right. Beautiful, clever, loving Patricia, the one and only woman he loved, had dared to disagree with certain of his opinions and he had actually wished to hit her lovely face, had dreamed of making those beloved lips bleed. It was not, of course, that she *was* right. It must be that he was going mad.

The last few weeks had been too much of a strain. He clearly needed a good rest.

He took a sleeping pill and fell asleep.

Successful men are able to keep different aspects of their lives in separate compartments, and Gerald was no exception. His work gave him enormous pleasure, the more complicated the problem, the greater the stimulation. Even though the nervous tension his private life had created did occasionally threaten to break through, he was able to complete his two days of work in Montreal without faltering. It was only when he returned to the hotel on Tuesday evening with nothing to do before flying to Chicago the next morning that he found himself overwhelmed with a sense of unreality.

He decided to walk, away from the bright lights flashing along St Catherine Street, up the hill towards the trees and large houses with gardens and the university. The sun had shone brightly that day in a clear blue sky, but it was now growing dark and he had to walk fast to keep warm. He no longer knew where he was or where he was going, for he turned left, then right, then left again, and kept on walking. He felt a pressure on his chest, and it was as though if he were to stop for a moment, he might burst out weeping.

If I could find a church, he thought, or a clergyman. Someone to talk to. Or he could go and sit inside a, church, and absorb the peace one always found there, and if the vicar happened to come in while he was there, he could speak to him if he chose. He did not think religion could take away his pain, but clergymen are used to death and might give him comfort.

He reached a major crossroads, and a bus was standing at the corner, waiting. It said "Cote des Neiges, St Joseph Oratory". He had heard of the oratory, a shrine visited by devout Catholics from all over the world, a great monument to the memory of a solitary hermit who had done great deeds of kindness, and had healed the faithful by the laying on of hands. Just what he wanted. The lights were against the bus so the driver opened the doors and let him on. He paid his fare, and the bus slowly climbed the steep hill, past the great hospital proud of its world-famous surgeons, along a great boulevard lined with apartment blocks.

Before they had gone far though, he saw a small church on the other side of the road, with a black cross on the roof, and unbelievably, standing beside it a house with "Vicarage" on the gate. He rang the bell. As he got off, he stepped into a pool of black water, soaking his good English shoes, and the wind caught him sharply. It was not freezing yet, but it soon would be. The bus drove off, spattering his trousers with salt and slush.

Gingerly, he made his way across the road and back to the church. The doors were shut. He pushed and pulled, but they were locked fast. He felt defeated and angry. In England, churches were not locked. Barbarous damned country. He walked all round the church, but there was no way in. He walked back to the gate with the plate that said "Vicarage" and stood looking at the small neat house. There was no sign of life, no lights in the window. Should he knock at the door? What would he say to a man who kept his church locked? He should have stayed on the bus, gone onto St Joseph's Oratory as he had planned.

Once more he crossed the road and walked along the boulevard, sloping downwards now. He turned round occasionally to see if there was a bus coming, for he did not know how far he had to go and would take a bus again if he could, or a taxi if one should come along. The wind was biting, knifing him through the overcoat that was warm enough in England, and patches of ice were forming on the pavement, making walking difficult. He walked a long way. His feet were very cold.

Just as a bus finally came in sight, he saw the Oratory. There could be no doubt about it. It was up there to his left, high on the hill, floodlit among the trees. He had almost given up after all, for he had just passed a cemetery, and had had a sudden vision of Madge lying in her coffin. But there it was, still a distance but not worth taking a bus now.

It was a huge domed edifice built to last a thousand years, a monument to man's endurance if not to his gift of beauty. Gerald hesitated, gazing up at the solid stone walls at the top of the hill, for he did not feel his soul could soar upwards to search the heavens from within that endowment of nineteenth French architecture, so firmly embedded in its rock did it appear. But he could not turn back having come so far. All he had to do was climb the hundreds of steps from the gates where he stood, tiers of wooden steps trodden by the faithful, and mounted by the devout and penitent on aching knees. He would walk, alone, not penitent nor devout, without faith, but he would climb the hundreds of steps to search for peace for his aching soul.

There were many doors, and many buildings or wings to the edifice, and many signs in French. Past a large souvenir shop, now closed, past a hot dog stand and coffee bar, unattended, past locked doors marked *Entree Interdite*, he began to wonder if this place too could be shut against him. But no, he found his way at last. Heavy doors opened into the sombre interior of this Catholic shrine, as big as a cathedral, built to mark the site of a hermit's hut.

But he did not find what he was seeking. No peace for the soul could be found here. Everywhere he looked were notices, in every possible language, and every one was a demand for money. In every possible nook and cranny, there were images of saints or the Virgin Mary, and beside each one a large money box and exhortation to buy a candle. The interior of the church was dark, but lit by flickering clumps of candles burning for men and women of more faith than he. Gerald was sickened and could not stay. He saw it was not a church of God, but a grotesque monument to North America's new idol, the dollar.

So God did not want to talk to him. Or could it just be that He was not here, he had simply not looked in the right place? But that was nonsense, God was supposed to be everywhere. If there was a God. Which there wasn't. But if there *were* a God, He would turn His back on Gerald anyway, and that was proof of his guilt. Jesus Christ himself wouldn't intercede for a man who had murdered his own wife.

There! He had said it aloud in his own mind, that terrible suspicion that had been growing like a tumour in his head.

But now that he had said it, it sounded ridiculous, melodramatic. Of course he hadn't done anything like that, hadn't touched the woman for heaven's sake. There was no need to over-dramatise. Secret fears were always worse than those you face fairly and squarely.

He had *some* responsibility towards the poor woman though. She was his wife. She had not loved him and he had left her and their marriage had failed, but she was his wife. Had been his wife for a long time. Twenty five years. A quarter of a century.

He had wandered away from the Oratory, not down the steps but behind the massive building towards a clump of trees. He found that this led him away into winding tree-lined streets at the back of the hill. The large and elegant houses were set well back in their snow-covered gardens, and reminded him of his own house of which they had been so proud. What had happened to them?

It was nearly nine o'clock, and not at all a usual thing for a man to wander aimlessly in this neighbourhood. A passer-by looked at him curiously, a house-holder about to shut his garage door thought seriously of calling the police. But luckily Gerald came upon a taxi depositing a young couple outside a large square house of white stucco, and he rode back into the city.

The rest of his North American trip passed in a daze. His Chicago host became concerned that Gerald was ill, and offered to take him to his country chalet, but Gerald refused. He would get through somehow. Like a wounded animal, he wanted to escape from his kind, to lick his wounds alone.

He thought unceasingly of Madge and himself, trying to remember why he had married her, trying to discover what had gone wrong. For he realized she was still inside him, still formed part of his unconscious, and until he could see their relationship as a whole he would never be free.

Why did he marry her? He remembered the first time he saw her, so smooth and clean and young, glowing among the teacups. His mind had been on death that day too, for his buddy Alf had bought it over the Channel two days earlier, and then that last night he'd had a telegram – their whole road in N.W.10 wiped out, Dad in hospital, Mother dead. German bombs on British cities, and he was dropping British bombs on German cities. Tit for tat, an eye for an eye, your mother's life for my mother's life.

All around him were men in uniform, weary, dirty, coarsened by the barbaric life, having fought and about to fight, about to die. And there before him he saw Madge, glowing with youth and enthusiasm, her light brown hair curling over her shoulders and swinging as she served a soldier and smiled. She was a picture of innocence, unsullied by the filth of war and the degradation of the human spirit when men destroy each other.

Her innocence, he knew now, was as much as anything a reflection of her not very high intelligence. She had kept her head when all around her lost theirs because she missed some vital information. But many women were like that, he remembered, sending their men off to battle in a romantic glow of chivalry, as to a crusade. She had been unsullied because she saw no real suffering, could not visualise death as other than a hero's end. Her mother was the same. Patricia would have laughed contemptuously: if she had been old enough and not a young schoolgirl, she would have driven a Red Cross van, he imagined, not been content to pour tea on Waterloo Station. What would I have thought of her then? he asked himself wryly. I'd have thought of her as crude and debased as the rest of us.

So he had been as romantic as Madge herself.

He had been proud of her too, and surely there was nothing wrong in that. The Leicesters were a well-to-do family far above him in the social scale, and even if such things no longer mattered and the war had broken down the last barriers, still he felt it was an achievement to win this girl as his bride.

He had thought too that this might be a short cut to becoming a cultured man, that he might be able to escape the sordid vulgarity of his grubbing, scrubbing working class family, whose books had been burned during the thirties when there was no coal, and the chairs and tables too. He had longed for beauty in his life, music, pictures, theatre, and above all, he longed for books and knowledge and intelligent conversation. Mr Leicester had the books, but they had few conversations, culture had not come to him through this well-to-do family.

It was Patricia who opened those doors he had never found, Tricia, whose background was just about as middle class, bourgeois and ordinary as you could imagine. Her father was a small time estate agent, and had the most fantastic collection of records Gerald had ever seen, all the classical names he could think of – Beethoven, Mozart, Handel, Elgar, Chopin, Britten, Vaughan Williams, lots of others. And her mother, a small neat lady with Tricia's eyes, was a teacher and loved books.

It just didn't make sense. They were just two very ordinary people you wouldn't look at twice in the street, and the Leicesters were of a long line of Leicesters and Wagstaffs who had served successive governments. Yet he had never been to the opera in his life before he met Patricia, or to anything more serious in the theatre than *Mame*. Not that there was anything wrong with that sort of thing, it was fun, lifted him out of himself. But when he did go to the opera and the theatre with Tricia, real highbrow stuff that terrified him, he found he was so stimulated he couldn't stop thinking about it for weeks. *Forty Years On*, for example, and *Abelard and Heloise* – he hadn't been able to get some of the scenes out of his mind, and must have been a real bore talking about them as though he had made an earth-shattering discovery. Probably everyone he talked to wondered just where he had been hiding all his life.

He felt as though his vision had cleared, and a curtain was drawn aside in his mind.

It was not so much Madge herself that he had loved as what she had represented. He had committed the ultimate insult to his own wife.

He realized now that he had never really intended to go so far as to leave her in the end. True he had been seduced by the vision of the new life he could have with Patricia, seeing doors open before him leading to delights he had never before felt capable of enjoying. But he had mapped out the life he wanted: safe, secure, humdrum perhaps and certainly lacking in sparkle, even his tentative approaches to the things of the spirit secretly and safely bounded by meetings at Lodge.

All he had hoped for was an affair, a true soul-searing love affair, a great love that could only end in a great renunciation. He would have felt he was turning his back finally, irrevocably on a major part of his life. Yes, very much as a man renounced the world of the flesh in days gone by and entered a monastery, and thereby saved his soul. It would have been dramatic. Heartbreaking. Only thus can ordinary mortals taste drama in their lives and hover around the fringes of tragedy.

33

June

The real problem was money, June thought.

There was no point in tipping the contents of her shoulder bag on the bed, she wouldn't find any more money there than last time. She knew exactly how much she had in the world after paying two weeks rent in advance for this grotty room: £3.14, an old penny and a silver threepenny piece. That was plenty if she was careful. She could make that last two weeks if she walked everywhere, but the thing was, how was she going to make more when that ran out?

Ruth had a point after all when she'd said she should get an education, learn something, get trained for a career. Trouble was she hadn't any special talents. The only way she'd ever made any money was working in a shop or babysitting. Babysitting – that was a funny one. Well, now she'd have to earn enough to pay her own babysitter, and how the hell was she going to do that?

There was Dad, of course. He'd always help her out if she got into a jam – that is, if his Lady Love hadn't got at him. But she was damned if she wanted to go to her father. He'd be bound to say, "Didn't I tell you you should have stayed at school?" and if she got involved with him now, she'd have to tell him about it in the end. She didn't want any more interference from her family, thank you.

Nor from Bobby either. It was probably a terrible mistake telling him yesterday. They had just bumped into each other in the street while she was searching for a room, as though London was a tiny village where coincidences like that happen everyday, and she had been so glad to see his dear old face again and to talk to someone for a change. They had talked for hours and hours in that coffee bar. He'd been glad to see her too, as though she was the only person who could understand he was consumed with this terrible anger, for the crime was not his, he said, the crime had been committed against him, against his will, against his very nature.

That was crazy, thinking that way. But then, because he was thinking crazy thoughts, she told him hers, how she thought she was going to have a baby, though it was really too soon to tell, and how she was going to start a new life on her own, with no one to push her around.

She was fed up with being pushed around, just because she was a girl. They wouldn't dare try it with Bob. They were a lot of phonies too – look at Uncle Bert. "Put your trust in the Lord," he'd say. "Take your troubles to God in your hour of need, lay your sins at His feet." And you could bet your last new P he doesn't take his sins to the Lord, he'd be too ashamed. Anyone who goes on about religion is a phoney, they have to be. No loving God could let the things happen to people you read about. And any other kind is not worth praying to. You hear that up there?

"You hear that up there?" she said aloud, looking up at the ceiling. "If there is a God up there, you should be bloody ashamed of yourself."

There was no thunderbolt, no flash of lightening. The ceiling did not fall in. Would have been quite understandable if it had fallen, with all those cracks, maybe it won't be safe sleeping here. But she lay back on the bed, her hands behind her head, prepared to risk it. If it did fall in, it would be an Act of God and therefore inescapable, and since there was no God, it would be fine. And she touched the wood of the rickety table as a charm, just in case.

The room itself was hardly an encouragement in her new life. It was so small and dark, with one bare light bulb in the ceiling, the bed lumpy, with broken springs, the linoleum cracked, the one bit of mat threadbare and none too clean. She hadn't dared look at the bathroom and kitchen she was to share with unknown neighbours. But it was just for two weeks, while she found a decent job, and then she'd get a nicer room than this, with light and space and maybe even her own washbasin and cooking things.

Better than living with George. That was a great joke, that was. He had been pleased to see her: when she telephoned from the station, he had sounded delighted, she was sure of that, and had said, "Stay here, stay here" when he learned she had nowhere to go. Oh well, it had been a lot of fun. He had been very busy in his last term, and obviously found it convenient to have someone around to look after him, prepare meals, wash his socks. And to keep off importuning women, she thought wryly, since his not inconsiderable energies were being consumed in a final effort to leave the Slade in a blaze of glory. There she had been, bubbling over with joy, all pure naive stupidity, while he didn't care for her any more than about a dozen others. No matter. She didn't want him. She wasn't getting married, ever, and certainly not to a self-centred narcissistic Don Juan like him.

No need to abuse him though. She didn't love him, even felt cold and disapproving of him, but that was because of her ridiculous expectations and inevitable disappointment. He hadn't changed. He was still her friend. She alone had changed, and it was not his fault.

Even the baby growing inside her was not his fault. It was his, but not his fault. She had just been careless, had forgotten to take the pill while in Nottingham, had got into a muddle and decided to leave it until next month, completely oblivious to the fact this left her more vulnerable than ever. And there she was. It was still too soon, she'd only missed once, but she knew. She even knew when it happened. She was sure she had felt the union of sperm and egg and the creation of new life inside her, even though anyone would tell her it was impossible to know, and of course it was impossible to prove. But she could remember the evening and how her body had glowed and he had loved her and they had been happy. If she was right, her baby was due on Christmas Day. Another virgin birth, dear Father, another immaculate conception. It would be a boy and she would call him Chrestos, simpleton.

"Listen," she said aloud. "Ugly cynicism isn't going to get you anywhere. You've got to decide what you're going to do."

"Abortion isn't so bad, Sis," Bobby had said. "Everyone has them. It's all a question of money, and Dad'll fork out. I'll make him."

"I don't want anything from him," she said. But he had insisted, his girlfriend knew a doctor who did them, no questions asked. She hoped he'd forget about it and thought he probably would. The sum of £140 was beyond the reach of either of them, and she was sure he wouldn't face their father feeling as he did.

"You don't really want it, do you?" George asked nervously. He had come to see her in her dreary room, and if he had had a hat, he would have been twisting it nervously in his fingers. She almost laughed to see him so tongue-tied and embarrassed, so enormous a contrast with his usual gay self-assurance.

"I see my damned brother doesn't know how to keep his mouth shut." A slow anger rose inside her. Even Bob was interfering in her life. She couldn't trust anyone.

"Hey, come on, don't talk like that. Surely to God you were

going to tell me, weren't you?"

"I don't know," she said truthfully. "It isn't even certain yet anyway."

"You mean it might all be a mistake? Phew, you had me quite worried there for a minute. Thought I might have to marry you or something daft like that. That *would* do my career as a great painter a lot of good, me old darlin'. Imagine trying to paint surrounded by damp nappies. Yucch!" George began to look quite cheerful, any minute he'd start waltzing round the room with her.

"Make a change from smelly socks and dirty underwear all over the floor. Shouldn't have thought you'd notice nappies." She masked her bitterness with a light tone, but his face drooped as her offensive hit home. Why did she want to hurt him? She felt ashamed. "In any case, it is true, you know. I don't need a doctor to tell me, I am expecting a baby. Our baby."

She was watching his face, hoping just for a moment, just for a few seconds, only the briefest time, that a miracle might happen. But she saw fear rush in. Oh well.

"Look, I sold a painting last week," George said in a great hurry. "I got thirty quid. Here, you take it. Sorry it isn't much, but maybe it'll help."

"Oh, George, how marvellous for you. Which one was it? Do I know it?"

"It's one of the seascapes I did in St Ives last summer, the one with the orange fishing boat." Pride in his transaction allowed George to relax for just a minute, but the horrors of the present soon recalled his attention. "For God's sake, take the money, it's all I can do. If you really are sure you're up the stump."

"Thought you were going to marry me, George," she said mockingly. "We were going to starve in a garret."

"Come one, June, don't play games," he cried, obviously becoming frantic. "I can't do more than this, you know I would if I could. If that's my baby inside you, and you say it is, the least I can do is help pay for your abortion."

"Help to murder your own child?"

They looked at each other in cold silence.

"Abortion isn't murder," he said at last. "It's legal these days, you should know that. And everyone has them. It's the only sensible thing to do."

"So I am told."

"You haven't any alternative, have you?" he said desperately. "I refuse to make a shot-gun marriage – that wouldn't be fair to either of us. Or to the child. You know that."

"I don't want to marry you, George."

His surprise and disbelief were so obvious she wanted to laugh. She felt strong, stronger than him and free. The ability to make a decision and stick to it come what may was exhilarating. The money, the fruits of his labour, lay on the bed between them. It would not become her fee, she was not his bonds-woman. She picked up the notes, folded them carefully and put them into his unresisting hand.

"Go away, George, take your money and go. Whatever I decide has nothing to do with you."

"Of course it has. You say that's my baby. Of course I'm concerned."

"Listen," she said firmly. "I didn't come whining to you, and I never will. And when my interfering brother tells you I'm expecting your baby, what do you do? You offer me money towards an abortion. So you are not interested. You don't want to marry me, and I certainly don't want to marry you. So go away and leave me alone. Become a great painter. Leave me to sort out my life by myself."

Getting rid of him was not too difficult. He probably meant

well, she thought, but that didn't stop him scuttling off like a scared chicken as soon as he had satisfied his anxious conscience that she really did prefer to be left alone. So the last door was closed. Now it was certain that whatever decision she made, it would be her own. No one was left to put on any pressure.

Perhaps after all abortion was the best solution. End it all, get rid of this unwanted life growing inside her and begin again. It should not be too difficult, surely. Newspapers said you could get one on the National Health. All she had to do was find a doctor and tell him the situation, and her problem would soon be over.

But she couldn't do it. There was no point in going through all the rigmarole, finding addresses and filling out forms or whatever, she just wouldn't go through with it in the end. She knew that. She wanted her baby. It was the best thing that had ever happened to her. Everything screamed to the world it was a disaster, the world DISASTER was written in letters six feet high and painted red and glowing with neon lights. But that was not how she felt. She was glad.

How other girls could have abortions she couldn't imagine. Perhaps they were pressured by other people. Who knew, perhaps they didn't really want one any more than she did, but accepted the role of victim without complaint, masochistically allowed another to violate their bodies for the sake of some mythical greater good. Or as punishment.

Ruth's words had not fallen on stony ground, that was for sure. But she had already hoed and fertilized the bed, had read Simone de Beauvoir and Germaine Greer, and was determined not to end her life as her mother had done, a worn-out dishrag tossed on a rubbish heap. Furthermore, she was going to think for herself. She might not be educated, but she had a brain. She could think. Women's Lib was against marriage and for abortion. She was against neither. Only for herself.

She could remember that last evening with Ruth with extraordinary clarity. Ruth's words were etched in her brain with fire.

"In a time of sorrow, you can choose how you will be," Ruth had said. "You can choose weakness or strength. The weak and helpless female will always find there are males hovering around, anxious to render assistance. Especially if she is pretty. It boosts a man's ego to find a woman entirely dependent on his stronger powers. But such women are like the vine which sucks the life of the tree, and when its sap is gone and the support dies, the vine must die too.

"If you choose to stand alone, you will always be alone. You breathe another air, speak another language from those who suck nourishment from others, and poison others' lives with their secret fears and inadequacies and their pathetic dreams of success. Only the company of others like yourself will break your solitude as, from time to time, they stand at your side."

So she had chosen, even though the way was hard, she wanted to be strong. Partly, she knew, it was because she was afraid of turning to her old friends, yes, even Hetty, only to find they did not care. She had to sort herself out first, find out who she was, maybe discover something of value inside herself, something worth giving to others. But more than that, she wanted to be able to live with herself with pride, to hold her head up high, to find nourishment from within, and drink deep from the well of life inside herself.

They temper steel with fire, she thought. The poor stuff cracks and is discarded, and she could fail. But she was not going to give up the struggle without even trying.

34

Gerald

For a long time, Gerald could not find the courage to go and see his daughter. His heart yearned for her as he imagined her in the desolation of some dreary bedsitter, awaiting a baby which nobody wanted. But she had made it very clear: she was to be left alone, and he did not dare interfere.

At the end of August, the money for the house came through, and then he realized he had to see her to hand over her share of her mother's estate. Madge's only real possession had been her jewellery, which he had put in the bank because he couldn't bear to see it. But it seemed to him, morally at least, half the house had been hers, and so he would give his children half each of her share of the proceeds of the sale. A handsome sum. The house had almost doubled in value in the ten years he had been buying it, and even after paying solicitors' fees and the like, there was still about £12,000 left to divide among them all. And £3,000 should be enough to make June an independent woman.

There were some advantages at least in being a successful business man. If the demands of business seemed sometimes to reduce one's humanity, there was still satisfaction in being able to give one's daughter a large sum of money. Especially at a time when she was in real need.

He learned she was working in a chemist's somewhere in South Kensington.

She smiled wearily when he turned up one airless August evening and asked if he could take her out to dinner. Her face was white and drawn, her long hair stringy with the heat, her shapeless cotton shift clinging to the sweat on her swollen body. There could be no doubt about her condition now.

"A drink would be nice," she said. "I'll be free in half an hour."

He hung around, watching her serve the after-work crowd, all in a hurry to get home, feeling the weary smile always on her lips. No longer did he know anything, only that this was his daughter and he loved her.

And when she came up to him, a shopping bag and cardigan over her arm, the same weary smile indelible on her lips, he put his arms round her shoulders and gently kissed the top of her head. It was easy. He was surprised at himself, Gerald Frederick Hunter, he had not lost his soul for he truly loved his own daughter. She felt it too, for the smile faded from her lips and a new one grew in her eyes as she said, "Hello, Dad." He directed their steps towards a Wheelers he knew in Brompton Road, and she added, "It's good to see you."

In the cool dimness, he watched her sink into the red upholstered seat and take the weight off her aching legs. There was so much he wanted to say to her, his daughter, but he didn't know where to begin. He ordered, a sherry for her, a gin and tonic for himself.

"How are you keeping?" he asked.

"As you see," she said ironically, glancing at her swollen body. "Still four months to go, at this rate I'll be as big as a battleship."

"I'm surprised at George letting you down like this. I always thought he'd be a responsible young man."

"Oh, Dad," she said laughing. "Don't be so old-fashioned."

"Is it old-fashioned to expect a chap to marry a girl when he gets her into trouble?"

"Yes, it is. And he did suggest it. Only I said No."

"Darling, I'm sorry," he said, taking her hand. "I'm a clumsy fool."

"Don't worry about it, Dad. It's nobody's problem but mine."

"That seems so wrong somehow."

"No, it isn't. I don't want to be tied to anyone through fear or guilt, I've had enough of being a child. It's time I grew up and stood on my own two feet. I shall soon have a child of my own."

He suddenly saw this might not be all over by the end of the year after all. Was his daughter capable of such foolhardiness?

"You *are* going to put it up for adoption?"

Her face changed and became hard. At that moment he realized she was his baby daughter no longer. She was a grown woman with a mind of her own, and he had nearly wrecked this meeting so barely started. What an evening of revelation this was turning out to be.

"June, darling. I'm sorry. I seem to be making a mess of everything. I just don't understand. Truth is, I feel rather helpless. Why don't you tell me your plans and maybe there is some way I can help? Without being interfering, I mean. How about it?"

Her face softened at once. "Poor old Dad." she said. But she didn't plan to tell him much, certainly nothing about her talks with the National Council for the Unmarried Mother and her hope of becoming a domestic somewhere, so that she could find a home for herself and her baby. She could not give anyone the chance to interfere. "Don't worry about me. I shall manage. I'm just not quite sure how at the moment, that's all."

"You know I sold the house?" he asked, to try another tack.

"Has it gone already?" she cried. "What about my things? Where are they?"

Can't I do anything right? he asked himself bitterly. It just hadn't occurred to him to think of her odds and ends, nor indeed of Robert's. Lucy had kept a watchful eye while the packers were in – he hoped to heaven she had had more sensitivity than he.

"They're in store," he said hastily. "When you left Ruth's, we didn't know where you were."

"That's all right then," June said, relieved. "I'll have a look sometime." It was amazingly difficult to turn your back finally on things, when you could dismiss a person from your life for ever. Of course, with people there was always the chance you might change your mind. Except when they were dead.

Gerald was anxious to get on and give her the cheque, but now he wondered what other things he had forgotten to do, what other sensitivity he might trample on. He offered her dinner, which she accepted, and they spent considerable time ordering and then talking about food in general. It was a pleasure to watch her evident enjoyment of good food well cooked, probably her first decent meal in weeks. His heart twisted in pain. In the end, he just took the cheque out of his pocket and gave it to her.

She gasped when she saw the amount. But she had the independent women's instinctive aversion to being given money she had not earned. Even her father might be suspected of trying to pay her off.

"What's this for?"

"Hush," he said embarrassed. A grey-haired business man at the next table was staring at them with a knowing smirk on his fat foolish face. Gerald would have to hit him in a minute. "It's your share of your mother's estate."

"I didn't know she was so well off."

Gerald glared at the prying fool, who turned away with the same idiotic smirk and ostentatiously lit a cigar. "In a sense, she wasn't," he said very quietly, leaning across the table so as not to be overheard. "It's just that morally speaking, half the house was hers, and so when I sold it, it seemed only right to give you and Robert her share between you."

"I see. Why didn't you take her share yourself though? I'm sure you must be legally entitled to it."

"Because I had left her."

A smile slowly bloomed on her weary face. "I see. I can take it then. Thank you, Dad." Carefully, she put the valuable piece of paper away in her bag. "How fantastic. Suddenly I'm a rich woman."

"Not rich exactly. But it should make all the difference to you now."

"I was always going to keep my baby. But it will make it easier."

They sat together in a companionable silence, glad at last to be at peace.

"Do you really love her?" she asked suddenly.

"Patricia? Yes, I do."

"What's it like, being in love I mean?"

"Chastening."

She laughed, and understood a little of what he meant. Love, she had begun to see, required humility and that was one virtue she did not need. Arrogance was what sustained her, and would carry her through the difficulties ahead. She dared not lose it.

"Would you like to meet her?" he asked hesitantly.

"Sometime perhaps. Not yet."

She refused to let him take her home, insisted that he walk her to the tube station and leave her there. She would not accept a taxi.

"Please don't disappear again," he said urgently. "You must let me know where you are. At least give me a phone number."

"I'll let you know when I move," she promised, and that was the best she would do, though she did accept a card with Patricia's address and phone number, and promised to telephone him soon.

Before she went through the ticket barrier, she turned and kissed his cheek.

"Bobby is in St Ives, with the hippies," she whispered, and then was gone.

35

June

I'd like to know love, she thought that night. She had imagined it was love she felt for George, but that had left her with nothing but a taste of ashes. Was humility an essential factor, as Dad seemed to imply? And how was one to achieve that? Did you have to believe that you know nothing, are worth nothing? Whatever good is that? That can't be right, she must have it wrong somehow. One day she'd asked her new-found father to explain. But not now. It was enough to wait alone for the birth of her baby.

At first, the cheque in her bag made no difference to her life. She continued to go to work in the shop, and to struggle home at night to the familiar dark room, to rest her aching legs and back on the lumpy bed. What did it mean, this paper which said: "Pay June Hunter £3,000"? Did it really mean that if she went to a bank, the teller would give her three thousand crinkly green pound notes? So much money was unbelievable, she dared not think too clearly what she might do with it.

That she must be sensible, save it for her baby, that was perfectly clear, but what was the best thing to do she did not know. It was not enough to buy a house, or a business, since she had no real income. She could not risk frittering it away, and could think of no one who could give her sensible advice. Ruth might, she supposed. Or even her father. But she was not ready to talk to either of them.

One day in September when she awoke, it was pouring with rain, her back ached unremittingly, and she realized she did not have to go to the shop at all. She could take her precious bit of paper to a bank and open an account, and she could find a doctor and go to a clinic like other expectant mothers, and stop pretending it would be all right in the end. She could go out and make it all right.

Indeed, she did not feel at all well. It was only the middle of September and she had three more months to go at least, but the kicking child inside her seemed to be draining all her strength. Probably she was not eating properly or something. It was time she put herself in a doctor's hands and stopped relying on youth to pull her through.

She would have to buy some new clothes too – she could only wear these two shapeless cotton tents now, and the weather had turned cold. She'd soon need her winter coat, and presumably it was now in store. Life was so damned complicated. It'd be so much easier to stay in bed and let the world get on without her.

She struggled into the cotton dress, which was so tight now it stretched at the seams, made herself a mug of tea in the filthy kitchen down the hall, and searched her bag for coins to make phone calls. That meant walking down the road and round the corner, for there was no phone in the house. She felt shivery now, and had a headache. She wouldn't take an aspirin though, too much risk. Just wrap up warm with a couple of jumpers and her plastic mac, then she'd go and phone the shop and Mrs Warren at the Council for the Unmarried Mother. Mrs Warren was not there, so she left her name.

Then, having come so far, she walked the fifty yards further on to the small branch bank and went inside. It was no wonder, she thought as she waited patiently for the necessary papers to be drawn up, they are having such furtive whispered conversations, I don't look exactly like the sort of person who should have that kind of money. Two referees were necessary to open a bank account, she was told, not relatives but people who had known her for some time and could vouch for her character.

"But I'm only trying to give you some money," she cried.

"But Mrs Hunter, it's the rules."

"*Miss* Hunter," she said. "Oh, go to hell."

She felt like crying and her head ached, and she felt such a fool. Who could have known there would be such problems? She should have gone to the Post Office as she always used to. Or someone should have told her about banks years ago. Perhaps this was the time to phone her father for advice. It was his cheque.

It was still raining, and she shivered as she walked outside. She had one more coin left. She'd just try him at the office, and if he was there she'd ask him what to do. Somehow it was more difficult than she'd bargained for being independent, there were so many things she didn't know.

To her surprise, she got through right away. But she felt so foolish, she nearly didn't tell him why she had phoned, just chatted about this and that until the three minutes were nearly up and she said hesitantly, "Dad, I've got a problem." Then the bleeps began. In the brief interval allowed by the G.P.O. for farewells, he said urgently, "Quick, give me your address," and she did, and then the dialling tone returned and she could not be sure he had heard her. But she had no more coins, and she felt so tired and woozy, it didn't really matter. She would just go back to her room and go to bed.

36

Gerald

Gerald was so gratified to hear from her at long last, his first instinct was to drop everything and rush to her rescue, even though he had a number of important engagements that day. He knew that if he gave himself any time to think rationally, he would talk himself out of this instinctive gesture, for what possible problem could she have that could not wait until the evening? But he did not want to fail her again. His own daughter in trouble was surely far more important than the report the two Senior Production Managers were expecting to give him in half an hour. Besides, he might well be back within the hour, it was probably something very simple. He couldn't let her down.

To prevent any more internal discussion, he buzzed his secretary, told her to postpone all his meetings until after lunch and to order him a taxi. He then took his coat and hat and umbrella and the piece of paper on which he had scribbled her address, and left before he could change his mind.

Traffic in London being as heavy as usual, it was more than half an hour before he reached her rooming house, and then he suspected that after all he had not caught the name of the road correctly. There were no names on the door and only one bell, which he pressed impatiently, peering through the grimy side window into a dark hall. But when he leaned on the door, it unexpectedly gave way and he walked inside. Was this really the place, and if so, how could his own daughter bear to live with that smell of rancid fat, boiled cabbage and ammonia? He felt as incongruous in this setting as he was sure he looked, and was not surprised when a short, slatternly woman in a hairnet, felt slippers and vaguely green overall greeted him with suspicious hostility.

"Well?" she demanded, standing in the doorway beyond the stairs. "Whadja want then?"

"Does Miss June Hunter live here?"

"Why?" She stepped forward belligerently. "What's it to you, then?"

"I'm her father," he said, carefully polite.

"Huh. A likely story, I don't think. Father? Father of that bastard kid more like. Go on, get out of 'ere. She don't want nothin' from the likes of you. Men." And she spat, narrowly missing his shoes.

Gerald was torn between a desire to laugh and a desire to belt her one in the chops. But he did neither, just walked towards the stairs saying, "Good. She *is* here. Just tell me which room she's in."

"'Ere you!" she shouted. "Whadja think you're doing? This 'ere's a respectable 'ouse, this is."

"Tell me which room she's in," said Gerald, walking up the stairs, "or I shall open every door until I find her."

"'Ave it yer own way then," she said sullenly. "See if I care. It's 'er lookout, not mine." She returned to her flat at the back. "Room 4." And she slammed the door.

The room was easy to find, but Gerald hesitated before he knocked. No wonder she had not wanted him to know where she lived. He was appalled by the dirty shabbiness of what he had seen so far, and was afraid of the squalor that might confront him in her very room. What had he done, how had he failed that his own daughter should be living in a place like this?

Snivelling coward, he growled to himself, this is not the moment for self-pity. But his heart was pounding and he trembled as he lifted his hand to the door. He saw himself standing there in the dimness, well-shined shoes on the torn linoleum, tall and broad of shoulder against the grimy brown paint, in his dark business suit and charcoal grey custom-made raincoat, furled umbrella on his arm and soft grey hat on his head. But inside this elegant facade, there was nothing. Like a Magritte painting, he was nothing beyond the elegant propriety of his carefully nurtured image. Gerald Hunter, Technical Director, appeared to stand there on an errand of mercy, but Gerald Frederick Hunter, human being, had crumbled to dust.

He knocked, and a faint voice called, "Who's there?" so he hesitantly opened the door. June was lying in bed, the covers up to her chin. She smiled vaguely, but said nothing. He walked over to the bed and bent down to kiss her forehead. That was all he needed. Her face was damp and burning to the touch, she was obviously ill, and no matter what she said about wanting to remain independent, the limit had been reached.

"Don't move," he said. "I'll be right back."

He hurried down the stairs and out the front door. The taxi had, of course, gone. He turned back and banged impatiently on the door beyond the stairs until it was opened by the same belligerent woman he had seen earlier.

"'Ere, 'ere, what the 'ell d'you think yore at?"

"Do you have a telephone here?"

"What's it to you?"

"Listen," he said impatiently. "My daughter is ill. I'm taking her away from here and I need a taxi."

"Takin' 'er away? You can't do that. What about my rent, eh? A month's notice, that's what I gotta 'ave. You 'ear?"

"Oh, for heaven's sake, woman, you'll get your money. Here, take this, here's £20. That's enough I should hope. Now for goodness sake, please call me a taxi."

"That's all right then," she said, hastily tucking the notes away in a hidden pocket. "Your daughter, is she? Yes, she'll be better off with you, poor soul. Why, I was only saying just that to 'er the other day, I said, you need yer own folks, that's what you need in your condition."

"Will you call me a taxi right now?" Gerald was so exasperated, he would have pushed the woman out of the way, but she capitulated. As soon as he heard sound of dialling, he hurried up the stairs.

June was exactly as he had left her, but as he rushed into the room she propped herself up on one elbow.

"Dad? What's going on?"

"I'm taking you away from here. You just lie there and watch me, and see that I get all your things together. Don't move – just tell me if I miss anything."

She shook her head, and then swayed and lay back with her hand over her eyes.

"Gosh, I don't know what's the matter with me. I feel rather peculiar."

"Yes," he said shortly, for he was packing things as best he could. "You've probably got flu or something." She did not appear to have much. It was as though she had just been camping out in this room and had not surrounded herself with the usual possessions that accumulate around one apparently in direct proportion to the time spent in any place. No books, no letters, no trinkets, the bare minimum of clothes and cosmetics, her secret life not available to anyone.

"Come on now," he said. "We must get you dressed for the taxi."

In a daze, she struggled to sit up and swing her legs down to the floor. She had not undressed properly, only dragged off her dress, so Gerald did not have much difficulty in restoring her clothing. But even with a heavy cardigan on, she shivered uncontrollably, so he put his own coat round her shoulders.

"It's on its way," said the landlady, poking her head round the door. Her practised eye rapidly took in the meagre furnishings of the room and none seemed to be missing.

"Good," said Gerald. "Would you be kind enough to carry this suitcase downstairs?"

Without looking at the woman further, he turned to June whom he picked up in his arms. The landlady raised her eyes at his peremptory request, but he ignored her, and he had paid her well and she had to go downstairs anyway and the sooner they were gone the sooner she could get someone else in, so she did as he asked.

Gerald was glad when he felt June in his arms, her body against his chest, her weight pulling on his muscles. She lay across his shoulder like a child, unprotesting, trusting, as he slowly made his way downstairs and through the dreary smell of the hall, into the open air. He felt like a knight who had rescued his lady, Sir Galahad with the Holy Grail.

And when they were in the taxi, he did not let go of her. He gently set her on the seat and sat beside her, and kept his arm around her so that she lay against his chest all the way to Hampstead.

37

June

Her head was thick and woolly, and didn't seem to function properly. The important thing was rest, she was sure that if only she could sleep, she and her baby would be perfectly all right in the morning. When her father came and carried her away from that grim and dreary room, it was just too much effort to protest. Besides, it was probably a good thing, she didn't belong there, had felt for all those weeks she had stayed in that room that the next week she really would move, it was only temporary.

But as she lay against his breast on that taxi ride, listening to the roar of engines and the squeak of brakes, the beating of her own heart and her father's heavy breathing, she began to ask herself where they were going. It could not be her former home, for it did not exist. Nor to Uncle Bert and Aunt Ena, surely not – they certainly wouldn't have her now, in her condition, thank heaven. Not to Ruth for she was too far away. To hospital then? But it was much too soon, there were more than three months to go. If her baby came now, he would surely die... She put her hand on her swollen belly, and her child answered her fears with gentle, rhythmic kicking. She could feel his limbs beneath her hand. She would keep him safe.

It was obvious, wasn't it? The one place she really did not want to go, that was where he was taking her.

"Dad. Where are we going?"

He looked down at her with a tender smile. "Home of course." And she knew he meant his new home, Patricia's flat.

He had not thought she would hate the very thought of the place. What was she to do?

If only her head did not ache so, it might be possible for her to think. Perhaps she really did have flu … It was just too much, she'd have to give in until she felt better.

She hardly noticed anything as her father lifted her out of the taxi and carried her into the building. It was unfamiliar, she knew she must be somewhere she had never been before, it must be that flat. But it didn't matter any more. All she wanted was to lie in a warm bed and sleep.

38

Gerald

A doctor was the next problem. His family doctor was in Godalming, he had not registered with anyone since he moved, and he had no idea who Patricia went to. Could be a gynaecologist, he thought, heaven forbid. And then it occurred to him that this might be just the sort of doctor June was in need of. How was a mere male to tell? Patricia was out all day, her secretary said, and there was nothing under *D* in her address book. He could not bring himself to search for anything in her desk that might give him a lead. In the end, he called the operator and told her his daughter was ill, and she gave him the numbers of three G.P.s who might be prepared to help. With the first two, he couldn't get past the receptionists, but the third promised to drop by in a couple of hours.

It was now about noon. He obviously wasn't going to return to the office, but he didn't phone. There was nothing for him to do but wait. He warmed up the dregs of their breakfast coffee in a saucepan, put some bread and cheese on a plate, and carried them into the spare room. June was huddled in a ball, her eyes shut, shivering.

There was a chest of drawers in the room, but no cupboard. He didn't know where the extra blankets were, looked in the drawers, and then in their bedroom where he found the car rug, which helped, and his heavy winter overcoat which he put over her. There must surely be a hotwater bottle somewhere, he thought, but his vague investigations revealed nothing. She had stopped shivering now, and her forehead was drenched. He wished he had a thermometer.

She did not wake fully until Dr Foster arrived, a young man who tapped her chest and back, and listened to the baby's heartbeat, and was shocked that she should be so near the birth of her child and not in a doctor's care. He left a prescription, and written instructions, and said to call him if there was any change. He'd be back tomorrow.

It was reassuring at any rate to know June was in good hands. He seemed very competent and obviously cared about his patients since he had offered to come round tomorrow, just like an old-fashioned G.P. They didn't do that these days. So why was he coming back tomorrow? Could she be dangerously ill? But surely he would have said so, and anyway he would have taken her into hospital, especially with the baby, that was two lives instead of one. Only hospital beds were scarce these days, especially in London, and why would he care specially about June? He'd never seen her before today. And what did he mean by "any change"? What was the matter with her anyway? Oh, why didn't he have the sense to ask the right questions when he was here?

Gerald sat in the old-fashioned fireside chair in Patricia's guest room, and stared at his daughter. She looked dreadful, thin about the face, with that same ugly old woman look he had found on Madge's face that awful day in the hospital. A deep red flush coloured her cheekbones, but the rest of her skin had a greyish pallor and dark shadows filled the sockets of her eyes. Her lids were sore, her nose pinched and thin, her tangled hair stringy and lank. What had happened to her youthful prettiness and her glowing vitality? It was worse somehow that she had no beauty lying there, the delight he had always felt in his young daughter's charms had vanished, leaving this anguished tenderness that made him long to pick her up in his arms, crush her to his heart, as though this might in some way assuage her hurt.

But she was sleeping. Perhaps he could leave her now, just for a while, to go and get the prescription filled.

39

Patricia

When Patricia returned home that evening, it was with a sense of relief that she would be able to shut the door and keep out the world. All she wanted was to collapse into a comfortable chair, put her feet up, sip a long drink and listen to some music. The petty squabbles, the jockeying for power, the idiocies and frustrations of business life had got her down. Gerald's worried face in the hall was a shock.

"June's here," he said. "She's ill."

She had changed her clothes and begun to brush her hair before the words really penetrated.

"She's in the guest room," he said hesitantly, for it had only just occurred to him that he had taken liberties with Patricia's home. It was not his after all.

June here? "Tell me what happened," she said, turning on the dressing table stool to where he stood in the doorway, the hairbrush still in her hand. Was this not what she wanted, to meet June and help her? Wherefore this sense of dread?

"I went to see her, and she was in bed, all hot and feverish, so I thought she couldn't stay there all by herself. And it was a terrible place. So I brought her here. You do understand, don't you?"

"Of course, darling. Of course you had to bring her here. Did you get a doctor?"

"Yes, eventually. And there are lots of pills and things."

"I'd better go and see her."

She was daunted by the realization that this young woman she was about to meet for the first time probably hated her.

That the last place she would want to be was here, in the Other Woman's

home. Patricia found her legs were trembling as she stood up. She wanted to be able to love Gerald's daughter, but she dreaded the inevitable hostility.

Slowly she walked down the hall and peeped through the door of her small spare room. When she congratulated herself six years ago on having a proper room for overnight guests, she had not bargained for her recent visitors.

June looked so like Gerald, she gasped. There was the same long oval face, the same set of the brow, the same well-chiselled mouth. The expression was different though, for she looked young and vulnerable and frightened. Her father had a firmness about his jaw which she lacked in sleep, for all her protestations of independence, and her face was drawn and thin. She was clearly ill.

The room looked dreary after Gerald's sojourn there, and she quickly collected the coffee cup and ashtray, the half-eaten bread and cheese, the pieces of newspaper Gerald had bought while he waited for the prescriptions. June was her guest and she must make her comfortable. She found two warm blankets, and removed the rug and coat. The sheets too should be changed as soon as she had a chance, for Robert had slept there last and she had left the bed made up just in case.

But as she covered her with a fresh blanket and tidied the covers, June stirred and opened her eyes. Here at last was the moment they had both awaited, and both dreaded, face to face, the two women left in Gerald's life. As she struggled to maintain her composure and smile in friendliness, Patricia found she was shaking. The self-control she exercised in business found no place in her private life.

June struggled to sit up. "I'm sorry," she said. "I don't know why I'm here." She put her hand to her forehead and swayed, and lay back on the pillow again. "I must go. Now."

"Oh, June, I'm glad you're here. Your father was right to bring you. You are obviously ill and need someone to look after you."

June lay back on the pillow, her eyes closed. Tentatively, gently, Patricia put a hand on her forehead, and was shocked at the fever she felt there. Quickly she removed the covers she had just put on the bed.

"I'd like to take your temperature," she said, and hurried to the bathroom to find the thermometer. "Darling," she called to Gerald, "Can you tell me what the doctor said, and what all the medicine is for." Then she hurried back to her patient, who accepted the thermometer under her tongue without protest, as though it was too much trouble to object any more.

Gerald showed her the doctor's written instructions, and Patricia settled down to nurse the stranger in her home as best she could, relying on common sense and some memory of a first aid course taken many years ago.

"We must get your temperature down," she told June for she was sure that 104o was far too high, and since June made no protest, she stripped the covers off and prepared to rub her down with cold water. As she stroked her arms and legs, she looked compassionately at this young girl who lay unprotesting in a stranger's hands, her belly swollen with a kicking child. The thin cloth of her nylon slip was stretched tight and Patricia could see the movements of this unborn life within.

What could it be like to carry a new life inside your womb? How was it that she, Patricia, had never had a child while June was to have one before her life had really begun? It was strange indeed, for often she had thought she would like to have a baby, yet she had never been able to face the ties this would entail, the other ties, not so much the baby itself as the need, as it seemed to her, for a husband and marriage and all the trappings of an ordinary life. Yet here was June, young, inexperienced, without a plan for a vocation or a career, setting out almost deliberately to begin her life with a millstone around her neck. Surely in this day and age one did not have to have a baby unless one really wanted it. Did one?

Patricia managed to reduce the fever by two degrees, and then she fetched a nightdress and helped June into it. Gerald came and helped her out of bed, and held her while Patricia changed the sheets and made the bed comfortable.

"Why are you doing this?" asked June as she lay back once more, apparently more tranquil. "You are being very kind to me."

Patricia laughed a little in embarrassment. "I'd be failing as a human being if I didn't," she said. "Now I'm going to make us something to eat." And she hurried out of the room.

But June could not eat, just managed to swallow her medicine and half a glass of orange juice before she fell asleep once more.

It seemed wrong somehow to leave her alone in the house for long, and so they planned the next few days together, trying to sort out who could spare time from the office when. By the end of the week she would be fine, but in the meantime they were worried. Flu was one thing – everyone had it once in a while. But what did it mean to have flu while pregnant? They neither of them had any idea, and Gerald had not dared to ask the doctor that day. Besides, it looked like a nasty attack with a temperature that high. It was reassuring that the doctor was to return the next day, but on the other hand, it was even more worrying, for did that mean that he too was concerned? The futility of such speculation was obvious, and all they could do was ask the doctor next day for more information.

But June was not better by the end of the week. If anything, it seemed to both of them she was worse. They dared not leave her alone during the day, yet neither of them could spare much more time from the office, nor did they know much about nursing. Gerald would stand by his daughter's bed, gazing at the tightness of the pale skin drawn across her cheekbones, the darkness of the grey shadows encircling her eyes, feeling utterly helpless. Patricia found she was afraid of this unknown young woman, and after that first evening seemed to know less and less about what she could possibly do to help her. She did not like to be left alone with her, for she felt a strange dread, as though in some way she, Patricia, for all her good will, only made June worse.

Dr Forster did not think that hospitalisation even entered the question, there were far too many people with far greater needs waiting for a bed. It was true her strength was low, and she was suffering a severe attack of influenza, probably a new viral strain, nothing one could do about that except wait. Secondary infections had been taken care of by his prompt treatment with drugs, she would be much better in a couple of days, and could perfectly well be left alone for a few hours. Viral infections were not welcome in any hospital, nor in private nursing homes, certainly not when the patient was in no danger. What they should be concerned about was who was going to look after her when she had her baby. It was too late to arrange for a hospital bed, he certainly had no hopes of managing that at this short notice. They might find a place in a private nursing home if they were prepared to pay, otherwise he could make arrangements with the local midwife, if they wished him to, but then someone would certainly be needed to look after her for a few days,

When the doctor left, Patricia and Gerald felt like a couple of school-children let out of the head's study after a whipping.

Dr Foster was younger than both of them, yet he had contrived to make them feel inadequate and incompetent as no other person in any other field possibly could. If their fears led them to exaggeration, it still seemed unjust for him to chastise them. Were his patients to make their own diagnosis before consulting him?

Patricia spoke to her own doctor, and she agreed to take June on as a private patient. She recommended a private nurse for a few days, to relieve their anxieties, and promised to take care of her pre-natal needs immediately.

40

June

Why do I keep on finding myself in the same embarrassing situation? June asked herself as she lay in bed a week later. Over and over again, things get too much for me and I get carted off to somebody's house like a toy doll, to be tucked up in a toy cradle until they get tired of the game. What's the matter with me? Can't I stand on my own two feet?

Well, no, she couldn't. She had tried standing without help that morning, and had felt very dizzy, and had been glad to have even Pat's arm around her on the way to the bathroom. Talk about undignified. Being with Ruth had been better, at least she liked the woman. Or even Aunt Ena, you could put up with her because she was so horrible you didn't feel guilty about disliking her. But Pat of all people ... what had she done to deserve being put in the clutches of a woman she hated?

Pat's gentleness was just a front, a show for Dad's benefit, June realized that. The woman was jealous only she couldn't show it, the two-faced bitch. That had to be it. A woman like that couldn't possibly have any real decent feelings. You only had to look at her, flashy and expensive, with what George called "bedroom eyes", no man would be safe within half a mile. Just the sort of woman I'd have disliked on sight, even if I hadn't known how she'd carried on with Dad.

If only she weren't so solicitous. That makes it hard. I mean, look at the way she keeps bringing me things like grapes and icecream and magazines, and that book about Natural Childbirth. It's as though she really knows what you want – that book is super. I just wish it hadn't come from her.

The appalling thought that perhaps she was mistaken about Pat, perhaps the woman was really genuine flashed across her mind. But she was feeling weak enough without the added burden of that sort of guilt, and a sudden revulsion against herself made her bury her head in the pillow and groan aloud.

Patricia came hurrying in. She had just returned from the office, and a visit to the hairdresser's. June's hackles rose immediately at the sight of this immaculately groomed woman with the careful make-up, scrupulously manicured nails, expensive trouser suit and discreet jewellery. June herself, however hard she tried, however much leisure she might one day have, would never look like that – her skin, her hair, her limbs were just not made that way. It was not fair, this contrast between the two women. Pat was ripe, voluptuous, glamorous, like a seventeenth-century French courtesan, you could imagine kings and princes throwing their crowns at her feet; while she, June, looked like what she was, a worn-out shop girl with incipient varicose veins, awaiting the birth of her bastard.

"Are you all right?" Patricia asked, bending anxiously over the bed.

June moved onto her back and opened her eyes. She could smell that expensive perfume again, it made her want to puke. But with Pat bending so close, she could see the lines and wrinkles on that oh, so beautiful face, she wouldn't have it for ever. "Yeah, sure. I'm fine," she said, closing her eyes again.

"I'll get a cup of tea," said Patricia with a sigh. "I expect you could do with one. And I thought you might like this."

She dropped a paper parcel on the bed and went out.

Another present. What could it be this time? In spite of herself, June felt a childish excitement at being given an unexpected gift, and her curiosity would not allow her to leave the parcel unopened. Languidly she pulled herself up onto her elbows and drew it towards her. Harrods, yet. It must be nice to be rich.

Damn the woman. Inside in tissue paper lay a baby's nightdress in white lawn, trimmed with broderie anglaise, and a white fluffy woollen jacket and bonnet and tiny bootees. June wanted to cry. Damn the woman, damn her. That was the most wonderful present anyone had ever given her, and oh heavens above, Lord forgive her, it was the very first thing she had for her baby.

What could she have been thinking of, waiting so long to prepare for her baby? Pretending it wasn't going to happen after all? Behaving like a fool certainly. An overgrown child. She had been playing at being brave, at being an adult, while all the time another life had been growing inside her, another human being who would be totally dependent upon her. And she couldn't even look after herself.

Oh, God, she said aloud, I feel so ashamed.

I know I'm not well, but who knows, that might be my fault too. I've behaved like a bloody idiot. And I haven't much time. I'm going to start right now, planning properly. Where's that *Mother and Baby* magazine? I'm sure I saw a list of what you need for a baby.

When Patricia brought the tea, she said, "Pat, that was the nicest present anyone ever gave me." She watched the woman's slow surprised smile, and thought, She looks tired too, as though she worries about things. Maybe it's me that's the bitch.

41

Gerald

House prices had got completely out of hand. Every day Gerald studied the real estate advertisements in the *Daily Telegraph*, and in the *Sunday Times* on Sunday, but every time he found a likely property the price was so outrageous, he never got beyond the stage of dreaming. Occasionally he would read aloud the description of a particularly exciting property, but Patricia never said the right things so he had not yet even suggested they might go and look around.

Things couldn't go on like this. This flat might be just right for one person, though it wasn't what he would have chosen, but it certainly wouldn't do for the two of them. Let alone three. Obviously, no man likes to live in someone else's home, and while Tricia did her best to make him feel welcome and part of the place, he always felt like a visitor. He had put up some shelves in the bathroom and painted the kitchen, imagining this might make the place feel more like his own, but really he was doing it as payment for being allowed to stay.

But the more difficult part was that he didn't like this way of life at all. You might even say he hated it, if you wanted to be dramatic. Of course that was an exaggeration. Nevertheless, he preferred living in the country. He liked to be able to lean out of the window in the morning, and breathe deep of the smell of grass and roses, and the strong fungusy tang from the woods up the hill. He liked to be able to stroll out of the house on a Sunday morning, in slacks and sports jacket and open-necked shirt, casually greet his neighbours who were working in their gardens or on their cars or just standing there enjoying the sunshine and the freshness and peace. He might simply wander up the hill and into the woods; or he might get in the car and drive for all of five minutes to Haydon's Heath, and walk through the woods there and climb the hill to the observation point and dream of a meaning that made sense of life and gave it value.

There was Hampstead Heath, of course, but it just was not good enough. It almost made things worse, for it was sooty and dusty and full of people, an oasis for Londoners in their desert of brick and cement, but for him a dreary, miserable apology for the real thing.

Before moving to London, he used to walk at least five miles every Sunday, usually alone for Robert had stopped accompanying him, to go off with friends, and he had assumed without asking that the females wouldn't come. He hadn't wanted Madge along anyway, so he hadn't asked June for fear of starting something. These days it was different, he wasn't trying to escape, and he would like Tricia to walk with him. But the exercise this had given him had become a necessary part of life and he felt flabby now.

His soul had been fed by a continuous intimacy with the untamed countryside, the changing seasons: the violets and primroses in spring and the bursting of buds and the songs of birds; the rich green of summer and the smell of heat and the dusty pine-needles and the buzzing of insects; the glowing glory of the autumn leaves before they fell and the crispness of the cornflake leaves in the frost; and then the growing sense of death when the new year began and still the trees remained motionless and dark, and the undergrowth snapped and crumpled lifelessly under his feet, and he began to feel that this time the earth had really died, there would be no spring this year. A primitive fear began to gnaw at his stomach and he understood that Early Man who prayed to the gods of the earth on whose good will he so utterly depended.

Here in London, the seasons were marked by varying degrees of discomfort. The heat of summer brought with it the smell of tar, one's lungs were filled with exhaust fumes and dust; rain was not refreshing, did not wash the world clean, but seemed rather to make everything dirty and muddy; and frost and snow were merely dangerous, held no beauty in cities for they had to be combated with salt and chemicals that wrecked one's shoes and trousers and made one long for a science-fiction world from which the elements had been excluded for ever.

He worked in the city and enjoyed it. The jostling crowds, the bright lights, the historic buildings were part of the flavour of his business life, his active creative life when he gave to the world all his talents and expended himself to the full. But there had always been an end to this, the journey home in the evening a time of transition and precious for his equilibrium, so that he became another person for that other part of his life, a more personal, self-indulgent part which included walking for miles through woods or over the downs, or lying in the bath for an hour on Saturday afternoon, or chatting to neighbours over a drink in the pub. Now these things were gone.

It was true that this half of his life had been less than satisfying and he had filled his time with good works in the community. Yet that had been more useful and relaxing than this stultifying life he had today, with nothing to do but lie around in a heap. Relaxation was just not as relaxing any more.

Was this whole thing a mistake? He had realized long ago that if Madge had not become hysterical and lashed out at him, he would never have left her in the end. Through cowardice mainly, but also because of his commitment. The consequences of his act had been so devastating, was there perhaps still a chance he might be able to salvage things by starting again where he had left off?

But what things? What could he salvage after all? Would a renunciation now bring Madge back to life? And what could it achieve except make everyone miserable?

Could it be perhaps that his misery these days, even living here with Tricia, was the result of a bad conscience? Of course it could. Objectively, he did not like living in this flat which was not his, in London and not in the country, surrounded by arty stuff he did not understand. But it could also be that his reaction to this new life was coloured by a sense of guilt. For how could be enjoy this new life while his daughter awaited her bastard, his son bummed around with hippies, and his wife lay rotting in the grave?

How far was he to blame? He had to answer this question, for otherwise he would never learn to live again. He could feel his life force ebbing away, each day he grew perceptibly older and wisdom seemed further off than ever. Her life had ended. Why should his not too? Had he the right to be happy now that she was dead? On the other hand, what good would it be to her if he was not happy now? The price had been paid – should he not justify her sacrifice?

Sheer romanticism, ridiculous melodrama! The important thing was, to be cold and brutal about it, how far was he responsible for Madge's death? Would she have died then anyway, or did his leaving her make her so unhappy she had given up living? Was that even possible anyway? Could you really die just because you were unhappy and tired of life? Surely the inmates of concentration camps must have felt like dying, yet they hung on unbelievably. Could it have been that they still nurtured some shreds of hope? Had Madge lost all hope then, despaired totally?

And if this were so, and she had died of despair, which he was not ready to grant, but if she had, was it entirely his fault? Did you take on total responsibility for another human being when you married? How appalling if this were so, for no one ever thinks of that. He at least had not thought of that, the other human being he was marrying he had thought was able to stand alone without his help. He had not intended to become the tree for the clinging vine, the prop for the parasite. He could argue that in this he too had been betrayed.

These questions and this terrible guilt were a result of her own weakness as well as his own. If she had not been so weak, had not collapsed as soon as things became difficult, they might both have been able to find a meaning to their lives. Her weakness could not surely be laid at his door. His mistake had been not to recognise it.

Poor Madge, she must have felt betrayed by all the men in her life - her father, her husband, her son. That was it, of course, she had felt completely worthless for a woman's value is measured by her men. Which was why Women's Lib would fail, for women needed men to give them value. Tricia needed him. And June needed him, for she had no lover now.

He would never be able to work out completely where his responsibilities lay, but the living had better claim than the dead, that was certain. In all this he had scarcely thought of Tricia, yet he knew she loved him. Could he say he no longer loved her? No. And her claims on him were stronger than any other's: he needed her too. The complexity of the thought was daunting, but he felt the truth lay inside this knot: one cannot be do better than one's best; one has to do what one can do. And so on. He had done everything he could for the best. He must leave the past now in the past, and concentrate on the present, and the future.

Which brought him back to houses. And June and her baby.

And Robert.

It was time to see about Robert. He had failed there too, he could see that now, the boy was too young to make sensible choices, too young to cope on his own. Reality was pretty grim for a sensitive lad like that, it was no wonder he had sought to escape in drugs. But I'll have to go and find him, Gerald thought resolutely. I owe him that at least. I must give him a chance to come back here with us, or show me some other way I can help him make a better start in life.

It was also time to make arrangements for June and her baby. Enough of her talk of independence. She needed a man to take care of her, and you didn't just turn your back on your own daughter when she was in a fix. The obvious thing would be to get a house for all of them somewhere in the home counties, and June could house-keep and look after her baby while he and Tricia went to work. It would be a good life for all of them.

Come on, you fool, pull yourself together, he told himself. Make this life worth all the disasters. Learn from your mistakes. And do not betray Tricia in the same way, by thinking of leaving her. You cannot leave her now, the commitment is made. You decided that a year ago, in the hospital room. It's time to buy her a ring.

42

Patricia

Patricia found herself more and more frustrated and increasingly irritable. But why? Did she not have everything she wanted? Only a year ago, she had thought she would be perfectly happy if only she could have Gerald too. And here he was, living with her, in her flat, just as she had wished. They were happy together too, perhaps not as deliriously joyful as in those first months, that was probably impossible, but in spite of all the heartache in the past year, glad to be together.

So what was wrong? He didn't like living in 'her' home, she knew that. His sense of not belonging had crystallised the day he brought June here. "We need *our* home," he said often enough, and "I'd feel more right if only I had somewhere to potter. I don't have anything to do." So obviously they were going to have to move. That was the crux of the matter.

Not that she really minded leaving this flat after all. It had suited her beautifully at first, but now her life had changed. She had no real objection to moving.

It was the prospect of making a choice that daunted her, as though whatever they chose to do now would be irrevocable, would direct the course of their lives until he retired in how many, fifteen years. Fifteen years! No, that was impossible, you could not promise away the years like that. Yet it was inevitable that at certain times in one's life there is a crossroads, and a choice has to be made.

The problem was that this choice would involve more than just where to live. It might leave her stuck in the same job for the rest of her working life, yet she was not ready to make a change for she did not know what she really wanted to do.

Recently she had found herself developing an aversion to the business world. Lying, cheating, manipulating people, using people for your own ends, these seemed to her necessary attributes for success. No longer was it like a game, a contest of skill like chess in which the quickest mind won. Now she saw her job, and those of all around her, as degrading to the human spirit. Values had been inverted, profit was more important than people, so much more important that thousands, tens of thousands could be put out of work without warning, just to keep the profit and loss figures moving in the desired direction. It was always the older men who got fired too, men in their fifties who would never find another job, and spinster ladies with the menopause and no resources. Friendship was no more. Trust had melted in the heat of realism, alliances were formed on the basis of fear and hate, dissolved instantly a more profitable association came in sight.

So why should this upset her? Business was just a bunch of human beings and human beings found it hard to be nice to each other. Just human nature, that was all, man was such a short way out of the jungle, he hadn't learned how to cope with his instinct to kill.

Don't take it all so seriously, she told herself. OK, so you can't trust anybody, but you can see what they are all up to, can't you? It doesn't take a genius to see that Barry is after your job, and Graham is empire-building, and Leo is bound and determined to break away with your best accounts. So what's so terrible? You know what to do. It's only a game.

But now she had begun to think that Vincent was right – she was wasting her life. What was it he said? That she was manipulating people, not for power, not even for money, but just for fun. Dear God, perhaps she was, but the fun had gone.

If only Vin had not gone back to Africa. If only he and

Gerald had liked each other better.

She had tried to explain to Gerald one evening her sense of gloom about where her life was heading, her inability to choose because she could not tell how to judge, trying to explain in order to apologise for her lack of response to his plans and dreams.

"You're just asking what is the meaning of life," he said. "The only answer is, of course, that it is for living."

She controlled a violent urge to scream. "But what does that *mean*?"

"There is no one answer," he told her. "That is why there are so many religions."

"And what if religion holds no meaning?"

"You're just asking questions which have no answer. It's a waste of time, and just makes you miserable."

"God, Gerald, don't you ever feel a need to question?"

"When I was a teenager," he said indulgently, "I asked 'Who am I?' I suppose everyone does. And I thought I was unique."

"And the question never arises again?" Were they so far apart?

Later he said he was sorry, he hadn't been feeling very friendly.

"But I do have profound thoughts too," he said. "You never give me credit for profound thoughts, but I do have them."

The terrible realization came to her that he was not after all the man she had thought. And yet she loved him. Strange that. Even though she knew he was not strong, as she had thought, was dull, pedantic, pedestrian, took ten weeks to read a book as though there weren't thousands upon thousands to read and digest and only a short lifetime, and yet thought he knew the answers to the problems of existence, just like almost every middle-aged middle-class Englishman – oh, these things made her rage inside at his stupidity, and made her wonder why, of all the men in the world, after waiting all those years, had she ended up with him. Yet still she loved him.

Projection perhaps, as psychologists would say, she had projected upon him her image of an ideal man. But there was more. Definitely more, for he had awakened such liberated sexuality in her, she had experienced such heights of physical ecstasy never before known with any other man, how could she not believe that he was at last the one for whom she had waited? Furthermore, when she met Gerald, she had just achieved another major goal, for she was given a directorship and met Gerald in the same week. So she came to believe that the magical synchronicity of these important events proved their rightness, not that she had imposed upon them from the outside a meaning they did not necessarily have.

Poor dear Gerald. She had expected so much of him, how could he not fail her in some way? But he was still Gerald. What really mattered was the fundamental structure, and for all his weaknesses, he was fundamentally a good man. Honest, true. There was an amazing dearth of adjectives, she realized, to describe those who chose the Good path. For she really did believe that there must be Good and Evil, for how else is it possible to explain the horror of men's inhumanity to other men. And she believed that somewhere in the middle of life, sometimes earlier, one must choose which path to follow. A cross roads is found, and the choice of Good and Evil then determines the rest of one's life. She knew she could love him because he was good.

Love was a life-giving force. At those moments in her life when she had needed love to carry on living, there had always been someone willing to offer the consolation another human being can give: her grandmother when Linda died and her mother was distraught with grief; Ellen after that terrible time with Martin; Vin the year she escaped from the world to try to find herself. If the power for good in these people could be multiplied several million-fold, then there would be hope. But the very nature of this power was its individuality, its lack of cohesion. No one who truly loved his fellow man could impose upon him any system of belief or conduct. Which left her exactly where she had started, with only the love of rare individuals to nourish her faith in human kind.

It had taken her a long time to question the values she had lived by, and she was not even sure why she no longer found satisfaction in her life. She had all she had ever wanted – a position of prestige, a high income, her own home and car, beautiful things, pots, pictures, music, expensive clothes, the best of food and wine. She had travelled. And now she was living with the man she loved, and he loved her.

Was it her age perhaps? A case of pre-menopausal blues? Or just the realization she had reached a crossroads? For living with another human being made life, not twice as complicated, but infinitely more so.

Could it be that she wanted a ring, marriage, a piece of paper, a signed contract? No. The truth was she did not want that at all. A ring, yes, she'd wear a ring as symbol to the world that she and he were united and one in love. But she would not submit to a legal tie. She had thought she would, but her soul rebelled. How then would she remain free? How could she remain an independent person if she allowed the law of England to tie her to another? While they remained together out of choice, out of love, that was good.

But why argue in her mind of matters that were not in question? Gerald had not mentioned marriage, had certainly not put any pressure on her. Was she then so perverse she wished he would?

She had thought this was what she wanted, to be sure. She could remember sitting in her bedroom, studying herself in the curved triple mirror, longing to change her status as the Other Woman into the Wife. But that was undoubtedly because as the Other Woman, she only had a position in relation to others, someone else outside herself called the tune.

She could not see how being the Wife altered the situation after all. In externals, obviously, but how did it change the fact that her status then would still remain a function of Gerald?

Yes, yes, the eternal argument of Women's Lib. Was it not the same for Gerald after all? And perhaps he had not talked of marriage, not since the funeral, simply because he could see that he would be exchanging one limitation for another. Yet this did not ring true. His silence was more likely a result of his struggle with his conscience. So it would be a shock to him when he did ask the question. He would not expect her to say 'No'.

She had never said to Gerald, "I live through you. I cannot live without you." That would be absurd. She would be ashamed to so far renounce her own self that she gave him responsibility for her life too.

How then did one resolve the problem of living together in equality? This must be the most important and the most difficult task she had ever undertaken. Here she was at thirty six, it was high time she evolved a workable and sane philosophy of life, and no philosophy could have any value if it did not allow two intelligent people who loved each other to live together in harmony and peace. If they could not manage it, what hope was there left for mankind? They might as well drop the bomb and have done with it.

43

An Autumn Picnic

It was October 1971, and the most glorious autumn many could remember. The sun shone, the skies were blue, the morning frosts melted swiftly and the trees flaunted leaves the colour of a costermonger's fruit barrow – red, yellow, orange, brown, purple, gold.

Gerald could restrain his impatience no longer. June was much better now, he said, and they all needed some country air, it was a gorgeous day, so they would go for a picnic in the woods. Since neither woman had any alternative suggestion, he would drive them all to Haydon's Ball in Surrey.

A sense of excitement, of festivity caught them all. Each one was filled with memories of child-hood picnics, and the sunshine and blue sky and the glowing autumn colours made them smile in friendship at each other, and laugh at the smallest joke as they drove out of London into the countryside.

It's a long time since I've done anything as simple as this, thought Patricia, and felt proud of her sophisticated acceptance. Walks in the country for her had usually been merely a charming prelude to wine and a three-course dinner at some food-guide recommended hostelry. It was not that she did not like the country, though flies, wasps, cows and mud inspired only loathing. She could remember enjoying picnics as a girl, and cycling for miles through Surrey and Kent. It was just that woods and fields were not part of her life any more. Perhaps she had missed something in her pursuit of stimulation among the bright city people. Perhaps the bucolic life had charm after all.

June felt like a young girl again. Here she was driving to her favourite spot with her father, and it did not even matter that Pat was there instead of Mother. Not very much. She and Bobby had played tracking on Haydon's Heath year after year, crawling through the tall bracken, scratching their bare arms and legs, but both of them able to move for miles without being seen, while Dad tried to find them before the sun went down. She would have loved to have tried it now, she was sure she could still move through the bracken without making it sway and give her away – well, if she were her usual slim self that is. And when they drove up the dirt track, she caught her father's eye and laughed in excitement, for it was all so familiar, they both knew it so well. And there was the old beech beneath which they always parked, and the branch on which she and Bobby used to swing, and the path where they found violets and primroses in spring.

Quickly she climbed out of the car, and stood gazing at the magnificent and ancient beech she had chosen as 'hers' many years ago, revelled in the golden glory of its leaves and the crisp carpet already beneath it, the green grass beyond dappled with sunlight and the secret darkness of the violet path. She realized dimly, with just a tiny piece of her mind for she was busy, that it was a long time since she had felt like this. She was happy.

Gerald and Patricia collected the picnic bags and the rug and began to climb the hill. June found to her dismay that her illness had sapped her strength, nor was she as agile as in her memories and had to rely on her father's assistance to reach the top.

The smell of pine needles and hot sand and the buzzing of insects filled Gerald's head, and he realized how much tension had been building inside him. He would need a great many more than this one day. Having companions was unusual too, and restricting at first. He was accustomed to striding along very fast, unencumbered by bags and rugs, with no demands on him but his own senses aquiver with fresh sights and sounds and smells. Then he would let his mind focus where it would, and found the hypnotic effect of his walking as relaxing as a yoga asana, and his mind clear ready for the refreshment of meditation. Today he could not indulge at once in total enjoyment of the scene, found that he had reached the top of the hill without having yet deeply felt the meaning of where he was, so preoccupied had he been with helping his daughter. But once at the observation point and gazing at the panorama of the downs, he found that these two women whom he loved beyond all others added a new dimension to his pleasure, that his gladness was increased by theirs. Patricia was delighted with the beauty of the view she had never seen before, the gentle rolling countryside, mostly wooded, glowing now in colours rarely seen in an English autumn. June was enraptured by everything she saw, and remembered her childhood as happy because she used to picnic here. Gerald knew he was right. It would work.

When they had settled on the far side of the hill, away from the many people who had also chosen this spot for their weekend outing, away from the sandpits echoing with shouting children, under a solitary birch on a carpet of moss, he told them his idea.

He would buy a house somewhere in the country, perhaps somewhere near here (though for obvious reasons not in Godbridge), he and Tricia would continue as before, working in London, and June would look after the house for them – be their housekeeper, so to speak, and at the same time make a proper home for her baby. For his grandchild.

They sat and gazed at the flowing bracken, and ate the cold chicken and French bread and fruit, and drank the wine.

"Why not indeed?" said Patricia. "Sounds a good idea."

Afterwards, June lay in the sunshine while Patricia went for a walk with Gerald. She told him how she had been looking for a new reason for doing things, that her present job no longer satisfied her, and how perhaps this idea of his was really the answer after all. It would give her a new motive, something beyond her very personal and selfish ambition. But she did not like the idea of commuting every day. It was not as though they would always be able to travel together, and she was appalled at the thought of spending two or three hours of every day struggling with crowds just to get from one place to another and back again. As far as she could see, it would be the same whether she took the car or the train. She would be exhausted after a very short time, to no useful purpose.

However, this was not a problem. She had already decided she was dissatisfied, had simply been looking around for alternatives. He should not think he was forcing her into a difficult decision. It was rather that he was giving her a reason to make a change that in any case she thought necessary. She would find something else to do, nearer their new home. Perhaps she would open a shop. In fact, the answer had just come to her in a flash: she would open a shop that sold pottery, she knew lots of potters she could call on, and really super kitchen ware, and new designs in furniture such as she saw in Italy last year. She could get really excited about this as a new project. She would love it.

Gerald was somewhat taken aback at the vehemence with which she was rejecting the job in which he had always known her. He had no wish to change anything except where they lived. He certainly did not want to feel responsible for her having relinquished a position where she was outstandingly successful. She would be bored without her kind of people to talk to. What on earth had got into her head that she should leave the agency?

And Patricia reiterated her wish to be no longer a part of the cynicism and downright dishonesty which seemed to her to have become necessary to a business life.

He accepted her view, for he too had been distressed by the inhumanity involved these days in keeping a business going. Many men he knew had lost their jobs – it was as though there was an epidemic. And he had certainly noticed that in many companies people did not matter much any more. His own company was still run on old-fashioned lines, where a gentleman's word was his bond and loyalty was repaid handsomely. But he did understand. He hoped she would think again before making such a drastic move, but he would be with her whatever she chose. If quitting and going into business for herself was what she wanted, then so did he.

44

June

The sun was very warm. Somehow it really did feel as though its rays were full of vitamins and goodness, those sunray lamps people bought might really have value after all. She certainly could feel vitality flowing into her limbs, so that when she moved, it wouldn't be yet, but when she moved, she would no longer need assistance in climbing hills. The weariness of that terrible job, the loneliness of that grubby room, the lethargy that had overwhelmed her with the onslaught of flu, all seemed to be draining away from her, through the rug, through the moss, deep into the earth for ever.

No longer would she be content to float down the stream, carried hither and thither by any wind that chose to blow. She remembered her childhood book of *Thumbelina*, and a brightly coloured picture of the tiny girl being carried away down the river on a lily leaf. A pretty feeble sort of person she was too, until she decided to care for the swallow, hardly deserved to be carried off to fairyland and be married to the King of the Flowers. Not that it would last.

So far, she had not made a very good job of standing on her own two feet either. Even if you discounted having flu, which after all was not her fault, and of course, it was sheer coincidence that Dad chose to come by at the crucial moment, when she couldn't defend her independence. Still, now she had lost her place in the Mother and Baby Home, Mrs Warren told her when she telephoned last week. It was perfectly reasonable, of course, there were lots of girls in need of assistance so if her family was prepared to help, then naturally she didn't need to take someone else's place. She couldn't help feeling fed up though, for she really had thought this thing through, and she could have managed on her own. Especially with the money.

The money! Great heavens, she had forgotten all about it till now. She still did not have a bank account, which was quite insane, she would get Dad to sort it out first thing on Monday morning. If she could find the cheque.

What was the matter with her anyway? She didn't seem to be able to keep hold of anything in her head for five minutes. And now Dad and his Lady Love were making plans for her without so much as a by-your-leave. It was a bit much.

Still, what was the difference? Let them get on with it. It made no odds. She would do as she pleased in the end, once she had had her baby. It was only that she did not know what she pleased.

Except that that was disgracefully selfish. Here was Dad trying to set up a nice home for her and his grandchild, and she was letting him go ahead without a word. She couldn't do that and then just walk out, as soon as she felt fit again. Could she? He obviously had a big thing about having a grandson. Imagine him being a grandfather ... he'd probably spoil the child silly. Yet he'd be good for him, I know. Or her. I must stop thinking it will be a boy, that's only prejudice.

I wonder if his idea is the best one after all, she said aloud, and sat up, hugged her knees as best she could. If I take a job, I'll have to leave my baby with someone else all day, and I certainly don't want that. If I take a job as a domestic, it will still be in someone else's house. Why not my own father's? Why ever not? He would even be a good influence for my child as he grows up, take the place of the father he hasn't got. It's the most marvellous chance I could get.

But then she lay down again, and thought about Pat. There

was the rub, the fly in the ointment. Disgusting expression. Why did everything nice have to be spoilt by something horrid? Not that Pat was quite as bad as she had once feared, she had to grant her that, she was certainly more human, not entirely a two-faced Jezebel. Still, there were limits. Just because she didn't exactly hate her any more, not to the extent of actually wanting to do her harm anyway, that didn't mean she wanted to live with her. George or Pat? She'd be better off with George! At least he didn't make her feel at a disadvantage.

Well, it was Dad's idea, she didn't have to decide anything yet. She'd like to please him though, if she could. It would obviously please him if she stayed with them until she had her baby, and as Mrs Warren said, if they'll have you, you stay put. She might as well do that anyway. Pat didn't seem to mind at all. Even if she did. It would serve her right. But in fact, she seemed to enjoy the idea of someone having a baby.

Someone *else*, that was the operative word. She wanted to have a baby vicariously. It was funny, if you thought about it, that she'd never had a baby, and she must be forty at least. Probably past it now, so she wants to enjoy mine. She'll be lucky.

The cracking of twigs made her sit up again and she saw them coming up the slope towards her. For a brief instant, Pat appeared almost vulnerable, from a distance small and careful somehow as she walked beside her father's tall bulk. But then all June could see was the Pat she knew, stunningly attractive, overwhelming in her competence, and her heart remained closed.

"Shall we do it, June?" asked Patricia gaily. "Would you like us all to live together?"

"Sure. Why not?" June answered indifferently, not looking at Pat at all.

Patricia turned to Gerald triumphantly, as though they had discussed how June would feel about the situation, and the woman had known the answer.

Gerald drew back so that he was looking down at these two women with pride. "I hope you realize," he said, "that I am the cleverest man you know. And that is, without doubt, the best idea I ever had."

45

Gerald

One thing was settled at least. He had given a list of requirements to all the reputable estate agents he could find in Surrey, Hants and Bucks, and already the lists were coming in. One or two places looked really promising. Not that there was any real rush, they could hang on until the right place came along.

June was blooming now, just as she should have been all along. It was a good thing he had rescued her. At last she looked like his daughter, more beautiful in fact than she ever had, with a fresh glowing complexion and her hair gleaming and lustrous. Having a baby was doing her looks the world of good. But still, there was not so much time left now, six or seven weeks by all accounts, and she was of course heavy and easily tired. So moving could wait a bit. They would just look.

November now, high time he went and found Robert. At least he could give the boy a chance to come back if he wished. And he must not forget the money to give him too. Best to open an account for him, then it would be there when he wanted it. He'd speak to the bank manager, it wouldn't do to give him the difficulties he'd given poor June. It was amazing how easily one forgot the little practical things which made all the difference.

June had last heard of Robert down in St Ives, so that was where he must go. Perhaps they could all make a weekend trip of it. But June said she certainly didn't want to see her grandfather at the moment, and what else would she go to Cornwall for? And Tricia seemed to think this was something he could handle best on his own. So the following Saturday he drove down alone.

Gerald had expected great difficulties in finding Robert once in St Ives, for not only did he not have any idea where to look, the boy might not be there anyway. But some higher power must have meant them to meet, he felt, for there was his son sitting on the wall overlooking the harbour, for all the world as though he was waiting for his father to arrive.

Distance both in time and space lent a certain objectivity, Gerald had to admit, though this was not what he would have wished, his son had a definite charm. At least, seen from a couple of hundred yards away he had charm, leaning there upon the wall unaware he was being observed, laughing gaily with a dark, long-haired girl and two distinctly scruffy young men. He was scruffy too, no doubt about that, but Gerald had to admit he exuded a certain virile attraction. He was lean and bony and very sun-tanned, his hair was long, he had grown a beard, was dressed in an ugly old army jacket and grubby jeans and thong sandals, yet he exuded a vitality, a zest for living. Gerald realized then that this was what had been missing for him: no one he knew took pleasure in living, except perhaps Tricia when she was not worrying about him.

There was pleasure in watching his son. He was in no hurry to approach him, for what would he say? The spell would be broken and they would be face to face. But then he had no choice, for they began to move away, and Gerald had to run towards them calling, "Robert, hey Robert!"

The whole group stopped and turned to face the disruptive noise.

"Man, this is some awakening," Robert muttered, and he did not look pleased.

"Hey, Rob, old son," said Gerald, panting somewhat. "Wait for me. How've you been?"

"Greetings, oh venerable ancestor," said Robert mockingly, for the benefit of his companions. They all laughed.

"Dig that crazy curly grey hair," giggled the girl. "Lover, if the old man is your true ancestor, I see where you get your remarkable powers of penetration. He just sends me wild." She sidled provocatively up to Gerald, but both hands on his shoulders, and offered in the most sultry voice she could managed, "Man, won't you dig me now?" Then she collapsed in a convulsion of laughter, in which she was joined by the two unknown young men. "Crazy, man, crazy," said one of them, digging deep into his repertoire of repartee.

"Cool it, Kitten," said Robert. He looked embarrassed. "What are you doing here, Dad?"

"I came to see you. Alone."

"Sure thing, Grandpa," said the other bearded youth. "We will melt into the earth like the snows of springtime. Hey, you cats, let's quit this scene."

"Crazy."

They skipped back to the harbour once more and along the wharf, punching each other and shouting with laughter among the lobster pots and fishermen's nets.

"If that's the sort of friends you hang around with," said Gerald angrily, "you'd be better off coming back with me right now."

"Oh, come off it, Dad. We haven't seen each other for a year. Can't you think of something new to say?"

Gerald sighed, and then shivered as a gust of icy wind caught him. "Isn't there anywhere we can talk in the warm?"

Robert took him to a small cafe just off the harbour and Gerald bought tea and saffron cake, and tried to explain to his son why he had come in search of him. Robert, it appeared, had been picking cabbages to make enough to live on, and had moved around with various groups of young people, sleeping mostly on the beaches which was great while the weather held. The police were tough in the summer time, and the locals were even worse – they thought that long-haired unwashed youths would ruin the tourist trade – but when the season was over, they were more or less left alone. They didn't plan to stay much longer, he and the girl. Some were setting up real communities and trying to live in true brotherhood, but the two of them were not ready for that. They probably never would be, no one had ever seen brotherly love last anywhere at any time in history.

"Why don't you come back to London with me?" urged Gerald. "You could make a new life there, try again, live with us while you study or something."

"Never change, do you, Dad? Same old arguments. I don't want to study. It's a waste of time trying to learn anything from dried up old people and dried up old books with nothing in them about what matters in the world today."

"What do you want then?"

"To destroy this corrupt society, break it down until there is nothing but rubble. Then build a new world with our own hands, a world where the smallest of us will have a say in how it runs."

"You don't have to destroy," said Gerald desperately. "You could start building in your own right, right now. You have £3,000 coming to you from your mother's estate. I will arrange for you to have the money now, and you could open your own business or something."

"You will arrange? What's it to you?"

"It's in a trust account for you. I would have to identify you, that's all, if only you want it for something sensible. Just think, three thousand pounds, that's a lot of money."

"Sure," said Robert indifferently. "Maybe I'll buy drugs with it. I could make a fortune with that sort of investment, selling junk. You should appreciate that, big businessman. Thousands of percent profit. You will be proud of your son."

"Oh, my God," groaned Gerald, putting his head in his hands. "Why do you hate me so?"

"Hate you? Do I? Maybe so." He leaned across the table and hissed into his father's ear. "Because you made a murderer of me, that's why."

Gerald's head jerked up, and his eyes were glazed.

"Murderer? What in heaven's name are you talking about? Who have you murdered?"

"You should know, fine upstanding citizen, you were there. Or don't you remember? You don't remember dressing up all in black and kneeling in a church and following a coffin with your head bowed low? Hypocrite! Bloody fucking hypocrite! There isn't any point in talking to you any more, I'm going."

Robert got up and pushed back his chair, but Gerald leapt up and grabbed his shoulder, hard.

"You sit down," he said fiercely. "You don't talk to someone like that and then get up and walk away. Sit down!" Robert sat, and they glowered at each other.

"So that's what's been eating you," Gerald said at last. "But I still don't see how you can feel guilty."

"Jeesus!" cried Robert in anguish. "It was my fault it all started, wasn't it? My bloody goddamn shoes. And I didn't mean it, truly I didn't, Dad. I just wasn't thinking when I put them on the kitchen table. I didn't mean *anything!* My god, I wouldn't hurt anyone, let alone my own mother." He buried his head in his hands in his turn, fighting desperately against the tears which threatened to overwhelm him. That would be the final humiliation.

Gerald was momentarily stunned, shaken to his very depths by the terrible revelation of his son's suffering. He must comfort him, if ever a father could comfort a suffering child, this must be the time.

"Oh, my son," he said gently and put his hand on the young man's shoulder. "You were not to blame in any way. You were not involved. Your shoes on the table were only one more occasion for your mother and me to have a row, they had nothing, truly nothing whatever to do with my leaving. Don't you understand? No one can break up a marriage, only the two people who made it. Your mother and I, we are responsible for what happened. You are not. You cannot be. You, my son, are only a victim."

"Why didn't you tell me this before?"

"Why?" cried Gerald, anguished in his turn. "Because you didn't ask. Because it never occurred to me that you might blame yourself. Don't you see? That must prove you have nothing whatsoever to do with it, for I never for one instant imagined you could possibly think such a thing. It never entered my head."

"I don't know whether I can believe it," said Robert, looking down at his hands. But he found he believed it already, for he had known all along he had never intended anything when he dropped his shoes, even if leaving them on the table was a pretty stupid thing to do. And he suddenly felt light, unreal almost, as though a terrible burden had just been lifted from his shoulders, and now he could leap in the fields, swim the rivers, climb the hills, reach the mountain top.

"Come with me," Gerald said urgently. "Come with me to London. Let's start again. It has been the most dreadful misunderstanding, but surely it need not wreck everything."

"I can't," he said. But the world held great possibilities now.

He had not thought there might be more than artificial excitement, the sort of earth-shaking, sometimes abjectly terrifying thrill you got from pot or taking acid. He had even begun to question why he should stay off the other more potent stuff, because it was obvious LSD was dangerous too, whatever the pundits said, otherwise Jake wouldn't be in hospital right now with brain damage. But crossing the road was dangerous. Why not live a short but exciting life? He had not gone so far yet, for he still had some sort of self-preservation instinct, it seemed. He didn't like the thought of brain damage or handing over control of his body to some foreign substance that would bring him visions, but eventually kill him. It was just that he could not see why not. Until now.

Suddenly it was perfectly clear. He had taken a wrong path, his original idea was obviously the right one. He would travel round the world, living rough, seeing everything. He would find out, feel for himself in his own body what it meant to be a human being, what it meant to be cold, to be hot, to be hungry, thirsty, tired, in the mountains and in the desert, in the forest and on the sea. And then he would write about it, give his knowledge to the world in poetry. Life was good. It was great.

He leapt up from the table and impetuously dragged his father outside, where a rain was blowing in sharp gusts of rain from the sea.

"See that!" he cried, his arms outstretched towards the ocean. "I am going to make it mine! Dad, I'm going round the world, don't try to stop me. The world will belong to me!"

Gerald was dragged back by the irate proprietor to pay the bill, and then they both bounded onto the beach left by the low tide, and in the wind and rain danced together in joy at having found what once was lost.

46

Gerald

Revolutions in the Board Room are usually bloodless. Heads roll, but the ankle-deep carpets show no stain, no victim was ever known to throw a punch at the chairman or knock him down, or even carve his initials in the gleaming mahogany table before being shown the door. Perhaps the thought of a Golden Handshake restrains vengeful impulses within these hushed walls, for the meek inherit a reward worth much humiliation.

Revolutions in the Board Room nevertheless bring in their wake widespread disorder and destruction. So it was in Gerald's company. Poor year-end results and dismal projections for the future resulted in an unprecedented *coup d'etat* in the Main Board Room, to which Gerald and his colleagues reported. The directors on this Board, which controlled the interests of a wide variety of companies of which Gerald's was but one, had for the most part acquired their positions through title (which brought influence in high places) or wealth (which bought influence) or inheritances of vast share holdings (influence being thrust upon them). Many of these men were in their seventies, and few had any practical experience of running a business outside the stock exchange. So it was that the rapidly changing demands of the business world left them fumbling, the bright young nephew of a titled Director was introduced in his uncle's place, and within a month it was ruled that all directors had to retire at sixty five. Not long after, shareholders were surprised to find a large American interest offering to take over what had become a somewhat shaky investment, and the offer was financially so welcome and so far outdistanced any rival British bid, all questions of national interest (now seen as blinkered chauvinism) were put aside. The bid was accepted. Within days the hushed panelled walls of the Main Board Room were bulging with Harvard Business School graduates, all trained in the bloodletting of American companies in Europe.

The bright young nephew was made Chairman of the Board, an American became Managing Director. Gerald's chairman, a man of fifty-five, was fired. An American, Jim Anderson aged thirty seven, took his place.

Gerald naturally expected to be fired too, as did all his colleagues. But his departure was not inevitable, it seemed, he was known to a number of very top men in the new parent company from his visits to Chicago. His stock was very high. If he played his cards right, he could hope for an even more successful future.

He determined to play it cool. The automatic *bonhomie* and good fellowship were overwhelming, so that he feared sometimes he might drown in a a sea of goodwill. And the arrogance, the immediate assumption of knowledge of the most complex aspects of the British market, the aggressive dismissal of production difficulties without discussion, the prompt high-sounding proposition on whatever topic which always proved on closer inspection to be without substance – these infuriated him at first. But it was easier now to be philosophical about the whole thing, now that he had sorted out his private life and regained his children.

These arrogant young men at least believed in something, exuded vitality. He could wait. They would find soon enough that the expertise they said they admired in him gained its fullest value through his years of experience.

Monday, 15th November was to be a Red Letter Day. This was when he was to present his own programme to his new bosses for the first time, not only to Jim Anderson, but also to the Executive Vice-President, Production World-Wide, who was flying in from Chicago specially. And it was Gerald's unbelievable good fortune that he had met this chap, Earl Swevenburger, two years earlier at an international cosmetics conference in New York at which he had even given a short paper. The coincidence was staggering. He could only believe the gods were smiling on him once more.

"Gerry, it's just great to see you," boomed Earl, pumping his hand amidst a swirl of after-shave. "Really. It's been too long. And how's Madge and the kids? Just fine, I know. Jim here has been telling me all about you. Doing a great job, Gerry, a great job."

"You remember Earl from the New York conference, of course," said Jim Anderson as he directed Gerald to a seat opposite the two men at the conference table. "He was just so impressed with your performance. That presentation you gave was just great."

Keep calm, you fool, he couldn't know, Gerald told himself as he silently checked his papers. It looked as though he was going to be the only one at this meeting with his new boss and a man who went straight into the President's office. This could be important. Nor did it appear that he was yet to be asked for his new programme, they obviously had more important things to discuss with him, for already Earl had started talking in detail about the "big numbers" which Gerald knew very well were "bad, very bad, Gerry", and against which he had been struggling for months.

"Gerry, I just know that you were not responsible for this crappy picture. I guess you were fighting a waterfall."

Chap seemed to know what he was talking about. Better

listen carefully. Sounds like my big opportunity.

"We know we can count on you, Gerry, to strip out the soft spots in your operation. Going through your numbers, it sure looks like the labour element of your Cost to Door is right off. That labour number is rough, Gerry. Sales per head is the key, and it's wrong. As I said to Jim on the pipe the other day, we're just gonna have to take a great slug out of that headcount."

I should have guessed. Talk about an innocent abroad. It's obvious they want to cut down on some of my projects, maybe get rid of some of my people, so they sweet-talk me first. Christ, what a life.

"Gerry, I know it'll hurt. Hurt right here. But I've got so much faith in you to do what you know is right. And this has got to be right. And because I know you will see it our way, I have already agreed with Jim here that we'll do it right away. Like Friday.

"Gerry, I want to have you get the letters out tomorrow, effective Friday. And do it personally, Gerry. It gets it in the right position, if you can do these things personally. A letter from you to each of them, tell them why it had to happen, say you're sorry and wish them all the best, all the very best for the future. We'll have to talk the details to make sure you agree with every step we make. Looks like an overall cut of around sixty percent.

"Gerry, I've been making a few notes, and I got a list here from Milt, who you know has been studying your side of the operation, and ..."

Sixty percent. That was more than half his people. Six out of every ten – they couldn't do that. Some of the men had been with the company thirty or forty years, they would never get another job now if they were turfed out on the scrap heap. Good god, there was enough unemployment without their adding to it. But of course, they weren't going to do it, were they? They expected him to do the sackings, do their dirty work for them, so that he would get the blame. He would have to tell them, it couldn't be done. As soon as that arrogant fellow stopped that monologue, he'd have to tell him. Sounded as though he had got no one left in the factories at all but the bare minimum on the production line and "enough Quality Control to make it look good". It was unbelievable.

But he *had* forgotten something after all. The unions! That was it, they would never manage to.   get away with it, an all-out strike could cripple them for good. There was hope.

"Looks like we could easily take a strike for a few weeks. Inventory is way up. Don't forget, a strike can save money if you play it in at the right time. That needs a delicate hand, but with your reputation, Gerry, I know you can handle it. Gerry, I feel we should have you take the union boss out for dinner – you'll know who's the right man. Take him somewhere good, and make a deal with him. If you need a sweetener, give him one. I'll sign it, no questions asked. Then we could get you Nationals, TV, the works. I cranked through a few of the key element numbers ..."

What had happened to him that he should have a reputation like that? How could they imagine he could possibly be capable of such chicanery? Were his scruples so much in doubt? Had he not always had an unblemished reputation for fairness and honesty? He had never given a bribe in his life. Should he start now, in order to deceive hundreds of men he had known personally for years? And that 'personally' wasn't phony either. He had worked in the factories, and many of the men were friends of his. That list of names produced by Earl was lying on the table, and just that top page – Affleck, Archer, Barker – these were men who had given nearly all their working lives to the company. The bastards probably put down everyone who might be due for a pension in the next five years.

Earl was still talking. The way these chaps could chunter on was unbelievable. Gerald got up from the table and went and poured himself a gin and tonic from the drinks cabinet though it was only ten in the morning. Both men stared at Gerald as Earl wound up his monologue … "So it's going to be a great opportunity for you to sell them all on Gerry Hunter. Feel free to call me any time. Keep in touch. You're a great guy, Gerrrry, a great guy. We believe in you."

For a few minutes there was silence. Gerald did not return to the table, but walked up and down with the filled glass in his hand, though he did not drink. The two Americans stared at him in astonishment which gradually transformed into indulgent amusement. These old-fashioned guys with their quaint ideas of gentlemanly conduct often took a little while to swallow the harsh facts of business, and this lean greying Englishman was just one more example. Fortunately they could rely on that even more old-fashioned instinct for self-preservation to prevent his making a fool of himself and forcing them to play one of the many trump cards they still kept up their sleeves. Pouring a gin first thing in the morning was a good one. They'd remember that.

He must be absolutely sure what he was doing. That was why he had poured that drink, more to gain time, give him something to do than anything else. Bob Durham, the official union leader, would never accept a bribe, he was certain of that, and if they were stupid enough to try it, he'd blow it to the press. But then he wasn't really the key person. Mac was, and he'd probably take anything that was going, he could shut down all the factories if he carried Transport with him. What about that young upstart Andrews, was his name on the list? Years of practice had given him the ability to read other people's documents at a distance, upside down, and he could see, yes, his name was there. Who could they have left off, for heaven's sake? The lad was only twenty-four, had years of hard work left in him. They probably wanted to get rid of him and his reputation as a firebrand. Good. He wasn't just an honest man, this one was an idealist. He could be relied on to stir up trouble.

"What if I were to tell you that this plan is impossible?" he said quietly, standing by the window, not looking at the two seated men.

"Gerry," interrupted Jim. "There's something I just forgot to tell you, I was so interested in hearing how you are going to sort out these bad, bad problems here. It just clean slipped my mind. I want to have you take a trip States-side, take a good look around our companies over there, get a feel for our kind of operation. And Gerrry, I want to have you take your lovely wife along too. It's real important she should know how much we depend on you, Gerry. Take a coupla weeks, see all over. Make a second honeymoon of it, ha! ha!"

Was there no end? First he was expected to give a bribe, now he was to take one. He had better keep a tight rein on himself or he'd give them both a punch on the nose. He must try to get out of this with his dignity intact. He still had to live with himself.

No, he couldn't save these men. If Big Brother in Chicago had decided, that was that. But he could get his revenge by putting Bob Durham and young Andrews in the picture. They would blow the thing sky high. He'd enjoy reading all about it in the papers.

He drained his glass, walked towards the two men sprawled in their chairs, waiting for him, put the glass on the table. The phrase that came to mind was vaguely familiar, but what the hell?

"You can stuff that phoney crap up your fucking arse," he said, and walked out. That was the first time he had sworn at a boss in his life.

It was strange no longer to have a job, not to belong in this building where he had spent so much of his life. He went round to say goodbye to those of his colleagues still left, and was gratified by their shock and concern, and their sympathy for him and bitter condemnation of the new regime when he told them briefly why he had quit. He telephoned Patricia, who was stunned, then spoke to Bob Durham in the North London factory. Then he cleared his desk of personal things, put the programme he had hoped to present in the wastepaper basket, and told his personal staff he had resigned. Mrs Mac burst into tears. And then he shut his office door for the last time, put on his hat and left. That was that.

He met Patricia for lunch, and they went somewhere very expensive and got very drunk. Perhaps he would join her in her shop venture, they thought, they could go into business together. He might well never find another job, but it didn't matter much after all. They would have to give him a handsome financial settlement, whatever they thought, he would put it into a solicitor's hands that afternoon, and in any case, his investments were pretty sound. He would manage.

The next day he set up a trust fund to be administered by himself and June, for the benefit of her baby. He did not want anyone to suffer because of his decision. June must have an income guaranteed even if he now had no job himself.

On Friday, the papers told him his company had shut down three of their five factories, and production had stopped at the other two because of an unofficial sympathy strike led by one "Mac" McCarthy. The early evenings reported violence outside the factory gates at the larger of the two remaining, two men were in hospital. Their names were Andrews and Durham. Later, two quality Sunday newspapers ran analyses in depth of the difficulties faced by the cosmetics industry because it was labour-intensive. On 6th December, after a two-and-a-half week strike, "Mac" led the lucky ones back to work.

So they had won. They were cleverer than he had thought. He had failed even in this.

Gerald lay in the bath contemplating his navel. A hollow which held water. A hollow in his flesh, he was a hollow made flesh, a depression in the earth. Depression. Sink deep into the bath, under the waters, why not drown? If only he could drown... if only he could weep, express the sorrow deep within him, flood the earth with his salt tears until he drowned, dead, dead for ever.

Self pity. Disgusting.

But who else would pity him now? No one could admire a man who had failed even in his attempted revenge.

What was he to do? Follow Patricia like a pet poodle, do her bidding, become a shop-keeper selling bits of pottery he did not even like because that was her will? Or forget his dreams of a house in the country, a home for his grandson, and remain here, a kept man in her arty flat? He loved her, admired her, but her tastes were not his. He liked to look on her pretty things, touch them tentatively from time to time, but these were feminine things, as books and music and theatre were female things. And how would he live now she would be taking the role of the man? She still had her job, her place in society. He did not. What could he do, for Christ' sake?

Throw himself off Westminster Bridge.

Yes, it might be better if he killed himself, there was nothing left. But it would look bad. He wasn't going to have those

American bastards jeer. For they would feel no remorse, he knew that with absolute certainty, he'd only earn their contempt. And Patricia's too, perhaps. He did not want to die having lost her love, having gained her contempt.

She was so strong, so self-contained, she did not need him. For all her gentleness, he knew she could not love him any more. He had failed her quite – morally, spiritually, and now materially.

The bathwater had turned cold. Hastily he climbed out, towelled himself vigorously, quickly dressed. He felt strangely as though another being had taken charge of his body. He was as though detached from himself as he packed his belongings into suitcases taken without thought from the cupboard, carried them out to the car. Patricia was at work, June was asleep. He had cleared the flat of all his belongings before he had quite seen what he was about. He had moved so swiftly, so quietly, within half an hour his presence in this flat had been obliterated, in less than thirty minutes his commitment to Patricia of the past sixteen months was blotted out.

47

Patricia

A letter in Gerald's handwriting was sitting on Patricia's dressing table when she returned that evening. She opened it with no presentiment, no sense of alarm, only a vague but pleasurable surprise.

My darling,

This is the most difficult letter I have ever written in my life. I know it will cause you pain, and believe me, I never wished to hurt you and would not if I could find some other way. Oh, Tricia my darling, you are the best part of my life and now we must part.

I must leave you. I know this will come as a shock to you, for we have not talked of this. But I believe you will understand. How can I remain with you now? You deserve better than me. Forgive me, my love, we had such beautiful dreams together. And now they are ashes, dust. All my fault.

I feel as though I am being punished for a terrible crime. But if only I can do the right thing now, perhaps I shall find a way through. Derek once said something about finding oneself on a mountain top, and I realize that is what I must do. I must find a mountain top. Perhaps I sound a bit mad. I feel so strange, as though something outside myself, another force has taken over my body and is holding this pen and writing this letter to you. But I can't fight it any more. If ever I do find what I am looking for – my self, whatever that may mean – then I shall return to you. And if you still want

me, my darling, I shall come back. Please forgive me.
And try to understand.

Goodbye, my darling. Tell June I love her, but cannot
write at the moment. I said goodbye to her this morning,
though of course she did not know. I know she and you
will be all right now – she will have her baby and the
trust account is in her name, that is all she needed of
me really. And you are so strong, you need nothing I
can give.

I love you.
Gerald.

What did he mean? He couldn't possibly mean he had left her.
She stood in her bedroom, their bedroom, staring at the letter
in incomprehension.

As she wandered about the room with the letter in her hand,
she could see nothing that was his, no sign of him anywhere.
June must know what had happened. He couldn't just have
left. She wandered down the hall and into the living room
where June was reading a magazine.

"He says he's gone," she said dazedly.

"What again?" June said, and her voice was hard.

"Didn't you know? Didn't you see him go? He says he's
gone to find himself on a mountain top. Surely you saw him
leave?"

"He'll never find himself on a mountain," said June
viciously. "He should look in the gutter. In the sewer."

June's virulence roused Patricia from her daze.

"No, no, don't be so hard on him. He says he loves us both
and I believe him. He says he said goodbye this morning, but
couldn't tell you and he leaves you his love."

"Yeah, sure. Great."

"I believe him. I believe he is doing that he must. But, oh, how I wish he had talked to me. I would not have held him back if he wished to go. But I wish I could have known I was kissing him for the last time."

"He's a liar and a cheat and a coward," said June, and she stood up. "I hate him. And so should you." She threw herself out of the room, and the house shook as she slammed her bedroom door.

Patricia sat on the edge of a chair and gazed around her, as though the familiar room had become strange. An immense sadness held her in its grip, her sorrow too deep for tears.

Poor, poor Gerald. He had failed, not just once but twice. He would be suffering, but she could not help him, not in any way. She could not speak to him, could not even write, so what would become of him as he struggled in agony entirely alone? Where could he have gone? Could he really walk out like that, leave her for ever?

She read the letter again, and this time it began to make more sense. He did not say he had left for ever, in fact he specifically stated that he had not, that he would return "if he found himself". What did that mean "if he found himself"? Could it be that he had never discovered the essential kernel of his being though he was forty-seven?

How terrible to know so little about another human being. She loved him, yes, she loved him as well as she was capable, more than any other living person, yet he had never told her this. They had never really talked of what matters most in all their years of love. In this she had certainly failed him. She had not thought that the man she loved, so successful in the material world, might not have succeeded in the inner one. Love should not be as blind as that.

Or perhaps he was off on a journey which would take him further than she had travelled. Once she had found that deep centre within herself, the strength to do what is necessary, she had not thought there might be a way beyond. She had not considered it at all. Was this the way of the Buddhist who left his family in middle life? She had always felt that was irresponsible, yet here was Gerald doing just that. Had he discovered something she did not know, something which would give her life more meaning, make it less selfish, more dedicated to others?

"Oh, Gerald, Gerald, why did you not talk to me?" she cried aloud. "Why? Why?" She knew she had been tried and found wanting.

Later that evening, June called to her in panic. The pains had begun, her baby was coming and she was not ready.

Patricia telephoned the obstetrician and the nursing home, packed June's bag and tried to comfort her as best she could. She had read as much as June about having babies, and knew there was little to worry about in having it three weeks premature. But June had left it so late to prepare herself with exercises, was so full of tension from anger with her father and fear of the imminent birth, it was difficult to know how to help.

She drove to the nursing home and sat with June once the nurses had finished the usual preparations and left her in a white cotton hospital gown.

"Relax, June," she said gently. "Don't fight. Let it just happen."

"I'd like to see you do it," June said resentfully, and then gripped Patricia's arm as she drowned in a wave of pain."

"So would I."

"I'm sorry," said June when the wave had subsided. "Forgive me."

For some reason, June was able to relax more easily now,

and though she held Patricia's hand when the waves swept over her, yet she did not grip quite so tightly. But her body was ill-prepared for the task it had undertaken, and she soon realized that labour was not just a vivid word. Bringing a baby into the world did not just happen, the whole earth shook and trembled at the approach of even the least of its members.

It took fifteen hours from the time June first called out in fear. On December 7th 1971, Miss June Hunter was safely delivered of a baby girl, 4 lb 12 oz. The baby was put into an incubator, the mother was allowed to sleep, and Patricia went home.

Already it was early afternoon of the next day. She had not slept, not even when the nurses sent her away at the end. She supposed she must have acted rather like an expectant father, pacing up and down, smoking countless cigarettes, and drinking dreadful cups of coffee from a machine, rushing to sit beside June whenever she could, to stroke her forehead and give her some comfort. She did not even know why she did this, the girl had made her resentment clear enough, but she seemed to need someone. It simply seemed to her that she must.

There was no sign of Gerald. The flat was just as she had left it. She took a couple of codeine to kill her headache, and went to bed.

In the week that followed, she began to feel battered. Everything seemed to depend on her now. She must endure.

It was fortunate they had not yet moved, and she had not yet resigned her position. She had planned to give notice only when they had decided on a house and she had found her shop. Now it was just as well.

The guest room was obviously too dark and small for both June and her baby. She would give her her bedroom, the cradle would fit in there much better, and would catch the morning sunshine. June would need the privacy too. She would use the living room most of the time and the small room just to sleep.

She was almost glad not to sleep in her beautiful bed any more, and moved into the guest room as soon as she thought of the idea. The black space beside her at night was too wide and too deep, it was like a yawning chasm that could never be filled. Unable to sleep, she would wrap herself in a dressing gown, hug a hot water bottle, even put a pillow there in that dark hole beside her where he should be. His absence was preposterous. What if he should never return? Her bones would never be warm again.

She kept hearing his voice, often it was almost as if he were in the room with her, and sometimes she spoke to him, expecting an answer. Often in the street, she was sure she saw him, even stopped the car and ran after one man, she was so certain it was Gerald from the back. And one night she woke up and leapt out of bed, for the telephone was ringing and it would be him. But again she found she was wrong. The ringing was only in her head. The telephone was as silent as the void into which he had sunk.

There was not a moment of the day or night when he was not present somewhere in her thoughts. She could not read, could not listen to music, paced restlessly up and down her living room, to the kitchen and back, sat in front of the television in search of distraction, leafed through magazines. Only once, just before Christmas, she found a short magazine article so entertaining, so funny that she read it through to the end, and actually laughed out loud, and realized that just this once, just for two minutes, she had escaped her obsession.

At work it was impossible to concentrate. Her secretary kept coming in with cups of coffee, wanting to help. Her colleagues asked if she were ill, or if there was anything they could do. But she kept them all at a distance. What could she say?

He could not know the agony he had left her, she was sure of that. Such cruelty could not be his. Yet was it not strange how people repeated things in their lives, as though their responses to any situation were limited by what they had done before.

But he had said he would return. As every day passed without a letter from him, without a phone call, she had to hold on to her faith with all her strength. She did believe in their love, it made sense that he would come back to her when he felt whole. Their passion, that miraculous blending of their bodies, that sense of unity could never again be found with any other partner. She could not imagine now making love with any other man. Occasionally she would think with a pang of fierce jealousy that he might be in bed with another woman, and she would hate him then for this would be the ultimate betrayal. Yet it was not possible that he would find with any other woman what he had found with her, such heights of passion, such ecstasy, such miraculous unity are vouchsafed only once in a lifetime, if ever. Which made it all the more incomprehensible that he should have wished to leave her.

If only he had talked to her before leaving, that was the cruel part. She did not understand how he could have left her like that, without a word. That he needed to leave she could understand. But leaving was surely clean enough. Could he not have let her know when they made love for the last time? Well, yes, she might have argued, she had to admit, she might have tried to persuade him to change his mind, to find some other way, that such a drastic solution to his inner problems was surely not necessary. Presumably that was why he wrote that letter.

But didn't he have any conception of the sorrows he would leave behind? Did he not think that June might be so upset, her baby would arrive early? That she, Patricia, might be so distraught her job, on which they both now relied, would be in jeopardy? She had to believe he had not thought of these things. Once again his imagination had failed to see the consequences of his acts.

Yet in the end, we are each of us alone. We can only do our best and hope that it is the correct thing to do. It would not be right for her to carp and criticise, and so destroy what they still had. Life was so complex and difficult to comprehend, there was only room for compassion.

She read no newspapers, no longer listened to the news. A military coup in a central African country brought bloody rioting, but she did not know.

Jill telephoned: Vincent Lemieux was dead. Though he was one of only five fully qualified surgeons in his country, the new regime did not like his politics. He was dragged from the operating room, tortured, shot. For a wild, insane, brief moment she wished she had gone with him as he so often asked, married him, died at his side. It made no sense.

Nothing made sense any more.

48

June

Nine days later, June was home with her baby girl. The baby was small but thriving, had been able to leave the incubator within three days. And June, who had hardly given the matter any thought, had chosen to breast-feed her baby because it was the obvious thing to do.

Those first three days had been agonising. As soon as she had been allowed out of bed, she would shuffle along the corridor to the nursery and gaze through the window at her tiny, tiny daughter, red and cross, fighting to keep hold on life. She had willed her to hang on, to grow, to reach five pounds so that she could hold her in her arms at last. And then that wonderful moment when Dr Parsons said, "She'll do," and she had held her close to her breast, and felt her own heart pounding and the power of life surging through her. It had been worth everything to reach this moment.

A new warmth, a new womanly competence accompanied June on her return, for she had found a maternal instinct awoke in her the moment she heard her baby's first cry, became established as soon as she examined the perfect female child that had so short a time before been a part of her own body. She did not know where it came from, this knowledge of what her daughter needed each time she cried, this gentleness, this sureness, this yearning to give comfort to another human being. She had read warnings enough that the so-called maternal instinct was not so instinctual in humans, had not expected to feel this way at all, had not thought she could love a tiny squalling infant at first sight. But it had happened.

There she was, an ugly girl without parents, without friends, foisting on the world her own potentially equally unlikeable illegitimate child, and yet this unpromising material actually showed signs of becoming a loving mother. The age of miracles could not have passed after all.

She noticed too how quiet and kind Pat could be. A grudging sort of admiration grew in her heart for this remote and beautiful woman who gave unstintingly of all she had. Extraordinary that she should have turned over that super bedroom: June felt like a princess some mornings, propped on pillows against that gorgeous peacock, nursing her tiny child. Suitable, Pat had said, for to her the peacock apparently meant, not vanity as June would have thought, but renaissance, rebirth.

She suspected she had been rather a bitch in the past, and tried very hard not to be too much of a nuisance now. But a new baby created an amazing amount of work, and the flat was scarcely designed for it – mountains of nappies to wash and dry each day, change of vest and nightgown and blanket each time, feeds every three or four hours all through the day and night. June began to feel dizzy from interrupted sleep. But she promised she would make it up to this strange, rather superior being one day. Not that she'd notice, she seemed so aloof. Didn't speak of Dad at all. You'd think she'd say something.

Christmas was coming. She decided to send George a card, telling him of his daughter's birth, as a Christmas present. And Ruth. No one else, a pretty poor show when you came to think of it. She thought about last Christmas, and sent Grandpa a card too. Who ever would have thought Mum would have gone first, with old Grandpa shuffling round like a semi-invalid for years? It was going to be a strange Christmas this year, just herself and the baby and Pat, and Pat's mother coming just for dinner. She would do her best to make the holiday pleasant, it was the least she could do. She would do the cooking too, or most of it, and start practising right now by baking a cake.

She was astonished at herself, and pleased. How much happier she felt now she had her baby. Someone to love. Perhaps that was it, at last she had someone who needed her, for no one else would do. She didn't care whether her love for her child was rewarded or not, that was not the question: it was not a need to be loved, it was a need to love. Had her mother felt this? She felt as though she had achieved something difficult of attainment, a level of maturity that would have been beyond her even a few months ago.

Going shopping, she walked along the streets pushing the pram, and was filled with a vague pleasurable sensation of well-being. Recent events seemed to have altered her perception. The buildings beside which she walked filled her consciousness with their solidity, the rough cruel strength of the stone, the hard durability of the glass and steel, the softer firmness of the wood, even the pulsing swirling emptiness in rooms and corridors behind these bricks and stones and panes of glass, the factual solidity of empty space. The pavement on which she walked pressed through the soles of her shoes, eternal rock, and in between the paving stones the separate grains of dusty soil and cement, resting, waiting, leaping to join her as she passed. The cars that zoomed past filled her ears with the sound of life, a non-living life, a mechanical life as real as her own and stronger, a roaring hungry blindness of pumping pistons and sparking fires and explosion of gases, a whirring and whirling of belts and gears and wheels, huge shiny bodies of coloured metal concealing the power within. And their lives would end. The trees, the sparrows and pigeons in the square, they would die. All that would remain would be eternal rock and steel. The non-living mineral world would remain, as it was in the beginning, is now and would be for ever more. Life would be dead. Why?

More than ever in her life before, she felt as though she belonged where she was, as though there was a place for her on earth. That made no sense either. Having just decided that all living things were doomed to die, or rather having just seen clearly in her own mind what others had said so often, how could she feel at the same time that she and her baby belonged, that it was good to be June Cecily Hunter?

Outside a large greengrocer's stood a small platoon of pine trees. She tucked her gloves under the pram cover, and brushed the pine needles to feel the sharp prickling, and the scent of resin was on her fingers.

"Good specimens, aren't they?" the red-cheeked shop keeper said. "How big do you want it?"

"Fairly big, please, to stand on the floor, and nice and bushy. I do love the smell, don't you?"

The man smiled and nodded. "Nice time of year this," he said. "I like Christmas."

"Oh, I'm so glad!" cried June. "So do I. But everyone seems to moan about it, and say it's phoney. I love Christmas, and the tree and the coloured balls and tinsel and presents and eating too much."

"Should be a nice year for you, eh?" he said, gesturing towards the pram with his bald head. "First one for the little'un and all that. Christmas is best when you have kids."

"She's a bit too young, really," June said ruefully. "You got any children?"

"I should say! Four still at home and two married, and the eldest has just made me a grand-father. Makes you think."

"Do you mind?" She was thinking of her own father, for he did not know he was a grandfather, and it did not occur to her she might be being rude. But the shopkeeper smiled indulgently.

"Bless you. Makes me feel I'm founding a dynasty."

She laughed. She then bought oranges and apples and chestnuts, which she stowed in the pram basket. But it was clear the tree was far too big. She'd have to choose – tree or baby? She couldn't have both. But the friendly shopkeeper offered to deliver it that afternoon, without charge, it would be no trouble. Her heart was light and joyous, for it was true, people could be kind to one another. Life was not all jungle warfare.

She almost danced now as she pushed the pram along, and people smiled. She bought a metal stand for the tree; because she wanted to please Pat, she thought of the colour scheme of that strange, attractive living room, and was careful in her choice of coloured glass balls; then she found thick ropes of tinsel coloured blue and green, and she knew luck was with her today.

That afternoon, she began to decorate her baby's first Christmas tree. It was important to do it right, there was a ritual to be observed, and since each item was new, it must be dedicated to the spirit of Christmas. She felt as though she were an initiate performing a mysterious ceremony.

Her baby lay in the cradle she had brought into the room, peacefully gurgling, She lifted each coloured ball from the box and savoured the colours and patterns of moving light, then tied it with black thread to a branch. At the top of the tree she tied a tinsel gold star. She had to fetch a chair from the kitchen to reach, and was afraid it would look bare, but the effect was better than she expected, a single five-pointed star shining at the summit. Very tasteful. She nodded, pleased. Finally the strings of coloured tinsel: she had never seen tinsel anything but silver, but these long, thick, fluffy, shiny garlands went perfectly with the colours in Pat's rug. It was just the sort of thing she would have chosen herself, June was quite sure. She felt strangely proud and touched, as though the woman had got inside her for a moment. Then she picked up her daughter.

The baby leaned towards the bright shining decorations, and she could see the coloured lights reflected in her eyes. Oh, she was glad, glad, glad. She hugged her child, and could feel the downy hair against her cheek, the soft skin and woollen jacket in her neck, could smell the mixed scents of baby powder and freshly washed wool, this was bliss, bliss.

"June, it's lovely." Pat said this with such simplicity, June knew she meant it.

"You don't mind?"

"Of course not. It's the most beautiful tree I think I've ever seen."

She turned away, but not before June had seen the tears in her eyes. How extraordinary. June realized with a delicious sense of power she actually had it in her to make Pat cry.

49

Gerald

A mountain top. At first, Gerald intended to go to Snowdonia, which seemed likely to offer the nearest thing that might be called a mountain. But as he drove, he thought that was to take the concept too literally. He did not need an actual mountain, that was just a metaphor, and what he really should do was go and see Derek, who gave him the idea in the first place. For the truth was, though he liked the idea of finding himself on top of a mountain, he wasn't exactly sure what that might mean. In a way, he felt absurd: "Derek, how does one set about finding one's self?" You couldn't ask a question like that out loud. But it was Derek who put the idea into his head, trying to explain why he was dropping out, going to do his own thing, so perhaps he would give some sort of guidance. Whatever finding one's self might mean, it must be better than this black depression, this sense of utter futility.

He telephoned and was invited to stay.

A beautiful interlude: he stayed with his friends in their large stone house, set in a sheltered valley, surrounded by fields of sheep, woods, a waterfall, a sparkling stream. The wounds to his ego were soothed by the balm of kindness, and he spent hours wandering through the beautiful valley, fed his soul by windy walks along the magnificent Cornish cliffs, watching seas crash against the rocks and seagulls swing on the wind, soothing his wounds and thinking as little as possible of what he had left behind.

One evening they sat together round the log fire, the big comfortable room filled with the scent of pine logs burning, the golden retriever stretched out luxuriously on the rug. Dinner was over. The boy was in bed.

"Being a shop keeper seems to suit you, Derek. Both of you, in fact. Who would have thought it?"

Derek smiled comfortably. "Yes, this life suits us. We work like crazy during the season, and then laze in the winter. But when the long hours in the summer get us down – and they do, let me tell you, we work seven days a week, often twelve hours a day, for months – then we remember, we weren't forced into it. We chose this way of life."

"It's worth a lot of hard work every day to have no boss," Tina said.

"Patricia talked of opening a shop," Gerald said. "But I'm a business man, a manager, I'm used to big operations on an international scale. I can't go into shop-keeping at my age."

"Age isn't the question, it's more a matter of temperament, I'd say." Derek leaned forward. "Look, Gerald, it's ludicrous to think of yourself as a failure just because you no longer have the same job. It's not even unusual these days either, lots of men your age find they have to think again, find something else to do. You have lots to offer, lots of abilities. I mean, it could be a marvellous opportunity to do something quite new. The world's your oyster."

"You could study," suggested Tina enthusiastically, "get a degree in, I don't know, law say."

Gerald sighed. "It's very good of you to try to cheer me up. But I need money, security. And at my age, who is going to employ me?"

"What do you want money and security *for*?" Derek exploded. "You *had* security, and what good did it do you? You have money, at least enough to live on. Come on, old chap, think. Think free! You're not a prisoner, except of your own expectations."

"Those he left behind are, though," Tina said.

"Hush," said her husband. But Tina's words opened the flood-gate of guilt he had been hoping to hold shut, and he knew he could no longer stay. Tina had not finished.

"What good is freedom if you make no use of it?" she demanded, and she sounded angry. "You walk out on those who depend on you for love, comfort, moral support, even financial help – and for what? A dream? A whim? Or was it because you felt inadequate? Or out of self-pity? OK, break your ties, take your freedom. It's your choice. But for God's sake, do something with that freedom. Make the pain you inflicted on those who loved you worth something."

"Tina, you shouldn't have said that. Gerald, I'm so sorry."

"Don't you apologize on my behalf, Derek Malley! I know what I'm saying, and it's time someone said it straight out. Gerald is afraid to take the consequences of his acts."

"Tina, that is too much.".

"Go on, Tina," Gerald said quietly. "I want to hear."

"I'm sorry it's hurtful, Gerry, really I am. But now I've started, I'd better finish, because I don't think you know what you're doing, and just once in your life … Oh dear. I listen to you and all I can hear is that you've tried to be a Good Guy, tried to act for the best. You wouldn't compromise your honesty, so you're out of a job. You loved another woman, so you left your wife. And then she died. And your daughter's pregnant. Sad, yes, but that's what *happened*. Can't you just once take the situation as you have made it, and *live* it? You stood on your principles when confronted by your new bosses, and refused to play their dishonest games. Good for you. We all admire you for your principles and your courage. But now you have no job, and you feel lost. Why? You *chose* no job, for heaven's sake, no job with principles rather than keeping it and losing your honour. *Take what you want, God said, and pay.* Your problem is, you don't want to pay full price."

"You mean, Madge's death was payment for Patricia's love?"

"No, I don't! You're so melodramatic, Gerry. Madge's life wasn't yours to give, was it? But maybe accepting your share of the *guilt* is part of the price. Accepting guilt, taking it in, living with it. Oh Gerry, don't you *see?*"

But he could see nothing except that his best friends had turned against him. What was the matter with him that everyone turned from him? First his mother, then his wife, his children, his colleagues, Patricia, and now his best friends. Who was left? No one. He was alone in the world.

"Gerry, please hear me," Tina cried in distress. "If I've gone too far, please try to forgive me, but you can't go on running away from yourself for ever. When you come to the end of running, you'll still be with you – you'll still have to face that dark side of yourself."

Very coldly he asked: "And what makes you so sure I am running away from myself?"

"I *saw*, that's all. I thought I might help. I'm sorry."

"We've been through it too, Gerry," Derek said. "We know what it's like."

He looked around the comfortable, wood-panelled room, glowing in the firelight, and laughed a bitter laugh.

He left next morning. He had no plans. He was polite and distant, for how would he be friendly when he knew their thoughts? But he didn't need them. He had his pride.

He got into the car and drove. Running away from himself, they said. That was a laugh. He was not so much of a fool that he didn't know as well as they that that was impossible, you couldn't escape from yourself. And the irony was he had actually gone to ask their help, Derek's help, in *finding* himself. Whatever that meant. Just as well he hadn't said anything after all. He'd been waiting for the right moment, because you felt such a fool, questions about 'finding yourself' could be so easily misconstrued. He'd been with them about ten days, and the opportunity had never arisen, and now he was glad. That would have given them one more weapon to use against him.

You didn't expect your best friends to turn against you like that. What was it they had said? Called him melodramatic when he had mentioned disaster; called him cowardly when he was facing up to failure; and called him guilty … yes, so they blamed him for Madge's death. As one would expect. They *said* they didn't, and then in the next breath spoke of his guilt. Very well, if that was what they thought ...

He found he was heading west. Following the direction his son had taken. Yes, there was meaning in that. At last he had begun to understand his son's extraordinary behaviour: Robert had felt branded, given the mark of a murderer, which was against his very nature. And now Gerald felt branded in his turn, given the names of coward, traitor, murderer.

Branded by his friends.

Branded by his business colleagues.

Branded by his new bosses, men who knew him not, who assumed without hesitation that he would give and take bribes. He, whose one strength in crisis had always been his sense of honour.

His whole body felt as though he were being tortured, muscles he did not know he had screamed at him, and he had to pull into a layby, stop driving. His shoulders felt as though pierced with red hot irons.

He was a prisoner of other men's expectations, expectations that wronged him as much as Robert had been wronged when he felt responsible for his parents' breakup, his mother's collapse and death. Evidently one did not need total war, tyranny or secret police for the innocent to suffer total loss. The innocent could be imprisoned in other men's lies.

Was he wrong then to have thrown away all he had worked for, nearly thirty years of struggling for financial and material success? When he refused to pass on the bribe, there were many ready, willing, anxious to take his place. What had he achieved? A few jokes at his expense … Mrs Mac would have lost her job … he had walked out on Patricia, on June, he had no future. And all those whose jobs he had hoped to save were, as planned, tossed onto the pile of struggling bodies of the unemployed. He was out of work, a failure, on the scrap heap.

His one strength was no strength now. In attempting to preserve his honour, he had been dishonoured. He had lost everything, and achieved nothing. His sacrifice had been in vain, without response from God. Like Cain, his offerings were not wanted.

He started off again, stopping some time later for beer and a pasty. It was true: he had given up everything, wife, children, home, love of a mistress, wealth, security, position in society. For what? Perhaps it was true, perhaps he was like Cain, doomed to wander the world, cast out from his people, a marked man.

He would drive into the setting sun. He would drive until he could go no further, until he came to Land's End. He had no plans. But he liked the symbolism.

The sun sank into the sea, and the sky was apple-green and pearl. Stars lit one by one as the darkness gathered in the late afternoon, for the year was ending, and a slender silver crescent moon rose slowly above the hills behind him. On and on he drove, until the road ended, and he parked beside the tourist kiosks, shuttered against winter storms, dark and silent. He was alone at Land's End. He walked towards the much-photographed rocky promontory at the tip of Cornwall, and could see himself, as though he was outside himself looking on as a spectator, he was alone among the rocks and mosses at the end of land, a lone figure in the expanse of moonlight and shadows.

It was surprisingly light as the crescent moon hung over the ocean in a clear sky. He found a comfortable rock at the edge of the world, and watched for a long time as the silver crescent rose, silvering a path across the ocean which lay all around him, swaying and sighing in its sleep. There was no wind, and though it was December, he did not feel cold. Darkness grew in the sky, and soon it was filled with myriads of stars, as countless as are the grains of sand under the sea.

He contemplated the vastness of the ocean, grey and deep, the immensity of the heavens, the infinity of other worlds, other suns, other galaxies, and his own puny insignificance. The immense impersonal grandeur of creation soothed him, and he felt at peace.

After a while, he smiled to himself. It had just occurred to him he had found what he was seeking without realizing it: this was his mountain top. A lonely rock at Land's End was where he would find himself.

A creepy feeling that he was not alone assailed him. He looked round. It had become very dark while he was sitting on his rock, and he could see very little. Moonlight and starlight were all very well, but if there were someone there … He was being absurd. He knew perfectly well he was alone, he was miles from the nearest habitation, and he'd have heard if anyone had come near.

But the creepy feeling grew that he was being watched from the shadows. Someone, some thing hostile was watching, waiting. He leapt up, turned round. Nothing. Nothing moved except the sea far below, slowly sighing.

He'd better go. It was a dangerous place to be all alone, miles from the nearest hope of help. Anything might happen. It was stupid of him to stay so long.

A wind suddenly blew in from the ocean, shaking it into waves, rustling the grasses on the cliff into footsteps. He shivered. He was cold, and had stayed too long. The wind grew stronger, and shreds of cloud covered banks of stars so that it became even darker. He must be very careful. Of course there was no one there; but if there were and he had to run, he might miss his way. The car was a long way away from here. The ground could end and he could fall over the edge of the cliff and into the sea.

"You can't go running from yourself for ever," Tina said. He jumped, and held on to a convenient rock to steady himself. He heard her voice. What was the matter with him? Was he going mad? She couldn't be here …

"Tina?" he said aloud. "Are you there?"

The only answer was a wave splashing on the rocks below, and a sighing in the wind. The clouds moved, and he could see that no one was near him on the cliffs. He was alone.

Was that what was meant by finding one's self? What Tina called turning to face the dark side of yourself? Was that out there in the shadows, his dark, ugly, shadow side? The part of himself he did not want to acknowledge? He had not thought that finding himself on a mountain top would be so frightening.

For he was shaking with fear. Part of his mind told him this was madness, which was occasion enough for fear. And this rational part told him to pull himself together, stop imagining he was hearing voices or seeing ghosts. He should pull himself together, fast, and get the hell out of there. If there was any danger, it was of a real and rational kind, like a wild animal or some criminal wanting to attack him for his money, and he wasn't equipped to deal with either, so why didn't he make for the car and drive away fast?

Another part of his mind though told him he had heard Tina's voice for a reason. She had been right when she said he was running away, and now he had come to an end of running, and where was there to go? He must come to terms with the wild animal, the criminal in himself.

Don't be absurd, cried Rationality. Are you cracking up or something? It's cold and dark out here, let's find a hostelry with a fire, and have a meal and drink some beer, and forget this nonsense.

If he let this go on, he'd sound like a mediaeval Morality Play in his own head. It was absurd to suppose that different parts of one's mind had different thoughts. Different attitudes. Different emotions. If that were so, who was he, Gerald? Which one of these different parts of his mind was him? Or if, as seemed logical, they were all him, being parts of him, why did he feel split up into fragments? How could part of him be haunting him in the shadows?

Yet who had not experienced arguments in his head? Who had not seen a child's book showing a devil on the shoulder of the hero and an angel on the other, each whispering in the hero's ear, and known this to be a picture of reality? Conscience versus Temptation: a Morality Play again.

Ah, but the devil was evil and must be chased away. Every child knew that. You don't come to terms with the devil.

And if the evil in you is part of you, do you chase away part of yourself? And spend the rest of your life running from yourself? Was that what Tina meant? That one must face the devil in one's self, because it is a part of one's self, and without it one can never be whole?

Trembling with almost overpowering fear, Gerald knew that Tina had told him this, not because she condemned him, but for love. She had seen his need, and tried to tell him what to do. If only he had listened. For though he saw now what she meant, he had absolutely no idea how to go about it. He must face the evil in himself, the darkness he had never wished to acknowledge, and he must assimilate it. Without his shadow self, he would never be whole.

But suppose his dark side were too strong?

He had an overpowering urge to run, though he knew he must not, it was too dark, he could not see where he was going, but – oh, God! If only he believed in God … if only God believed in him … Was he not forsaken of God, cast out?

Alas, Tina was right. He *was* melodramatic, and that was perhaps the least of his sins. He sat down again on the rock, since he was not going back just yet, and thought, Yes, ever since that time in Montreal, he had known in the back of his mind he had a tendency to dramatise. Melodrama was a way of experiencing tremendous emotions superficially, allowed him to skirt the edges of reality.

What else? What else had she said? Was she right about everything? That he was guilty, she had said, guilty of Madge's death. A murderer.

No. She had not said that. That was part of his own dramatisation. He was not a murderer, even if perhaps it might satisfy some part of himself to think he might have been. What she had said was, "Accept your share of the guilt."

He began to feel cold then, cold through and through. If he were to accept his guilt in Madge's death, it was the smallness, the pettiness of his guilt that made him feel unclean. Guilty of murder, that at least had some size to it, some dramatic impact. But his true guilt was so little, so petty, had more to do with marrying the wrong person for the wrong reasons, the small cruelties perpetrated by his possessiveness, his selfish misplaced pride, his own self-pity.

He sat for a long, long time as if turned to stone. He looked on the face of Medusa. She might smile on him one day, when he had swallowed his pride, assimilated his cowardice, eaten humble pie. But she did not smile on him yet.

50

Patricia

Patricia stood looking down at the baby in her cradle, trimmed with white and pink frills, She had not picked her up, had not done more than caress that tiny cheek with her fingers and brush that tiny hand with her own.

But today was Christmas Day and June was with her, in her flat, and now she felt an overpowering urge to take this small human being in her arms. She would never be a mother now, would never feel life leap in her womb, never feel the earth moving in her body and the eruption of new life from hers. But she was a woman, if she could not do that woman's work. She longed to feel this tiny body against her breast. She had not taken up the baby before because she knew June had only remained with her out of need, and had sensed that she would object. But now, surely it would be all right.

Slowly she bent over the cradle and the baby looked up at her, eyes wide open, hands waving. She was quiet and awake. Patricia gently put her hand under the baby's head, and felt the soft golden down against her skin. It was easy to lift a baby into your arms. She could feel it. She slid her arm under its head to steady it, and then with her other hand she lifted the baby up out of the cradle and into her arms. Oh, the warmth, the joy of it. It was not strange, it was right and natural. She lifted her higher until the baby's little head was resting on her shoulder, in the crook of her neck, and she felt as though she had never known such happiness as this. Just holding a baby, someone else's baby? That was ridiculous.

She slid the baby back down into the cradle of her arms

and looked at her, smiling. They said new-born babies were always ugly, but this little one was beautiful. There was no doubt about it. Her skin was not really wrinkled and had the bloom of a peach, her eyes were blue and she had perfectly formed eyebrows, very faint, and a tiny nose, and her hands were so beautiful, each finger had little knuckles and a minute shell-like nail. A tiny perfectly formed human being.

"Hey! What do you think you're doing? Don't you dare touch my baby!" June strode angrily into the room and snatched her baby from the other woman's arms. Patricia offered no resistance, let her take the baby and then walked to the window, stunned and hurt.

What good was all the love she felt, all the kindness she had shown, if in the end they were totally rejected? What had she done that was so terribly wrong it could never be forgiven? But no, she did not honestly think that she was so much at fault. Surely goodwill was not so freely available to the world that June could afford to reject what she had offered.

And suddenly she was angry. She turned to face June who was bending over the cradle. It must be said after all.

"How dare you talk to me like that? You have been living in my house, eating my food, sleeping in my bed, for months now. All the time you talk of independence and living your own life and not wanting to be pushed around, and all the time you just sit there, waiting, as though life is going to come to you on a plate. I have been kind to you as far as I know, I have not asked anything of you, have cared for you when you were in need, and have offered you a home for yourself and your baby. And then you have the effrontery to tell me not to touch your baby, as though I were a criminal or something. Your baby is not a toy. She is a human being. And I am a human being. It is natural for two human beings to want to make contact, to learn to know each other."

June had gone white. "I'm sorry," she said.

"Not only that, I feel I should have the right to touch that baby of yours. Once in a while. Don't worry, I don't want to take her from you or harm her in any way. It's just that she is Gerald's grand-daughter and I love him, and I want to love that baby because she is part of him." Her voice broke. "And why shouldn't I hold a baby in my arms? Tell me that. I'm a woman too."

To June there came an illumination, and she suddenly felt a tremendous desire to smile, to laugh, for it was as though something had broken inside her and set her free. She could not laugh, not yet, for she could not let Pat think she was mocking her distress. But suddenly she was, oh, so happy, and she wanted to put her arms round this lonely woman, that other woman who had never had a baby. She wanted to comfort her.

But it was not a sudden superiority she had found, it was rather the revelation of their oneness, that they were truly sisters on this earth. It was the sort of revelation vouchsafed but once in a lifetime, sometimes sooner, sometimes later, to every person who honestly strives to understand. Special gifts are not required, all that is necessary is an approach to suffering, and who among us is preserved from that to the end? June knew then with joy that this new-found knowledge gushed forth from the springs of life itself. She had found love at last.

Tears filled her eyes as she saw for the first time the loneliness and the courage of that other woman, her sister.

"Oh, Pat, Pat, what a rotten bitch I've been. I want you to forgive me, but I don't know how you can. I just didn't understand." Impulsively, she walked towards her with her hand outstretched and Patricia clasped it tightly, held it in both of hers. For the first time, they looked into each other's eyes, and they were dimmed with tears.

"How difficult it is to live with another human being," said Patricia sadly. "And yet, surely, with good will ..."

With the tenderness of a lover, June stroked Patricia's cheek.

"Don't worry, Pat. It won't be the same any more. Believe me. You made me see the light. Do you realize that's the first time you've ever told me what you really think?"

Patricia gently dropped June's hand and turned back to the window.

"I hate fighting," she said, looking out at the leafless trees. "I always hoped that anger not expressed might pass. It doesn't seem right that raising your voice at someone should change anything, except for the worse."

"When you've got someone as dim as me, maybe you have to raise your voice. Don't feel bad, Pat. I'm at fault, not you. You've only known me a few months, and heaven knows I've been badly enough behaved. And yet you've treated me better than anyone else in the world. Better than anyone. I really mean it. I think you must be the nicest person I know."

Patricia turned round slowly, scarcely able to believe what she had heard.

"It's true," said June defiantly, "so don't try to deny it. I don't go round saying that to everyone, you know." She picked up her baby and carried her carefully over to Patricia, who was still standing by the window. "What's more, while we are having this crazy conversation, I want you to know I am going to call this child of mine Pat, after you."

Patricia relaxed suddenly, and laughed aloud. "Oh, you crazy girl, June."

June silently and very carefully and gently put her precious bundle in the other woman's arms, then stood back and looked at her triumphantly.

"Oh, June, you make me want to cry." Patricia looked down

at the centre of contention, who had surprisingly not picked up the tension in the room, but instead had fallen asleep. "I'm very flattered. Really. I shall never forget what you said today. But Patricia is really not the right name for this lovely girl." She smiled, and the humour of the situation assailed her. "I don't suppose we'll have another conversation like this in a hurry, do you?"

"I shall call her Miranda, to be marvelled at," said June, and they both laughed, smiling into each other's eyes.

Patricia did not believe in miracles, and was sure that this sudden understanding would dissolve in the future under other pressures. But the joy of it grew in her heart, and for this while she was happy. It was almost worth all the heartache to have moments like this.

The Porcupine's Dilemma
**published 2016, just as the author ended up
in hospital seriously ill!**

Katie Isbester, Founder of Claret Press
Falls into a well-recognized genre of a comedy of manners, set in a genteel English cottage, with a theme of gross injustice and lack of autonomy expressed with considerable good humour. Similar to Jane Austen - writing is witty and charming and all the barbs are gently swathed - only here the injustice is a bright old lady denied control over her own life. It's a fabulous updating and pertinent given our ageing populace.

Jacob Ross, Fellow of Royal Institute of Literature
A remarkably accomplished, wholly absorbing portrayal of family, love and the tensions that bind them, and ultimately an old woman's gracious retreat from life. *The Porcupine's Dilemma* is not only about ageing and dying, but also life: the gift of offspring and perpetuity through those who come after.

Cherry Mosteshar, The Oxford Editors
Great story line that should appeal to the 'sandwich generation', those taking care of both children and parents while having their own mid-life crisis. Gentle and moving, with dialogue that is totally natural and believable.

The Amazon's Girdle
Published 2015 by Genver Books

Dennis Hamley, author of *Spirit of Place* (and many others)
An absorbing, many layered story, beautifully written...To keep hold of such a subtle plot is a high novelistic skill.

Barbara Lorna Hudson, author of *Timed Out*
Complex fascinating characters and a plot to match. Elegantly written with a strong feel for place... If you like Ruth Rendell writing as Barbara Vine you will love this.

Martin Ouvry, *Wingate Scholar of Literature*
A harrowing tale of love and loss, jealousy and betrayal, with a mystery at its heart. Through a tantalising weave of character and plot, Mapstone keeps us guessing to the end... The qualities in her prose are worth reading for alone.

NON-FICTION
War of Words: Women and Men Arguing
First edition Chatto & Windus, 1998
Second edition Vintage 1999
Also published in German
Warum Manner und Frauen sich nicht verstehen
and in Mandarin Chinese (but no copy available)

Stop Dreaming, Start Living
Discover your hidden powers - and transform your life
Vermilion 2005
Also published in French:
Changez votre vie! Un programme unique pour vivre pleinement vos reves.
in German:
Traumst du noch oder lebst du schon?
in Dutch:
Geniet van het levan En maak je dromen waar

Lightning Source UK Ltd.
Milton Keynes UK
UKHW011351151221
395647UK00001B/23